Every
Hidden
Thing

Books by Athol Dickson

Garr Reed Mysteries
Whom Shall I Fear?
Every Hidden Thing

Every Hidden Thing

athol dickson

ZondervanPublishingHouse
Grand Rapids, Michigan

A Division of HarperCollinsPublishers

Every Hidden Thing
Copyright © 1998 by Athol Dickson

Requests for information should be addressed to:

ZondervanPublishingHouse
Grand Rapids, Michigan 49530

Library of Congress Cataloging-in-Publication Data

Dickson, Athol, 1955–
    Every hidden thing : a Garr Reed mystery / Athol Dickson.
      p. cm.
    ISBN: 0-310-22002-5
    I. Title.
    PS3554.I3264E93 1998
    813'.54–dc21   98-9594
                                             CIP

Published in association with the literary agency of Alive Communications, Inc., 1465 Kelly Johnson Blvd., Colorado Springs, CO 80920

Printed in the United States of America

98 99 00 01 02 03 04 /v DC/ 10 9 8 7 6 5 4 3

For God will bring every deed into judgment,
including every hidden thing,
whether it is good or evil.

Ecclesiastes 12:14

Chapter 1

UNDREDS OF STRANGERS JAMMED THE winding driveway of Jackson County Memorial Hospital, squatting cross-legged on the pavement to block the front door. Over five hundred of them had descended upon us like a plague of carpetbaggers, intent upon disturbing the peace. For a backwater community like Mount Sinai, Texas, the crowd was enormous. They came to our little town on the Louisiana border from as far away as New Orleans, Dallas, Houston, and Shreveport, gobbling up every motel room and public camping site in the county, and creating our first traffic jam since we quit holding the annual Miss Cotton Festival back in 1973. Most of the local churchgoing people had given up a Sunday afternoon of raking leaves and watching football to be there. And while some of us just stood by and watched, others joined in, strolling over to the seated gathering and hunkering right down among them.

Standing near the street, I sniffed burning leaves in the air and wondered what was keeping Mary Jo. She'd gone inside the hospital twenty minutes ago to powder her nose, and should have come back out by now. As I scanned the crowd, a television crew wandered alongside the drive. A blond reporter in a gray suit bent down here and there to ask a question, pointing his microphone at the person he was interviewing while the cameraman followed his every move. A sheriff's deputy in a brown uniform paced beside the driveway on the opposite side of the mass of seated protesters, pausing now and then to speak to them, warning them to abandon their sit-in and clear the road, or face arrest. Each person he spoke to answered with a rueful smile and a negative shake of the head.

Across the lawn, a small group of people held round blue picket signs aloft and stared at us sullenly. Most of them were women. They were very few compared to the crowd on the driveway. Squinting my eyes, I read the messages on their placards: "N.O.W." and "Keep Abortion Legal."

I thought I heard a car backfire once, then again.

Waiting patiently for Mary Jo to return, I watched the dappled shadows on the hospital lawn shift with the autumn sun. Above us, a crisp breeze stirred the pines, and a pair of cardinals chirped brightly from a sweetgum branch nearby. Happy voices drifted across the lawn like the hum of an audience before the curtain goes up.

For the first time since we had arrived almost an hour before, I separated myself from the small group of onlookers near the street to approach the hospital. Inching alongside the driveway, I searched the peacefully resolute faces of the seated demonstrators for Mary Jo. Mostly, the crowd was made up of outsiders. Many of them wore an odd uniform of red berets, black T-shirts, and combat trousers. Others wore identical white T-shirts pulled right over their long sleeved shirts or blouses and emblazoned with the words, "Thou Shalt Not Kill." I thought of how far they had come to be here, of their willingness to tour the Jackson County Jail the hard way. Whether singing softly, holding hands, or simply staring across the lawn toward the distant cotton fields at the edge of town, everyone seemed so peaceful. But they held crude signs with words like *murderer* and *shame* and *damnation*. An elderly woman waved a hand-painted placard slowly above her head. It read "Christians Don't Abort Babies."

I felt something rotten gnawing at my gut.

Some of the hometown folks I recognized in the crowd were priests, ministers, elders, and deacons. Mostly, these were good, God-fearing people. So why did I feel so uncomfortable? Only a year had passed since I had decided to become a Christian, so maybe my uneasiness with this mixture of faith and social issues was simply due to inexperience. Still, the worm in my belly turned when I looked at their signs. Was I falling away from my newfound faith so soon?

The thought dripped like poison into the calm pool of my mind, sending concentric ripples of doubt to the horizon. It was an unexpected challenge. But then, everything that day was unexpected. I always pictured protests as noisy, frantic things. Yet the crowd on the lawn of Jackson County Memorial Hospital was peaceful and serene. So when the wild man in the bloody white lab coat burst from the hospital doors, he was as conspicuous as a chainsaw at the dinner table.

The man almost tripped over the first row of protesters seated just outside the doors. Struggling to regain his balance, he rose to his toes, poised above the sea of bodies with arms thrust back like a diver. He glanced around frantically. For an instant our eyes locked, and my breath caught in my throat. I had seen that look before.

It was the look of terror.

Chapter 2

THE MAN IN THE WHITE LAB COAT TURNED left and right, searching for a way through the throng of people littering the hospital drive. Unable to find an opening, he plunged into the protesters anyway, stepping on hands and legs, leaving a stream of outraged complaints in his wake. He stumbled over a seated teenage girl, rose to hands and knees to glance around desperately, then leapt to his feet and resumed his headlong charge through the crowd. Once he reached the lawn on the far side of the driveway, the man trotted across the grass until he reached a deputy. They spoke in quiet, urgent tones, the deputy touching the man's arm, calming him. Then they both hurried back together toward the hospital entry. Along the way, the deputy waved two other uniformed men to his side. The four of them retraced the route through the seated crowd, taking care this time to avoid stepping on the protesters. Once across the driveway, they disappeared into the hospital. In a flash of intuition, I guessed why.

Then, I prayed I was wrong.

All around me, people wondered aloud about the strange actions of the man in the white lab coat. More than one person mentioned the terrified look on his face. I checked my wrist watch. What was keeping Mary Jo? If what I suspected was true, I had to find her.

I moved on, reaching the portico without spotting my wife. Up near the hospital entrance, a man climbed onto the hood of a parked car. Someone handed him a bullhorn, and he began to address the crowd, his amplified voice echoing against the hospital wall. He was a young man, with steel wire-framed glasses and freshly scrubbed cheeks the color of skim milk. Like so many seated on the driveway, he wore the strange paramilitary uniform of camouflage trousers and a black T-shirt. As I drew closer, I saw that the front of his T-shirt bore the word "C.H.A.R.G.E." printed in blood-red letters. He had tucked a red beret in his rear pocket, revealing a crisp part in his light brown hair. The cuffs of his camouflage trousers rode too high, exposing argyle socks above his black running shoes. A preppy Christian soldier. I smiled to myself as he spoke encouraging words to the crowd, his prominent Adam's apple bobbing in time with the syllables. Then I heard Mary Jo's voice above his bullhorn.

"Garr! Over here!"

I turned toward the voice. Mary Jo sat on the curb in the shade of the portico, smiling and waving. I realized why I had missed her when I first looked that way. She had left my side earlier with her hair up in a ponytail, wearing a plaid cotton shirt. Now her hair fell to her shoulders, and when she raised her arm to wave at me, the red letters on her T-shirt stretched tightly across her ample bosom, spelling the words, "Thou Shalt Not Kill." Even after twenty years, she could excite my libido with a casual shift in position. She'd been pretty when we married. She was breathtaking now. A single streak of gray had appeared recently, just to the right of her forehead. She never mentioned coloring it. Her pale skin had a translucent quality, a clear veneer that softened her features and welcomed intimate inspection. Mary Jo was a listener. A watcher. A city-raised country woman, comfortable with herself both physically and mentally.

Or so I thought then.

With careful tiptoed steps I inched across the driveway. After I settled to the curb beside her, she took my hand and pulled it onto her lap, gripping my thumb with one hand, while the other squeezed my fingers. Both of her hands together were the size of one of mine. I bent down to kiss her freckled cheek, nuzzling her auburn hair. She smiled and snuggled closer. It was chilly in the shade.

I said, "Where'd you go?"

"I'm sorry, baby," she said. "I just meant to go inside for a minute to use the rest room and change into this shirt, but when I came out I ran into a friend from New Orleans, and . . . well, here we are."

"I wish you hadn't left me alone so long. You know I'm not comfortable about all this. I wouldn't even *be* here if it wasn't for you—"

"I said I was sorry, Garr."

"It's all right. I just feel so out of place, you know?" Her face darkened a bit, so I squeezed her hand and changed the subject. "Hey. You said you ran into a friend from New Orleans?"

"Oh! I forgot you don't know her. Meet my friend, Faye Slydel."

The woman sitting on the other side of Mary Jo leaned forward into my line of sight and smiled tentatively, as if smiling might not be the thing to do. Her smile exposed two front teeth tilted one behind the other. She was dressed exactly like the man on the car.

Mary Jo said, "Faye, this is my husband, Garrison Reed. Everyone calls him Garr, like the fish."

The woman smiled at that and said hello. I returned her greeting. Her voice was surprisingly soft and warm. Honeysuckle sweetness and Southern charm. A Scarlet O'Hara voice. She was small, with thin brown hair parted in the middle and swept back to a low ponytail, pulled tight against her skull. The mottled brown skin below her eyes sank into her thin face. I wondered if she was ill or recovering from an illness. Her black T-shirt draped loosely on her bony frame. She pushed nervously at the hair behind her ear, as if afraid her ponytail was coming loose. Her fingernails were short and dirty. Crossing her arms across her sunken chest, she rubbed her hands against her biceps to warm them. We made eye contact for an instant. She quickly looked away. But in her eyes I caught a wounded look, like the backwards glance of a stray dog running with its tail tucked.

Mary Jo said, "Faye is married to James."

"James?"

She waved the back of her hand vaguely toward the crowd. "The man on the car over yonder."

"Ah."

"Faye and James came all the way from New Orleans to help organize the protest."

"So did you meet each other recently?" It was a natural question. Mary Jo had been down to New Orleans a lot lately.

My wife looked away from me. She said, "Yes, a few months ago."

"That's nice."

"They're going to stay here all night."

"Here? On the driveway?"

Faye leaned forward again, to look around Mary Jo. She said, "We want to be here early in the mornin', in case he tries to bring in a pregnant girl while ya'll are home or in jail."

Jail? Me and Mary Jo? It took a moment for me to realize that she meant we might be arrested for joining the sit-in. Suddenly I understood how serious all of this was.

"When will you sleep?" I asked.

She looked up at her husband. Then she turned to me. Above the dark smudges, the wounded look was gone. Her eyes burned with a fierce brightness. "How can we sleep when he might be in there murderin' babies? How can *any* decent Christian sleep while this is goin' on?"

I didn't know how to respond, so Mary Jo and I made small talk, something about the back of her white jeans getting dirty from sitting on the ground. I offered to dust them off. Mary Jo giggled. I told her I was serious. She pinched me and changed the subject, leaning close to my ear.

"You should have been here a few minutes ago. It was the strangest thing."

"What happened?"

"I was standing over yonder by those doors watching James, and from out of nowhere this nurse grabs me by the arm. When I turned around to see who it was, she takes one look at me and says, 'You're not her.' Then she started cussing and ran back inside."

"Weird."

"Yes. But it wasn't what she said so much as how she said it. I was frightened by the look on her face."

"How so?"

"She was furious. I thought she would hit me."

"But why? Have you ever seen her before?"

Mary Jo looked toward the doors. "Maybe . . . she could be one of the women who works for Dr. Rideout."

I squeezed her hand. She looked back at me. An unspoken message passed between us, a communication of mutual misery. Dr. Rideout had diagnosed Mary Jo with breast cancer less than a month earlier. He was undecided about the treatment he would recommend. She had undergone several tests during the last few weeks. It was torture, waiting for the results, not knowing how far the malignancy had progressed, whether she would lose her breast . . . or her life. Being at the hospital reminded me of her cancer. I did not want to be here, and had agreed to come to the demonstration only after much persuasion on her part.

Christians are not supposed to worry. Either you trust the Lord or you do not. Worry is a sure sign that you do not. But I was living through a hellish cycle of remembering the cancer with a sharp stab of fear, then remembering that I should not feel afraid, then committing the whole miserable situation to God again, then experiencing sweet relief from fear, leading to a few moments of peace, followed by remembering the cancer again and so on and on and on. I wondered if I could keep my newfound faith if God took Mary Jo. I felt guilty for wondering, but the doubt was there.

Mary Jo said, "James is a pastor down in Metairie, Garr. He and Faye brought a hundred and twenty people up here."

I looked at Faye. "How did you find out about all this?"

Faye said, "Oh, we was after that Doctor Milo back home. He's from New Orleans too, you know." She pronounced it as one word: 'Nawlins'. Then she said, "James thinks the doctor wants to move up here to get away from us. But it won't work. He can't never get away. God's wrath is everywhere for such as him."

She looked toward the hospital doors, her haunted eyes following some motion there. Whatever she saw seemed to make her uncomfortable. She quickly turned away and bowed her head to stare at the concrete between her feet. Perhaps she was praying.

Shifting position, I looked over my shoulder. Through the sliding glass doors I saw the man in the white lab coat standing with the three deputies. They stared out at us, scanning the crowd. The man in the white coat said something. The deputy who had been trying to talk the protesters into moving earlier answered him.

A woman walked behind them, paused, and tilted her head as if listening. Then she strolled out through the doors. They were automatic doors, the kind that slide to the side when you step on a rubber mat. The woman stopped near us, glanced around, then crossed over to stand beside the car. She spoke to Faye's husband. He looked down at her from his position on the hood of the car. She spoke again. He squatted and leaned toward her and said something. Perhaps he asked her a question. She shook her head and spoke again. James Slydel turned his face toward the sky and closed his eyes. Then he looked directly at Faye. Even across forty feet of crowded pavement, the look was intense. I heard Faye suck in her breath.

James climbed down from the hood of the car and made his way through the seated crowd toward us. When he reached Faye's side, he kneeled and whispered in her ear. Her thin shoulders seemed to curl inward as she listened, as if they bore a great weight. She touched his arm and said, "You can speak freely. These people are our friends."

James looked at me and Mary Jo. He said, "Someone has tried to kill Doctor Milo."

Mary Jo's fingers tightened around my hand. I said, "*Tried* to kill him?"

He nodded. "Shot him. I'm told he will survive."

Mary Jo said, "Thank God."

James looked at her strangely, as if she'd reminded him of something. He said, "Yes. Well, it seems a man was standing near the doctor. An innocent bystander. The man was shot, too. I'm afraid he's dead."

We sat in silence for a moment. I remembered the backfires I'd heard a few minutes earlier. I said, "Who did it?"

"I don't know. A woman."

"They catch her?"

"I don't know. I've told you all I've heard." He sighed and stared across the heads of the faithful toward the television crew standing out in the sunlight. He swallowed. His Adam's apple danced up and down like a tiny elevator zipping between chest and chin. From across the lawn, the blond reporter watched us closely. So did most of the faithful.

James Slydel said, "I suppose I should make an announcement."

"Maybe you should wait to see what the sheriff wants to do."

He looked at me, then something caught his eye and he turned toward the doors. "Here they come."

The three men in uniform marched through the door behind us, followed by the man in the white lab coat. The first deputy turned left. The next one turned right. The third deputy, the one I saw earlier, halted just outside the door with Lab Coat at his side. I had the uneasy feeling they were watching us and trying to hide it. The first two men took positions on opposite sides of the portico, blocking both ways out. After they were in position, the deputy and Lab Coat came in our direction.

I decided they must want James to help them work the crowd.

They mumbled apologies as they picked their way between the hands and legs across the pavement. As they came closer, Faye Slydel clutched James's arm. The knuckles of her bony fingers were white from the pressure of her grip. I glanced at her face. She was watching the approaching men like a deer frozen in oncoming headlights. What was she afraid of? James said the shooter was a woman. Perhaps it was not James they wanted after all.

It was obvious the men were coming to us. They had to watch the ground to place their feet, but between steps they both looked our way. The deputy's eyes connected with mine, and something unexpected happened. I felt an old familiar swelling in my chest. The feeling was one part panic, one part guilt. It said run. Run *now*.

Perhaps I would always carry the fear within me, in some deeply hidden corner of my mind, a vestige of the insanity I lived through once, when they thought I had murdered my best friend. If the foundations of your world have crumbled, and you are lucky, you survive and build again. But the cracks are always there.

I told myself it was not me they wanted. It was Faye. Then I prayed a short and selfish prayer, to ask the Lord to protect me, to keep me from having to go through it all again. I believe God always answers prayers. He answered mine that day.

It was not me they wanted.

It was Mary Jo.

Chapter 3

THE DEPUTIES RUSHED MARY JO INTO THE hospital as James Slydel's metallic voice sliced through the autumn air outside: "Brothers and sisters, something terrible has happened . . ."

I followed as closely as they would allow. When the automatic glass doors whispered shut at my heels, even Slydel's bullhorn could not penetrate the seal. For the moment, no sound remained but the lock-stepped rhythm of the deputies' polished boots slapping the terrazzo floor.

They gripped her elbows, one on either side, and marched her down a sterile corridor. She had to break into a trot to keep up. They wouldn't let her talk to me, but they couldn't stop me from calling to her, "Mary Jo, don't say a word! I'll call Winston Graves. Don't answer any questions until he comes! Don't talk to them!"

As they escorted her into a room on the left, she glanced back over her shoulder. I'll never forget that look. Her emerald eyes wore fear unnaturally, like an overcoat in August. Nothing was the same for me after that. It marked the dividing line between peace and war, heaven and hell, then and never again.

When they slammed the door behind her, the deputy bringing up the rear put his back to it and faced me with his arms crossed.

I said, "Listen, there's been some mistake. Let me in. I'm sure I can straighten this out."

The deputy shook his head. "I can't do that, sir."

For the first time, I really looked at his face. I said, "Look, your name's Jason isn't it? Jason Crittenton? You're Cyril and Edna's oldest?"

He smiled. "Yessir."

"I thought so. I coached you in Little League, what—nine years ago?"

Rubbing his chin, he said, "No sir. You must be thinking of my little brother Tommy."

"Oh, Tommy. Yeah. Tommy Crittenton. He was a pitcher."

"Yeah. Tommy had an arm on him."

"Well, look here, Jason. Since you know me, and—"

"Mister Reed," he interrupted, "You got to understand, the sheriff would have my hide if I let you in there just now. I'd like to, but I just can't."

I argued with him for two or three minutes, then rushed back to a row of pay telephones near the lobby. Stopping at the closest one, I flipped through the slender directory and punched the buttons.

A woman answered, "Ryan residence."

"Sorry. Wrong number."

I hung up and took one deep breath. Then, more carefully, I pressed the numbers again.

The phone clicked in my ear, with a clatter and an antique rattle. I visualized the handset on the other end of the line: black Bakelite and a rotary wheel, brown cotton insulation around the cord and handwritten numbers on a disk in the center, the exchange spelled out the old-fashioned way: Adams 5–7208.

"Winston Graves speaking."

"Winston, this is Garr. I need your help."

"Of course you do, Garrison. Agatha is bringing the car around now. I will be there shortly."

"Here? How can you already know—"

"Garrison, you underestimate me. Again. It is becoming tiresome. Stay as near to her as they will allow. Instruct her to remain silent on the subject of Father McKay's murder. I will be there in twenty-three minutes."

A dial tone hummed in my ear.

There was nothing left to do. I wandered the halls aimlessly, thinking of Mary Jo in that room with the two deputies. They would be flinging questions like stones, demanding answers she could not give. I knew what it was to be falsely accused, to be assaulted by their questions, to feel your will being eroded by their unyielding skepticism until you longed to say whatever they wanted to hear, anything to make them stop.

I turned corners without thinking, a part of my mind idly focused on the immaterial: a blue stripe on the floor, an unbroken handrail along the wall, a stainless steel cart filled with trays of uneaten food. Then I remembered something Winston Graves had said.

Who was Father McKay?

The hallway stank of urine. A man and a woman slumped against the wall outside a patient's room, staring at nothing, faces limp, clothes wrinkled. I drifted through their line of sight, attracting less attention than a speck of dust in a ray of sunshine. Turning another corner, I found my path blocked by a yellow plastic tape, strung across the hall at waist height. Beyond the tape, a man sat cross-legged on the floor with his back against the wall, his head bent over a clipboard in his lap. He wore a brown deputy's uniform. Further down the hall, three more men worked behind a second yellow ribbon stretched tightly from wall to wall. Two of them also wore brown uniforms. They held opposite ends of a white cord. The third man sighted along the cord with one eye shut like a hunter taking aim. He wore an immaculate blue suit, with the jacket buttoned.

The man in the suit said, "Amos, move your end a little bit higher. That's it. Hold it right there. All right, Hank, come shoot this one, will you?"

The man on the floor said, "Excuse me."

I stepped back as he rose to his feet. He stooped under the yellow ribbon. Reaching into an open suitcase lying on a gurney, he traded his clipboard for a camera. I stepped up to the ribbon for a closer look. One of the men stood with his back to me, his arm about chest high, holding the cord between his thumb and first two fingers. The other one knelt near the wall, holding his end of the cord against a bloody smear about two feet above the floor. On the vinyl floor below the smear, someone had drawn a crude pattern in blood, like a child's attempt at finger painting. It was a star—a pentagram—surrounded by strange symbols. An open eye. A swastika. Others I did not recognize. The camera flashed. A red river flowed from a pool on the floor beside the symbols. It disappeared between the wheels of a food cart parked further along the corridor. I wondered how anyone could have bled so much. This was a hospital. Why couldn't they stop the bleeding? The camera flashed again.

I called, "Hey, Ernie. Why couldn't they stop the bleeding?"

The man in the suit turned to look at me. He wore a crisp white button-down collar and an expensive burgundy silk tie. His tasseled loafers sparkled with polish. He smiled, his eyes lingering on my face. He was a big man, as big as me, with the wide shoulders and trim waist of a swimmer. The olive color of his skin was a gift from a Greek grandfather. It contrasted starkly with the thin white scar stretching along his jaw from just below his left ear to the center of his chin. He once told me that the scar was a souvenir from a knife-wielding Peruvian smuggler on the docks of the Houston ship channel. The Peruvian's aim was off. He was trying for Ernie Davenport's throat.

Ernie said, "Garr, you shouldn't be here."

"They won't let me be with Mary Jo."

"I know. I told them to keep her isolated until we get this thing sorted out."

"Ernie, you know she didn't have anything to do with this."

He lifted the tape to step closer to me. His gentle brown eyes searched mine for a moment before he said, "Garr, we have a witness."

"Witness?"

"Someone who said they saw her do it."

My chest caved in around my heart. I said, "I don't care. You know her. You know she wouldn't do this. She teaches your kids in Sunday school, Ernie. You and Helen have been over to our house for dinner. You *know* her."

Ernie Davenport put his arm around my shoulder. He smelled of Old Spice. He said, "You're right. You're right. I know her, Garr. But I've also got a job to do, and we have a man who says she was the assailant here. Now, you tell me, what am I supposed to do? Ignore something like that? Come on, Garr. What would you do?"

I started to speak but he interrupted me. "Listen, you and I both know this is nothing but a temporary thing. A mistake. Give me an hour or two to sort it out, and you and Mary Jo can probably go on home and forget it ever happened."

"Probably? *Probably?* That's not good enough. Ernie, I thought we were friends."

He removed his arm from my shoulder and looked back at the men working the murder scene. Running spread fingers through his short black hair, he said, "I'm sorry, Garr. I really am. But I didn't cause this problem. And because we *are* friends, I have to be careful to do everything by the book here." He turned back to me, his eyes flicking across my face. "When you've calmed down a little, maybe you'll understand. This is the best way for Mary Jo. And you, too."

I said, "What about these people I've seen all over town? The ones dressed like soldiers. Maybe they're ready to act like soldiers, too. Maybe they're ready to shoot doctors."

Before he could answer, a silken voice called down the hall, "Sheriff Davenport! I hear you've already made an arrest. Can you tell me the name of the suspect?"

Ernie glanced past my shoulder and whispered, "Garr, I'm already onto those people. Don't worry. Now, here comes the press. You'd better go." Then he smiled and called to the approaching reporter, "You boys are sure enough on top of this thing, aren't you?"

I turned and walked back the way I'd come, looking away from the blond reporter and his cameraman. They ignored me as they hustled by, firing questions at Davenport. As I turned the corner I heard Ernie say, "No, we haven't made an arrest yet. We are questioning a suspect, but until an arrest is made, I can't give you a name. You fellas know the rules. . . ."

It gave me hope. They had not arrested Mary Jo. They were only asking questions, after all. I hurried through the starkly lit halls, back to the room where they held her. A left turn, a right and two more lefts. Up ahead of me a pair of stainless steel doors crashed open and an orderly rushed a gurney into the corridor with a nurse following close behind. They careened my way, shouting questions at each other. The nurse held a plastic sack full of clear liquid at shoulder height as she ran. Limp tubing spiraled down to the unconscious man on the gurney.

The nurse saw me and yelled, "Stand back. Stand back!"

I flattened against the wall as they stampeded by. The nurse was a beauty. Full figure, blond hair in a bouncing ponytail, clear white skin with a sprinkling of freckles, striking green eyes that glared at me for getting in the way. Ribbons of blood crisscrossed the front of her white gown. Strangely, she seemed to be crying. Or perhaps the red in her eyes was from lack of sleep.

The man running beside her could have passed for twelve years old. He was short, with full round cheeks scrubbed to a rosy glow, and a stiff red cowlick on the back of his head. He had blood on his chest, too. On the gurney, the unconscious man's skin had turned to ashes, his lips to cold blue ice.

I turned to watch them rush the gurney around the corner out of sight.

Dear Lord, I prayed. *Please get us out of this.*

Turning to continue down the hall, I began to ask myself how this had happened. These people were strangers. Why should anyone believe Mary Jo would be involved? Why, they weren't even from Mount Sinai! All of them, the doctor and those fanatics outside, they were all from way down in New Orleans . . . Wait. New Orleans. I thought of all of the trips down there that Mary Jo had made lately. At least half a dozen in the last few months. She said she was talking business with a gallery owner. And there was the time her mother was sick. So many trips, all for good reasons, but all so recently. Could there be a connection?

Garr, what are you thinking?

As I passed my hand across my eyes to remove the traitorous thoughts, I heard a familiar voice call from down the hall. "Garrison! I told you to remain near Mary Jo. Why are you standing here?" Facing back toward the stainless steel doors, I saw Winston Graves coming in my direction.

Winston Graves did not walk, he advanced, measuring his progress with an ivory handled cane. Were he not a childless bachelor, he would be the quintessential Southern patriarch. His bourbon-infested eyes squinted behind frameless glasses. A soggy cigar stub jutted Winston Churchill style from the corner of his thick-lipped mouth. In spite of the season, he wore a linen suit as white as his hair, with a black bow tie and a pair of well-shined burgundy wingtips. He used his considerable midriff to forge a passage through crowds, intimidate witnesses, and create a dignified and trustworthy image with jurors.

Winston was the best attorney in East Texas or West Louisiana. Unfortunately, he was well aware of that, and seldom let anyone forget it.

I said, "Mary Jo's in a room around here somewhere. Let's go find her."

"Garrison, she is no longer there."

"You already got her out? That's great, Winston! Where is she?"

"She is en route to the courthouse, but I did not effect her release. They have formally arrested her. I arrived too late to intervene."

His florid face drifted out of focus, an incidental image at the edge of my consciousness. I watched his mouth move, substituting my thoughts for his words. It was happening again, the helpless feeling you get when the ground peels away and you find yourself tumbling through the air without warning and you hope you will wake up with your hands clutching the edge of the bed, breathing hard and fast and trying to calm yourself, taking comfort from the thought that it was only a dream, but knowing all the time it was much too real.

It was happening again, but this time was worse.

They had never arrested me for Ernest's murder. Through all the harassment and intimidation, I was comforted by the thought that they never had enough evidence to arrest me. But now they had taken Mary Jo straight to jail, less than an hour after the murder. What evidence could they possibly have to make them so certain? How could they think she would do something like this?

I said, "What can we do?"

Winston sighed. "As I have been saying, Garrison, I only remained here in order to advise you of the situation. I will now proceed to the courthouse to be present at her interrogation. You may accompany me; however, be advised that they will not allow you to have contact with her until we have arranged bail."

"When will that be?"

He checked his watch; a gold railroad watch on the end of a chain that he fished from a vest pocket. He said, "It is five after three in the afternoon." He clicked the watch shut and replaced it in his pocket. "I will almost certainly fail in my attempt to arrange a hearing today. Let us say tomorrow, perhaps in the morning."

"But that means she'll have to spend the night in jail!"

He placed a hand on my shoulder. "Garrison, the Jackson County Jail is hardly Gore State Penitentiary. They will isolate her from the male inmates, of course, and I very much doubt that she will find herself in the company of another female. At worst, it will be a long and boring night. Your wife is an intelligent and resourceful woman. She will be fine."

"Can't I do anything? Anything at all?"

"Perhaps a book. A change of clothes. I will see if it can be arranged."

He patted my shoulder once and turned and walked away, his ivory handled cane measuring every rolling step. I watched him go like a castaway squinting at a departing ship, knowing my hopes were going with him.

Chapter 4

ASIENNA BLANKET OF FALLEN LEAVES LAY upon the limestone plaza. More leaves trickled like gentle snowfall from the looming ring of ancient oaks around the square in front of the courthouse. I hurried past the gazebo and the iron benches and the bronze Confederate soldier high upon his pedestal, my heavy footsteps muffled by the leaves, my thoughts dulled by shock.

The red granite courthouse dominated the plaza, its arched black windows watching my approach with unblinking malevolence, a Romanesque remnant of Mount Sinai's faded eminence, a relic of the days when cotton was king. It squatted like a fat red spider at the center of a web of roads and two-lane highways, all of which led inevitably from the surrounding countryside of Jackson County to the old town square.

I took the stone stairs in front of the courthouse two at a time and yanked open the scarred oak door. Stepping into the lobby, I realized that the building manager had not heard that it was autumn outside. Cold air wheezed from the ceiling ducts in the lobby, air conditioning left over from the hot weeks of September. Sometimes we can't believe our luck when the seasons change and the intense, dripping heat of a humid East Texas summer finally recedes.

As I crossed the marble lobby floor, I rolled down my sleeves and buttoned the cuffs of my plaid cotton shirt. Sergeant Julie

Masters sat at the reception desk just beyond the frosted glass Sheriff's Department door. She wore a glossy brown nylon uniform jacket with a fuzzy black collar and a nameplate pinned above the left breast pocket.

I said, "Hello. I'm here to see my wife."

"Mister Reed, right?"

"You remember me."

She smiled. "From the last time."

It was like visiting the family dentist's office with a recurring toothache. I said, "I don't know what to do. Can I get to the jail through here?"

"No, sir. The public entrance is back out and around to the right. But your wife's not in jail yet. They're questioning her in the interrogation room."

"Where's that?"

"You can't go in there, Mister Reed."

I sucked in a deep breath. "Is Winston Graves with her?"

"Well, I did see him here a while ago. I imagine he's back there with everybody."

"Would you let him know I'm here?"

She said, "All right," and pushed away from the desk. I watched her weave through a small collection of desks and chairs, one of which was occupied by a uniformed man talking on a telephone. She disappeared through a wooden door at the far side of the room. I rubbed my hands together and stuck them in the pockets of my blue jeans. Shifting my weight from foot to foot, I turned to look at a wall covered by plaques and framed photographs. Ernie Davenport's collection had replaced our previous sheriff's. Ernie's was smaller. In most of the pictures, he stood beside rows of smiling children in baseball uniforms. There were Little League awards and citations from the Houston Y.M.C.A.'s Indian Guides program. His predecessor's collection had focused on shots of himself with various governors, mayors, and high-profile business leaders. I liked Ernie Davenport's photographs much better.

"Mister Reed?"

I turned and saw Sergeant Masters approaching her desk.

"I was able to poke my head in and let Mister Graves know you're here. He said you should wait."

"Thank you."

She looked at me closely, eyes searching my face. "They seemed to be taking it easy in there. More like a conversation than . . . well, you know."

I nodded. "Thanks. I appreciate that."

Two scuffed and cracked brown leather club chairs stood on either side of a small plastic table against the wall. I sank into the chair on the right and picked a magazine from the pile on the table. Thirty seconds later I put it back on the table. I crossed my right leg over my left. My left over my right. I sighed softly. Sergeant Masters looked up from her paperwork curiously. I smiled. She smiled. I studied the palm of my right hand. I selected another magazine. I flipped the pages, idly glancing at the photographs. I replaced it on the table.

It seemed like a good time to pray. But when I closed my eyes, the words wouldn't come. It wasn't fair. After all those years of lying to my wife and to my God, I was finally a believer. But looking back, life seemed easier before. The construction business had gone smoother then. The choices in life seemed easier. And now I faced the loss of my wife. Even if we got her through this insanity there was . . . the other thing. At the thought of her cancer, I gave in to a fog of sorrow. Where was God? Why was he allowing these things to happen to me? Was this faith real?

I shuddered. Folding my arms across my chest, I clutched at my elbows and willed my mind to turn from such perilous contemplations. It took a few minutes, but finally, with relief, I sank into a pool of memories, to a better place. A better time . . .

• • •

MARY JO WAS NINETEEN AND NEW ORLEANS WAS sweating under a harsh September sun on the day we met. I sat cross-legged on the sidewalk outside an old firehouse at the corner of Broadway and St. Charles, sketching the building for a freshman design studio. She rode her bicycle over my left foot. It was fate, pure and simple.

She careened out of control toward the granite curb, with her feet off the pedals. Her long auburn hair flew back like a soft red flag on a windy day. Muttering "Oh dear! Oh dear! Oh my goodness!" she made wobbling motions with the front tire and at the last moment, managed to steer away from the street to halt abruptly beside the gnarled trunk of a huge live oak. With her back to me, her long runner's legs spread wide, her hands on the handlebar grips, and her rib cage heaving with deep breaths, she straddled the bike, calming down. After five or six seconds, she whipped around suddenly, twisting at the waist and fixing me with a penetrating stare over her shoulder. Green eyes, shining with intensity, hair flowing back from her smooth forehead like a lion's mane, that piercing look, that fierce beauty—it was a vision frozen forever in my memory. Even then, I knew the image would brand the cells of my brain, to be carried among my collection of mental snapshots for life: the Grand Canyon, the Rocky Mountains, Golden Gate Bridge, the Manhattan skyline—and my first good look at Mary Jo.

"How's the foot?" Her first words to me.

"I'll live." But not without you.

She nodded once and began to maneuver the bicycle away from the tree. Her cut-off shorts rode high on her thighs. I stood and stumbled a bit, faking it. I sat back down and said, "Wait a minute. Maybe it's worse than I thought."

She leaned the bicycle against the tree and hurried back to kneel beside me. I couldn't take my eyes off her. She knelt at my side, the muscles of her legs strong and well toned. She said, "Here, let me look at it," and began to loosen the strap on my sandal. It was the late sixties and sandals were very fashionable. She wore a multicolored tie-dyed T-shirt. Tie-dyed T-shirts were also very fashionable. Hers was several sizes too large. Girls with full figures wore baggy shirts in the sixties, because full figures were definitely not fashionable. I could not have cared less about fashion.

Her hair was frizzy from the humidity. It fell on either side of her head as she bent over my foot, an apple cider waterfall defining the space between us, a copper tunnel connecting her face and mine, creating an illusion of privacy on the busy street corner. I felt an almost irresistible urge to kiss her.

She took the sandal off and massaged my foot, feeling for broken bones. In my fascination with her beauty, I forgot to flinch. She said, "Well, there doesn't seem to be any real damage." I remembered too late and winced a little as she rubbed my foot. She smiled at my delayed reaction and said, "Maybe a cup of coffee would make it all better?"

I smiled too, and said, "Absolutely."

She rose, dusting off her hands. "There's a cafe around the corner."

I gathered my sketch pad and my tackle box full of pastels and conté crayons, and we walked together around the old firehouse toward the cafe. She steered the bicycle easily with one hand on the handle bars. I longed to hold her other hand. I did not bother to limp. We ordered *cafe au lait* and a dozen oysters on the half shell. Ella Fitzgerald's version of "April in Paris" played softly on the jukebox. We talked for three hours. Sometimes Mary Jo sang along with the jukebox. She knew the words to all the jazz numbers.

I learned she was originally from a small town south of New Orleans. Her father was a minister, her mother a professional minister's wife. She had one sister. For some reason, she did not want to talk about her sister. She was studying fine art at Tulane, concentrating on painting. She had always loved to draw and paint, ever since she could remember. Her parents moved the family to New Orleans to run a storefront mission down by the river. When she was a teenager, she began walking to Jackson Square to watch artists draw on the sidewalk with colored chalk. Some of the men had been there for thirty and forty years, drawing scene after beautiful scene on the French Quarter pavement for dimes and nickels in a paper cup. She became a regular. One day they gave her some tiny pieces of leftover chalk and a small section of sidewalk back out of the way. In time, they taught her everything they knew.

She said, "They call it 'painting,' you know. Only people who don't know better call it drawing. Drawing is in black and white, or monochromatics, like contés."

I said, "I was working with contés when you, uh, ran over me. It's for an elective art class. I'm an architecture major."

"Could I see?"

I showed her my sketch book. Foolishly, I reveled in her flattering critique of the crude images. Several weeks later, when I saw her work for the first time, I realized her praise was akin to Leonard Bernstein complimenting a child's fumbling efforts at the major scales.

By the age of seventeen, she had graduated from pastels on pavement to oils on canvas. The work she showed me at Tulane was part of a series she'd begun in high school. We stood side by side in her carrel at the fine arts studio, considering a three-by-five painting on a wooden easel. She had captured the Vieux Carre in the morning.

Tendrils of fog drifted above the granite curbs. Sparkling drops of dew quivered on the tips of ferns dangling in baskets from delicate wrought iron balconies. Stucco walls and ancient brick defined the perspective and enclosed the image. It was the same jaded scene they sold to tourists by the hundreds from sidewalk kiosks piled high with cheap color. But in Mary Jo's hands, the tired old view came to life, and more than that, assumed a sense of place, an aura that captured the mystical feeling of generations lived and died, of lives forgotten and tragedies on the distant edge of memory. It was more than an image of the Vieux Carre. It was an encapsulated piece of history. One look and I knew she was a genius.

But there was something vaguely disturbing about the painting. I looked at it silently for a minute, trying to define the feeling. Finally, I said, "It's so . . . sad."

"I suppose."

"Why have you made it feel so gloomy?"

"Oh, not gloomy. Sad, maybe. Or mythical. Maybe even ominous. But gloomy? I hope not. The Quarter doesn't feel that way to me, and I always paint what I feel."

"I didn't know until now that it was mythical or ominous, but you've proven your point. I'll never look at Dauphin or Bienville the same way again."

She took my hand and squeezed it. As she showed me her other paintings that day, I realized every canvas conveyed intense emotion. How or why, I couldn't say. But to look at them was to feel something strongly.

She pulled them one by one from an open wooden box against the wall, showing them to me in chronological order. "This is one I did last year. It's the Bayou St. John." Then, "Here's one of an old shack on the Atchafalaya. I did it early this year." She brought out the others, each an image from South Louisiana, each a vivid statement about more than just the view. I began to see a pattern. The older works were bright and lively, painted in full sun with laughing men and women and children inhabiting the landscapes and the buildings. As she withdrew the newer paintings from the box, darker colors began to intrude upon the light, edges became frayed and muddy, the people disappeared, and the landscapes took on a barren, haunted quality. She might not like the word, but to me they felt gloomy.

I said, "Why the change to such an, ah, ominous feeling in the later stuff?"

"It's just how I feel. Picasso had his blue period. I'm in my gray period."

I nodded. Gray period described the feeling well, if not the colors. I said, "But your older ones are so . . . happy. Why the change?"

She placed the last painting back in the wooden box. With her back to me she said again, "It's just how I feel. Could we talk about something else?"

Perhaps that was when I first knew something was wrong.

• • •

WINSTON GRAVES, ERNIE DAVENPORT, AND DISTRICT Attorney Jacob Steiner emerged through the wooden door on the far side of the sheriff's office, yanking my thoughts back to the here and now. Winston's red-rimmed eyes rested on me as he crossed the squad room, bumping his cane against the desks and chairs like a blind man.

He said, "Garrison, as I suspected, it is too late this evening to effect your wife's release on the strength of a bail bond. Did you bring clothing and reading material as we discussed?"

"It's out in the truck."

"I will accompany you."

Together, we descended the courthouse steps and strolled across the plaza in the rusty light of an early autumn dusk. It was good to get out of the cold interior air. Crows and grackles were alighting on the old oaks around the square by the hundreds, their guano pasting the flagstone, their calls like cruel laughter, heckling me as I led Winston to my truck. We crossed the red brick road. Out of habit, I had parked in front of the Reed Construction office building across from the square. I was glad it was Sunday and Mrs. P. was not working. I did not want to discuss this with her. I did not want to discuss it with anyone. Talk makes things more real sometimes, and I preferred to put off facing this particular reality as long as possible.

We reached the truck. I opened the passenger door and removed a cable-knit sweater, a pair of khaki slacks on a hanger, and a paper bag packed with a pair of brown leather shoes, a bra and panties, and some of Mary Jo's cosmetic things. Winston stood leaning on his cane, catching his breath from the hundred yard walk across the plaza. I held the clothing in my left hand and reached into the truck again for the books.

Behind me, Winston wheezed, "May I be of assistance?"

"Yes. Thanks. Will you hold these while I lock up?"

I handed him the books. One of them was a Bible. The other was a copy of *The Swiss Family Robinson*. Winston glanced at the title and looked up at me, eyebrows raised.

I said, "She just finished *Robinson Crusoe* and before that she read the Bounty trilogy. Her parents didn't let her read novels. They said fiction was too 'worldly.' So she's catching up, choosing books by subject matter. Last year it was *Rebecca* and *My Cousin Rachel* and *Frenchman's Creek*—that kind of thing. This year I guess it's sea and survival."

"Indeed."

I slammed the truck door. "Let's go."

"It is not necessary for you to accompany me, Garrison."

"What?"

"You might as well return home. I will deliver these items."

"But I want to see her!"

"As I told you at the hospital, that will not be possible until tomorrow at the hearing."

"Are you sure? I mean, Ernie and I are pretty good friends. . . ."

"Garrison, I am sorry, but I asked Sheriff Davenport if you could visit your wife after the interrogation. He specifically requested that I tell you it was a regulation he could not abridge. He also asked me to convey his sympathies. I believe he was sincere."

I nodded, my eyes dropping to the brick pavement at our feet. "How did the . . . interrogation go?"

"She did quite well. I doubt very much if they learned anything of substance. The district attorney expressed some frustration with my intervention at times."

"Did they ask her about New Orleans?"

He looked at me curiously. "What do you mean?"

"She's been spending a lot of time down there, and these people all seem to be from there, and . . . I was just wondering if there was a connection."

"I see. Well, the subject did arise, of course. Mister Steiner, the prosecutor, wanted to know if she had been in New Orleans recently, and if she had had any contact with the Milos, or the, ah, C.H.A.R.G.E. organization, such as it is."

"And? What did she say?"

"She said nothing. I instructed her not to answer. Now, if there is nothing else, I must deliver these items and return home. Agatha serves the evening meal promptly at seven."

"All right, Winston. Listen, there's something you should know. Maybe it will help you to get her out."

Impatience showed in his rheumy eyes. Perhaps he was overdue for his evening bourbon. He said, "I really must be going."

"All right, I'll hurry. It just that ... Mary Jo has cancer. Breast cancer."

He turned to look toward the courthouse. "I see."

"I thought you should know."

"Yes. You were wise to tell me, Garrison. I may be able to use that fact in future negotiations."

"I hope so."

We stood silently for a moment. Then I cleared my throat. "Do me one more favor, will you?"

"If possible."

"Will you ask them to turn down the air conditioning? Mary Jo hates to sleep in a cold room."

"I will see that she is as comfortable as possible."

He walked across the brick street, loaded down with clothes and books. The back of his white linen jacket was crisscrossed with wrinkles. At the far curb he stopped and turned back.

Peering over the top of Mary Jo's sweater he called to me. "Garrison, how bad is it?"

"We don't know. We're waiting on some tests."

He stared at me for a moment. Then he said, "I am very sorry." Without waiting for a response, he turned and walked toward the jailhouse door.

Chapter 5

I LAY UPSTAIRS IN THE DOUBLE BED WE HAD shared for almost twenty years, squeezing my eyes shut, counting to one hundred again and again, telling myself I needed rest for tomorrow. At two-thirty in the morning I slipped into a robe, went downstairs, and shuffled out through the French doors to the deck. We live in a large two-story cedar house on top of a gently sloping hill above Martin Pool. Except for the clearing in front, our house is surrounded by dense woods. There is a covered porch in front and a partially open deck in back. The deck stands ten feet above the ground because of the way the hill falls away toward the lake. In summer when the sunlight strikes the water just so, you can see the shimmering quicksilver reflection through the branches. But now, with winter approaching, the deciduous trees had shed their multicolored canopy to reveal a panoramic view of Martin Pool lying cold and blue in the hollow down below. The water wound to the left and right for miles, a narrow, wandering lake with hundreds of hidden coves and tributaries.

I slumped on the porch swing and stared across the moonlit valley. Boathouse lights glistened on the water along the opposite shore, their reflections dancing like fairies on the waves. Insects chirped rhythmically among the moldering pine needles on the forest floor. In the treetops, a whispering breeze coaxed the last of the autumn leaves to the ground. Bare branches sketched jagged black lines against a powdered spray of stars. My breath came in steamy puffs. I shivered.

My heart was breaking with worry for Mary Jo.

I shuffled back inside and fell onto the leather recliner she had given me for our tenth wedding anniversary. The house felt so empty. I pointed the remote control at the television, hoping for an old movie, something to distract me for an hour or two. What I got was the Cable News Network, showing the scene outside Jackson County General Hospital. Mount Sinai had made the national news. The picture was a bit snowy, like it gets when I put off cleaning the pine needles out of the satellite dish. But I still recognized the blond reporter in the gray suit staring at me from the screen as he described the events of yesterday.

"For the third time in just under two years, a medical doctor has been assaulted by anti-abortion fanatics. The hospital you see behind me in this sleepy little town of Mount Sinai, Texas, was the scene of a vicious attack this afternoon, in which Doctor Melvin Milo was shot and seriously wounded, and Father Michael Q. McKay, a Catholic priest, was killed."

The reporter's face was replaced by the scene in the hospital hallway. I saw Ernie Davenport's men working behind the yellow tape.

"The attack took place here, in this hallway outside an operating room at Jackson County General Hospital, while pro-life advocates demonstrated outside. Authorities have arrested a local woman who was present at the demonstrations. They believe she slipped into the hospital to wait in this hallway, where she allegedly shot both men as they walked around that corner. Doctor Milo was shot one time and is in stable condition, while Father McKay, apparently an innocent bystander, was shot twice and lies dead tonight in the county morgue in the basement of this same building."

The camera zoomed in on the pool of blood beside the wall. The reporter's voice continued, "Today, Doctor Milo was visiting Jackson County General, where he had hoped to escape the controversy that surrounded him in his home of New Orleans, Louisiana." The picture changed to a crowd outside a building in a place I did not recognize. People were holding placards and chanting a slogan. The reporter's voice-over continued. "Doctor Milo has been the focus of a long-standing battle between pro-life and pro-choice factions here in New

Orleans. His medical clinic was the scene of repeated demonstrations like this one, in which up to two hundred people participated. The clinic building in the background was repeatedly vandalized, and Doctor Milo had reported receiving telephone threats. It was this kind of harassment that he came to Mount Sinai to avoid. But he found that his detractors were waiting for him here, as well."

Again, the scene changed, this time to the crowd outside Jackson County General. The reporter chose footage from the moment the crowd was told about the murder. I saw faces I knew, faces made ugly by the intensity of their emotions. The reporter's voice continued, "This was the scene just moments after the doctor was attacked and Father McKay was killed. Many of the demonstrators in this crowd made the trip from New Orleans to be present at the hospital on Doctor Milo's first day here. They were led by this man, Brother James Slydel, a minister from Metairie, Louisiana."

James Slydel's face filled my television screen, his eyes large and wild behind steel-framed glasses, his cheeks flushed, his hair perfectly parted. He was speaking to someone off to the side with his face turned at an angle to the camera. He said, "We condemn this kind of thing. It is a sin to kill, and that applies to everyone, from unborn babies to the men and women who murder them for profit. But I cannot help wondering how many innocent children's lives will be saved by what happened here today."

Another man's face appeared on the screen, and the reporter's voice continued, "Not everyone here agrees with Brother Slydel, including this man who was a demonstrator at the hospital yesterday."

The man on the screen began to speak in a thick East Texas accent. "Well, I'm against killin', I surely am. But you gotta defend them that can't defend themselves, and if that means you gotta get tough now and then, why I say fine. The Good Book says an eye for an eye, and a tooth for a tooth. It also says to shed the blood of them that sheds blood. And brother, you better believe I'm gonna follow the Good Book right on down the line."

The reporter said, "In this case, the prosecution believes Mrs. Mary Jo Reed agrees." They showed some footage of Mary Jo being led by two deputies from a squad car to the side entrance of the courthouse. She wore handcuffs behind her back. She glanced at the camera just before they walked her through the door. The cameraman zoomed in for a tight shot, and her face filled the television screen. In her eyes was that lost and fearful look I had seen at the hospital.

I moaned out loud.

Against the backdrop of Mary Jo's fearful expression, the reporter's relentlessly neutral voice continued, "Mrs. Reed, a prominent artist and social activist in this part of East Texas, was arrested less than one hour after the murder. Rumors are circulating here in Mount Sinai that she was a member of a shadowy cultlike organization that is sworn to fight abortion by any means necessary—even violence. Strange symbols were found at the scene of the crime. The authorities are not releasing any information about the—"

I shut the blasted thing off. Staring at the blank screen, I tried to think of something I could do, a plan of action. I decided to try to pray again.

Leaning forward with my elbows on my knees and my hands clasped together, I shut my eyes tightly. I spoke of my fears out loud, listing them one by one. Please keep Mary Jo safe while she is in jail. Please don't let them hurt her there. Please do something about this terrible mistake. This murder. This false accusation. And please deliver her from the cancer in her breast. Please don't take her that way.

I tried to feel God listening as I prayed. But distractions flitted through my skull like winged demons, giggling and mocking my feeble faith, gleefully chanting a coda of worry and doubt. Who was I that the Creator of everything would attend to my puny concerns? I struggled against the demons, eyes squeezed shut and knuckles white, until finally, the horrible thought that God was not listening made it impossible to continue and I surrendered instead to the strange memories dancing through my mind, memories of something that happened not long ago, of a moment when I first realized Mary Jo's old sorrows might be back to haunt us both . . .

• • •

IT HAD BEEN JUST A MONTH AGO, JUST A MONTH before the murder at the hospital. I awoke early on a weekday morning, rolled toward Mary Jo's side of the bed, and reached for her as I always do. She was not there. "Honey?" I called, thinking she might be fixing coffee down in the kitchen. She did not reply. I rose and padded through the house, searching for her. But Mary Jo was gone.

Wrapped in my flannel robe, I stepped onto the back deck. Perhaps she had decided to fill the bird feeders. I scanned the nearby woods but saw no movement, no Mary Jo. I began to worry. It was something she had never done before. Where could she be?

As I was about to enter the house a shot rang out, muted and distant. Then I heard another, and another. Perhaps it was a poacher, firing at a buck or a doe. I hurried inside and pulled on a pair of faded jeans, a red and black plaid cotton shirt, a pair of white crew socks, and buck leather walking boots. I went to the study and lifted my Browning twelve gauge from the rack. Back outside, the shots continued. They were off to the west, toward the dam. With the shotgun loose in the crook of my arm, I set out through the woods.

The birds were silent that morning, afraid of the gunfire. A heavy carpet of leaves and pine needles muffled my footsteps as I followed the path toward Mary Jo's studio. When I reached the solitary building, I peered in through the tall glass on the north side. The studio was vacant. Worry gnawed at the edges of my mind. Where could she be? The distant shots resumed, echoing through the woods. Closer now, I could hear that they were probably not deer rifle shots. The sound was too delicate. Someone was firing a target pistol, or a light gauge rifle, perhaps a twenty-two or something a little larger. I resumed my search, moving more slowly since I was leaving the well-traveled path between our house and the studio and striking out through the underbrush. As the sound of firing grew closer, I began to place each footstep carefully, searching for the mossy spots or the all-too-rare places not covered by freshly fallen leaves. The firing was very near, somewhere directly ahead. I knew I was approaching a deep ravine that fell away to a creek. I reached a place beside an ancient oak that marked the sudden drop to the bottom thirty feet below. Shots rang through the woods from just beyond the tree. Clutching the shotgun with my finger on the trigger and the safety off, I peered over the edge of the ravine.

Just below, about halfway down the slope toward the creek, was a broad level place. Mary Jo stood there, facing the other side of the ravine, her head about a yard lower than my feet. She held a chrome-plated .32 automatic pistol in both hands, her arms extended, her feet spread and knees slightly bent. She fired. Across the ravine, the soil erupted beside a rotten log. She fired again and a new crater formed beside the log, an inch to the right. If she was aiming at the log, it seemed to be safe. The plateau where she stood was littered with brass shell casings, but the log was completely intact. An open yellow cardboard box lay at her feet, almost empty. I watched as she squeezed off three more shots. When she ejected the clip, I spoke.

"What's going on?"

She stiffened, then turned and looked up at me. Her eyes were rimmed in red. She said, "How long have you been there?"

"Long enough to see you turn the ground around that log into Swiss cheese," I said. Staring at her eyes, I asked, "Have you been crying?"

"No. It's just hay fever." Then she smiled and knelt to reload the clip.

I took a deep breath, inhaling through my nose. The damp, clean air felt good going in. I said, "Why the sudden interest in target practice?"

"Oh, I just woke up early and thought about it. It's been a long time since you taught me how to do this. It seems like a good idea to stay in practice."

"Why?"

She slipped the clip into the handle of the .32. It went home with a dull click. She worked the slide with a practiced motion and took aim across the ravine again.

"It just seemed like a good idea. That's all."

She never could look at me when she lied.

Chapter 6

AFTER A SLEEPLESS NIGHT I ARRIVED AT THE courthouse before dawn. They told me the hearing wouldn't take place until ten that morning. I could not visit her at six A.M. The sky was just beginning to blush when I left the building and wandered across the street to the Reed Construction offices.

My father and grandfather started the family business at the time Martin Pool was built, during the Great Depression. Since then, our old red brick building on the Mount Sinai square has always been Reed Construction's headquarters. It is sandwiched between two nearly identical commercial buildings, part of a line that makes up one of the four sides of the square. Cantilevered canopies shelter the raised sidewalks. Rows of second story windows, empty as a blind man's eyes, stare out beneath tall parapets inscribed with the name and date of the original tenants: Meany Mercantile, 1893; James and Sons, 1904; First National Bank, 1878. I saw *Fantasia* and *The Wild Bunch* at the Esquire Theater across the square a generation ago.

In those days, downtown Mount Sinai was a vital, active place. On Saturdays, the sidewalks around the oak-shaded courthouse plaza teemed with country folk, come to town for the shopping and the fellowship. Apache 31 pickups with streamlined fenders nosed to the curbs around the square. Farmers and ranchers and wives and kids piled out of their trucks to spend the day window shopping and strolling and catching up on the comings and goings of friends from the other side of the county. Nobody worried much.

The Reed Construction building is small for a company our size, but I remain there out of nostalgia, working at the same desk my father used in the ten-by-twelve room with a view of the courthouse square. Out front in the reception area, Mrs. P. adds her own bit of nostalgia to the atmosphere. She was my father's secretary during his last few years and stayed on after he died. That was almost fifteen years ago.

Ethyl Polanski is a short and wide black woman who is fond of floral muumuus and nylon wigs. She selects her wigs according to the day's events: a white pony tail with velvet ribbon in honor of George Washington's birthday, or a black one with leather ties to express solidarity with Native Americans on Thanksgiving Day. One may well ask how a black woman came to be named Polanski, but one would not ask twice. Questions along those lines make her angry, and when she is angry, bad things happen. It is rumored that a man's ears once bled spontaneously from the ferocity of an Ethyl Polanski tongue-lashing. I knew that the Polish name is a vestige of an ill-fated marriage. But Mrs. P. has shortened it to the single initial as fair warning to all that the subject is taboo.

I expected an empty office at that early hour, but Mrs. P. was there, enthroned behind her antique desk, pudgy hands folded on the blotter. She granted me an imperial nod as I stepped through the front door.

"Look like we got another problem, don't it, Garr?"

"Problem?"

She snorted. "Why you wanna play games with me? I saw her on the TV this mornin'."

"Oh."

I went to the chair in front of her desk and sat heavily. She rose with a grunt and a two-handed shove at the desktop and waddled toward the door that leads to the rear.

"You sit there, Garr. I'll go get us some coffee."

There are many tasks that Mrs. P. considered to be below her station. Chief among them was making coffee. I always handled that for myself. And she never arrived at the office before nine in the morning. Offering me a cup of coffee at six A.M. was a sure sign of the severity of the situation. My depression deepened.

She returned almost immediately, with two steaming mugs. She placed mine beside my elbow and settled into her chair with a grunt. We sat in silence. She sipped her coffee; I stared at mine. Time flew. At five after six she said, "You gonna let us help you this time?"

"What?"

"Don't *do* that! Don't play dumb with me, boy. You know exactly what I mean."

"What?"

She sighed. "Leon an' I want to help, Garr. Last time you wouldn't let us help. This time we want to do what we can."

"Thank you."

"You welcome."

Another thirty seconds crawled by. Outside the storefront windows, the rusty red glow of dawn was giving way to a clear white light. A pale blue van pulled to the curb near the courthouse. Painted on its side was a big yellow number five.

Mrs. P. said, "What we gonna do?"

"What?"

"Oh, come on, Garrison! Snap outta it! You sure 'nuff tryin' my patience, an' I'm not likely to be this nice again for a coon's age. Listen to me when I talk."

"I'm sorry, Mrs. P. What did you say?"

"I asked you what we gonna do about this mess?"

I returned my gaze to the scene outside the window. Two men and a woman had emerged from the van. The woman looked like she was wearing a thousand dollars worth of clothes. As I watched, the men opened the side door and began removing equipment from the van. Without looking at Mrs. P., I said, "I haven't thought about it. I don't know what to do."

"You got to fight, Garrison. That's what you got to do."

"How?"

"Same as last time. Get out there an' find out what's going on. Who did this. Why they did it. Only this time you let us help. I got a feelin' you gonna need lots of help this time. This town been full of them crazy people in those silly red hats with the pants look like they's covered with leafs. They all wrong, Garr. Don't ask how I know. I just know they wrong people. Remind me of Nazis, in them black shirts an' all. Got the same lowdown dumb-as-dirt look on they faces them red-neck Klan boys used to have. You don't try to work this out alone. You let us help."

"But you don't even like Mary Jo. You don't even say her name."

She looked straight at me, and in her eyes was something I'd seldom seen before. Perhaps it was sympathy. Maybe even love. She said, "Garr, I know what she mean to you. It the same with you an' her as it is with me an' Leon. An' we gonna help you this time, whether you like it or not."

"All right."

"*All right?* That all you got to say? Shoot, I got to get me some help over here."

She lifted the telephone handset and punched the numbers. Looking away from me, she spoke into the handset.

"Hey, sugar. How's everything out there? Uh huh. Listen, I'm here at the office an'. . . now don't interrupt. A girl don't need much beauty sleep when she come with my fine natural equipment. Ain't that right, sugar? Uh huh. You come on over an' I'll explain why I'm here . . . right now, sugar, an' don't make me wait . . . all right." She hung up the telephone and said, "Leon's on his way."

"But he's got to pour the ground floor on that school this morning."

"That's not near as important."

"But we've been waiting a week for the ground to dry."

"Garr, you 'bout to tick me off. They's only so far I can push this good mood. I said Leon's coming over, an' that's what he gonna do."

Objections were pointless. I said, "I'll be in the office," and walked away.

I closed the door behind me, sank into my father's leather chair, and propped my boots up on my grandfather's desk. To my left, through a full-height glass window, I looked out across the raised sidewalk and the brick road that lay between our building and the courthouse. Two more vehicles had arrived and parked across the street beside the van. A sudden gust scattered golden oak leaves along the plaza. The well-dressed woman clutched at her skirt while she and the camera crew loitered at the foot of the courthouse steps. Another group stood near the gazebo. As the third crew emerged from their car, yet another van slowly pulled to a stop at a parking place on the far side of the plaza. This vehicle had a folding satellite dish on top. It was six-thirty in the morning and already over a dozen reporters waited on the square. I felt the acid in my stomach begin to boil.

Time passed. Several more reporters arrived before a dirty white pickup truck nosed into the stall right in front of my window. Leon Martinez slid out of the truck and gave me a friendly wave. I was surprised at the relief I felt.

Leon was fifty-seven years old and sixty-seven inches tall. A wrinkle etched his bronze face for every year spent in the East Texas weather building roads, bridges, schools, and warehouses. His faded blue jeans hung loosely around a pair of skinny legs as bowed as the handles of a pair of pliers. Leon boxed in Golden Gloves during the late fifties. He went all the way to the nationals, where he lost on points in the semifinals to a kid from Queens, New York. Leon liked to say it took a national champion to beat him, and if it was a real fight with the gloves off, the kid would have been down in the first five seconds. I had seen Leon lift solid steel reinforcing bars and piles of timbers and watched him drive nails with a two-pound framing hammer, pounding on and on for hours to the double-time beat of a *Tejano* polka on the radio. I believed him. The kid from Queens would have been history.

My father hired Leon as a laborer thirty years ago. Leon's intelligence and natural people skills soon made it obvious he was bound for better things. Dad promoted him regularly until he was in charge of all field operations. Over the years I had begun to rely on Leon for more and more support in the business. He considered himself to be a kind of uncle or godfather to me, and I thought of him as family.

The door to my office opened and he and Mrs. P. walked in. They were a strange couple. Mrs. P. outweighs Leon two to one. She is as caustic as he is gentle. Leon is a simple, what-you-see-is-what-you-get kind of ol' boy. Mrs. P. wears wigs and makeup like disguises, changing her appearance from day to day. But there is love between them. Anyone can see that.

"Garr, this is just terrible. Ethyl called me, and then I turned on the news and saw Mary Jo. I just had to sit right down and get collected, it shook me up so bad."

"Yes."

He walked around the desk and placed a huge hand on my shoulder. "Don't you worry, son. We gonna get this fixed. There's been some kind of mistake, that's all."

"Thank you, Leon."

He patted my shoulder twice and removed his hand, shifting positions awkwardly. He said, "What's supposed to happen next?"

I looked through the window toward the courthouse and said, "Winston Graves will try to get her out on bail today. Then I suppose we'll have to sort this out. Find out why they think she did it."

"When you gonna go over yonder?"

"I already tried to get in to see her once this morning. I'm going back at ten to try again."

Mrs. P. said, "We gonna go with you."

"All right. Thank you."

Small talk was impossible and we had two and a half hours to kill, so I did some paperwork while we waited, and Leon and Mrs. P. went over some invoicing. Other Reed Construction employees began to arrive about seven-thirty. I heard the familiar ritual, with Mrs. P. grunting hellos to those brave enough to speak to her. Finally, Leon opened the door.

"It's about time, Garr."

I checked my wrist watch. Nine forty-five. I stood to go. The easy part was over. The rest of the morning would be a nightmare.

Chapter 7

A FIENDISH FACE LOOMED LARGE IN MY vision. It was the devil, with short bleached white hair, blood-red lips, insane eyes, a felt-tipped pen, and a note pad. The roar of voices surged and ebbed around me. Hands clutched microphones like sharpened spikes, stabbing them at me, pushing, shoving. Answers were demanded, commands issued. I was in hell.

"Did she know him, Mister Reed?"

"Can you tell us how long she had planned this?"

"Is she a part of a pro-life group?"

"Will she plead insanity, Mister Reed?"

Leon plodded ahead of me, a short but unstoppable ice-breaker chopping through the sea of reporters. There were at least fifty of them. I stayed as close behind him as possible, with Mrs. P. toddling beside me, holding my arm, pushing me along like a tiny tugboat guiding a rudderless ocean cruiser. It took maybe three minutes to walk from the plaza curb to the bottom of the courthouse steps. It seemed like hours.

Mrs. P. was magnificent, turning the full brunt of her acerbic wit upon them, a match for any and all. But they were seasoned professionals and had been insulted by the best. They persisted.

A young woman thrust a tape recorder at arm's length toward me and shouted, "Mister Reed, tell us your position on abortion. This is your chance to reach thousands of readers with the whole truth."

Mrs. P. said, "Honey, you better move yourself out *my* reach. An' *that* the whole truth."

A man in a bright green sport coat pushed forward carrying a handmade sign that read: *Keep Abortion Legal.* He yelled, "How could your wife do such a thing? How *could* she?"

Mrs. P. said, "Mister, only thing louder than you is that jacket. How could you *wear* such a thing? Get out the way."

We ascended the steps, with Leon doggedly pushing and shoving people aside up above and Mrs. P. falling back to protect me from behind. At the top, Sheriff Ernie Davenport and two deputies met us, joining Leon in pushing back the crowd. Turning to look across the plaza, I saw a cluster of waving placards above the sea of heads. They read: *My Body, My Choice* and *Free to Choose.*

As he stiff-armed two reporters, Ernie had to yell back at me over his shoulder to be heard above the babble of questions. "Next time, maybe you better call us first, Garr. We'll come over and walk you around to the side entrance."

I shouted back, "How is she, Ernie?"

"I looked in on her about six-thirty. She was sleeping like a baby."

The well-dressed woman who had arrived early in the van pushed through the throng and presented herself before us with the air of a person accustomed to getting her way. Although we were just a few feet apart, she screamed her question to be sure it was heard above the roar of her competitors. "Mister Reed, I'm Petra O'Connor from CBS. Could we meet someplace later today? I'd like to ask you a few questions about your wife. Try to get her side of the story."

Sheriff Davenport said, "Oh, for pete's sake. Come on, Garr, let's go inside."

The reporter said, "But I've come all the way from New York, just to interview Mister Reed."

Mrs. P. wedged her considerable bulk between us and said, "You should've called first. Made an appointment, honey."

"Appointment? Called? What do you mean?"

Mrs. P. took the woman's arm and turned her away. Speaking in a patient tone, she said, "I'll explain everything, honey. Now an appointment, that mean you ask when can you talk to Mister Reed, and I say never. And calling is when you use the telephone to try to talk to Mister Reed, and I hang up on you."

I entered the courthouse and took a seat on a bench that was almost an exact match with those in the old church where Mary Jo and I worshiped every Sunday.

The crowd in the courtroom murmured loudly when Mary Jo was led in through the side door. She searched for me with a frightened look as the deputy walked her across the marble floor in front of the raised judge's bench. I caught her attention with a little wave. Winston Graves, our attorney, had saved a seat for me behind the defendant's table in the first row of the gallery.

The room was packed. Leon and Mrs. P. had to stand near the rear. It was a traditional dark oak-paneled courtroom, with a pair of heavy doors leading in from the hallway and a row of tall narrow windows along the outside wall. Benches lined both sides of a central aisle. Just below the softly glowing windows, the double-tiered jury box contained a dozen empty barrister chairs. The judge's bench was a raised monument to the woodworker's craft, with deeply recessed panels and artfully mitered dentils and moldings. High above, mica shades on the old bronze light fixtures tinted the room with a sepia glow.

Only a low oak balustrade stood between me and Mary Jo after she was seated. Winston had warned me that they would not let us touch, but I leaned forward and slipped my hand between the railing anyway. She seized it in both of hers and held on tight. We whispered short, rushing sentences over the wooden rail; eager to talk, eager to listen.

"Are you all right?"

"Yes. It wasn't so bad."

"You're very brave."

"No. I prayed a lot."

Looking down to avoid her eyes, I said, "Me too."

"Oh, Garr. I'm so glad you're here."

"Tried to get in last night."

"I know. Winston told me."

"Tried again this morning."

"Oh, I missed you so much."

"It's very hard."

"Yes."

We squeezed each other's hands and sat silently for a moment. I said, "Do you have any idea why they think you did this?"

"There's a man, an employee at the hospital, who says he saw me do it."

"They must have more than that."

"That's all they told me."

But there was more. When they started the hearing, the judge introduced Winston Graves and Jacob Steiner, the district attorney. After the formalities were complete, Steiner began his argument against releasing Mary Jo on bail. The district attorney had the look of an undertaker: tall, thin, pale, and somber. His pasty scalp glistened like the white underbelly of a catfish. He wore a simple black suit and a boring tie. He wore huge, scuffed black wingtips like twin canoes. In slow, hollow tones he asked that bail be set at half a million dollars. When Winston Graves objected on the basis of Mary Jo's lack of a criminal record, Steiner described the shootings as a "savage and merciless attack." He said the prosecution would show a long list of proofs that Mary Jo was the murderer. They had witnesses—more than one apparently—who would testify they saw her at the scene. They had forensic evidence to prove she had fired a weapon.

Finally, he pointed a bony finger at my wife and said, "The people will prove that the defendant had a personal relationship with one of the victims. This heinous crime was only partly motivated by the defendant's intense beliefs about abortion. Are such strong beliefs reason enough to commit murder? There were hundreds of people at the hospital yesterday who felt as strongly as Mrs. Reed. No, your honor, we will show that there were more personal issues at stake here, motives that drove this woman to the attempted murder of Dr. Milo. This was no violent act of social conscience. This was a premeditated and highly personal crime with roots in the defendant's shrouded past."

I assumed it was all bluster and bluff, of course. How could Jacob Steiner know some deep, dark mystery about Mary Jo that she'd never shared with me? Preposterous! If that was all he had, this thing would be over before it began. I stared at my wife's back, silently willing her to turn so I could smile to reassure her. But what I saw destroyed my short-lived confidence.

When Jacob Steiner finished making his statement, Mary Jo's shoulders dropped, as if a heavy weight had been lowered upon them.

Chapter 8

I WASN'T ABLE TO ARRANGE BAIL THROUGH A bondsman in Dallas until eight-thirty that night. Winston had warned me that they would not release Mary Jo until the following morning if we did not deliver the bond before five. So Mary Jo spent a second night in the Jackson County Jail, and I spent a second night without sleep.

On Tuesday morning, as I waited outside the side door of the jail, a crowd of reporters flung noisy questions like a vaudeville crowd pitching rotten tomatoes. I kept my eyes on the closed jailhouse door and ignored the reporters.

Finally, Mary Jo emerged, blinking at the morning sunlight, with a deputy at her side. We hugged briefly, an awkward embrace, closely watched by the crowd of strangers.

With my lips against her ear, I whispered, "Let's go home."

She nodded and we turned with my arm around her shoulder.

The experience of wading through a pack of rudely shouting men and women was new to Mary Jo. After my walk to the hearing with Leon and Mrs. P., I knew the best approach was to keep eyes forward and move with a steady determined pace. I guided Mary Jo along. She moved like a sleepwalker, her eyes glazed and the muscles of her face limp. We made it to the white Reed Construction pickup truck. I opened the passenger side door and helped her in. A large man wearing blue jeans and an NBC jacket stuck a video camera in my face, while his partner, a smaller man in a dark blue suit, tried to push his way past me.

I said, "Buddy, are you planning to get in my truck?"

The man in the blue suit ignored me, focusing instead on Mary Jo. She sat with her hands in her lap and her eyes on the floorboard. He put his hand on her shoulder. "Just a few questions Mrs. Reed. Please. People everywhere want to know."

I said, "Get your hands off my wife."

Perhaps I said it too softly. I tend to speak softly when I'm angry. Perhaps he heard, but chose to ignore me. He continued to touch her shoulder.

I turned, put both hands against the cameraman's chest, and pushed hard. He fell backwards against the crowd, landing at their feet. I swiveled quickly and gripped the reporter's shoulders and pulled him away from the truck. His feet got tangled in the cameraman's legs. He fell too. I slammed the truck door and strode around the hood toward the driver's side, shoving the reporters aside. The shouted questions stopped. In the new silence, cameras clicked all around me. Strobe flashes sparkled like fireworks against the windshield. The reporter's voice rose from below the crowd, clear and alone.

"Did anybody catch that? Did we get that? I want shots of that!"

I got in the truck. Mary Jo sat with her eyes lowered and hands clutched together in her lap, sobbing quietly. My first instinct was to slide across the seat and wrap her in my arms, but the reporters outside had recovered from their momentary shock and begun hurling questions at us again. Gritting my teeth, I turned from my wife, put the truck in gear, and managed to drive away without running over any of them. As we neared the edge of town, I reached over and wordlessly pulled Mary Jo against my side. She buried her face in my chest, her tears flowing quietly. The primal urge to protect her rose within me, bringing churning emotions of tenderness and anger. I gripped the steering wheel tightly with my left hand as I gently stroked Mary Jo's shoulder with my right, and allowed the bittersweet feelings to fill my mind. To my surprise, the strange emotions brought memories, unbidden memories, from a day that hadn't crossed my mind in almost two decades . . .

● ● ●

A MONTH AFTER MARY JO AND I MET, MY FRIEND Ernest B. rented a ski boat and we put it in at Bayou Beau Bois. It was a sixteen-foot white fiberglass Chris Craft, with padded bow seats, a triple vee hull, and a Johnson one-fifty outboard. Mary Jo and I sat in the bow. Ernest B. played captain at the steering wheel, and his date, a buxom blonde from Lafayette, sat behind the windshield, tuning in Merle Haggard on the radio. The girls wore bikinis, Ernest B. and I wore blue jean cut-offs. We cruised the bayou doing about thirty, bow high in the air, rounding the gentle curves, trailing an expanding wake that slapped the trunks of cypress trees along the shoreline twenty seconds after we passed. Merle Haggard sang "Okie from Muskogee," his voice echoing from the levies. The looming walls of tan dirt to our left and right were clothed with honeysuckle and ferns and densely populated by cottonwoods and ancient cypress trees draped with Spanish moss. Mary Jo and I watched for snags and fallen trees and floating lily pads or hyacinth. It was easy to steer around them in the bayou. The olive-green water was as wide as a four-lane highway.

As we neared the Gulf, the bayou spread out and cypress islands appeared on the left and right; large clusters of trees standing two or three feet apart, with water flowing between and around them. Ernest B. reduced our speed. The bow settled and Mary Jo leaned over the side to trail her fingers in the deep green water, carving a narrow swath through the duckweed. Bayou Beau Bois was little more than an extension of the Gulf now, slowly flowing through the scattered stands of cypress, spread out for thousands of feet in both directions with dozens of identical twists, turns, and tributaries. Ernest B's. date used a pencil and a scrap of paper to jot down landmarks as we passed. It was the only way we would be able to find our way back upstream through the maze. Mary Jo and I searched for identifying features in the swamp.

"There's a Jax can nailed to that tree."

"Red ribbon hanging from a branch on the right."

"Turtle shell wired to that limb on the left."

It was a lazy day. A gently flowing day. A day of blue herons and mallards, of shyly peeking does, of drifting cottonwood fluffs. It was a day of whispered endearments and stolen kisses.

Mary Jo and I were in love, but we had not slept together. Somehow, whenever we were alone at my apartment, the mood was not right. Something in her body language, the way she rose from the sofa when I sat beside her, the way she stiffened just a bit when I kissed her, told me she was not ready, or so I thought. I was twenty years away from becoming a Christian, and did not understand her beliefs. To me, her attitude about sex was nothing but a facade concealing some deeper reason for refusing my advances. I was patient, but the sight of her in a bikini that day was almost more than I could bear. I remember being driven almost mad by the sight of a single bead of perspiration slowly flowing across her tan, flat stomach to join a puddle in her navel. She seemed completely unaware of the power she exercised over me. Even when I looked away, her body lingered in my mind's eye. I became obsessed with the idea of making love with her. But somehow I knew she would be offended if I simply sat and stared, so I stole glances at her all morning, rationing them like a drunk with a secret flask.

The blond with Ernest B. had arranged for us to meet her brother and some friends at a restaurant and bait shop on the west bank of the bayou. When we nosed up to the wharf, her brother stood looking down at us with his hands on his hips, an odd expression on his face. The blond turned to Ernest B. and said, "Something's wrong." Mary Jo and I remained aboard while Ernest B. and his date stepped up to talk with him. She pulled a T-shirt on and slipped into a pair of blue jean cut-offs. After a few minutes, Ernest B. hopped back down into the boat.

"Their momma's sick," he said. "Got some kinda heart thing. Their daddy had to take her to the hospital."

I said, "You going to drive back to town with them?"

"I hate to leave y'all alone here." He was smiling.

I said, "We'll be all right."

He smiled wider and said, "You betcha."

Mary Jo and I ate boiled crawfish and pan-fried channel cat with French fries and white bread at an outdoor table covered by a week-old copy of the *Times-Picayune*. A gentle breeze from the Gulf cooled us. We used our Dixie longnecks to weigh down the fluttering edges of the newspaper. The bayou lapped at the pilings beneath the wharf and oozed away toward the deep water. Gulls complained loudly from the air above, reeling on the wind in an intricate ballet. The proprietor, a thin white man with a thick Cajun accent, pushed an eight-track tape into the stereo and Clifton Chenier's brand of zydeco pop joined the screeching gulls. The French words meant nothing to me, but the music tied everything together, sweetening the moment like thick corn syrup congealing in a papershell pecan pie. I finished my meal and scooted my rickety wooden chair around the table to sit beside Mary Jo, our backs to the faded gray kitchen shack, our feet on a lower rung of cypress railing, my arm around her shoulder. The thin man came out to clean up. He rolled up the leftover fries and crawfish shells in the newspaper and shoved the whole mess down through a hole in the center of the table. I looked around and saw trash buckets under every table on the wharf.

"Got some fine-fine pecan pie, me. You wanna piece maybe? Good pie, mon."

Mary Jo shook her head and I said no.

The thin man nodded and said, "They no one else out here. Fine day and you so friendly. Stay right here if you want. I goin' inside, me. Holler loud-loud if you gonna need something, you."

We sat for a few minutes, watching the lake. Mary Jo rested her head on my shoulder. I touched her cheek, turning her face toward mine. I kissed her gently. We held the kiss. Her lips parted. It seemed like an invitation, a yielding, so I turned in the chair and reached across her, pulling her close with my hand on her shoulder. Our kissing became frantic. I began to move my hand, to slide it under her T-shirt. Suddenly, she pulled away, looking around at the empty wharf.

I said, "No one can see us, baby. But if you want to, this ol' boy has some cabins in back. We could—"

"No, Garr."

"Mary Jo, I love you. You love me. I don't understand."

She looked away, staring out across the gray-green water. She was silent.

I waited three or four minutes, then said, "Do you really think God would care?"

She did not answer.

After a moment I said, "Isn't that the reason?"

"It's part of it."

"What's the other part?"

She shook her head, staring down at her hands which were clasped together on her lap. The sunlight danced in her lovely auburn hair. I said, "Are you on the pill?"

"No."

"That's okay. I brought something."

"No, Garr. That's not it."

"What then? Please."

"I'm not afraid of getting pregnant. I love children. I love you. I'd love to have a child with you."

"Having a baby wasn't what I had in mind."

"Don't you want children, Garr?"

"Well . . . sure. I want to have a son someday. But—"

She sobbed then, suddenly, without warning. Raising her hands to her face, she abandoned herself to whatever it was, crying loudly, with heaving breaths and shaking shoulders. Startled, I hugged her close, murmuring little condolences, softly whispering to her, patting her back and shoulders as they heaved within my embrace. Her cries joined the merciless shrieks of the gulls, echoing from the weathered wooden walls of the Cajun's shack.

For half an hour, I held her as she wept, longing to understand, yet afraid to voice the question. What could it be? What was so terribly wrong? Had I caused this?

Finally, when the sobs subsided, I lifted her chin with two fingers and searched her liquid green eyes for the answer. Thinking I saw it there, I said, "If you believe that strongly that God disapproves, we'll wait. I don't have to make love to prove how I feel."

Her eyes flashed wide, filled with new emotion. But it was not relief I saw in the windows to her soul.

It was grief.

Chapter 9

THE SILENCE IN THE PICKUP CAB WAS SOOTH-
ing and welcome after the confrontation at
the courthouse. Mary Jo and I cruised slowly
along the old narrow road, winding parallel to
the Martin Pool shoreline, catching occasional glimpses of water
like quicksilver through the woods on our right. We held hands.
I squeezed her hand three times. I love you. She smiled and
squeezed mine twice. Me too. The road dipped between moss-
covered embankments, so ancient they supported red oak trees
with trunks four feet wide. The branches spread above us,
draped with Spanish moss and alive with autumn color, a burning ceiling of scarlet and orange. A quarter mile from the turn-
off into our driveway, we passed the rotting remains of an
armadillo in the center of the road. Its shell was split and
crushed.

I thought about asking if she knew Father McKay or Dr.
Milo. I thought about asking if there was a connection between
her trips to New Orleans and this disaster. But when I turned and
opened my mouth, her profile held such an expression of grief
that I found I could not bring myself to risk adding to her sorrow.
We continued down the narrow blacktop road in silence.

They were waiting for us at home, dozens of rental cars and
television vans parked along both sides of the blacktop road. I
slowed and turned the truck in at our gate, tapping the horn
lightly to encourage the reporters loitering in the driveway to step

aside. As we rolled down the long twisting drive, two men ran along-side shouting questions, their heavy footsteps pounding across a fresh carpet of gold and brown leaves, their harsh voices echoing unnaturally beneath the cathedral rafters of naked branches like the blasphemous laughter of pagans. I resisted the urge to steer into them, kept my eyes forward, and ignored their questions. Mary Jo did the same.

At the end of the driveway, the forest spread away from the edges of the road to surround a small meadow. Our two-story house stood at the edge of the clearing, waiting like an old friend. Five or six cars were parked near the front porch steps. I pulled to a stop beside a blue Ford Taurus with Louisiana plates. The two reporters loped up beside me as I stepped from the truck and walked around to open Mary Jo's door. Both men were out of shape and out of breath, but the younger one managed to ask annoying questions between wheezes. I ignored him, fighting a rising anger as I helped Mary Jo from the truck. We hurried to the front steps. The men followed one step behind. As Mary Jo turned her key in the front-door lock, I turned to face them.

"This is incredible. Would y'all just barge right on into the house behind us?"

The older reporter, still huffing, said, "Mister Reed, we're only try-ing to do our jobs. Won't you and Mrs. Reed please answer a question or two?" I followed Mary Jo through the door, turned again, and said, "Our property starts back at the gate. You've been trespassing since you set foot on that driveway. Get off my porch and off my land or I'll call the sheriff and have you thrown off."

The younger reporter said, "But Mister Reed—" as I slammed the door in his face.

Mary Jo fell against me, limp and exhausted. I wrapped my arms around her. We stood silently in the entry hall, thankful to be alone. She nuzzled her cheek against my chest and pulled herself tightly against me. I squeezed her hard, looking down at the top of her head. Together again. It was as if the world ceased to exist when we held each other. It had always been that way. I felt so peaceful that I didn't hear the voices at first.

Mumbling against my chest, Mary Jo said, "What's that sound?" Listening, I heard the low murmur of a distant conversation and clinks of silverware and the scrape of a chair across the floor. We walked down the entry hall, through the living room, and into the kitchen.

Outside the kitchen window, eight or nine people were gathered on the back deck drinking coffee from our wedding china. Tape recorders and cameras were piled on the table or hanging around their necks.

Mary Jo said, "Garr, don't do anything you'll regret." Without answering her, I stormed into the study, seized a shotgun from the cabinet, and charged through the living room to the French doors. I flung them open. They slammed against the wall as I strode onto the deck.

I pumped a shell into the chamber, pointed the gun at them, and said, "You people get off my property. Now!"

They turned to look at me with smiles frozen on their faces, and coffee cups halted in mid sip.

I said, "Move it. I won't tell you again."

From somewhere behind them, a strong voice said, "Garrison Reed, don't you dare speak that way to these gentlemen. They are here at my invitation."

It had been almost two years since I last heard it, but I would have known her West Bank accent anywhere. It was Lucretia Granier, Mary Jo's mother.

• • •

"SUCH BEHAVIOR. HONESTLY. POINTIN' A *SHOTGUN* AT those poor fellas."

It was later that night. We had just finished eating dinner, and Lucretia Granier and I stood side by side, washing dishes at the kitchen sink. Lucretia clucked her tongue as she wiped a dish with a blue plaid towel. "I was absolutely petrified. Petrified." She opened the wall cabinet on the left, pushed some cups aside, and set the plate on the bottom shelf.

I said, "Those plates go in the cabinet on the right."

"What on earth possessed you? What *could* you a been thinkin', you?"

"Those reporters were trespassing."

"Dey were not! I invited them in for coffee."

"Why would you do something like that?"

"It didn't seem right to leave dem all standing 'round outside. Besides, *someone's* gotta speak to dem news people for Mary Jo. Dat fo' sure." She stopped drying a plate and fixed her eyes on me. "Why am I the one doing the explainin'? You're de one pointed a shotgun at me, you."

"I didn't realize you were here, Lucretia. Maybe if you'd called ahead—"

"No one bothered to call *me*, no. Had to see my dear girl in handcuffs on de television. Found out on de midnight news like everyone else, me." She put another plate in the lefthand cabinet.

"We already went over that. It's been hectic, these last forty-eight hours. I just didn't think to call anyone. I am sorry, Lucretia. I really am."

She avoided looking at me, shrugging at my apology as if to say she had considered the source and found it lacking. She was a tall, thin woman with a square jaw line, deeply tanned skin, and startling green eyes below thick black eyebrows. Her short gray hair still showed signs of its former crow-feather black. Her nose was long and narrow, a remnant of her Acadian French heritage. The tight curls in her hair and something about the lines of her face hinted at the possibility of some Creole in her bloodline, although she would vehemently deny that interracial relations existed in her family tree. The tendons in her age-spotted hands and neck were very pronounced, as if the skin had been stretched too tightly over her frame. She wore a simple cotton dress printed with small red and yellow flowers and a pair of square-toed black leather shoes with one-inch heels. It was the way women dressed during the Great Depression. She had always dressed that way. She was proud that her simple wedding band was made of stainless steel. Back in the sixties when we first met, she told me her steel wedding band meant that more of God's resources were available to feed the itinerant men at her shelter. She was not favorably impressed when Mary Jo and I showed her the tiny diamond on the engagement ring we purchased a few months later.

Lucretia Granier had seen everything down at her mission behind Canal Street. If Satan was behind it, she had dealt with it, and the experience had slowly rubbed the loving-kindness off her and left a thinly concealed core of anger. Lucretia Granier was a hard-hearted Christian woman—a walking contradiction, constantly looking for opportunities to point a bony finger and unleash her scriptural half-truths like a weapon, as if by accusing someone else of sin she was absolved of her own. No one had seen the things she had seen, or learned so much from life. Those who disagreed with her were relegated to the rubbish heap of ignorance, or worse, condemned with the vengeance of a judge at the Salem witch trials. When her views were challenged, Lucretia Granier became a fury, her deeply tanned face flushing, her hands clenched in tight fists, her bright green eyes betraying the depth of the anger that twisted her soul.

It had not always been so.

Something had seized her spirit, gradually distorting it over the last two decades. Sometimes it seemed to me as if a demon rode upon her back, claws wrapped around her head, whispering angry distortions and falsehoods. Mary Jo and I prayed for her every day, asking God to soften her heart and return her to the gentle goodness the Creator wants us all to enjoy. But so far, our prayers had not been answered.

Lucretia and I stood side by side at the counter. I was rinsing. She was drying. Lucretia sniffed and put a third plate in the wrong cabinet. "My girl wasn't raised dat-a-way. Forget to call her *maman* dat-a-way. Me and Alphonse, we raised her proper, we did."

"I suppose I've been a bad influence on her."

"Didn't say dat, just said you should-a called, you."

"Well, neither of you called me when you were in jail, Lucretia."

"That different."

"Why?"

"Just is, that's all. Dey didn't arrest me for no *murder*, no."

Spoken aloud in our home, the word seemed to infect the air like a sulfurous vapor, poisoning the atmosphere with fear. To shift my mind away from the horror, I said, "Tell me again why they arrested you. I never did quite understand all that."

"Wasn't nothin'. Jus' de godless government tryin' to stop Christian folk from standin' up for what's right."

"What does that mean? Standing up for what's right? What did you *do*, exactly?"

"Same thing Mary Jo been doin'. Protestin'. Organizin'. Supportin' those got de guts to stand against de godless in this country."

"You got arrested at a protest? Is that what happened?"

"Somethin' like dat."

"Well, then what, exactly? What did you do?"

She turned her ice cold green eyes upon me for a moment. "I did my duty, Garrison. Just like my Mary Jo done." Then she returned her attention to the dishes.

I asked again for specifics, but she refused to speak, meeting my questions with stony silence. All I knew was that Lucretia's hired man called from down in New Orleans a few weeks back. Mary Jo was to come down as soon as possible. No further explanation was offered, in spite of my questions. I was not invited. That was the last time Mary Jo had been to New Orleans. It was only after Mary Jo's return that I learned she had arrived to find her mother in jail for some crime related to the local pro-life movement. Apparently it was a minor infraction, since Mary Jo was able to deal with the matter by paying Lucretia's bail and a fine.

But why were both of them so secretive about the details?

Knowing Lucretia's temper, I guessed there was probably some misbehavior on her part, something she would be ashamed to have me know. I decided to drop the matter. If it was important, Mary Jo would have told me what I needed to know. And if she chose to support her mother's desire for secrecy, I would respect her choice.

Earlier that night, dinner had been a disaster. Mary Jo had somehow found a way to rise above the shock and exhaustion of her own ordeal to cook the evening meal, refusing my offers to help. Perhaps it made her feel better to be busy. Lucretia had chatted away between delicate bites, offering a running account of the recent "doin's" of Mary Jo's cousins, aunts, and uncles. Some were ill, some divorced, and others struggled with the demon alcohol. Mary Jo and I ate quietly, nodding at the appropriate times, forcing smiles when she mentioned how clever little Jacques Benoit had grown up to be. Jacques was the second child of Edna Benoit, Lucretia's first child. Edna still lived down in Barataria where Lucretia and Alphonse first met. Lucretia frequently mentioned her husband Alphonse as if he was still alive. "I don't think Alphonse would care for dat woman," or "Alphonse would not allow de sun to set on a job undone, no." The Reverend Alphonse Granier had been dead for eleven years, but Lucretia carried on without him down at the mission.

Lucretia's conversation did not require a response for the most part. When it did, I was the one who spoke. Mary Jo ate little, her eyes on her plate, her fork absently pushing at her food. At the earliest opportunity, she excused herself and said she would walk through the woods to her painting studio. She stopped in the open door and glanced back at me, an odd look in her eyes. I moved closer. "There's something we've got to talk about," she whispered.

"Is it about what they said in court? About this being something personal for you?"

She paused, then said, "Yes."

"Mary Jo, does this have something to do with all those trips to New Orleans you've been taking?"

With a glance at Lucretia across the room, she lifted a finger to her lips and whispered, "We'll talk later, after Momma's asleep." I nodded and stood in the door watching until she disappeared into the shadows beyond the moonlit tree line.

Her words would haunt me for weeks.

Chapter 10

FIFTEEN MINUTES ALONE WITH LUCRETIA Granier was more than enough.

I said, "Listen, why don't you walk over to the studio to see Mary Jo while I finish the dishes? I know she'd like to show you some of the paintings she's done lately."

"I'll stay and help. I don't want ya'll feelin' like you have to clean up after me."

"Don't be silly."

She turned her fierce green eyes upon me and said, "Silly?"

"Well, I meant, of course we don't feel that way."

"What way?"

I shut off the faucet and lifted a skillet out of the sink, stalling for time. I did not want any trouble. After a moment, I said, "Lucretia, really, I think Mary Jo would like to show you her work. She's had great success with this latest series. They're selling fast in Santa Fe and New York."

She wiped her hands with the dish towel. "All right."

I opened a drawer and removed a flashlight and handed it to her. "You'll need this to find your way along the path. Do you remember how to get over there?"

"I imagine so."

"Okay. I'll see you when ya'll get back."

I returned to washing the dishes. Lucretia put on a thick gray sweater and walked to the kitchen door. Behind me, just as she was about to step outside, she paused and said, "De Lord will forgive her. One of dem was a-murderin' little babies and de other . . . well, a priest is still a man of God, I suppose. He with his Maker now, and doin' no more harm with his papist lies."

I turned slowly. Indignation and anger rose within me. How could she believe her own daughter was capable of such a crime? How could she pollute my home with her prejudice on this difficult day of all days? My tactful veneer dissolved. I opened my mouth to shame her with a righteous tirade. But the look in her eyes stopped me. Lucretia Granier was afraid for her daughter, and, just for an instant, the naked fear flashed across her hard brown face. Her open concern touched me more strongly than any honest appeal she could have made.

Softly, I said, "We're going to get this thing cleared up, Lucretia. Don't you worry about that."

The fearful look evaporated. Her features hardened again. She said, "Worry is a sin against de Lord. You'll not find me committin' it."

The screen door slapped the jamb behind her and she stepped into the night.

I dried the dishes with the towel, rubbing hard, as if to wipe away the frustration she had left behind. Why did she have to come at such a time? Wasn't it enough that Mary Jo and I had to deal with cancer and murder? I removed the plates from the left-hand cabinet and put them in the right one. I wiped the counter and hung the dishtowel on the refrigerator handle. Then I walked to the door, selected a tan windbreaker from the coat rack, and stepped out onto the deck.

It was a dark night. Clouds rushed low across the sky, so low they were illuminated by the distant upcast lights of Mount Sinai, glowing yellow on the horizon. At the bottom of the hill a boat sped along the lake, the roar of its motor shouting down the whisper of the wind in the trees, masking the gentle chirps of the crickets and the songs of the few tree frogs still resisting the urge to hibernate. I struggled with my conscience. Lucretia was a mother, come to protect her child, responding to one of nature's strongest imperatives. My hands slipped into the pockets of the windbreaker. I shivered. It was callous of me to resent Lucretia's presence here. She had a stake in this, as strong as mine. An owl called in the distant woods, like an old man moaning in his sleep. The boat's motor noise faded as it sped toward the far end of the lake. I could hear the crickets again. I wondered what Lucretia had told the reporters as they drank coffee on our back deck.

A bobbing light flashed through the trees to my left, Mary Jo and Lucretia returning from the studio. I smiled. It had been less than fifteen minutes. Mary Jo was no more in a mood for Lucretia than I. The light panned the path as they approached, swinging side to side. They were coming slowly. I imagined Lucretia, an old woman after all, picking her way carefully along the narrow pathway, clutching Mary Jo's arm for support. The light drew near, no longer disappearing behind tree trunks, coming straight for the house.

I called out. "Hey ladies. How about a cup of decaf and some buttermilk pie?"

They did not answer. I called again. "Ya'll want some dessert? I'll make coffee."

No answer.

I descended the stairs and walked along the path to intercept them. As I neared, I realized they were not speaking. I reached a wide spot on the trail and stopped. Lucretia approached first, holding the flashlight. The path behind her was empty.

I said, "Is Mary Jo working late tonight?"

Lucretia did not pause, walking on past me toward the house. Without looking back, she replied, "Mary Jo ain't there."

"What?"

"She left a note. Come along, I'll show it to you at de house."

"Let me see it."

"At de house, I said. I need to sit down, me."

I followed her back toward the stairs. She climbed them one riser at a time, pausing between steps to take several breaths. Finally, up on the deck, she sat heavily on the porch swing. The flashlight dangled loosely between her knees, still on and shining at one of her shoes. It illuminated a red oak leaf stuck to the ankle of her stocking.

I said, "Can I please see the note?"

"You ain't gonna like it, Garrison."

"Just give it to me."

She handed it up without looking, her head bent, her eyes on her lap. I took it over to the French doors to read in the yellow light spilling out through the glass.

Garr—

I need to be alone to finish with Melvin Milo. I'll call you as soon as I can. Please understand, it is something I have to do. Don't worry.
—M.J.

I looked at Lucretia. "What is this?"

"What it look like, I imagine."

"Mary Jo didn't write this."

"Her handwriting."

"Yes, but she wouldn't do this. She'd tell me . . ."

I read the note again. And again. So short. So final. I would read it many times in the next few days, but always it amounted to the same thing.

She was gone.

Chapter 11

L UCRETIA PULLED THE GRAY SWEATER CLOSER to her neck as she gazed across Martin Pool and said, "It don't much matter where she is, long as she safe."

I said, "They'll think she did the murder. They'll think she's trying to escape . . . jumping bail."

"We know better."

"Sure. But we've still got to find her."

Lucretia nodded and continued to stare through the early mist above the water. We stood on the old fishing pier my father and grandfather built together when the lake was new. Neither of us had managed to sleep. We had checked the garage and discovered that Mary Jo's Volvo was gone. Somehow, she had managed to drive it away without either of us hearing. But she had not taken any of her clothes. When the sun began to rise, we walked down the hill through the woods to escape the emptiness of the house. Stepping from the tree-line, we surprised a great blue heron standing one-legged on the far end of the pier. It spread its awkward wings and clawed its way into the air, flopping toward the dawn with loud angry squawks. Lucretia Granier followed the flight of the heron with her electric green eyes, commenting on its large size. When she spoke the word heron, she pronounced it "air-own," the Cajun way.

Turning toward me she said, "How we gonna find dat girl?"

"I guess we'll just have to start looking."

"Lookin' where?"

I rubbed the stiff gray and brown stubble on my cheeks and chin. My hand passed up to my eyes and I rubbed them too. "If she really wants to be alone, she'll leave the county. Everybody knows her here. Let's think about places she might go. You have any ideas?"

"She might go home. To New Orleans."

"Yes. Maybe. But it's been a long time since she lived there. It's not really home for her anymore."

"Place you raised up is always home."

"She has been spending a lot of time down there . . . do you think those trips have anything to do with this?"

"How would I know?"

My eyelids burned from three nights in a row without any real sleep. I rubbed my eyes again, thinking that I had to have patience.

"So you're saying you don't know?"

"Dat what it sound like, don't it?"

I counted to ten silently. Twice. Then I said, "I was thinking about her agent. Her name is Julie Berger. They've been working together a long time. Julie opened the New York market for Mary Jo. Whenever they get together, they seem to play as much as they work. Shopping, shows, that kind of thing. They're friends. Maybe Mary Jo went to New York."

"Driving all dat way?"

"She would go to Shreveport or Dallas and fly from there. Probably Dallas."

The sun rose higher as we stood on the pier. A flock of mallards winged in from the west, following the bend of the lake. They sank single file into the mist a hundred yards out, splashing down loudly below the soft blanket of white. Lucretia would call them French Ducks— their Cajun name—if she noticed them at all. Her hard green eyes did not seem to register their approach. She stared across Martin Pool as we talked, clutching her arms across her chest, her square face almost masculine in its severity. A tiny yellow elm leaf settled onto her shoulder and stuck in the fuzz of the sweater she had borrowed from Mary Jo. I looked beyond her at the aluminum boat hanging above the water in the boathouse, suspended on wide fabric straps and covered by a tan tarp. Mary Jo and I had gone for a moonlight cruise on Friday night, the night before the murder. I saw she had not fastened the tarp properly on her side of the boat when we returned. The wind had lifted a corner and exposed the passenger side seat. Her seat.

I pulled the tarp down over the side of the boat and said, "Mary Jo always leaves things undone."

Lucretia said, "Ain't changed since she was little. Left dem brushes of hers stickin' in a paint pot up there in dat shed last night."

"She didn't clean her brushes?"

"No."

"Do you think she went to Edna's?"

"No. Least I hope not."

"Why not?"

"Because I won't go lookin' for her there."

I sighed. "You still won't speak to Edna?"

"Not while she worships Satan, I won't."

I said, "Voodoo isn't exactly Satan worship."

She laughed. A low, hollow sound. "You a fool."

"Well, it isn't. It's more like the ancient Greeks and Romans. The way they believed in mythical gods."

Lucretia looked away. "You talkin' 'bout things you know nothin' about, boy. I thought I showed you better, me. But you won't believe what you seen with you own eyes."

"I've never understood what that was—what you showed me."

She flipped the back of her hand at me as if shooing away a fly. "Never mind that. What difference do it make now? One of my girls is lost to Satan, whether you believe it or no. An' now de other one just plain lost. You go to New York. I'll go home, me. Maybe Mary Jo gone home."

"Lucretia, I need you here."

Her pale eyes settled on my face, cold, calculating, sizing me up. She said, "Why should I stay here with my baby gone?"

"We can't let them *know* she's gone. Someone's got to arrange things so they'll think she's still at home."

"Do dat yourself."

"Lucretia . . ." I stopped to calm myself. She was a smart woman. She could see the obvious: if I was out looking for Mary Jo and the house showed no signs of life while I was away, they would know she was gone. It wasn't that Lucretia didn't understand. It was her way of assuming control. Lucretia was making me beg. I clenched my hands into fists. I unclenched them and looked down on the tight gray curls of her hair. I forced myself to see more than a cantankerous old woman. I forced myself to see a widow, a mother, a woman with a missing child. I said, "I need you. I can't do it without you."

She snorted, turned her back to me, and walked along the pier toward the tree line and the shore. The heels of her heavy black shoes cracked against the old gray boards as she went—a stark, unnatural sound.

I called after her, "She has cancer."

At the end of the pier she paused without turning. After a moment's hesitation, with her back still to me, she said, "What kind?"

"Breast cancer."

I saw her shoulders drop. She lifted her head toward the sky and took a deep breath. Then she said, "All our time together back home these last few months, why didn't she tell me?"

I said, "Maybe she didn't want to burden you. You were sick yourself."

Lucretia said, "I ain't been sick a day in fifty years."

I stared at her. Was it true, or was it her pride speaking? She had a lot of pride. "But isn't that why Mary Jo spent so much time at home last summer? I thought you were sick and she was taking care of you."

"What difference do it make now? What do de doctors say 'bout Mary Jo?"

"They just found the cancer. We haven't seen all of the test results yet. Her doctor said the treatment would depend on how far it has spread. He said it doesn't look too bad."

She turned to look at me. "She gonna be all right."

I nodded. "Lucretia, I really do need your help."

We stared at each other silently for moment, then she said, "I'll stay a spell, me," and she stepped onto the bank to begin the climb to the house.

I stood at the end of the pier long after the sounds of Lucretia's slow ascent through the woods had blended with the morning calls of the sparrows. The last twenty-four hours had been a roller coaster of emotions, ranging from fear for Mary Jo's safety in jail, to intense relief at seeing her and being able to touch her again, to sorrow at her misery and frustration at being unable to help. But now I felt something new. As the sun warmed the water out on the main lake, I watched the lacy blanket of cotton white mist grow thin and rise.

I thought about that morning when she snuck out of bed for target practice. About the trips to New Orleans. She had said they were to nurse her mother. But I had seen in Lucretia's eyes that that was a lie. What was this emotion growing within me? Why was it so hard to define? More mist flowed out from the shaded coves as I stood silently, wrestling with my emotions. I stayed until the last of it evaporated, then turned to follow Lucretia, having arrived at an answer to my question.

I was intensely worried about Mary Jo. And I was quietly furious with her.

• • •

"YOUR TURBAN IS SHOWING."

Mrs. P. poked at her curly blond wig with a pudgy hand, shoving it back in place to cover the pale tan Spandex underneath. "That all you got to say? Come in here off the street, stand in front of my desk, and I don't get no hello, no good mornin', just, 'Your turban is showin'?"

"You asked me to let you know when your wig slipped."

"Ain't no excuse for rudeness. You oughta say mornin' first."

"Good morning."

"Too late now."

"Lovely day, isn't it?"

"Said it was too late."

"How was your evening?"

"Stop that."

"Can I get you a cup of coffee?"

"All right, that's enough. Here's your messages. Get on in there and return some of them calls and leave me be."

"Have a nice day."

Returning her attention to the papers on her desk, she snorted and said, "I got other plans."

I walked past her desk to my office door, sorting the phone messages. Most were from reporters and friends. Only two were business calls. Pausing at the open door, I turned and said, "That's a fine wig."

She smiled and pushed at the platinum curls above her ears. "It is, ain't it? I picked it up last night at Kathy's Kuntry Kuts. Got me a discount 'cause that silly old Kathy sold my red wig out from under me."

"What a shame. Red looks good on you."

"I know *that's* true, sugar. I was fit to be tied when I found out Kathy sold it. Ordered that one special for Leon. Month or so ago he mentioned he liked your Mary Jo's hair, so I thought I'd surprise him."

"Mary Jo's hair isn't red, it's auburn."

"That a school in Georgia."

"It's a color too."

"What color?"

"Sort of brownish red."

"Which is it, brown or red?"

"It's in between."

"It ain't red?"

"No."

"Wonder why Kathy tried to sell me a red wig?"

"Didn't you order it?"

"Ordered one that look like Mary Jo's."

"Mary Jo doesn't wear a wig."

"Don't get sassy now."

I smiled and said, "Did you ask who she sold it to?"

"Why should I care?"

"Maybe you can still get it."

Mrs. P. shoved her blond wig back and slid two fingers under the turban to scratch her scalp. The turban and wig shook violently with the motion of her fingers. When she was done, she pushed the wig back in place with both hands. Her long fingernails were painted pale orange. Her fingers were the size of Vienna sausages. Patting the hair piece delicately, she said, "I wouldn't dream of wearin' a wig after somebody else had it on their head. Wigs is private things, honey."

I closed the office door, got on the telephone, and called American Airlines, Delta, PanAm, Continental, USAir, and Southwest, pretending to be calling for Mary Jo, changing her reservations to a later flight. They told me they had no reservations for Mary Jo Reed. I said perhaps they had mistakenly set her up on an earlier flight. No, there were no reservations for her on any other flight today. Obviously there had been some mistake. They were sorry.

I called Julie Berger in New York. She had seen it all on cable television, and was just about to call Mary Jo. I told her not to bother, that Mary Jo was not at the studio. I said I was surprised Mary Jo had not already called.

She said, "Me too, Garrison. I've been so worried. I didn't know whether it was appropriate for me to bother you or not. But you know, they printed a picture of her in the *Times* today. Everyone's been ringing me up, wanting to know how this happened."

"Yes. I've got a lot of messages here, too."

"It's all so shocking. I mean, I opened the paper and there she was on page three, above the fold. They were leading her into some building, She was wearing handcuffs. I mean, *really*. Handcuffs?"

"I know."

"How is she, Garr?"

"She's . . . distant."

"Poor thing. How could this happen?"

"Well, you know . . ."

"I mean, it's not like she's a violent person. She's always been so quiet. And private. Not one to get involved in something like this."

"She didn't really mean to get involved, Julie."

"Oh, of course not. She'd never do it deliberately. But you know, sometimes in the heat of the moment . . . I mean, we all find ourselves in situations . . . oh, dear. None of this is coming out right."

"It's okay."

"I know she would never hurt anyone, Garr."

"No."

"But they're trying to make her out to be some sort of fanatic. One of those terrible Moral Majority persons. It's like they're making her a symbol of that whole anti-abortion movement . . ."

There was a pause, the line hissing in our ears. I had already decided Mary Jo was not with Julie in New York. Julie was not that good an actress. After five or ten seconds, I said, "Well, I just wanted to call to put your mind at ease. Mary Jo said you'd be worried."

"Give her my love."

"Sure."

"And tell her all of us up here are pulling for her."

"She'll call soon."

"Garr? What *was* she doing at that hospital?"

What were either of us doing there? If only we'd stayed at home, read the Sunday paper by the fireplace, walked in the woods . . . anything. I said, "I guess she was hoping to do some good."

"She never mentioned anything about abortion to me. I didn't know she felt strongly about it either way."

"She feels strongly about it, Julie."

"Do you?"

"I don't know."

"Yes. Well, I guess I'm asking too many personal questions."

"It's all right. You're a friend."

When she spoke again, it was in a rush, as if something pent-up was finally being released. She said, "A woman should be able to decide what happens to her own body, Garr. She shouldn't be forced to go through nine months of nausea and sore backs and swollen ankles and all the rest of it without an alternative."

"What about the baby?"

"It's not a baby until it's born."

"Are you sure?"

The line hummed for a moment. I heard her breathing. She said, "I had one fifteen years ago."

"An abortion."

"Yes."

I said, "Why are you telling me this?"

Another pause, then, "I'm not a murderer."

"Of course not."

"Those people . . . they say it's murder. It's not murder. It's just a procedure you go through to remove some tissue."

"Don't be too hard on yourself, Julie."

"Thank you."

"You're welcome."

Another long pause. There was nothing to say.

"Good-bye, Garr."

"Good-bye."

I hung up. Before I could remove my hand from the telephone, it rang. Without thinking, I picked it up and said hello.

"Is this Garrison Reed?" The voice was oddly hollow, with a slight tremor to the final syllable and an odd lift to the way she said my name, a slightly exotic way of pronouncing it.

I said, "Yes, this is Garrison Reed speaking."

"It is your wife who tried to kill my Melvin."

I clutched the handset tightly. After a moment I said, "Mrs. Milo?"

"Like an animal she shot him down."

"No, ma'am, she did not. Mary Jo would not do that."

"Don't lie to me. They *saw* her do this thing."

"Who saw her?"

"That orderly and Melvin. Melvin saw her too."

"It's just not possible."

"You lie to me. Isn't it bad enough without lies?"

"Mrs. Milo—"

"Oh, shut up. You can say nothing I want to hear. Just listen." I shifted the handset to my other ear, wiping the sweat off my palm onto my blue jeans.

She said, "I am taking Melvin home. We should not have left there. If those people follow us . . . you tell them to leave us in peace. If they follow us, I will come for you, Mister Reed. Like she came for my Melvin. Remember this."

I wanted to tell her that I did not know them, that I had no control over the pro-life fanatics who had followed her from New Orleans. I wanted to tell her how sorry I was for the suffering she and Doctor Milo were undergoing. But it was too late. She hung up and I found myself listening to a dial tone.

Chapter 12

COULD NOT ASK THE POLICE TO HELP ME look for Mary Jo. They would search for her as a fugitive, not as a missing person. I could not ask my friends to help. In a community as small as Mount Sinai, the police would hear about it somehow. I could not ask around town for the same reason. Wednesday passed, and all I could think to do was to drive across the county aimlessly, searching for her Volvo. I checked the parking lot at the Hideaway Inn, the Motel Six, and the McCleary's Bed and Breakfast. I cruised alleys in town, hoping to find her car parked in a friend's back driveway or garage. I walked the sales lot at Jim Adams's Used Cars, thinking she might have traded the Volvo for cash.

At the bank, I found she had withdrawn three thousand dollars the Friday before the murder. It made sense if she knew she would be on the run or hiding. Mary Jo was smart enough not to leave a trail of credit card receipts. Suddenly, I realized what I was thinking. This was not some criminal. This was my wife.

Was this really happening?

"Mr. Reed? Mr. Reed? Are you all right?"

The bank teller's face seemed to swim into focus. She stared up at me curiously. I forced a smile. "Sure," I said. "Everything's fine."

Balling both of my hands into fists, I turned and walked out.

While I was away, Lucretia had remained at the house, opening and closing drapes, turning lights off and on and playing music on the stereo to make it seem as if there was enough living going on inside those walls for two people. We both knew the reporters would begin to wonder why they had not seen Mary Jo. It was a question of putting off their questions for as long as possible.

On Thursday morning, I drove the Reed Construction pickup truck out the drive. Near the road I tapped the horn and the reporters at the gate slowly parted to let me pass. After four days, they had dwindled to a handful of diehard photographers and freelancers hoping to snatch a shot of Mary Jo clutching an ax or engaging in satanic rituals. I was trying not to hate them.

The reporters were no longer alone. A group of women and a few men had joined their vigil on the roadside. They carried placards that read "murderess" and "hypocrite" and "free to choose." They lined the road as I pulled out of the driveway, their faces screwed down tight with anger. One of them called out, "Why not kill us too?"

A reporter shouted, "Mister Reed, where is your wife? We haven't seen her since she drove away last Monday night."

I ignored them and turned onto the blacktop, grateful that I could drive away without letting them see the worry in my eyes. So the reporters saw her Monday night as she left the house. It was a relief in a way, a validation of my mental health. Since she left I had struggled with a nagging sense that none of it was really happening, that I was living a fantasy in which strangers manipulated the truth. The murder seemed real enough, and the nights Mary Jo spent in jail, and the hearing. It was her leaving that pushed at the edges of my sanity. How could she do that to me? Other than the note and an empty spot in the garage where her Volvo should have been, no evidence existed that she was gone. She had not even packed a bag. And yet I still could not think of a reason why she would leave without warning. It did not fit within the natural order of our lives. A silent voice raged within me, flinging furious accusations at Mary Jo. Betrayal. Abandonment. Lies and treachery. I tried to tell myself it was something I would never do, but memories of the night I slipped away to hunt down Ernest B.'s killers mocked my righteous indignation.

After two days of searching, completely out of ideas, I drove to Granddaddy's Spot, bumping along a seldom used dirt road that wound to the levee of the Big Muddy Bayou, just downstream from our land. I scrambled to the top of the levee above the place where a row of giant red boulders block the bayou, piling it up like thick molasses, only to unleash a twenty-foot waterfall, tumbling over the back side of the limestone into a foaming pool below. Since childhood, I had believed that somewhere in that frothy pool lay Granddaddy, the biggest catfish of them all, the one I never caught. Three decades ago, Ernest B. and I named it Granddaddy's Spot after the mythical fish. This was the one place in Jackson County where the bayou betrayed the powerful presence sleeping below its surface. The pounding waterfall raged at the indignity of such a rude awakening, rumbling low and constant. It was a comfort to me. The continual roar had not changed since my earliest memories. I went there for assurance that the world was still the same, that my sanity was untouched, that I could count on certain things to be a certain way, no matter what. I knelt on the top of the levee and basked in the vacant rhythm of the falling water. When my heart felt still enough, I shut my eyes and prayed.

At first, it was as if I spoke only to myself. The worry and the images of the past days drifted in and out, breaking my concentration. In the good times, after my epiphany with Christ but before Mary Jo's diagnosis, I had learned to keep praying, to continue to call on the Lord, knowing he would answer, would clear away the distractions until it was just us two in sweet conversation. I longed for my prayers to slip into that quiet place, to feel the anger and the anxiety melt away, replaced by a familiar sense of confidence. It is one of the finest gifts he gives us: the certainty that everything will work out according to his plan, if we simply trust in him.

And I wanted to trust in him.

But then it came: that small nagging voice. Why did this have to happen? Why did God let this go on? Mary Jo's cancer. Her arrest and disappearance. Was there some higher reason, some hidden agenda that God alone understood? And if so, why couldn't I just relax and rely on that? Mary Jo would have been standing here, praising her Maker for the good to come. What kind of faith was this that drove me to my knees on the top of a levee, clenched fists knuckle-white with fear, tension roiling in my stomach like a simmering acid vat?

I remained kneeling, head bowed, ashamed of my weakness, with guilt underlying everything. Did my pitifully feeble faith bring on this trouble? God, no. Please don't let it be that. Don't inflict the sentence for my doubts on Mary Jo. Please remove them. Give me confidence. Give me faith. Give me a sign.

Finally, with no prayers left to pray, I rose to my feet and dusted off the knees of my blue jeans. I felt better, as if I had been heard. It surprised me. Perhaps the Lord allowed for the fact that I was new at this. I had never faced disaster at his side. Perhaps he would honor my request and offer a sign, in spite of the weakness of my faith.

With a final look at the waterfall, I turned to descend the levee. Then, just as I took the first step down, I got the sign I asked for. From my vantage point twenty feet above, I saw a square of white, concealed among the trees and brush to one side of the road. It was about fifty feet away from my truck, and so buried in the vegetation I could never have seen it from any other angle. I rushed down the side of the levee, boots slipping on the soil, groping at limbs and bushes to maintain my footing, pushing into the woods below, ducking low to avoid branches, and gingerly stepping through thorny clumps of vines. After several minutes, I found it.

Mary Jo's Volvo was scratched and filthy. The driver's-side door was open, and the driver's seat sprinkled with damp leaves. A raccoon had investigated the interior, leaving delicate muddy paw prints on the dashboard and the top of the seats. I walked around the car, peeking through the windows. Other than the leaves and the signs of the raccoon's adventure, the interior was immaculate. Mary Jo always kept it clean and tidy. She was that way about things she enjoyed.

Behind the Volvo, I saw an abandoned roadbed leading back through the woods. The car had been driven along it and parked where the old road came to a dead end at the bayou. My eyes rested on the trunk. Perhaps I should check inside. An image of a tightly curled body flashed through my mind. I pulled my keys from my pocket. Praying fervently, I turned the key in the lock and lifted the lid. The trunk was empty. I sighed out loud and whispered, "Thank you, Lord."

An irregular circle of something brown had stained the carpet on the left side of the trunk. I touched it. The fabric was matted and dry. I leaned close and sniffed, my nose an inch above the carpet. Nothing. Was it blood? Paint? As I stared into the trunk, a house fly landed on the stain. My heart sank. A fly would never be attracted to paint.

I closed the trunk lid and stood beside the car for several minutes, thinking hard. Ernie Davenport and his men could check the car for fingerprints, take a sample of the stain in the trunk, find clues to help me learn what had happened here. But what if the only fingerprints they found were Mary Jo's? What if the stain was only paint? If I told them what I had found, they would know she was gone. But they would not search for her. They would hunt her down like a common criminal, a murderer. I could not allow that to happen.

I closed the driver's door, turned my key in the lock, and walked back along the abandoned roadbed, forcing my way through hip-high weeds and bushes, some of which still showed signs of the car's recent passage. It took fifteen minutes to reach the intersection with the main road. Pushing through a final mass of brush, I found myself standing beside the ring road that encircles Martin Pool and our property. I turned to the left and walked along the bar ditch beside the blacktop until I came to the old dirt road that led back to Granddaddy's Spot. Following the dirt road, I came back to my truck at last.

I drove away, praying for Mary Jo's safety. Then my prayers were interrupted by old memories. Like waves of sorrow, they washed away all thoughts of God, and although I did not want to do it, I remembered the first time Mary Jo caused me pain . . .

• • •

"I'LL HAVE A SHRIMP PO BOY, PLEASE."

"Go ahead and order something special."

Mary Jo smiled at me over her menu. "What's the occasion?"

"I feel fine, and Dad's check came in, and you're as beautiful as a fawn in dappled sunshine. Is that good enough for you?"

The waiter smiled.

Mary Jo looked at him and said, "Did you serve this boy a couple of drinks when I wasn't looking?"

The waiter said, "No, ma'am."

"Then I guess I'll have one of Miss Hilda's salads and the stuffed flounder."

The waiter, a black man in his sixties wearing a black bow tie, starched white shirt, black slacks, and a peach-colored vest, said, "Ya'll want gumbo or turtle soup au sherry with that?"

I said, "Is it seafood or chicken gumbo?"

The waiter said, "Do somebody make it with chicken?"

I smiled. "In that case I'll have the gumbo, please."

After he collected the menus—which were peach colored to match his vest—Mary Jo said, "I guess this is sort of turning into our special place, isn't it?"

"It will be after tonight."

She smiled at me, resplendent in a green silken blouse with a short strand of faux pearls. The green was a close match with her eyes. A black velvet hair band lifted her shimmering auburn hair up and away from her forehead. Her cheeks were still flushed from the nip in the air outside. It was Christmastime, we had the weekend ahead of us, and as usual she was easily the most beautiful woman in the room. I was on top of the world.

She said, "So, really, what's so special about tonight?"

"You'll see."

Mandina's dining rooms were divided by a long bar populated on the left by people who were waiting for a seat and on the right by lawyers and cab drivers who were drinking their dinner. For obvious reasons it was not wise to hail a cab on upper Canal or anywhere else nearby after five in the afternoon. New Orleans residents loved Mandina's for its history, its cuisine, and its location far away from the French Quarter tourists. Mary Jo and I loved it for the noise and the press of the crowd and the shouting bartenders and the slow waiters who maintained their unhurried pace no matter what.

Mary Jo said, "Come on, tell me what's going on."

"All things come to she who waits."

"You pig."

"Such talk."

"Why won't you tell me?"

"It's more fun this way."

"Maybe for you."

"Definitely for me."

She stuck her lower lip out, pouting. I loved it when she did that. It made me want to nibble. I told her so one time. She laughed so hard I knew she liked the idea. So I had a pet name for her: Nibbles.

The waiter brought my gumbo and her salad. At the bar, a lawyer and a cabby argued about the perfect martini. I slurped my soup loudly, watching Mary Jo. She made a big production out of cutting her salad and ignoring me and my crass eating habits. I added three drops of Mandina's Original Habanero Pepper Sauce to my gumbo. World's hottest. We ate without speaking, surrounded by a cacophony of shouts and clinking silverware and chairs scraping on quarry tile and wheezing heaters and Dean Martin singing Christmas carols on the hi-fi in the corner. She did not look at me until her salad was a memory. I smiled winningly.

She said, "Garrison Reed, whatever it is, you tell me, and you tell me right this instant or I'll go over there and drink myself silly with those awful men at the bar."

"What's the hurry?"

She calmly folded her napkin and placed it beside her plate and slid back her chair to stand. I said, "All right, all right. I'll tell you." She pulled her chair up to the table, retrieved her napkin, and looked at me expectantly.

"Well?" she said.

"Well . . . I really wanted to wait until after dinner."

"It's better this way."

"How do you know? You don't even know what I want to say."

"I know because if you don't come out with it I am never going to speak to you again."

"All right. Why didn't you just say so?"

"That's it. I'm leaving."

"Will you marry me?"

She looked at me hard, all signs of frivolity gone in an instant. "What?"

I said, "Will you marry me?" and returned her stare. The noise faded and the crowd disappeared and it was just we two, alone across a table filled with dirty dishes and saltine cracker crumbs.

Mary Jo looked away first. She bowed her head. And then, very quietly, she broke my heart.

She whispered, "No."

Chapter 13

URPRISE!"

Leon and Mrs. P. stood side by side in my office, clutching black balloons.

Leon said, "All things considered, we weren't sure if you'd want this stuff, but we already bought everything and we figured . . ."

He stepped aside so I could see. On my desk was a small cake covered with candles—way too many candles—and a couple of gaily wrapped packages. I smiled.

"Thanks, ya'll. This is nice."

Mrs. P. said, "Blow out them candles before the wax covers the cake." I leaned over and blew hard. It took three tries to get them all. She said, "Now open that one on top first."

I said, "Yes, ma'am," and began to unwrap the gift.

Leon said, "She's sure 'nuff bossy, ain't she?"

Mrs. P. said, "Somebody got to keep things movin' along."

"He just walked in, Ethyl."

"Got no time for this foolishness here. Hurry up with that present, Garrison."

I said, "Yes ma'am," again and withdrew the gift from the wrapping. It was a flannel shirt from Hoover's Big and Tall Shop. I said, "Thank you, Mrs. P. It's great."

She sniffed. "Thought you could use something warm."

"You betcha. I'll go put it on right now."

"No. Open them other ones first. Leon got you somethin'. It's that little one there."

I picked up the second gift and unwrapped it quickly. It was a copy of *Fodor's Mexico*.

Leon said, "I knew you and Mary Jo were thinkin' about going down there this winter and . . . well, maybe you'll still be able to."

I said, "Sure we will."

Mrs. P. said, "'Course you will."

We stood silently for a moment. Finally, Mrs. P. said, "Well, that's enough of that. You boys get on to work now. I got books to tend to this mornin'."

Leon said, "But there's a couple of other presents here, Ethyl. And he didn't cut the cake."

"We got no time for that."

He said, "Don't mind her, Garr. She's just embarrassed 'cause we have something to tell you. Don't we, honey?"

Mrs. P. said, "Oh, all right. But make it quick."

They stood shoulder to shoulder, looking at me and smiling, both short, both dark, one hard as nails and the other plump and soft as a bowl of chocolate pudding. Nobody said anything. Their smiles got wider. I said, "What?"

Mrs. P. said, "We gettin' married."

Leon said, "And we want you to be the best man."

I sat down behind my desk, feigning astonishment. I said, "No! *Married?* But you're coworkers. Isn't there a rule against that?"

Mrs. P. said, "He not takin' this well."

Leon said, "About as well as we expected."

I said, "And you . . . you're Mexican American. And you're African-American. Isn't there a rule against *that?*"

Mrs. P. said, "Boy, gettin' personal now."

Leon said, "We're gonna be a multicultural family in the finest tradition of the American melting pot."

I said, "Won't your children be confused? I mean, they'll be Mexican African-American Republicans. Who can remember all of that?"

Leon said, "I vote a straight Libertarian ticket."

Mrs. P. said, "*Children?* Honey, them days is *long* gone. Besides, I'd rather have hives."

I said, "Have you considered the religious differences? A Baptist and a Catholic? Leon, you'll have to sell your stock in Coors, and Mrs. P., you're going to have to kneel in church."

Leon said, "I already sold Coors high and bought Lipton low."

Mrs. P. said, "Honey, they gonna have to raise that floor up to these knees, 'cause they ain't bent in twenty years."

I said, "You've thought of everything."

Leon said, "You bet."

"And you are determined?"

Mrs. P. said, "We are."

"Then I suppose I have no choice but to give you my blessing."

Mrs. P. said, "*Blessing?* Who cares about that? We just want you to give us a couple of weeks off so we can honeymoon right."

"Where will you go?"

Leon smiled and said, "Wichita."

I said, "Wichita?"

"Yessir."

"Wichita, Kansas?"

Leon said, "Yep. It was either there or Mexico."

Mrs. P. said, "Or Africa."

"But Wichita?"

Mrs. P. sniffed and said, "It's neutral ground, sugar."

• • •

I WAS DRIVING OUT TO THE ELEMENTARY SCHOOL JOB later that day when the telephone in the truck rang. I lifted the handset to my ear and said hello.

Winston Graves said, "Garrison, I have just received word that the grand jury hearing will occur next Wednesday. We must prepare. Bring Mary Jo to my house on Monday morning at ten."

"Ah, that might be a problem."

"Please explain."

I said, "Anything I tell you is just between us?"

"Of course."

I paused, reluctant to go on. But it had to come out sometime, so I said, "Mary Jo has been missing since Monday night."

I heard his labored breathing over the telephone. It was a relief to tell someone. Perhaps he would have an idea. Perhaps discussing it would help me to overcome the sense of unreality that had troubled me since I first read Mary Jo's note. I accelerated onto an old blacktop farm road.

Winston said, "Have you informed the police?"

"Do you think I should?"

"I shall assume that is a negative response. Did Mary Jo indicate where she was going or why she would choose such an inopportune time to depart?"

"She left a note. All it said was she needed to be alone." I decided to leave out the part about dealing with Melvin Milo.

"I see . . . is there any reason to doubt the provenance of the note?"

"It was her handwriting."

"Was it her phrasing?"

"What are you after, Winston?"

"It seems to me that Mary Jo is a singularly intelligent woman. Yet this is a singularly unintelligent thing to do. I am simply trying to account for the situation."

In a sudden flash, I saw where he was going, and relief surged through me like that first deep gasp for air when you've been under water too long. Maybe she didn't lie. Maybe she was forced to leave me . . . But then, when the thought was fully formed, I felt ashamed. I drove a few hundred yards in silence, trying to master my emotions. When I felt ready to speak again, I said, "You think she was forced to write the note?"

"It seems possible. There is a murderer loose in our county, after all."

"But why would they take her? She's against abortion. Everybody knows that."

"True. In view of the apparent motive for the slaying, it does seem unlikely that the perpetrator would have anything to gain by seizing her."

I steered mindlessly, my left hand clutching the wheel, my right holding the mobile phone to my ear. I lifted two fingers in response to a wave from a man in an oncoming pickup.

Winston said, "Perhaps she simply panicked and ran."

"I hope so." It was a lie, but what could I say? Could I admit that I hoped she was kidnapped, because the alternative was too hard to bear?

"Yes. Well, it does little for our cause in any event. We shall be unable to plan a defense, and our position will be untenable if the authorities learn of her departure."

"We won't tell them."

"Of course."

"And we'll find her."

"Shall we engage an independent investigator?"

"I thought of that. There are too many reporters hanging around. They'd spot him and they'd make him an offer he couldn't refuse."

"You are most probably correct."

I steered to the left, following a wide bend in the road. Above me, the intricately interwoven branches of live oaks obscured the sky with deep green. The autumn sun shone through in places, dabbing shimmering puddles of white light on the road ahead. I could see further through the woods than the week before. The last leaves had fallen from the deciduous low-lying brush, allowing glimpses deep into the heart of the forest. Soon, the deer would begin their annual struggle for survival against the hunter's thirty-ought-six, wandering among the naked poplars and elm, searching for berries and a haven from sudden death.

I said, "If I gave you a sample of something, would you know where to send it to have it analyzed? Like, a forensics lab. Some place like that?"

"Of course."

"In that case, I'll come by your place in an hour or two, if that's okay."

"I shall be here."

I was passing Pedro Comacho's land. Slowing, I bent to see through the foggy glass on the side window. About a quarter mile beyond the turn-off to his house I swung left, bounced across the bar ditch, and plowed over a tall row of bushes. I followed the abandoned roadbed through dense brush and overhanging branches until I came to the end. I was planning to get a sample of the brown stain in the trunk of Mary Jo's car.

But the Volvo was gone.

I parked and stepped from the truck. A woodpecker's odd scream echoed through the trees, like an exotic call in an African rain forest. I blew into cupped hands, warming them. Dew dripped from the bare twigs and branches overhead and clung to the fallen leaves underfoot. I walked the area where her car had been parked. A pair of deep ruts sank into the soft humus of the forest floor. They were filled with water. I found a Marlboro butt about ten feet away. Other than that, there was no sign that anyone had been there for years.

And no way to tell whether the stain in Mary Jo's trunk had been paint or blood.

Chapter 14

T HAD BEEN OVER A YEAR SINCE OLD MAN
Martin took a bite out of my ear. They did a
fine job of reconstruction at Jackson County
General Hospital, but the scars were still bad.
I wear my hair long on the sides and try not to think about his
foul breath curling hot against my cheek or the pain as his teeth
gnawed through the cartilage.

Standing at the reception desk, I considered the fact that our
local hospital has been the scene of many unpleasant experiences
in my life. My mother died there. I once discovered the body of
a murder victim in the basement. After Victor Sickle shot me, I
spent many painful days recuperating in a bed on the second floor.

And somewhere deep within the bowels of the awful place
was the examination room where they discovered that Mary Jo
had cancer. A skin graft and an ear full of stitches was nothing
compared to that.

I rapped the small silver bell on the desk to call for assistance. While I waited, it occurred to me that I should be more
thankful. They managed to save my life when I was shot. My ear
would be half gone without them. And at least they had been
skilled enough to find Mary Jo's cancer before it spread into her
lymph system.

But it was difficult to feel thankful with Mary Jo gone and the
front of the hospital staked out by a furious pro-choice crowd that
would like nothing better than to see her dead. I had entered

through a gauntlet of sullen women, positioned alongside the door. They shuffled along in a large oval, eyes quietly blazing, united in their grim determination to fight the murderous trend that threatened doctors, nurses, and patients at every abortion clinic and hospital in our nation. Their placards were professionally printed, in blue and white, designed and produced by the National Organization of Women. I had looked away and hurried into Jackson County General, praying they would not recognize me.

The pro-life advocates assembled beside the patient wing across the lawn, probably hoping to be seen from Doctor Milo's window. Some of them were dressed in the odd uniforms of camouflage and black. They stood silently, perhaps in consideration of the other patients suffering within the hospital, but their hand-lettered signs said it all: "An Eye for an Eye" and "Defense of the Innocent Is Not Murder."

How must the doctor feel, knowing these so-called Christians wanted him dead? I was relieved to see that the pro-life group on the lawn was made up of strangers. No one from my church had joined their protest.

Our town had become a battleground for outsiders.

Perhaps not all of my fellow believers agreed with these people after all. Perhaps I was not alone in this growing sense of unease with their tactics. And yet, I was so new to this faith, with such a frail belief. Was my reticence merely the insecurity of a novice who was lost in the complexities of this new religion?

"How can I help ya'll?" A candy striper smiled behind the front desk and looked at me expectantly. She drew the word *help* out to two syllables—"hey-yelp"—as only a girl from Dixie can do.

I said, "There was a man here, an orderly, who said he saw the priest and doctor get shot."

Her smile dissolved. Her smooth forehead creased at the thought. She said, "Harry Attwater."

"Yes. Harry Attwater. Where can I find him?"

She looked at me closely. "Say, aren't you that lady's husband?"

"Yes."

"I thought so. I've seen ya'll around town a lot. My name's Tammy."

"It's nice to meet you, Tammy. I think I've seen you around, too."

"Ya'll don't have any kids, right?"

"No. No, we don't."

"That's what I thought. Because if you did, I'd probably have met ya'll before, like at an open house up at school or someplace. I'm graduating this spring."

"Tammy, I'm in a bit of a hurry here. Do you think you could tell me where I can find this Attwater fellow?"

She said, "I believe he's on the third floor this afternoon."

"May I go up? I won't take much of his time. Just a few questions they forgot to ask. You understand." I smiled my most engaging smile.

"Why, sure. I suppose that will be all right."

The elevator squeaked and trembled and opened to a brightly lit corridor with solid gray carpet, white vinyl wallcovering, and a vaguely unpleasant smell. I looked left and right and turned down the hall to the nurse's station. Two women in nurse's uniforms sat on rolling chairs behind the counter. Both were filling out forms. One was black and in her fifties, the other was young and blond. I knew the blond—she went to our church—but I couldn't remember her name. Neither of them stopped writing when I leaned on the low wall in front of their counter.

I said, "I'm here to ask a Harry Attwater some questions."

The older nurse kept writing. She said, "He's around here somewhere, isn't he, Nancy?"

Without looking up, the other one said, "Over in the lounge most likely. Watching the television."

"Isn't he on duty?"

"That doesn't stop him from enjoying himself."

"Which way is the lounge?"

The blond fixed beautiful blue eyes upon me. Recognition flashed in them, and she smiled a greeting. Then she made a circular motion with her pen and said, "It's a big loop, Garr. Just walk either way until you get to it."

As I walked away, I heard them whispering behind my back.

The lounge was right around the corner. Two sofas lined adjacent walls in the small room, and a television hung from the ceiling in the opposite corner. There were no windows. An old man sat on one of the sofas. He wore a clean pair of blue and white striped pajamas. Beside him stood a tall chrome contraption, like a hat stand on wheels. A brown plastic box with buttons and glowing numbers was mounted about waist high on the stand. Two clear plastic bags hung from hooks at the top. Slender tubes trailed down from the bags and disappeared between the buttons of the old man's pajama shirt. The box clicked every couple of seconds. I suppose it was pumping fluid through the tubes. The old man smoked a cigarette and stared at the television. His face was the color of soggy oatmeal. When I stepped into the room, he looked at me without interest.

The orderly sitting on the other sofa could have been playing hooky from grade school. He wore his bright red hair short, with a cowlick in back sticking straight up like a rooster's comb. Beneath a liberal scattering of freckles, his cheeks were candy-apple red. His small nose turned up to show a lot of nostril. His white uniform was clean, but his Nike running shoes were scuffed and worn. He sprawled across the love seat with his legs crossed and his fingers laced behind his head, intent on the television show. I recognized him immediately as the man in the white lab coat who had identified Mary Jo to the deputies on the day of the murder.

"Harry Attwater?"

He flicked his eyes away from the television, looked me up and down, and said, "Yeah?" His voice was very deep. Coming from such a boyish face, it was as unexpected as a barking canary.

"I need to ask you a few questions."

"Oh, man. Not now, okay? I'm right in the middle of somethin' here." He gestured toward the television, where a woman in a tight evening dress stood on a moonlit balcony with a man in a tuxedo. The woman said, "I saw her do it." The man said, "It just isn't possible." The red-headed orderly had returned his full attention to their conversation.

I said, "It's about Father McKay and Doctor Milo."

His eyes remained on the television screen. He said, "I told you I'm in the middle here."

I said, "It's important."

The woman on the television said, "Darling, you must believe me."

The orderly, speaking to himself, said, "She saw it, man. You better believe she saw it." The old man on the other love seat grunted.

I said, "We're having trouble believing part of your story."

The orderly said, "Who's 'we'?"

I said, "I work for the county." It wasn't a lie, strictly speaking. Reed Construction did a lot of work for Jackson County.

On the television screen, the man in the tuxedo said, "Dolores is just not capable of such treachery."

The old man in the pajamas snorted.

Without removing his eyes from the screen, the orderly said, "I work for the county too, buddy. And right now, I'm on my afternoon break. Do you mind?"

"When is your break over?"

"When that idiot up there believes that Dolores poisoned James and not a second sooner."

I sat on the love seat to wait. The woman in the evening dress said, "Darling, I know how much she has meant to you these last two years, but you must believe me, Dolores has changed. When James entered law school and Sidney decided to wait for his graduation to announce the new partnership, it did something to her. She has been manipulating you to try to influence their arrangement. When you left for the Sudan, she moved in with Terry, and things went from bad to worse."

The tuxedo said, "I think I finally see ..." and the picture got fuzzy around the edges. A silky masculine voice-over said, "Thus continues ... *The Turning Tide*. Tune in tomorrow to see Edward and Terry discuss Jillian's startling revelations. Until then ..."

The orderly pointed a remote control at the television and the screen went blank. Turning to the old man he said, "Well, Mister Miller. Didn't I tell ya? I knew James would believe her if she just kept trying."

The old man said, "Hogwash."

Laughing, the orderly stood and moved to a position directly in front of the old man, holding both of his hands out as if they contained twin offerings. The old man stabbed his cigarette into an ash tray and took Harry Attwater's hands. Attwater pulled him to a standing position. The old man grasped the chrome rolling stand with his shaking right hand, put his left hand on the orderly's shoulder, and took a tentative step toward the hall, leaning heavily on the shoulder. The orderly turned to me and said, "I'll be right back, mister."

I sat alone in the little room, waiting. On the wall above the sofa where the old man had been sitting was a large framed poster of vague pastel shapes with jagged black lines. Perhaps it was intended to be a mountain scene, something light and cheery. Its mediocrity had the opposite effect on me. A stack of folded brochures lay upon the low table between the love seats. I picked one up. It contained promotional information for the National Nursing Association's hospice care program. When you are too ill to treat, they call in the hospice. It is their job to treat the pain, not the disease, until death removes your suffering. I read about their combination of psychological counseling, pain-killing medications, and in-home nursing—all designed to make the final days as comfortable as possible. I read with detached curiosity, until I reached a brief list of the types of illnesses most often leading to the hospice program's care: AIDS, Alzheimer's, Lou Gehrig's disease, leukemia, cirrhosis of the liver, cancer of the lung, cancer of the colon, cancer of the cervix, cancer of the breast.

I closed my eyes.

Dear God, please don't take my love that way.

Harry Attwater cleared his throat with a deep bass rumble. I opened my eyes to see him standing in the doorway looking down at me.

"Mister, are you all right?"

"Yes. Thank you. I was just resting my eyes."

"Well, here I am. What was it you wanted again?"

I rose. We stood across the little room from each other. We were complete opposites; one a short, pale, redhead and the other tall and tanned with brown hair. Harry Attwater smiled, aware of the comical differences between us. I liked him for that.

I said, "I lied before. I'm not really with the county."

"Oh?"

"I'm Garrison Reed. Mary Jo Reed's husband."

The smile remained, but for an instant a puzzled expression joined it on his face. He said, "And?"

"Mary Jo Reed. The one you identified to the police."

His smile evaporated. "I never knew her name."

"Mister Attwater—"

"Call me Harry."

"Harry, my wife is a gentle person. She would never hurt anyone deliberately."

He held up his hands, palms out. "Hey, I never said she hurt anyone."

"But you identified her to the police."

"All I told them was that I saw her leaving the, ah, scene of the crime."

"You didn't actually see her shoot those men?"

"No, sir."

"But you think you saw her . . . what? Running? Walking? How was she leaving the scene?"

"I *know* I saw her run down the hall, away from those guys."

"Where were you at the time?"

"I was running toward them."

"And she was running away? Or was she running toward you?"

"She was on the other side of them, running away."

"So you couldn't see her face."

"That's right."

"Then how could you see who she was?"

"She had shoulder-length auburn colored hair and she was wearing a pair of white slacks and one of those white and red T-shirts they were passing out to the demonstrators. Besides, I saw her in the lobby earlier that morning. I'd remember her anywhere. Your wife is a knockout."

I smiled. "I think so too, Harry. Did you see anyone else?"

He said, "You mean hanging around the lobby, or later, after the shootings?"

"Either, I guess."

"Yeah. Milo's wife was there."

"Doctor Milo's wife was there at the scene?"

"Uh huh."

"Was she there when you arrived?"

"Nah. She showed up a minute or two later. While I was working on the priest."

"What did she do?"

He shrugged. "I wasn't paying that much attention, what with trying to resuscitate the father and all. But I do remember one thing . . . a really weird thing, actually."

"Yes?"

"Well, she was crying, of course, and screaming a lot, mainly in some other language I couldn't understand."

"That sounds pretty normal to me."

"Yeah, but she was also drawing in his blood."

"*What?*"

"Yeah. I told you it was weird."

"She was drawing in her husband's blood?"

Harry Attwater nodded. "Yeah. Finger painting, like."

"What did she draw?"

"I dunno. A star, I think. And a bunch of other stuff around it."

"Did you ask her why she did it?"

"No. But I heard one of the deputies ask her later on. She said it was some kinda healing ritual. Like, a special sign to keep death away or something." He shook his head again. "That lady was really weird, man."

I said, "What were you doing before that?"

He looked at me oddly, tilting his head a bit. "Like I said, I was trying to stop the bleeding."

"I mean, you said you were running in that direction as this other woman ran away. Were you nearby when the shooting happened?"

"I was in the E.R. cleaning up."

"And that's nearby?"

"Around the corner."

"Was anyone else in the E.R. with you at the time?"

"No."

"What if there had been an emergency? Who was going to help you?"

"Well, Doctor Milo was on emergency duty that day, standing in for Doctor Rideout."

"Doctor Milo was *working* here?"

"Not really. He was just standing in for a couple of days to get the feel of the place."

"How come Doctor Milo wasn't in the E.R. with you?"

"No reason for him to be there, Mister Reed. There was no emergency at the time." He glanced at the sofa behind me. "At least, there was no emergency until he was shot."

I followed his gaze to the seat. "Would you like to sit down?"

"All right, but I've got to keep this quick."

"Won't take much longer. I promise."

We sat on separate sofas. I had dropped the hospice brochure on the seat when I rose to greet him. I picked it up and refolded it and replaced it on the stack on the table. Harry Attwater watched my every move. He said, "Are you sure you're all right?"

I said, "I would be, except for this problem with the shooting."

"I'm very sorry about all that."

"Yes. Well, is there anything else you can think of that I might want to know? Anything about what happened that day?"

He stared at the far wall, thinking. Finally, he said, "I don't think so."

I said, "How about the nurse?"

"What nurse?"

"Didn't I see you and a nurse running down the hall with a sick man on a gurney a short while after the shooting?"

He looked me up and down. "I remember . . . that was you blocking the hall?"

"At my size, it's hard not to get in the way sometimes."

"Yeah. I wouldn't know."

"So who was the nurse?"

"Uh, that was Lizzy. Lizzy somebody. I don't know her last name. She was a temp."

"Was she working the emergency room with you that day?"

"Yeah. I forgot. She was there."

"Was she with you when you heard the shots?"

He said, "I think she might have been across the way in the ladies room. . . . Yeah, I think I remember her saying she had to powder her nose."

"So she was nearby when the shooting started?"

"As close as me, really. Just on the other side of the corridor."

"Did she come to help you with the doctor and Father McKay?"

"Sure. After a while."

"How long?"

"What?"

"How long were you there with the doctor and the father before she arrived?"

"Oh, I don't know . . . maybe four, five minutes. Hey, it's hard to tell in those circumstances, you know? I mean, we don't get that many shootings here. And I never saw one right at the, ah, scene like that. I was agitated."

"I can understand that. Anyone would have been agitated."

"You bet."

"But even though you were . . . agitated . . . you're sure the woman you saw was my wife?"

"I'm sorry. Yes."

I stood and stuck out my hand. He rose to take it and we shook hands quickly. "All right, Harry. I appreciate your time."

Harry Attwater said, "You bet, Mister Reed. It's the least I can do, what with your wife's problems and all."

"Yes, well, thanks again."

As I stepped out into the hall, Harry Attwater said, "Doctor Rideout is a fine oncologist, Mister Reed. You shouldn't worry."

I stopped and looked back at him. "You know about that?"

"It's a small hospital."

I stared at him for a moment, trying to decide if I was angry or embarrassed. I felt as if someone had eavesdropped on a private conversation or read an intimate love letter. He must have seen the strength of my emotions in my face. He said, "I saw you reading the hospice stuff. It reminded me about your wife. I just thought you'd like to know there's no reason to think along those lines. From what I heard they caught it real early."

I said, "I thought you said you didn't know her name."

"I didn't. I just heard that the woman they arrested had breast cancer . . ."

"Who told you?"

He said, "I think it was Lizzy."

"The nurse?"

"That's right."

"How would she know?"

"I guess she was assisting Doctor Rideout when they made the diagnosis."

"Everyone wears a lot of hats around here."

"Like I said, it's a small hospital."

"This Lizzy. I seem to remember she was crying when you two ran past me in the hall. Why would she do that?"

"I don't know."

I looked at him in silence for a moment. Then I said, "Harry, who was the man on that gurney?"

"I thought you knew. That was Doctor Milo."

"Is that why Lizzy was crying?"

"What?"

"Was she crying for Doctor Milo?"

Harry Attwater said, "Beats me. Who knows why women act the way they do? I have to get back to work, Mister Reed. I really am sorry about your wife."

Chapter 15

WITH HARRY ATTWATER'S DESCRIPTION OF the murder scene spinning through my mind, I stepped from the elevator onto the second floor instead of descending to the lobby. I had just realized my mistake and begun to spin back toward the elevator when I saw Mary Jo turning a corner at the far end of the hall. She was already out of sight when I called her name.

"Wait!" I yelled as I sprinted toward the corner. I took the right-hand turn fast, sliding sideways on the vinyl floor just in time to catch a glimpse of her auburn hair as she stepped through a door about halfway down the corridor. As I approached the door, a boiling alphabet soup of questions swirled through my mind. Where have you been? What happened to your car? What do you know about the murder? And the one question I feared, yet longed to ask before any other:

Why did you leave me?

I stepped through the doorway, prepared to face her with righteous indignation. It was a private room, with a single bed along the far wall. A man reclined beneath the white hospital sheets with his face turned toward a pair of windows flanking a square column just beyond. She sat in a chair in front of one of the windows, her head and shoulders outlined in crisp silhouette against the glare of the sunshine beyond. I realized my mistake even as I spoke her name.

"Mary Jo . . ."

Rising, she said, "What? Who are you? How did you get past the guard?"

It was not Mary Jo's voice.

As she came closer I tried to explain. "I'm sorry. I thought you were someone else. My wife, Mary Jo." As the woman moved away from the light, I could clearly see the lines of age beneath her eyes, the darker skin, the wider cheekbones. How could I have been so mistaken? She was Mary Jo's height, and like Mary Jo, she had shoulder-length auburn colored hair. But the resemblance ended there. The hair was frayed at the ends from too many permanents. And this was an older woman with a body that showed the effects of gravity and a life lived in defiance of the rules. Too many cocktails had cast their net of tiny red capillaries across the whites of her eyes. Too many idle days had left their legacy in the sagging of her upper arms and the atrophy of her calves. The skin stretched unnaturally tight across her lower face. I could just make out the fine line left by a surgeon's knife at the fold where her neck met her jaw. She stood very straight, her shoulders square, her ample bosom thrust up proudly. A strange necklace cascaded across her chest, rows of thin, pale gray bones and small silver coins hung from a length of ordinary brown twine. In the center of the necklace hung what could only be a mummified monkey's hand.

Beside her on the windowsill and bedside table, I saw dozens of candles, interspersed with crude clay bowls and brightly colored drawings of saints, with hands uplifted or folded in prayer. In one of the clay bowls, a powdery substance burned slowly, emitting a thin spire of smoke. In another, I saw a large bird claw, floating in a pool of dark red liquid. Could that be blood?

The woman stared hard at me as she leaned both hands on a strange walking stick, carved and painted to resemble a miniature totem pole. Suddenly, her eyes grew wide and she screamed, "But I know you! You are the husband of that murderer!"

The man on the bed watched us with a detached expression, the faraway gaze of a man on barbiturates. I recognized him immediately as the man on the gurney. Doctor Milo. I returned his stare, surprised to realize for the first time that his skin was as dark as a black man's. But his features were Caucasian, with a long, narrow nose and thin lips.

I said, "I am very sorry. I honestly didn't mean to intrude—"

She screamed, "How could you come here? Get out!"

She pounced on me, arms raised, fists clenched around the strange walking stick. The stick cracked against my forearm as I lifted it for protection. A flurry of blows came with incredible speed. The stick was a blur, whistling through the air around my head and cracking against my skull twice before I realized I was in a serious fight. I parried the blows with my forearms, moving in close to make it harder for her to get a backswing. The woman grunted like an animal with every strike. Her eyes shone with a malicious delight. Her teeth were bared, the incisors long and sharp and glistening white against her blood-red lips. A large diamond on her left hand slid across my forearm, slashing a thin red line from wrist to elbow. She aimed the stick at my cheek. I deflected it again, but her heavy rings bit into my hands like a viper. Then she began to scream in a language I did not understand.

I backed away, warding off her stick and her bejeweled fists as best I could. Then someone grabbed my arm from behind and pulled me toward the door. The woman landed three quick blows against my ribs.

The man behind me shouted, "That's enough, ma'am!"

Panting like a jaguar, the woman backed away. The monkey's hand hanging on her chest rose and fell like a living thing with each breath.

"All right, buddy. What are you tryin' to pull here?" I turned and saw a man in a brown deputy's uniform.

Between breaths the woman said, "He just walked in. Where is it that you were?" Her accent was odd, a combination of nasal French consonants and something I could not identify. Perhaps it was Cajun.

The deputy said, "I'm sorry, ma'am. I just went down the hall to take a—ah, to use the rest room."

The woman screamed, "You allow the crazy woman's husband to come here like he is the owner of this place! Who can know what he intended?"

I said, "Wait a minute. This was a mistake. I thought you were—"

"You bet it was a mistake, partner," said the deputy. "Come on out to the hall here where we can talk without botherin' the doctor." He pulled on my arm again, steering me out to the hall. The woman followed and stopped in the open hospital room doorway. I glanced back. Out of the corner of my eye, I thought I saw the shadows shift in the darkness behind her, almost as if something was looming there, leering at me. I shivered and looked again. There was nothing but thin air. And the woman's eyes, so empty, yet so full of hatred that I dared not meet them directly.

The deputy said, "Missus Milo, you mind stayin' inside until I get Mister Reed's story?"

She said, "I do! I want to know why it is acceptable for them to kill the people but wrong for my husband to save the lives of the innocent girls. I want to listen to his lies! I want to hear him explain why he and his wife are persecuting us."

I said, "Nobody's persecuting you."

She sneered. "Tell this to my husband. He is lying there with the hole in his side and still you will not give him peace. You people have made of our life the living hell. Standing outside our home, standing outside his clinic, shouting your slogans, waving your signs, printing the number of our telephone on posters and talking of him on the television as if he was some kind of an animal, a *Tom Tom Macute* or a serial killer or a . . ."

She slumped against the doorjamb, propped the stick against the wall, and broke into tears, clutching her hands together over her face. If the diamonds on her fingers were real they were worth a fortune. I glanced back at her bedridden husband. He lay perfectly still, head turned away from us, looking toward the eerie altar of blood and candles on the windowsill.

Her tears touched me. "Mrs. Milo, my wife and I have never been a part of those things."

With her face covered she said, "Liar. I saw you here last Sunday. You were with those animals out front. Those *Christians*." She spat the word like a curse.

"But I was just watching. I wasn't part of it."

"You were here. You and your wife. She shot my Mel."

The deputy said, "Hold on here. Are you sayin' this is that woman's husband?"

She looked at him and said, "You idiot." I realized that her eyes were completely dry.

The deputy's grip on my arm tightened. He said, "Mister Reed, we better see if we can find us a quiet room somewhere to wait on the sheriff. I got a feelin' he'll want to come talk to you."

We were several steps down the hall when I heard Dr. Milo's weak voice call from within the room. He spoke in the language his wife had used earlier. I understood only one word.

"Juliette?"

Mrs. Milo turned toward the doorway at the sound of her husband's voice. I saw something unexpected in her face. It was not a look of love or compassion. It was not worry or concern. Whatever it was, I pitied the man who received that look.

She spoke to him with words I did not understand and with a final glare in my direction, she stepped inside. I felt an immediate sense of relief to be out of her line of sight.

The deputy and I waited in an empty room down the hall. I sat on the edge of the bare mattress while he watched me from a position near the door. He leaned casually against the wall, arms crossed, boots lined up side by side. His brown uniform shirt was wrinkled, but his boots, holster, and Sam Brown were shined to a sparkling luster. I said, "Didn't you get much sleep last night?"

"Why?"

"Your shirt looks like you slept in it."

He glanced down at his chest, then back at me. "Yeah."

"What's your name?"

"McCracken."

"Been with the sheriff's department long?"

"Long enough."

"Don't think we ever met."

"Nope."

"You're not much for conversation, are you?"

"Nope."

I nodded and turned to look out the window. Down below, the pro-life crowd stood silently, oddly dressed in red berets and bearing their ugly signs. On the far side of the hospital lawn, a row of tall pines defined the edge of the property. Beyond the pines lay a barbed wire fence and beyond that a thousand parallel rows of plowed soil—a cotton field lying fallow. I watched a white plastic garbage sack blow end over end across the field. It caught on the barbed wire just beyond the pines and fluttered there, at the mercy of the unceasing wind.

Ernie Davenport stepped through the hospital room door like he was entering a funeral home, looking left and right, wiping both palms on the front of his blue pin-striped suit coat.

He said, "Man. I hate to touch things in here. Who knows what kinda germs are on this stuff?"

I said, "Hi, Ernie."

He smiled. "Hey, Garr." Turning to the deputy he said, "Charlie, you got anything to add to what you told me on the radio?"

Deputy McCracken said, "No, sir."

Sheriff Davenport said, "All right then. Why don't you head on back to Doctor Milo's room and keep an eye on things there."

Deputy McCracken said, "Yes, sir," and left the room.

Ernie returned his dark brown Mediterranean eyes to me. "What on earth were you trying to accomplish here?"

"It was a mistake. I thought Mrs. Milo was Mary Jo, and I followed her into the doctor's room before I realized I was wrong."

"Why would you think an old woman like that was Mary Jo?"

"Well, first of all, she's not that old, and second, she was walking away from me when I saw her."

Ernie shot his cuffs and looked around the bare hospital room. "I never thought they looked alike. But I never watched the two of them walking away. Interesting . . ." He seemed to drift away for a moment, deep in thought. Then he fixed me with a straightforward stare. "Garr, I'm gonna tell you something I shouldn't. Because we're friends. You won't tell anyone where you heard this, will you?"

"Not unless I have to. But Ernie, you know I'll do whatever it takes to protect Mary Jo. Maybe you shouldn't tell me anything that might get you in trouble."

"It'll come out directly anyway. One of our witnesses, an orderly here at the hospital, said he saw Mary Jo at the scene. Picked her out of the crowd in front of the hospital that day. But it turns out he only saw her from the rear, going away." He adjusted the knot of his red paisley tie and went on with a smile, "Get my point?"

"Like I said, I made the same mistake just now. So it's pretty obvious the orderly saw Mrs. Milo and thought she was Mary Jo. Is that what you're saying?"

He nodded. "If the orderly was our only witness, I'd say that's what happened for sure."

I frowned. "But what about your other witness?"

"Doctor Milo."

"What does he claim he saw?"

Ernie Davenport said, "That's not so good. He picked Mary Jo's photograph out of a dozen that we showed him."

It was as if demons had wrapped steel cable around my chest. I could almost hear their evil laughter as they twisted it tight. I said, "He was positive about the picture?"

"Pretty positive, yeah."

The demons' mirth drove up my blood pressure. I could feel the throbbing in my ears. I turned to look out through the window. It was just not possible. Mary Jo would not do such a thing. Somehow, I had to prove her innocence, yet the doctor's accusation lay like a gaping chasm across my path, exposing the burning stench of hell below.

I said, "Ernie, she didn't do it."

"I believe you."

I looked away from the window for a moment, my eyes meeting his. There was sympathy there, like an offering. I said, "How can I help you prove it?"

"You might start by being honest with me."

"What does that mean?"

He broke our eye contact first. His hands were in constant motion, pulling down on the front of his coat, smoothing his tie, adjusting his cuffs. He said, "You could start by telling me where she is."

I returned my gaze to the scene outside the window. Beyond the crowd, the white plastic sack still fluttered on the barbed wire, like a flag of truce. Or surrender.

"I don't know where she is, Ernie. Somewhere around town, probably. Why is that so important?"

"I went by your house this morning. Met her mother. Hard woman. Wouldn't let me get a peek past the door, much less set foot inside."

"Lucretia is a very private person."

"Yeah. Well, after our little talk, I wandered over to the studio, thinking Mary Jo might be working. I wanted to ask her a few more questions. Thought maybe she could tell me something that would put us on the right track. Something that would help us to clear her."

"I appreciate that."

"Don't mention it." He moved to the wall, looking closely at a framed print. The long thin scar along his jawline lay white against his olive skin. He said, "Of course she wasn't there, either. I went inside. Hope you don't mind."

"Not at all."

"The paint was dry on every canvas." He touched the print. "It takes a while for oil paint to dry, doesn't it?"

"A day or two."

He turned his dark eyes toward me. "Where is she, Garr?"

I looked at a spot an inch above his eyebrows. Ernie Davenport was a friend. I did not want to lie to him. I said, "Ernie, the judge told her to stay in Jackson County until the grand jury hearing. He didn't say she had to stay at home."

"Do you know where she is?"

"Not right at the moment, no."

"Is she coming home tonight?"

"I hope so."

He leaned closer to me. I saw real concern in his eyes. "Garr, are the two of you all right?"

I laughed bitterly. "Of course not, Ernie. She's been arrested for murder!"

"That's not what I meant. Helen and I always thought you had a model marriage. But something like this happens, it puts a heck of a strain on things. I've seen it a hundred times."

"Thanks, Ernie, but it's not like that." I decided to try to change the subject. "Have you learned anything about those strange markings on the wall?"

"Markings?"

"Yes. The finger painting on the wall where the bodies were lying."

"You noticed that, did you?"

"Hard to miss, Ernie."

"Yeah, I suppose so. But to tell you the truth, we don't know what to make of it."

"Maybe you should ask the Milos. Have you seen the stuff they've got set up in that room down there? The candles and the incense and all?"

"I thought it was a Catholic thing."

"A Catholic thing? With bowls of blood and chicken claws?"

"I didn't see any blood or chicken claws, Garr. Just a few candles and a picture of a saint."

"When were you in their room?"

"Just now. Right before I came in here."

I stared at him for a second, trying to understand. Why would he say it if it was not true? And if it was true, why didn't he see the things I had seen? Did the Milos hide them?

He walked to the door. With his fingers on the handle, he said, "Garr, Mary Jo has got to be there at the hearing. It would be a big mistake if y'all were planning to do anything else."

"Right now we have no plans, Ernie."

"Just so you know. If they indict her and issue an arrest warrant, it will be better if she surrenders voluntarily. Otherwise, once we have her in custody, not even Winston Graves could talk the judge into letting her out on bail again. She'll have to stay in the county lockup until her trial. That could be months."

"I understand."

He nodded. "Just so you know."

The door closed softly behind him.

I stared outside again. It always surprises me how quickly autumn nights can fall. In the sudden twilight, I saw that the relentless wind had ripped the white plastic sack in two. Along the line of separation, tattered pieces of the remaining half fluttered frantically, impaled upon the barbs as if beckoning the missing half to return. For the hundredth time, I wondered why Mary Jo left.

Behind me, the door opened and Ernie Davenport stuck his head back in.

He said, "Garr, I forgot to tell you—stay away from Melvin and Juliette Milo, all right?"

I nodded absently without turning to look at him, my attention on the trash outside.

Chapter 16

IN THE AFTERGLOW OF THE EARLY SUNSET, hands buried deep in my pockets against the nip in the air, I strolled along the sidewalk between the hospital and Saint Sebastian's, Jackson County's only Catholic church. As I stepped over the cracked and uplifted slabs where the roots of an ancient oak swelled above the ground, it occurred to me that I was retracing the route Father Michael McKay had walked to his death.

The rectory was a large white clapboard house on Tyler street, five blocks from the hospital. The door was opened by a woman with short brown hair and a round face cruelly scarred by acne. She wore a simple black skirt to mid-calf, a pair of white canvas sneakers, a white long-sleeved blouse, and a tiny silver crucifix on a silver chain around her neck. A large pair of thick-lensed glasses with tortoiseshell frames magnified her curious brown eyes. I introduced myself, offered condolences, and explained that I was there to learn what I could about Father McKay. With a touch of reluctance, she invited me to step inside. We stood in a narrow hall beside a formal sitting room. A small shelf hung on the wall to our right. The shelf supported three burning votive candles and a framed print of the Virgin Mary. The items on the shelf reminded me of those on Doctor Milo's bedside table.

The woman shook my hand and said, "My name is Sister Anne Marie Carlisle. Please accept my apologies for making you stand outside like that. I thought you were another one of those reporters."

"Have many of them come here?"

She nodded. "Oh my, yes. All week long. They've made it difficult to get anything useful accomplished since I'm the only one here right now. Sister Ruth is in Shreveport at a conference on child abuse, and Father Carson and Sister Constance Augusta have been spending their days across the way at the Knights of Columbus hall preparing for tomorrow's clothing drive."

"Did you know Father McKay well?"

"No. He was new here."

"Really?"

"Yes. He only arrived this fall."

"Do you know where he was, uh, stationed before he came here?"

She smiled at my ignorance of Catholic terminology and said, "I'm not sure, actually. We never discussed it. Isn't that odd? But I think maybe he served somewhere down south."

"Why is that?"

"He had a strange accent."

"Could it have been a New Orleans accent?"

"Perhaps. Or maybe he picked it up when he did his mission work in Haiti."

"Haiti?"

"Yes. The Father ran a small mission for orphaned boys down there."

"When was that?"

"After he left the seminary, I think. But I'm not sure. He didn't speak much of his background. But I seem to recall he mentioned some bad experiences there, in Haiti I mean. Something he found shocking because he was fresh from the seminary and a bit naive about other religious practices."

"Other religions?"

She looked at me, her eyes large and guileless behind the thick glasses. She said, "Yes. I believe he said he encountered some strange beliefs down there."

"How about you? How long have you been here, Sister?"

"Let's see . . . I came down from Cincinnati the same winter we had that terrible freeze. You know, when it dropped below zero for three or four days? I remember because everyone was in such a panic. I thought they were silly, being from up in Ohio, until I realized it hadn't happened here before."

I said, "It was awful."

She smiled. "Nobody was prepared for it, that's for sure."

"Our water pipes broke in seven places."

"Ours too. I remember mopping up with Sister Ruth after the thaw."

"So that would mean you've been here for seven or eight years."

The candlelight flickered in her glasses, obscuring her eyes. "Oh, my. Has it really been that long?"

"Time flies when you're having fun."

"Fun," she sighed. "Yes, I suppose."

Something in her tone inspired my next question. "Are things comfortable for you here?"

"Comfortable? Do you mean here at the rectory, or here in Mount Sinai?"

"Either, I guess. I wouldn't ask, except you sounded a bit unhappy."

The nun stared openly at my face for a moment, then she said, "I've seen you around town, I think, but I haven't seen you at Mass. Are you a Catholic, Mister Reed?"

"No. But I am a Christian."

"A Christian. Yes. We Catholics are strangers in a strange land here in Mount Sinai, Mister Reed. That is not a comfort to us."

"I am sorry."

She flipped her hand back and forth, a dismissive gesture. "It's not important. We are not called to lives of comfort and leisure. The Church requires more of us than that."

"Amen."

Smiling, she said, "There, you see? Already we have reached an understanding. I persevere in my calling. Perhaps one day we will celebrate Mass together after all."

"You're a missionary."

"Sometimes it does feel that way."

"Speaking for all of the Protestants in Mount Sinai, I promise not to add you to our stew."

"Ah. Next you'll be covering your nakedness with a loincloth and removing the bone from your nose. God does perform his wonders."

I grinned. "Did Father McKay feel as you do? Surrounded by heathens and infidels?"

"Why don't we sit down?" She gestured toward the sitting room. When I had settled onto an overstuffed chair and she had perched on a sofa, she said, "Father Mike was an unusual man. He could have been comfortable anywhere."

"How so?"

She studied her hands, which were clasped primly on her lap. "He was a friendly man. A man who fit in well."

"You almost sound as if that is a bad thing."

"Oh, it can be a blessing I suppose. But one can be too friendly."

"Forgive me, Sister, but aren't we Christians supposed to be accepting and loving? How can we be too friendly?"

Her eyes remained firmly fixed upon her hands. "There are some kinds of . . . friendship . . . that are forbidden to us by our vows, Mister Reed."

"Are we talking about relationships between men and women?"

"That is one kind, yes."

In a flash of intuition, I said, "You're telling me Father McKay was involved with a woman."

She looked up, her eyes huge behind thick lenses. "I am not telling you anything. We are simply having a conversation."

"Forgive me if I misunderstood."

She smiled and said, "You are forgiven, my son."

I laughed. "What was Father McKay doing at the hospital that day?"

"We often visit our ill parishioners."

"Could he have been there in connection with the pro-life protest?"

"It is possible."

"You don't sound as if you think so."

"No."

"Was he involved with the pro-life movement?"

"That would require that he take a firm stand on the issue. Father McKay was not one to take a stand."

"But you said it was possible he was there because of the protest."

"He did have beliefs on the subject. He called himself a moderate. He felt that both sides, pro-life and pro-choice, were ignoring the possibility of a compromise."

"How's that?"

"You understand, his opinions did not agree with the Church's position?"

"If you say so."

She nodded. "He believed that we should establish guidelines to define when a fetus has developed the mental and emotional characteristics of a human being. Once we identify that stage of fetal development, we could morally condone abortions prior to it."

"That sounds reasonable."

"Yes, it does, doesn't it?"

"I wonder why nobody has offered it as an option?"

She leaned back against the cushions on the sofa and crossed her arms. A collection of modestly framed small oil paintings hung on the wall above her head; a hill country field of bluebonnets bordered by live oaks, a mysterious moss-draped bayou scene, and a prickly pear desert vignette. Someone had a penchant for Texas landscapes. She said, "There is a catch. Sonograms often show fetuses sucking their thumbs as early as fourteen weeks. All of the vital organs are formed by the twelfth week. And it's pretty well established that the nervous system development begins in the area of the brain by the sixth or seventh week."

I did not respond. She looked closely at me and leaned forward an inch or two. "Do you understand? It is very possible that the fetus has developed a human consciousness by the end of the second month."

I said, "Some women wouldn't even have been tested for pregnancy yet."

She nodded. "Exactly. A woman would have to abort within two to three weeks of the first indications of pregnancy. Many women don't go in to their doctor until they've missed their second cycle."

I stared at the field of bluebonnets in the painting above her head. She watched me closely. I said, "Did Father McKay ever try to present his compromise idea to anyone who was actively involved in the issue?"

"I don't know. These are just things he and I discussed."

"Could he have been at the hospital that day to make a case for compromise?"

"Perhaps. He was there to see someone."

"Someone in particular?"

"I believe he was."

"Do you know who?"

She shook her head. "I'm afraid not."

"Sister, if Father McKay was moderate on the abortion issue, whoever shot Doctor Milo may have killed him because of his views. It's important that we know why the Father was there. Could he have gone to see Doctor Milo?"

"No. It wasn't the doctor. I overheard him speaking to someone the day before. Making an appointment."

"On the telephone?"

"No. Here at the rectory."

"Did you see the person he spoke with?"

"Yes."

"Did you hear what was said?"

"Bits and pieces. I really wasn't paying much attention."

"Did they discuss abortion?"

"I heard the word being used, yes."

"Could you describe the man he spoke with?"

She looked at me for a moment before answering. Then she said, "It was a woman, actually. She was about forty years old, quite attractive, about five and a half feet tall, with shoulder-length reddish-brown hair."

I returned her stare. The silence between us grew awkwardly long. Finally I said, "That description matches my wife perfectly."

"I know. The police said that, too."

"They were here?"

"Oh yes. Several days ago. Just before the reporters began to arrive."

I looked away from her innocent eyes, focusing my view on a lamp across the room as I struggled to regain composure. Mary Jo and the dead priest, speaking together here, where he lived, just a day before the murder. And the police knew it. A roiling black cloud of depression rose on the horizon of my mind. It would poison me if I let it, paralyzing me with doom. But I couldn't let that happen. I had to fight it, to hold onto hope with all of my strength.

Remembering something Ernie Davenport had said, I asked, "Did they show you photographs of suspects?"

"Yes, several."

The demons were at work again, twisting their hot iron straps around my chest. I could barely ask the next question for fear of the answer.

"Did you pick a photograph?"

She said, "I could not. As I told them, I was not wearing my glasses that morning. They are heavy, and I like to give the bridge of my nose a rest sometimes. I'm afraid the woman's face was a bit blurred."

I leaned back against the chair's plump pillow and said, "Thank God."

She looked at me strangely and said, "You are ... unsure of your wife's role in these events?"

With my head thrown back upon the pillow, I stared at the swirls of texture on the sheetrock ceiling and said, "I am unsure of everything."

She had the grace to let me sit in silence while the fear and confusion subsided. Finally, I thanked her and rose to go. As we stepped into the entry hall, I again noticed the votive candles and the picture of Mary. I said, "Sister, what would it mean if you saw a display like this, except with bowls of blood and chicken body parts mixed in among the candles?"

Here eyes were wide behind the thick lenses of her glasses. "Have you seen such a thing?"

"Yes. Do you know what it means?"

She stared at me before answering, the reflections of a dozen candles dancing in her glasses. Finally, she said, "I have heard of such things, Mister Reed. In fact, Father McKay told me of them. It sounds like certain religious practices he encountered in Haiti."

"You mean voodoo, don't you?"

"Yes."

I nodded. "That's what I was afraid of."

She chuckled. "Oh, I wouldn't waste any time being afraid of *that*, Mister Reed."

"You don't believe in it?"

"Certainly not!"

"But I thought the Catholic church conducted exorcisms."

"Only in the movies, as far as I know."

"So you don't believe voodoo is real?"

"Oh, I know there are people who practice such pagan religions. But I hardly think we have anything to fear." She looked at me closely, her eyes amused. "Surely you don't *really* believe in that kind of thing?"

I stared at the flickering candles. "I have seen ... well ... things that are hard to explain by natural means."

"How intriguing. What kinds of things?"

I started to speak, but found myself strangely unwilling to give voice to the specters of the past. Instead, I said, "Nothing really. Just a few odd people in the streets of New Orleans during my college days."

"I'd love to hear more, Mister Reed."

I smiled and shook my head. "Another time perhaps. I really have to be going."

"Oh, that's a shame. Just when the conversation was becoming exciting."

As I opened the door I said, "Sister, I really don't think you want to have anything to do with that kind of excitement."

Her laughter followed me as I walked away, filling my heart with a growing sense of doom.

Chapter 17

AT MIDNIGHT, STANDING ALONE BENEATH the moonlit treetops outside our home, I heard the call of a distant owl, an oddly human sound. From somewhere off to the left came the rustle of newly fallen leaves, nosed aside by a blindly foraging armadillo. And overhead, the soft breath of a north wind whispered high between the pines. These sounds usually filled me with a deep sense of the love of God, but tonight they were simply distractions. I longed for silence, so I could sort through the facts undistracted. I longed to discover why Mary Jo was gone.

For days I had thought of little else, puzzling through the maze of conflicts. The target practice. The trips. The note she left behind. But all my thinking led inevitably to just two possibilities, neither of which was acceptable:

Either she left for reasons beyond her control, or she had deliberately abandoned me.

After a silent dinner with Lucretia, I had decided to walk alone through the woods to think. But thinking was apparently beyond me, so I pressed on to Mary Jo's studio. It would not be the first time since she left that I had searched there for a clue. With little hope, I entered the concrete block and glass-walled building through the side door. I touched the light switch, and a bank of fluorescent tubes bathed the studio in stark white. Feeling uneasy, I opened drawers and searched one more time through storage closets. With its high sloping ceilings and paint-splattered walls, the studio was Mary Jo's private world, the one part of her life I did not share. She never asked for privacy. It was just the way we were. Her art was something she discovered deep inside, at a place I could visit, but never understand. In everything else, we were a team. But she lived alone with her muse. Even during the years when I lied to keep her, when I pretended to share her spiritual center, I made no pretense of understanding the source of her inspiration. So I gave her space to work, both physically and emotionally; rarely visiting her studio deep within the woods. I learned to expect her long absences, sometimes lasting through the night. And I loved her all the more each time she led me down the studio path between pines and poplars to stand silently while I gazed at her new painting, hope and worry melting away and shy pride shining in her eyes when I told her how it felt to be the first to share such beauty.

Now I stood before her current work, a five foot by four foot canvas on a paint-encrusted wooden easel draped with a cotton sheet. The painting was not finished. If it had been, she would have tilted it against the wall, ready to crate and ship to one of her galleries. She would have shown it to me.

I had never seen one of her unfinished works without her permission. To look at the painting without her in the room would be a violation of a long-standing tradition, if not a trust. But I had searched the studio completely and found nothing more unusual than a few paint brushes lying on the counter near the sink, ruined because she forgot to clean them. The surface of the canvas was the only remaining possibility. So, although it felt like a betrayal, I lifted the cotton fabric away from the painting.

If what I saw was a clue, it led to more questions than it answered. Mary Jo had built her professional reputation on a long series of landscapes that captured the joy of being alive and aware in the center of beautiful forest dawns and dew-covered meadows. But the painting on the easel was a return to that disturbing period of ominous visions she had painted at Tulane so long ago. It was a forest scene from a Wagnerian nightmare, with twisted tree limbs and moldering rot in the roots. The sky was overcast and forbidding. A terrible storm loomed just above the treetops. An unnaturally straight path led through the menacing woods to a tiny dot of red, barely visible at the middle left of the canvas.

It was worse than her note. In a way, it hurt me more than her absence. After two decades of painting light and joy, Mary Jo's gray period was back. Was this agony born of the cancer in her breast, or did it stem from something else? And if it was something else, why hadn't she shared it with me? I always assumed she had revealed all of her secrets, but clearly, she had not. I stared at the painting for a long time, trying to understand the message she had hidden within the layers of oil and pigment. Finally I understood.

She had painted death.

It reminded me of a time when I struggled against demons of my own, battling a depression so desperate I could only think of suicide, a time of sorrow so intense I had tried to purge it from my memory forever . . .

• • •

MARY JO'S REFUSAL OF MY MARRIAGE PROPOSAL HAD been final and nonnegotiable. She would not tell me why. I knew from the tears and the pain in her eyes that her choice was not an easy one. At least she gave me that much. But when I asked for a reason, she simply shook her head and said, "It's not fair, I know, but I can't bring myself to marry. I love you. If I could marry, it would be you. But I can't . . . can never marry. Anyone." She would say no more.

We left Mandina's in silent misery.

The Mississippi carries obvious allegorical messages for anyone faced with sorrow. Life goes on, and all of that. I spent much of the following week squatting near the top of the levee down below the Quarter, watching rusty barges plow the filthy gray-brown waters, counting empty Jax cans as they drifted right to left, considering my options. The Peace Corps came to mind, but I had no desire to be helpful to anyone. The Army was a possibility, but killing my fears in Vietnam seemed redundant, when oblivion already lay all around me, as simple as a cocktail on Bourbon Street or a needle prick in Jackson Square. If the pain she had caused me was insurmountable, I might end my life quickly, or with a lingering habit that left me sprawled on the slate sidewalk, hand extended, haunted eyes pleading mutely for enough change to buy one last portion of peace. At least the drunks and addicts could escape for a time.

I shifted my position. The dampness of the levee soaked my blue jeans and crept into my joints. The ancient sweat of slaves mixed with the morning dew and rose through the soil from the decomposed bones of the poor devils who had piled this ground between the wealthy Vieux Carre and the slumbering fury of the river. I pondered the passing of time.

Ernest B. found me somehow. I was lost in my lethargic contemplation of the river, alone with my sorrow, and then he was there beside me. He could have been there for a minute or an hour. Who cared?

"Buddy, you ever comin' back to the apartment?"

I shifted my gaze to the soil between my feet. A smooth black pebble lay against the withered grass, as out of place as an East Texas country boy in the Big Easy.

My roommate tried again. "It's been awful quiet without you around. Sink's full of dirty dishes. We're runnin' out of frozen dinners. I can't find the can opener. Hey, look at me over here. I'm losin' weight. When you gonna come home?"

I lifted the pebble and rubbed my thumb over its smooth surface. My thumbnail was as black as the stone. I said, "Can you tell me why someone would push away the one they love?"

Ernest B. grinned at my sappy question. For him, all feelings for women were passing infatuations. But then he saw the pain in my eyes and his expression changed to somber thoughtfulness in an instant. He was a true friend, willing to overlook his philosophy and take my situation seriously. He said, "Could be lots of things, Garr. What did she say?"

The pebble was cold to the touch. "She said she loved me. She said she could never marry anyone, but if she could, it would be me."

"Couldn't marry?"

"Couldn't. That's strange, isn't it?"

"Maybe she's got some kind of a problem. Somethin' you don't know about."

"Of course. But what could it be?"

"Lots of stuff. Could be sick, like with a real slow disease, you know?"

"Oh, dear God." I buried my face in my hands.

"Now don't get like that. It could be somethin' else ... maybe she's afraid. Worried about makin' such a big change."

"No. She is very strong."

"All right. How about her family? Maybe her old man wants her to marry a Cajun boy, keep the traditions goin' and all that hogwash."

I looked at my old friend. "That could be . . ."

He smiled his lopsided, goofy smile. "Sure. You could go over yonder an' talk to the ol' boy. Maybe ya'll can come to an understandin'."

I returned my attention to the river, staring intently at the sluggish flow. My thoughts struggled to rise from the morass of self-pity and consider this new possibility. It was worth a try. Anything was worth a try.

The damp and cold of the levee had sapped my strength and stolen every sensation but sorrow. If I had been less concerned with the moment, I might have remembered another time, by another stream of water far smaller, when my friend comforted me in the death of my mother. Here was my personal history repeating itself: women, loss, and rivers. The swirling eddies of the Mississippi called silently, offering the final solution. I had almost succumbed to its languid allure, but Ernest B.'s suggestion was a reason to hope. At least it was a reason to move. My legs were numb when I stood.

Ernest B. said, "You goin' over to see her folks?"

"Yes."

"Good. Come on home afterwards, all right? I'm gettin' tired of cleanin' up after myself."

I smiled—my first smile in a week—and skipped the black pebble across the river. It hopped three times and sank. It was good to have a plan.

• • •

I SHOOK MY HEAD TO CLEAR IT OF THAT TERRIBLE time and left the studio, setting out through the woods. The path between the house and Mary Jo's studio is well beaten from her daily trips. I once offered to place stepping stones along the way, but she preferred to leave the woods as natural as possible, insisting that the leaves and pine needles were pavement enough. I worried about copperheads. Even water moccasins were a possibility so close to the lake. But in all the years she painted there, Mary Jo never saw a snake. Or perhaps she was wise enough not to tell me, knowing I'd have had the path paved with concrete and strung with lights within a day.

My boots shuffled through the soft blanket of leaves, the plodding of my footsteps matched by the dullness of my thoughts. Mary Jo's new painting exposed a misery I thought she had conquered long ago. There could be no other explanation for the thing I found on her easel.

It represented a backward slide to a period of bitter struggle for us both. But if the evil was upon us again, I could handle the struggle. It was her failure to warn me that was difficult to accept. Why had she allowed me to blunder in unprepared, to charge knee-deep into the misery before I saw the danger signs, like a tourist blithely strolling through the worst of neighborhoods? My hands clenched into fists as I strode between the trees.

When I saw the woman on the path ahead and stopped, only fifteen feet separated us. She was a vague silhouette, frozen in a slender moonbeam.

"Lucretia, is that you?" My voice sounded too loud in the quiet of the forest night.

Her answer was a dull pop, like the crack of a breaking bone. Death whispered in my ear. I had heard the sound before, but the unexpected fact of it in that peaceful place delayed my reaction. I turned to run just as her pistol barked a second time. A dull thud announced the bullet's impact in a tree just inches to my left.

A moonlit walk along a familiar path is one thing. A wild charge through the dense and untamed forest is another. There was light enough to avoid the trees, but briars and brambles clawed at me like spiked tentacles closing in on frantic prey. I heard three more shots, deliberate and well spaced. The dreaded whisper hissed by my ear each time. She knew enough not to fire too quickly, taking time to adjust her wrist to the recoil, aiming with care. I would have preferred a rapid series of shots; lead flying wildly through the woods. But she paced herself, getting her range. And she was using a silencer. I was in trouble.

My only hope was distance. With feral grunts and no regard for stealth, I stumbled through the brush for three or four minutes before I realized the firing had stopped. I leaned against the trunk of an eighty-foot pine, panting like a hound in July and listening for sounds of pursuit. Could she hear my labored breathing? I measured every breath, mouth wide, sucking in air and hating the sound it made. My heart danced wildly, drunk on adrenaline. Touching my wrist with two fingers, I felt my pulse, willing myself to be calm, to clear the pounding of my heartbeat from my inner ear, the better to listen for a broken twig or the soft rustle of leaves underfoot.

Minutes passed. My pulse returned to normal. I prayed silently, offering thanks for my survival and asking for help. It was good to know the massive pine trunk stood between me and her last position. I prayed she was not as adept at stalking as she was at aiming her weapon. Too many of her shots had come within inches of my head. It was a miracle that she had missed. As I stood listening to the normal sounds of the woods, I felt my confidence return. I thanked God again for throwing off her aim. I had no doubt that he had protected me. And now, his forest creatures would be my bodyguards, warning of the killer's movements by their sudden silence. I waited, reluctant to shift position for fear that she waited too, somewhere within range. My thighs and forearms had taken a vicious thrashing from the undergrowth. Blood trickled down my cheek from the slash of a thorn.

Then a sound I had never heard before whispered through the brush to my left. It seemed to fondle the undergrowth, drawing a moist tongue along the leaves as it passed, like a jungle cat licking blood from its prey. Yet its hissing advance touched nothing. No branch or limb quivered in the moonlight. The sound grew, throbbing now, more of a buzz or a rattle than a whisper. And suddenly my imagination was seized by the unnatural image of thousands of insects, hurtling straight toward me.

I pressed myself against the trunk of the tree, frantically looking left and right, searching the darkness for a better place to hide. Fear welled within me at a primordial level beyond logic or control. A voice screamed from my deepest being, screamed at me to bury myself in the earth, to pull down the hills upon myself, to do anything to hide from the approaching evil.

Suddenly, her pistol barked five times in quick succession. All five slugs slammed into the tree trunk less than six inches above my head. I did not have time to react until after the final shot. By then, of course, it was far too late.

Her voice came softly through the trees. "You see? You cannot hide. I know your mind. I can kill you easily. Stay away from Mel. I will not let you hurt him anymore."

The voice seemed to grow from the buzzing thing, beginning with it, and fading back into it. Then, suddenly, she was there, less than ten feet away. I saw her silhouette clearly, a black form against the forest background, devoid of details except for the cold and sulfurous burning of the moonlight in her wild hair and its twin reflections glowing red in her eyes.

Trembling with fear, I sank to my knees beside the huge trunk. The evil noise receded. After perhaps half an hour, I heard the distant but familiar sound of a car door closing and an engine coming to life.

When I moved, it was away from the house, toward Pedro Comacho's land.

Chapter 18

PEDRO IS AN OLD MAN. HE MOVES AT AN old man's pace and hears only what he cares to hear. At first, I tapped lightly on his door, hoping to wake him without making enough noise to be heard from the woods beyond his house. He did not respond. Starkly exposed by the yellow glow of a bare porch light, I kept my eyes on the tree line, alert for any motion there. I was far from certain that the car noises I had heard meant the woman was gone. Perhaps it was a trick, designed to get me out in the open. I glanced up, wishing I could unscrew the light bulb, but it hung out of reach against the wooden ceiling high above. I knocked again, louder this time. Which was more dangerous: standing in the light or making too much noise?

I decided to risk pounding on the door. Soon afterward, Pedro peeked out with sleepy eyes. He cleared his throat and said, *"Que pasa?"* in a gravelly voice. I don't think he recognized me.

"It's Garr, Pedro. Let me in."

"Que pasa?"

"Let me in, Pedro. I'm in trouble."

Immediately, he opened the door wider and stepped aside, making a small motion with his free hand, sweeping it inwards toward the hall. He said, "Of course, old friend."

My relief must have been obvious when the door closed behind us. He stood with his head cocked quizzically to one side, his hazy brown eyes expressing the questions that his old world manners would not allow him to ask.

I have known Pedro Comacho all of my life. Some of my earliest memories are of lunches in his cafe with my parents. Pedro's Cafe is near the Reed Construction office on the same side of the town square. It's as much a landmark as the courthouse, serving down-home cooking since the end of the Second World War. Pedro himself was a landmark of sorts, with his bushy white Zapata mustache and a reputation for speaking his mind. He had been there at the hospital on the day of the murder, sitting in the crowd, surrounded by his grown-up nieces and nephews. It had not surprised me to see him there. His language got a bit salty now and then, but he was a strong Catholic, with strong views.

Over the years, I'd often strolled over to his restaurant for commonsense advice when I was in a tough spot. In earlier days, to get a moment of his time, I stood in the kitchen, sweating and shouting questions over the roar of the exhaust hoods and the cacophony of crashing pots and pans. These days our talks were easier, since he no longer cooked. He was too old for such hard work and had taken to operating the cash register while perched on an ancient chair near the front door. It was considered a compliment for him to rise to show you to your seat, something reserved for old friends and beautiful women of all ages.

Pedro was a ladies' man, a bachelor, a sage advisor, and a local hero of the civil rights movement. He was the first Mexican American to own a business in Jackson County, something which cost him many broken windows and some sleepless nights with a shotgun during the early fifties. Pedro was the only one who had courage enough to warn me about the cocaine dealers when I tried to find Ernest B.'s murderer. In the days of segregated rest rooms and drinking fountains, he welcomed blacks into his restaurant and demanded that they sit where they liked.

I was proud that Pedro Comacho was my friend and neighbor, both in town and out on Martin Pool. When old man Martin put his homeplace up for sale to pay his legal and hospital expenses, Pedro offered him cash through an attorney. The deal was done before the old man knew it was a *Tejano* that got his land. They say allowing the Martin homeplace to fall into "Mexican hands" was one of the things that finally killed the old man. When he heard that rumor, Pedro shrugged elegantly, dismissing such deeply ingrained bigotry. Smiling his toothless smile he said, *"Asi es la vida"*—such is life. But Pedro was there at the old man's funeral; him and me and Clyde Barker and the undertaker, just we four beside the Martin family crypt in the cemetery down next to the Big Muddy Bayou.

I said, "Do you have a gun?"

"Of course. Who don't?"

"Shotgun?"

"What you huntin' this time of night, *amigo?*"

I told him of my narrow escape. The curious look in his eyes did not change. When I was done, he turned without a word and shuffled deeper into the dark rooms of the old house. I stood in the entry hall, careful to keep away from the window. When Pedro returned, it was with a pump-action twelve gauge crooked under his left arm and an ancient .44 revolver the size of a cannon in his right hand. He had pulled on a pair of Redwing work boots and wrinkled chinos. His pajama top was tucked into the chinos.

I said, "I'm no good with pistols, Pedro."

He handed the shotgun to me and said, "That's okay. I am."

Chapter 19

PEDRO DROVE ME HOME IN HIS BATTERED red and white Ford pickup, going past two reporters sleeping in their parked car out by the gate. He killed the motor and the lights about three hundred yards up the driveway and coasted in on the downhill slope to a position just at the edge of the tree line of the meadow surrounding our house. We sat silently, watching and listening for ten minutes. Then we stepped from the truck, crossed the clearing, and climbed the steps of the front porch. Inside, Lucretia sat reading her Bible by the fireplace. When we entered the living room, she looked up, her long finger marking her place, eyes narrowing slightly at the sight of my neighbor.

Nodding toward Pedro, she said, "What'd you bring him in here for?"

I told her what had happened. When I finished, she returned her attention to the Bible for thirty seconds, her lips moving slightly as she finished reading the passage we had interrupted. Then she closed the Bible, rose slowly, pushing at the arms of the chair for support, and said, "I'll make coffee."

I called Ernie Davenport at his home to report the attack. He said he'd be over right away. As we drank coffee at the kitchen table with the blinds drawn, I told Pedro and Lucretia of my suspicion that the shooter had been Juliette Milo. I asked Lucretia if the woman had come to the house. She said, "No. I never heard a thing."

I said, "You wouldn't have. She moved like a ghost. After her first round of shots, I hid behind a tree trunk and listened as hard as I could, but somehow she got right up beside me, just ten or twelve feet away."

Pedro whistled. "How could she come so close in the dark without you would know?"

I remembered the frightening noise I had heard whispering through the underbrush. But how could I describe it to someone who wasn't there? I would sound like a child afraid of the dark. So instead of telling them, I shrugged and took a sip of coffee. Then I said, "The shots weren't very loud. I think she was using a silenced .22."

Pedro nodded. "Makes sense. Is a woman's gun. Easy to control."

"She was very good. Good with the pistol and good in the woods. She could have killed me any time she wanted."

Lucretia said, "Wonder why she didn't?"

"I don't know. Maybe she wasn't the killing kind."

"Someone on the side of them abortionists and you sayin' they ain't de killin' kind?" Lucretia snorted. "They're all murderers."

Pedro nodded again.

We returned to silence, rough and clumsy and laden down with things unsaid. Pedro slurped his coffee loudly. Lucretia would not look at him. I thought I heard a car door close outside and went to the front hall to peek through the blinds. It was nothing. When I returned, Lucretia was saying, "What's the difference?"

Pedro said, "Just ain't the same, is all."

Lucretia snorted again and deliberately turned away from Pedro, snubbing him with her body language. I said, "What's going on?"

She said, "None of your lookout. You'll only take his side."

"What side?"

Pedro lowered his eyes, studying his coffee cup. Neither of them spoke, so I said, "How do you know I'll agree with him when I don't even know what you're talking about?"

She fixed me with her cold green eyes. "You ain't got de backbone to agree with me, else you would've helped my girl do it proper."

"Do what?"

"Fix that doctor."

"Lucretia, you don't really believe Mary Jo shot him."

"And why not? Ain't she her momma's girl, flesh of my flesh and bone of my bone? I reared her to know right and do it when she had to, didn't I?"

Pedro said, "Right? Ma'am, are you sayin' murderin' *Padre* Miguel and shootin' the doctor was right?"

"Of course. Look at de babies it saved, just in this last week."

Pedro said, "Murder is not right. It don't matter why you do it."

"They murder little babies every day, and you won't do nothin' to stop them, you?"

"I will not murder. I will protest. I will vote against them. But I will not kill or threaten or try to hurt them for what they do. *Dios mio*, if we murder them, what is the difference between them an' us?"

She glared at him, something intense and frightening in her eyes. "It ain't murder. It's defense of de innocent."

Pedro said, "*Señora*, it is murder and you know it. God don't want us killing each other."

She pointed at the .44 on the table and said, "Talk is cheap."

He said, "It's not the same thing. I can not do nothing while some *loco* kills my neighbor."

Jerking her thumb toward me she said, "Is he more important than an innocent baby? You're sayin' he's worth killing for, but a baby ain't?"

She had him. Feeling strangely disappointed, I said, "It's different, Lucretia."

"No. No difference. None at all."

Pedro said, "This is about where she and I were when you came in, *amigo*."

I stared at Lucretia Granier's hard brown face, searching for something. Something that seemed to be missing. She was the widow of a minister. She had devoted her adult life to feeding the hobos and bums of New Orleans. For decades before they took to calling them "homeless," before it became a popular cause to help them, like saving the whales and the rain forests, Lucretia Granier was finding them bedding and medical care, and teaching them about the Lord. What else but love could explain her desire to undertake such a thankless task? Surely there was Christian love behind her harsh facade. All I had to do was appeal to it.

As if he was reading my mind, Pedro said, "God is love, *señora*. Do you truly think he wants us to kill?"

"Would he ask me to stand by and do nothin' while an innocent life is taken?"

"But that is what happened when they took him to be crucified, no? Saint Peter tried to defend him with a sword, but Jesus wouldn't allow it." He pronouced the name the Spanish way: "Hey-soos."

Stressing her own English pronunciation, Lucretia said, "*Jesus* had a job to do. It was God's will for him to die on de cross. No one had a right to interfere with dat."

I said, "How do you know God's plan for Doctor Milo? Maybe he wants the doctor to go on living."

"Go on killin' you mean. See. I knew you'd take his side."

Pedro said, "*Señora*, it is not Christian to use violence in that way."

She waved the back of her hand at him, looking away as if dismissing a child. "You think what you like. I know my Scriptures. Read Psalm one-thirty-nine. Read Jeremiah one. God knew us before he formed us in the womb. He set us apart for a special purpose, each and every one of us. No one has a right to interfere with our birth."

Pedro said, "Do these things not include Doctor Milo? Did not God have a special purpose for him?"

She rose and walked to the hallway door. When she turned to look at him, what I saw in her eyes was not love. Far from it. What I saw was intense, smoldering anger—perhaps worse. She pointed her finger at Pedro and said, "You, sir, do not know what you are speakin' of. I am a scholar of de Scriptures, me. I have lived my entire life in de service of de Lord. I have experienced things you could never imagine. Don't you lecture me on what *God* wants, you. I *know* what God wants." Her voice rose as she spoke. A vein beneath the tight brown skin at her left temple throbbed visibly. She shook her finger in time with her words. "Every *decent* Christian hates abortion and de scum that do it."

Pedro said, "*Señora*, if I thought for one second that *El Señor* wanted me to hate anyone—anyone—I would know he was a false God and I would never call myself a Christian again. But that will not happen, because *El Señor* is a God of love."

In spite of myself, I mumbled, "Amen."

She trembled as she looked from me to him, her finger still pointing at his face. Finally, she said, "It's a wonder to me that my girl had the strength to do what she did, burdened down by cowards and foreigners."

With that, she turned and stomped down the hall. Pedro and I sat silently together, awash in her wake of anger. Why did this new faith of mine have to be so complicated? Pedro's words resonated in my heart. A loving God, a Creator that cares for all of us—that was the

God I thought I had joined when I committed myself to Christ. Yet Lucretia—and so many others—were full of passion for their cause, and certain of the holiness of it. She knew so much more than I about theology and Christian traditions. She had invested a lifetime in serving God, living among drunks and addicts and insane people at the mission in New Orleans, feeding them, clothing them, sharing the Word of God with them. Who was I to say such a woman was wrong? Who was I to feel as I did? Perhaps my reservations about Lucretia's passionate actions and words were merely the uninformed instincts of an immature faith. Perhaps I *had* no faith—not really. Was it possible I had deluded myself?

After a long pause, Pedro said, "My family has lived in *Tejas* for over two hundred years. Who's she callin' a foreigner?"

"We Reeds have only been here four generations. Maybe she meant we were the foreigners . . . Of course, that would mean you were the coward."

"Oh." He smiled his toothless smile. "That's different."

We sat together for a minute or two, sipping coffee without speaking. Suddenly Pedro glanced around the room and said, "Hey. Where is Mary Jo?"

There was nothing I could say.

Chapter 20

RNIE DAVENPORT ARRIVED WITH ONE deputy. I told him Mary Jo was asleep upstairs. He turned his soft brown eyes upon me sadly and nodded, acknowledging my lie. Then he took my statement, said he'd station a man outside for the rest of the night and come back himself after sunrise to check the woods for evidence. Pedro went home about three in the morning. I slept fitfully. At dawn the next day, over a breakfast of sweet rolls, orange juice, and French roast coffee, Lucretia curtly informed me that she was leaving for New Orleans. I did not ask her to remain. She was packing her single bag when I left for the office. Our parting words were brief and carried no emotion. It seemed we shared nothing in common but our love for Mary Jo and our desire to see her safe.

At the office, Mrs. P. greeted me from her usual position in the front room. A new diamond ring twinkled on her pudgy finger.

"Hey, will you look at that rock," I said.

Holding her hand at arm's length with fingers spread she said, "This little ol' thing? I suppose it'll do for now."

"Do you mind if I ask how big that diamond is?"

"Oh, it's just an empire cut in a couple of carats . . . nothin' special."

"Holy smoke. That must've set Leon back a couple of months' pay."

She fixed me with a pair of cold black eyes. "You got a problem with that?"

"Of course not . . ."

"'Cause if you don't think I'm worth it . . ."

"Of course you are."

"No, I'm *not*. I'm worth lots more than this here measly ring. I got my self-respect. I got my dignity. I ain't somethin' you can put a value on."

"Of course not, Mrs. P."

"An' that another thing. I ain't changin' my name, just 'cause some scrawny Mexican gave me this here thing. No sir, I am *not*. You men best get that through your thick heads right off."

"Nobody's saying you have to change your name."

"Well, all right then."

I turned toward my office and said, "Okay."

She said, "That's right."

Stepping through the door, I said, "You bet."

She waited until the door was almost closed, then called out, "Better believe it."

Determined to get the last word, I mumbled, "Uh huh" just as the door shut.

As I settled in behind the desk, the phone rang. I picked up the handset, and Mrs. P's voice came over the line, "Just so we got that straight. That's all." Then she hung up before I could respond.

I stared at the handset for a moment, then, shaking my head, I forced myself to focus on the growing pile of invoices, change orders, bid requests, and contracts that lay neatly sorted on my grandfather's old oak desk. At about nine, Mrs. P. poked her head in and said, "Garr, Tyler Quint is on the phone. You wanna take it?"

"Sure. Put him through."

In a moment, I heard my banker's voice say hello.

I said, "Hey, Tyler. What's up?"

"Well, you know. Just tryin' to make a livin'."

I laughed. Tyler Quint's idea of making a living had quite a few zeros attached. His daddy had left him with ten thousand acres of nicely producing oil leases and a huge quarter-horse ranch with a reputation for taking ribbons at Ft. Worth's Fat Stock Show. Tyler's daddy also left him with majority shares in Mount Sinai First National Bank and Trust, a bank my grandfather helped to found. For all his money he wasn't a bad ol' boy, but he did love to talk. I leaned back, crossed my boots on the desk, and shrugged at Mrs. P. through the open office door, ready to listen to at least five minutes of small talk before Tyler Quint got to the point.

First I got a rundown of his health, his darling Tammy's latest shopping tour of the Galleria in Dallas, and the state of his twin daughters' college education in Houston.

He said, "They're makin' pretty fair marks down there at Rice, Garr. But I ask you, does the name of that college make any sense at all? What in the sam hill was those fellas thinking? Shoot. Most folks I know like a plate full of *frijoles* or a juicy steak a durn sight better than a bowl of rice. Why not name it Beans or T-Bone?"

Then, after he described the birth of a particularly promising colt and the firing of a ranch foreman who overdid the tequila and underdid the payroll, Tyler Quint got down to business.

"Uh, listen Garr, I hate to pester you with this, but I called over to the house and your mother-in-law told me Mary Jo wasn't home, so I figured I better go ahead and give you a holler."

"What's the problem?"

"Oh, no problem. I already took care of it. It's just that we got a check in here that Mary Jo wrote and ya'll don't have quite enough in the account to cover it. That is, right at the moment."

"Oh, not again. I'm sorry, Tyler. You know how she is."

I heard a chuckle over the line. Mary Jo was never diligent about balancing the checking account, yet she insisted on maintaining control of the family finances. Her natural tendency to leave things undone sometimes led to a rubber check or two.

I said, "Let's just move some cash over from the money market account, all right?"

"You betcha. I'm gonna transfer you over to Tilly or Marge. They can do that for you."

"Thanks for the personal attention, Tyler."

"What I hear, you and Mary Jo got enough troubles these days. No need to worry over a little thing like this."

"Thank you."

"Stop thankin' me so much, Garr. We're buddies, right? Y'all don't come around enough. Now that the girls is down in Houston, we oughta get out more. Just as soon as you get that hospital thing straightened out, we'll cut a rug or two down at the V.F.W. Or run over to Bossier City, play a little blackjack."

"The V.F.W. sounds good."

"Oops. Forgot about that religion thing of yours."

"It's not just that, Tyler. I never did care for it."

He laughed. "Man, from what I hear, your daddy must've been a heck of a poker player. Shame he didn't pass along the gift."

"He did love a good poker game."

"Forty years of Saturday night games at the Reed house is what my daddy said. Those ol' boys swapped greenbacks and planned elections and pretty much ran the county around the card table."

"Times change."

He snorted over the telephone. "Bet your sweet patooty they do. Can you imagine what the A.C. to L. with U. would do about those poker politics nowadays? Shoot. They'd burn ya'lls house down."

"Pesky liberals. What's next? Free elections? One man, one vote?"

"Oh, you laugh, Garr. Go ahead and laugh. But I'm tellin' you, times were simpler back then. Our daddies got things done right, without all this interference from Washington. Doggone Federal bureaucrats make runnin' a business harder than pickin' cotton in a West Texas twister."

"What's the deal, Tyler? Auditors on your back again?"

"Well, now you mention it, yeah. There's some Federal boys down the hall here with their calculators and their number-two pencils and their pointy little heads."

"It's your cross to bear."

"Why do you suppose they all wear suspenders?"

"Keep their pants up?"

"Exactly. They got so much of my money stuffed in their pockets a belt won't do the job."

I laughed and said, "Sorry to hear it."

"Yeah. Well, listen, we really oughta get together more often."

"That would be nice, Tyler."

"Yes . . . uh, Garr? This is none of my business, and if I'm feedin' at the wrong trough here, just say so, but I'm about as curious as a preacher at a peep show."

"What is it?"

"Well, what the heck are ya'll gonna do with a tow truck?"

"A tow truck?"

"Right."

"You lost me."

"Well, it says right here on Mary Jo's check, 'tow truck.' Down on the memo line, you know?"

"She probably had a flat or something and needed a tow."

"For eighteen hundred ninety-three dollars and sixty-seven cents? That's a heck of a tow."

I pulled my boots away from the desktop and sat up straight. What did it mean?

He said, "Uh, Garr? You there?"

"Yes. Sorry. I was thinking."

"I shouldn't of pried this way."

"No, no. It's all right. I just . . . Tyler, who did she write the check to?"

"Lemme see here . . . ah, looks like a 'Crescent City Towing Service.'"

I rubbed my forehead. It was damp with sweat. I dried my palm on my blue jeans, picked up a pencil, and made a note of the name of the garage on a piece of paper. It was hard to keep the anger out of my voice when I said, "I never heard of them."

"Lemme see somethin' here . . . yep. Transaction was wired in from a New Orleans bank. Dated two days ago."

Underneath the name of the garage, I wrote "New Orleans" in capital letters. I glanced through the window at the courthouse across the street. A pair of deputies climbed the side steps together. One of them laughed and punched the other's arm. My thoughts turned to Mary Jo. So all this time she was down in New Orleans, leaving me alone to wonder why . . . I heard a snap and looked down to see the pencil broken in two on the desk.

I said, "Tyler, I'm going to ask for a big favor."

"Sure."

"It's a lot to ask."

"Garr, we go back a long, long way. If it's about that thing at the hospital . . . I know you and Mary Jo. Neither of you would do what they been sayin'."

"Thank you, Tyler. Please don't show that check to anyone. Handle the transfer yourself. I can't tell you why, but I think it would mean more trouble for Mary Jo."

"You got it, Garr. Anything else ya'll need, just ask. You know that."

"I'll let you know," I said as I hung up the telephone. But I was thinking I would need much more help than Tyler Quint could provide.

Chapter 21

L UCRETIA'S BLUE FORD TAURUS ROLLED around the last turn in our driveway as I pulled in from the blacktop road. We stopped, facing each other bumper to bumper. Several reporters watched us from across the road. I sat behind the wheel for a moment, hands at ten and two, staring at her through the windshield. Was it worth the trouble? I could always fly.

I opened the truck door and stepped out onto the gravel. The morning was bright and crisp. I ignored the reporter's shouted questions. A crow cawed from the high branches deeper in the woods. Behind the wheel, Lucretia glared at me. With a small smile and a wave, I walked around the front of her car. She stared straight ahead, even after I stood alongside the driver-side door. I tapped on her window.

"Lucretia. Roll it down."

Without looking at me, she pushed a button and the glass slid away. She said, "What do you want?" Her single suitcase lay on the backseat.

"I'd like to ride with you."

She lifted her eyes toward me. For a brief instant, I saw interest there, a hint of the old electric green. Then the dull glaze returned and she said, "Are you sure?"

But that flash in her eyes was enough. It reminded me of a different Lucretia Granier, the woman I'd met so long ago, before twenty years of sorrow had turned her heart to stone. It had been a long time since I remembered that other Lucretia. The woman sitting before me now had completely erased her from my mind. Perhaps that was my fault. Perhaps I should fight to remember her as she was.

And so, as I stared at her profile, I felt myself traveling back in memory . . .

• • •

IT WAS A SHORT WALK ALONG BLUE SLATE SIDEWALKS from the levee to Canal Street, past antique shops and four-star restaurants with gilded lettering on plateglass windows. Crossing Canal, I left the sedate storefronts and granite curbs of the French Quarter behind and entered a neighborhood of tall brick and stone office buildings. A few more blocks brought me to parking garages, diners, five-and-dimes, and secondhand clothing stores. Eight blocks from the Quarter I made a left toward the piers along a street dominated by liquor stores and peep shows. Skinny men sprawled across the cast-iron thresholds of vacant buildings, their heads cradled in arms lined with the scars of a thousand needles. Two women giggled from the doorway of a pornographic bookstore. One black, one white, they wore identical pink hot pants, low-cut sequined blouses, and black fishnet stockings. They tottered along behind me on stiletto heels, calling softly, offering their services. I ignored them until their propositions became profanities and they gave up the hunt.

It was a hard neighborhood, dusty and bleak, lined with broken glass and chain-link fence, bound above by a random web of power lines and telephone wires and below by the drifting stench of rotten fruit and the indiscriminate defecations of dogs and drunks. It fit my depression perfectly. As I ambled through the Big Easy's underside, fantasies erupted from my festering wounds. I dreamed of joining the lost souls who populated this world of oblivion. It was oddly comforting. I was approaching a crossroads. Soon it would be necessary to choose between a path that led to a permanent place in the gutter and . . . what? What other choice was there if Mary Jo would not have me? I could not envision a life without her. I might as well face the future one bottle at a time. Already I was adopting the posture: shuffling along the garbage-lined sidewalk, hands buried in the pockets of my blue jeans, shoulders stooped beneath a thin cotton shirt, sinking deeper and deeper into the sickly sweet allure of dying emotions and expectations.

A line of gray and brown people extended from the door along the facade of the ramshackle two-story building. A dull smudge across the storefront marked years of greasy heads and shoulders leaning against the woodwork, waiting. I joined the end of the line. No one said a word. No one looked at me.

We filed inside slowly. A big black man with a huge afro stood smiling and nodding just inside the door.

"Welcome, brother," I lifted my eyes to his. He said, "My name is Handy. You never been here before." His eyes were interested in me, in who I was.

I said, "I want to see the Graniers."

Handy laid his hand on my shoulder. "You gonna see 'em directly, brother. Just follow the line."

He turned his attention to the man behind me. "Welcome, brother. Remove your hat, please."

We passed down a wide hall. Black and red words sprawled across the walls. Jesus Saves. Trust Jesus. Frozen trickles of paint dripped from the letters. I thought of the bloody messages left by the Charles Manson family a couple of years earlier. Helter Skelter. Trust Jesus. What was the difference? None of it meant anything to me.

The hallway emptied into a tall room, perhaps fifteen feet to the ceiling, with bare light bulbs suspended on naked black wire above rows of battered folding chairs. I followed a filthy old man in line ahead of me to a chair on the far side of the room. We sat facing a blank wall. In front of the wall was a music stand. A scarred and scratched upright piano stood in the corner. Behind me, more of Crescent City's lost souls drifted into the room to take their seats. Between the old man to my right and a younger one to my left, the body odor was almost overpowering. The old man slid his right hand under the top of his trousers and scratched himself. I sighed and kept my eyes straight ahead.

The room hummed with mumbled conversation. A short man with stiff red hair in a butch cut walked to the front and stood behind the music stand. He wore a black Nehru jacket—perhaps it was a priest's jacket without the collar—and a large wooden cross on a brown rope around his neck. His white trousers flared at the knee into bell bottoms that almost covered his leather sandals. He lifted both arms above his head for silence.

"Good morning!" he said, smiling wide. A few in the crowd returned his greeting. Everyone else shut up. "For you newcomers who don't know, this is the Prodigal Son Mission, and I am Pastor Alphonse Granier. My lovely wife Lucretia is at the piano."

I hadn't noticed her when she entered. The woman at the piano wore her curly black hair in a short ponytail. The simple cotton shift and lack of makeup did nothing to detract from her beauty. Her profile was regal: high forehead, proud straight nose, firm chin, and a sweet smile that hinted at a kind, good-hearted nature. The skin of her face was an unblemished deep bronze. I thought perhaps she was part black or Indian. When Pastor Granier introduced her, she turned toward us and smiled wider. The brightness of her straight white teeth was extraordinary. But it was nothing compared to the sparkling green of her eyes.

"Lucretia is going to lead us in song, then I'll say a few words. After that, we'll have a nice hot meal and ya'll can get cleaned up and stay the night if you like. Lucretia?"

She smiled again, looking from side to side across the crowd, her remarkable green eyes resting on each of us briefly. Her beauty shone like a spotlight. Old men and young, ragged, unshaven, and unwashed alike; all sat a little straighter as her gaze rested on us one by one. She announced a hymn, I think it was *The Old Rugged Cross*, and we stood to sing. We were awful, but she smiled anyway, beaming like a mother swaddling her newborn.

After six or seven old-time hymns, Pastor Granier stepped up to the front and began his sermon. He sounded a lot like the Baptist preacher at my parents' church back home in Mount Sinai. I tuned him out immediately and concentrated on breathing through my mouth. The old man beside me smelled like a garbage dump.

Then something Alphonse Granier said caught my attention.

"Brothers, when I say we are in a fight with the devil, I mean that the evil one is right here, in this room today. I mean Lucretia and I and even our darlin' little girls struggle against him and his demons every moment. There's a plague on this town! A plague of evil! Some of you know what I'm talking about—I'm talking about strange religions and pagan beliefs. I'm talking witchcraft. I'm talking voodoo. I'm talking Satanism!"

He stood silently for a moment, catching his breath. He seemed to stare straight at me as he continued in a loud voice, "My family has dedicated itself to fighting this curse upon our city, and the battle wages on. Angels protect this place, called here by our unceasing prayers. But we have strayed and been wounded in other places. Satan has invaded our very bodies. He has stolen the life of my darling child. And Satan can reach each of you outside these walls. If he can harm the ones I love the most, what makes you think you can escape? But here, his powers are as chaff in the wind against the Lord God's will."

Quietly, he said, "We are safe now, in this place."

Beside me, the filthy old man snored quietly. Alphonse Granier's warnings of satanic threats seemed to fall upon deaf ears. At least I was unconvinced. For all of my life, the so-called Almighty God had never been more than a subject of mild interest in times of trouble. And Satan was merely a boogeyman that mothers used to scare disobedient children.

I would think of him very differently after the next few days.

Forty more minutes of pleading, cajoling, yelling, and fist waving, and then Alphonse Granier let us go with an admonition to "turn from your evil ways or go to hell." You couldn't fault him for subtlety, but except for the strange message in the middle of his sermon, he was not a creative preacher. With sighs of relief, we rose and shuffled toward the cafeteria across the hall. I tried to shove my way against the crowd, but by the time I reached the front of the room, the Graniers were gone.

The mess hall was a mirror image of the chapel: high ceilings, bare light bulbs, and white plaster walls covered with blood-red slogans. The hobos, winos, bums, and addicts were lined up along the far wall, waiting to pass in front of a row of folding tables laden with cold-cut sandwiches and large steel soup kettles. I took my place at the end of the line. As we approached the row of tables, I saw Lucretia Granier in a clean white apron, standing with two young women behind the kettles. She was ladling soup into plastic bowls and chatting with the men up ahead.

"Afternoon, Mister Grosbeck. How's your arm today?"

The man smiled crookedly, exposing a dentist's nightmare. He said, "It's better, ma'am."

She said, "I'm pleased to hear it," and turned her attention to the next man in line. "Mister Pineman, it's nice to see you here. How ya'll been makin' out, you?"

Mister Pineman reached across the table to take the bowl from her outstretched hand. He said nothing. Lucretia Granier's radiant smile and laughing eyes remained unchanged. She said, "It's always good to see you, Mister Pineman. Ya'll let us know if you need seconds, hear?"

The man ignored her and moved on.

Lucretia's lovely smile and honey-toned Cajun accent bathed each man in turn, creating an aura of warmth and civility that was all the more wonderful for its contrast with the squalor lying just outside. The stooped shoulders of the street people straightened as they grew near to her, then fell again as they moved away, as if her loving-kindness physically supported their frames. I found myself frustrated with the slowness of the men in front and wanted to hurry to her end of the line. Surely she would understand. Surely such a woman would find a way to help me.

When I stood across from her at last, her lovely green eyes rested on mine, and I saw Mary Jo within them. I said, "Mrs. Granier, I came to talk to you about your daughter."

She said, "Which one? I have three." Then she looked down briefly and said, "I mean two. I have two daughters, me." Before she lowered her eyes, I saw the sunny light within them fade. It was a bleak sunset.

"I'm here about Mary Jo."

She said, "You're dat boy from de college."

"Yes, ma'am."

"I'm sorry things ain't gonna work out for you two."

"Can you tell me why?"

She glanced up. "Why?"

"Why she won't marry me."

"Mary Jo didn't tell you, no?"

"No, ma'am. She only said she'd marry me if she could, but it wasn't possible."

"If she didn't tell you, I'm not sure I should, me."

"Mrs. Granier, this is driving me crazy. I love her. If I don't find a way to deal with this, I'm going to end up like them." I inclined my head toward the men hunched over their plates behind me.

Lucretia nodded as if I had confirmed something. She wiped her hands on her apron, then removed it and began walking. I followed her toward the rear of the building. The flat heels of her black leather shoes clapped against the wooden floor like a carpenter's hammer. Beneath the simple cotton shift, her body was lithe and fluid in motion. I wondered why such a beautiful woman would wear such a simple dress and such ugly shoes. We passed a straight stair on the left. I glanced toward the second floor, thinking, *Mary Jo grew up above all this*. Near the end of the hall, Lucretia knocked lightly on a door to the right. A muffled voice responded, and we went inside.

Alphonse Granier sat behind a scarred brown wooden desk, scribbling on a yellow legal pad with a ballpoint pen. After we entered, he continued to write without raising his eyes. Lucretia took a position directly in front of his desk. I stood at her right side. There was no place else to stand. It was a small office; just the desk, a window looking out on a narrow side yard, and a bookshelf. Alphonse Granier sat in the only chair. The view through the window was filled with tall weeds woven through rusting metal odds and ends strewn across the narrow yard. Half of an oil barrel, the metal skeleton of a bunk bed, and an ancient lawn mower without the engine lay cockeyed and abandoned. Across the yard, a blank brick wall rose from the weeds. On our side of the window the pine floor was immaculate, the white plaster walls without blemish, and the glass itself crystal clear, without a speck of grime.

After Lucretia and I stood silently for two or three minutes, Alphonse Granier sighed, laid the ballpoint on the paper, and looked up. A pair of what were then called granny glasses rode low on his nose. He stared at Lucretia over the top of the glasses with small, piglike eyes. His red hair stuck straight up from his head like the bristles of a brush. It was so short I could see the pale flesh of his scalp reflecting the bare bulb above us. He barely glanced at me.

He said, "You know I don't want you in here when I'm workin', Mother."

Lucretia said, "This here is dat boy Mary Jo told me about."

He did not look at me, keeping his eyes fully upon her face. Staring over the top of the glasses gave him a curious and benign appearance. He said, "Which boy? There's been so many."

She said, "Dat's not true."

His expression did not change. He looked down and opened a desk drawer and removed a pack of chewing gum. He withdrew a single stick, replaced the pack in the drawer, and slid it shut. He offered none to me or the woman. Without looking up, he unwrapped the stick of gum. He opened his mouth wide, closed his eyes, and placed the gum on his extended tongue, receiving it like the body of Christ. His fingernails were perfectly trimmed. His hands were immaculately clean. They moved with surgical precision as he carefully folded the empty foil wrapper to resemble its original condition. As he refolded the wrapper, he chewed quickly, the muscles in his jaw bunching up with every bite. He seemed content to let us stand silently and watch. Or else he had forgotten us for a moment.

At last he raised his tiny blue eyes to his wife. "What does he want?"

"Ask him yourself."

"I don't allow them in here, you know that."

"He's not from off de street, Alphonse. I told you who he is."

"I don't want him in here."

"You got to tell him, you."

"No."

Lucretia said, "You tell de boy or I will."

"He won't believe me."

"You don't *know* that, husband."

Alphonse Granier spun in his chair and stared out the window, his jaw muscles clenching and relaxing. After a moment, he said, "Must I go through it again? Every time we mention it, I feel such . . ." He interrupted his own statement with a deep sigh.

Lucretia said, "Husband, this boy is sufferin'. He loves our Mary Jo and it's hurtin' him, not to know de truth."

The missionary's head bowed slowly, as if he lacked the strength to hold it high. Finally, without turning to face us, he said, "All right, Mother. Leave us."

Before she left the tiny office, Lucretia Granier placed her hand on my arm. I looked down, and our eyes met. Hers were large and clear and devoid of guile. I looked deeply into them and saw sorrow and pity there.

I should have savored her concern. Because over the next twenty years, bitterness and indignation would purge her of such weakness, until there was nothing left but ice-cold judgment.

Chapter 22

"SLOW THIS THING DOWN!"

I sighed and lifted my foot from the pedal. It was over three hundred miles from Mount Sinai to New Orleans. We were only halfway there and already I wanted to scream, or burst out laughing. Lucretia Granier was driving me crazy.

"Lucretia, I'm only going seventy. They won't give you a ticket for five miles over the speed limit."

"Oh yeah?"

"Yeah!"

It was ridiculous. Three and a half hours alone with her had reduced my conversational skills to grade-school level. By the time we reached Lafayette, I was doing my best to avoid speaking at all.

"You gonna get us killed, runnin' this thing so fast. 'Sides that this here is situational ethics. What kinda Christian are you?"

"All right. I'm down to sixty-five. How's that?"

She set her jaw and said, "I never go faster than fifty-five, me."

I slowed. The pine trees and billboards crawled by. I began to add highway signs, a road trip game my mother taught me when I was young. You add the numbers of every highway and farm road sign you see. The trick is to try to get them to add up to an even multiple of a hundred. An even thousand was better. Even multiples of ten thousand meant you got to stop for a malt at the first opportunity. I was working on sixty-five hundred when we reached Baton Rouge.

Lucretia rebuffed every attempt to strike up a conversation. Never one to make small talk, she stared straight ahead and said nothing. I turned on the radio and dialed in a talk show. The topic was homosexuality in the public schools. A Baton Rouge teenager was suing the school district because its sophomore sex education course was not offering information on AIDS and the proper use of condoms. We drove ten or fifteen miles, listening as the callers voiced their opinions. Mostly they were for expelling the student and fighting the law suit all the way to the Supreme Court. Then a man with a pronounced lisp called the station. He wondered why the other callers were so opposed to educating young homosexuals in the practice of safe sex. The result of the school district's policy might well mean death for many boys and girls. Was their motivation genocide?

With absolutely no warning, Lucretia slapped the dashboard and screamed, "Dat's it!"

I almost steered into a bridge guard rail. Frantically looking left and right I shouted, "What? What's the matter?"

She pointed at the radio and said, "Dat there man and his kind are gonna take over this country. Gonna drive it straight to hell."

I should have agreed with her just to keep the peace, but it was hard to pass up the opportunity for a conversation after three hours of silence. I said, "I don't think they have that kind of power."

She snorted. "Dey sure do. Dem namby-pambies give it to 'em. In my day, de menfolk would have taken dat boy out to de swamp and nobody would've ever heard his evil trash again. Den dey would've torn dat school down board by board."

"Torn down the school? Why?"

"For allowin' dat garbage to mix with decent children."

"But don't you think the boy has a right to go to school?"

She snorted. "Right? Dat *boy* has a right to join his master in hell. Dat de right *he* got."

I sighed and turned off the radio. "Oh, come on, Lucretia. You don't really mean that."

"Don't I? Mister, you better wake up, you. Dem people is takin' over. Dey teachin' in our schools, runnin' de military—dey even startin' dey own so-called church!"

She leaned back and crossed her arms, watching me with her head tilted to the side. She seemed so smug I decided to egg her on just a little. I said, "What's the matter with that?"

Nodding her head she said, "Dat's about what I'd expect. Just about what I'd expect from you. You ignorant about children, you. Don't know what a mother feels like. How you like to have one of dem teach *your* child, alone in the same room?"

"Leonardo da Vinci was gay. Michelangelo was gay. I wouldn't mind taking an art course from either one of those guys."

"*Gay?* In my day dat word meant happy! Now it mean sick! And you would let dem kind alone in a room full of children?"

"What do you think they'd do?"

"Seduction! Rape! Unnatural acts with defenseless children."

"Oh, for pete's sake."

"Go ahead. Turn your nose up and join dem liberal scum. It's a known fact them homosexuals hunger after young boys. Dey can't control themselves, no."

"So all homosexuals are child molesters?"

"Of course!"

"Lucretia, that's ridiculous."

"It is a fact. Why do you think God singled out their sin in de Bible?"

"What?"

"Why did he make such a point of sayin' their sin was de worst?"

"I don't know that he did."

She looked at me with her eyes wide, feigning amazement. "Are you tellin' me it ain't a sin for men to lie together?"

"No. I know the Bible says it's wrong, so I believe it is."

"You *better* believe it. It's the worst, most heinous thing there is in God's eyes."

"I thought all sin was the same in his eyes."

"You read your Bible. He leveled Sodom and Gomorrah because of it. He flooded de whole world because of it."

"Don't those passages mention other sins, too? I think I remember a long list."

"He hates homosexuality de worst. It's de cornerstone of Satan's plan to turn de world away from him."

"What about murder? Is it worse than that?"

"Absolutely."

"Oh, Lucretia. How could that be?"

"You read your Bible. You'll see."

We drove several miles in silence.

She was so filled with anger. I turned it over in my mind, looking at it, trying to make some sense of it. How did it happen? What could have made her this way? What could I do to help her? I prayed that God would show me a way. I said, "So what should we do? You said they would have killed that boy and leveled the school in the old days, as if you think that's all right. Do you think it's right?"

"Is it right to let them go on with their wickedness?"

"Don't avoid the question. What should we do, exactly?"

"Do? We should do God's will, of course."

I reminded myself to be patient and repeated the question. "Was it God's will in the old days when they solved these kinds of problems by violence?"

She looked away from me. We passed the stacks of a refinery just beyond the treetops, spewing orange smoke into the sky. She said, "Boy, sometimes violence is de only way. When de Lord rained hot coals down on Sodom, dat was violent. When he dropped de sea on Pharaoh's army, dat was violent, too. Violence ain't necessarily a bad thing. Just depends on what and why."

I didn't know what to say, so I said nothing. Again, the doubts crept in. Much of what she said seemed to support what I'd read in the Bible. Did that mean she was right to condemn abortionists and homosexuals so vehemently? Was that what the Bible taught? I regretted the lost years, my Bible on the shelf, unopened, positioned somewhere between *The Collected Works of Shakespeare* and *Webster's Dictionary*. If only I had studied it, learned what it really had to say . . . As a child, I was taught that God did destroy entire cities because of such sins. He flooded the earth to rid it of men and women who broke his laws. Moses and the Levites killed three thousand sinners at the foot of Mount Sinai for worshiping the golden calf. Should Christians now do the same? Was my heart wrong to rebel at such notions? I remembered an Old Testament verse. It went something like, "The meditations of man's heart are evil from his birth." I passed my hand over my eyes, trying to rub away the confusion.

This newfound faith was not a simple thing.

We drove closer to New Orleans, parallel to the river now, passing signs for turn-offs to Gramercy and Lutcher. Lonely clumps of dead or dormant trees stood against the backdrop of refineries and factories that lined the river. Now and then we passed small carefully plowed fields. In season, they would be green with Perique tobacco, but with winter approaching, the rows were naked. Industrial billboards proudly proclaimed the names of companies that had raped the land along the Mississippi, often demolishing plantations that had existed for two hundred years before the discovery of their products. Dow Chemical. Kaiser Aluminum. Nalco. DuPont. LaRouche. Miles of indistinguishable rusted pipes, smoke stacks, boilers, low-slung steel sheds, and huge factories lined Route 61 and the river, choking the terrain like tar on a chain smoker's lungs. The land west of New Orleans was once covered by cypress trees so large they rivaled the giant sequoias of Northern California. After the Civil War, logging companies slashed their way through the primeval forests, leaving thousands of acres of massive stumps in their wake. In less time than it takes for a cypress trunk to expand a quarter inch, they stripped four parishes bare of trees that had lived for five hundred years. Huey Long and his cronies brought more "progress" to the state, cutting deals with one global corporation after another until the land that once supported an ancient moss-draped forest of giants was choked by a thousand smokestacks spouting filthy chemical-infested fumes. The locals sometimes call it the "cancer corridor." For sheer destruction of natural beauty, it is matched only by what the oil companies and the Corps of Engineers have done to the Atchafalaya Basin, where abandoned pipelines and pumping platforms hang cockeyed and rusting above the swamp, and the concrete weirs and manmade levees are choking the bayous with silt.

Careful to stay well below the speed limit to avoid antagonizing Lucretia, I followed the highway north of LaPlace. In 1818, six hundred slaves revolted there. Those that survived the white militia's counterassault were executed and their heads were placed on poles along the road. I wondered if Lucretia would line Highway 61 with the heads of abortionists and homosexuals. Didn't Nero do the same to Christians? I did not have the courage or the energy to ask. As we neared the hazy skyline of New Orleans, I remembered the day we met. She'd been kind to me then. She had seemed to care, not only about me but about the men and women living on the streets of New Orleans. They were drug addicts and alcoholics, thieves and murderers. Some were probably homosexuals. Yet she cared for each of them, with love and kindness.

We reached Metairie, the sprawling suburb west of the Crescent City. Commercial jets came in low over the freeway, adding their exhaust to the haze in the air. As traffic pressed around me, I forced myself to concentrate on the drive.

It was difficult.

I was wondering what had gone wrong with Lucretia Granier. I was wondering if she was right after all, and I was simply too weak or foolish to obey the will of God.

And I was wondering where to start looking for Mary Jo.

Chapter 23

THE SUN WAS SETTING AS WE DROVE THROUGH the city to the shelter. Lucretia did not invite me in. Handy rushed out to the curb to get Lucretia's bag. Handy had changed in the twenty years since he'd greeted me at the door on the day I met Lucretia and Alphonse Granier. He'd cut his hair long ago. Now his hair was short and speckled with gray. And with Alphonse dead, he ran the place for the most part. Lucretia still lived upstairs and helped with meals and played the old upright piano, but it was Handy who preached the sermons and held the Prodigal Son Mission together. I never knew his last name. I don't think anybody did.

As I stood outside watching Handy remove Lucretia's bags from the trunk, a girl opened the door and peered out at us. She was dressed in black jeans, with a pair of scuffed black square-toed boots. She wore a brass stud in her left nostril and had cut her bleached blonde hair close to her scalp. Her black T-shirt stretched tight over her belly. She was about eight months pregnant. Handy saw me watching her and raised his eyebrows.

I said, "When did ya'll start taking in women?"

He said, "Didn't Lucretia tell you? We changed our ministry a couple of years ago. No more bums. Now it's teenage mothers with their kids. And battered wives."

I was stunned. Why hadn't I heard about this? Why hadn't Mary Jo told me? The pregnant girl closed the door.

I said, "No. Lucretia didn't tell me."

Handy lifted the bags. With a wide grin, he said, "She's funny that way."

"Yes. She's funny all right."

I took a cab to the airport, where I rented a neon blue Pontiac. I drove to the French Quarter and took a room at the Hotel Provincial, hoping Mary Jo might show up there. It was her favorite hotel in New Orleans. After a meal of brisket Creole around the corner at Tujague's, I went to bed. About three in the morning, I awoke when a couple of guys marched down the hall singing *Old Man River* at the top of their lungs. At three-thirty, they walked back the other way, still singing, only now it was *Rolling on the River*. *A river medley*, I thought. *How nice*. You get used to drunks in the Quarter.

I tugged at the sheets, trying to put thoughts of Mary Jo from my mind. Visions of her fearful backward glance as they led her into the courthouse competed with the hollow echo of her doctor's words, "It's breast cancer, but we think we've caught it early." They had put me in the room she and I shared on our last long weekend at the Provincial. It was the kind of morose twist of fate that is guaranteed to keep you up nights, with or without a drunken choral section stalking the halls. I rose to look out of the window and saw a view Mary Jo had adored: a long barge slipping downstream on the Mississippi beyond the moonlit rooftops of the French Market.

After watching the river for half an hour, I returned to bed, but sleep was still impossible. Images from the past rose with fearful moans from the fertile soil of my subconscious, driving the sweet release of slumber before them like zombies pursuing their prey.

I tried, but could not stop the flood of images. Mary Jo squeezing off shots at a rotten log. Smiling sweetly as she offered another explanation for so many visits down south. Whispering that we would talk later as she slipped out of the kitchen door and out of my life. And then there were the other memories, from further back, the ones I'd hoped to put behind me forever . . .

• • •

THE DAY AFTER MY CONVERSATION WITH ALPHONSE Granier, I stood beneath a lichen-spotted live oak at Tulane, watching the doors of the fine arts building as students clutching books and portfolios emerged in twos and threes. Some descended the stairs with intent expressions. Some laughed or read as they walked. They were living the moment, free from the morass of misery that enveloped me.

She came through the doors alone. Anticipation had boosted my pulse rate and drenched my palms with sweat. Almost a week had passed since she refused my proposal. In the intervening time, I had thought of nothing else. In my imagination, she had assumed the qualities of a goddess, an unattainable ideal of womankind. Now there she was, flesh and blood, descending the steps and looking my way. Her beauty lived up to all of my fantasies. I breathed deeply, sucking in air like an amateur with stage fright. Nausea tickled my insides as I caught her eye. I smiled and waved. When she returned my wave with a smile of her own, I thanked a God I did not yet know.

"How have you been?" I asked, hoping to hear a story of misery as deep as my own.

"All right, I guess," she said. "How about you?"

Oh, how could she be so calm when I was nearly insane with missing her? I said, "You know. The usual. Working late at the design lab and not getting enough sleep."

She nodded, her ponytail bobbing long after her head was still. She glanced at something past my shoulder. I searched her face anxiously. She would see my pain if she looked back at me. I did not care. The lovely green of her eyes drew me from myself for the first time in a week. I basked in her aura, content to stand with her forever under the swaying Spanish moss. She wore faded blue jeans, a brightly embroidered Guatemalan blouse, and a pair of brown leather sandals. Her toenails were painted pink. It was a warm New Orleans winter day. Hundreds of Tulane students passed beside us, walking calmly to class or rushing to the trolley stop in the neutral ground along Saint Charles. With her beside me, the world felt normal again at last.

She said, "Garr, I've got a class in five minutes."

I said, "Political science."

She smiled. "You remember my class schedule?"

"I remember everything about you."

"I can't offer anything new, Garr."

"Maybe."

She checked her watch, a Mickey Mouse Timex with a black leather band. I had won it for her at the City Park Christmas midway. She said, "We could walk there together."

We set off, strolling away from Saint Charles and Audubon Park, following concrete sidewalks between towering Romanesque limestone buildings with dark slate roofs and French dormer windows. Oak trees sheltered the grounds, some of them older than the buildings. Tendrils of ivy crawled across the limestone facades. I took her books like a schoolboy. And like a schoolboy with his first crush, I could not think of where to begin. We were halfway to the poli-sci building before I made my plea.

I said, "I went to see your parents."

She said, "They told me."

"Did your father tell you about our talk?"

"Yes. I'm not sure how I feel about that. I think I might be angry with you."

"Why?"

"It feels as if you've . . . I don't know . . . invaded my privacy."

"I just wanted to find out why you won't marry me, Mary Jo. I had to know and you wouldn't tell me."

She stopped and turned to face me beside a wrought-iron bench. "And what did you learn?"

"I'm not sure."

"What did he tell you?"

"He quoted Genesis and Saint Paul about marriage and procreation."

A fleeting and humorless smile drifted across her face. She said, "Procreation."

"Yes. And being fruitful."

"Fruitful."

"And marriage as a holy burden. A commission from God."

"A commission to be fruitful, right?"

"Yes."

"And did he tell you why I cannot marry?"

I looked at my feet, embarrassed. "We discussed it, yes."

"You and my father discussed my . . . my reproductive system?"

I lifted my eyes to hers, pleading. "He said you were sterile. But Mary Jo, I don't care. I don't understand all this. We can live without kids. I don't buy all his mumbo jumbo about having children being the only reason to marry."

"Mumbo jumbo? Garr, I was raised to believe those things." She looked away from me and said, "I *do* believe those things."

"You believe that having children is the only reason for sex? You believe that having children is the only reason to marry?"

She said, "Yes," but her voice was small and sad. "In the book of Genesis, God made it clear he expects us to bear children. Having children or avoiding adultery are the only acceptable reasons for marriage that are mentioned in the New Testament. But I can never have children, and I know better than to commit adultery. Saint Paul said it is better not to marry, so that our attention will not be distracted from the Lord."

"Your father told me that. I read it. Paul also said it was better for a woman to marry than to burn with passion. Can you deny having those feelings for me?"

She looked away for a long time.

I said, "And love? Where does love enter into all of this?"

She whispered, "I don't know."

I called upon memories of every sermon I had heard in Mount Sinai's small Baptist church—on every Bible verse, every bit of dogma. I said, "Do you believe that God is love?"

"Yes."

"Do you believe he put us here to be happy?"

"Yes, but—"

"Do you believe he wants you to love those that despise you and use you?"

"Yes."

"Then how can you believe he would not approve of you loving someone who thinks you are the most wonderful person on earth?"

She glanced at me, a quick look that held something hopeful.

"Do you love me, Mary Jo?"

"Oh, yes!"

"But you believe this loving God wants us to deny our feelings for each other because of an accident? Because of some stupid medical accident?"

Tears welled in her eyes, filling them, washing her cheeks, trembling on her lovely chin and dropping to the multicolored yoke of her blouse. Unashamed, she stared deep within me, through the tears, deep into the essence of me. She said, "It was . . . not . . . an accident."

"But your father said—"

"He could never face it."

"Face what?"

She shook her head, sobbing openly now. People passing us averted their eyes. I didn't care about them. I didn't care about anything but her and me and working it out somehow. To do that, I had to know. I had to know everything. I said, "What, Mary Jo? Tell me! You've got to tell me!"

She sank to the bench, hugging her knees and rocking back and forth. I knelt beside her and wrapped my arms around her shoulders and held her silently for what seemed like hours. Slowly, she calmed herself, sniffling and rocking and wiping her eyes with the back of her hands. When she seemed herself again, I said, "I can help. We can beat this together. We can beat anything together. But I have to know what we're fighting. You have to tell me, Mary Jo."

Still looking at the ground, she whispered, "I had an abortion. I killed my baby. That's why I can't have children. That's why I can't marry you. I don't deserve to marry you."

Chapter 24

I PACED THE SIDEWALK OUTSIDE THE CRES-
cent City Garage from six in the morning until
they opened at seven, trying to shake a lingering depression left behind by the memory of
Mary Jo's tearful confession. The garage was tucked away in the
thick fog between a dry cleaner's and a stucco apartment building in the *Faubourg Marigny*. A single overhead garage door
faced onto Burgundy. Beside that was a wooden door and a grimy
window. I tried to peek inside, but the view was obscured by
faded pieces of paper of all colors and sizes taped to the inside
face of the glass: bills, bad checks, postcards, and pinups. I
knocked on the door. The thin young man who opened it was
almost my height, but about half my weight. I explained who I
was and why I was there, leaving out the murder. He invited me
into the office. The glow from the bare fluorescent tubes overhead shimmered in his greasy black hair. His skin, pale as the fog
outside, seemed to absorb the blue flickering light. He wore dark
gray slacks streaked with motor oil, a filthy gray shirt, and size
fourteen shoes. A name was machine-stitched above his shirt
pocket: *Elmer*. He wore no belt. He had no hips. I wondered
how he kept his trousers from falling to his ankles. His eyes were
bright with interest when I asked about Mary Jo's Volvo.

"White 940, all the way from Texas? You better believe I'm
gonna remembah dat. Yessir."

You could have cut his West Bank accent with a knife. I said,
"Did you meet the person who asked ya'll to pick it up?"

"Lemme see . . . I was heah, so I must of."

"Can you describe the person?"

Scratching the black stubble on his sunken cheek with the first three fingers of his right hand, he stared up at the water-stained cypress ceiling. After a few moments of thought, he said, "That's strange. I don't recall . . . I'm really sorry, mister." Suddenly, his eyes lit up with an idea. "Tell you what, let's go look out in the files."

He opened a battered wooden door and led me deeper into the building; along a dark and narrow hallway past a wall-mounted time clock and rows of yellow time cards in angled racks, then through another door. I stopped walking and stared with my mouth open.

We had entered a room the size of a train station. The ceiling was three stories tall and dotted with filthy glass skylights. An acre of concrete slab sprawled before us sprouting cars at various elevations on hydraulic lifts, like a field of giant steel blossoms. Along one side wall, a network of metal racks and catwalks rose two stories tall, piled with a haphazard jumble of tires, belts, hoses, and mufflers. The air sang with the zip-zip of pneumatic wrenches. A hidden radio spewed the nasal twang of an announcer: "Yeah mon, you on the Bayou with WBYU." Men in dark gray uniforms were everywhere. The huge facility was completely unexpected after passing through the tiny office and single-garage door off the street. Unaware of my amazement, the skinny man walked on without me, turning left along a row of old oak filing cabinets against the wall. I hurried to catch up.

He talked to himself as he walked, "Lemme see now . . . lemme see. Yep. Heah she is . . ." He stopped at one of the cabinets—we had passed at least twenty—and opened the second drawer from the top. The golden oak had been stained black around the drawer handle from years of contact with greasy fingers.

I had to shout to be heard above the radios and intermittent buzzing of the tools. I yelled, "This is amazing."

Without looking up from the drawer, he said, "Surprised ya, did we?"

"Why do you only have one door off the street with such a big operation?"

He said, "Open dat drawer there beside you. The top one. Go ahead. Now, look at any of dem papers there an' tell me what ya see."

I pulled a yellowed paper from the haphazard mess within the file cabinet drawer. I said, "It looks like an invoice. For some body work."

"Look at the date."

I scanned the top of the page until I found the date. It was December 13, 1932.

The man said, "Shoot. I was hopin' you'd pull out an old one. We go back to 1889." He waved his arm expansively. "This heah was an open yard back then. We was a combination livery and wheelwright operation. The street door was the carriage way. Then my great grand-daddy bought a 1911 Cadillac an' decided automobiles might be a comin' thing. He started repairin' cars; was the first in the city. My granddaddy built dat roof up theah. Daddy had the lifts installed. But we was locked in by neighbors up front so today we still only got one garage door. Yep. Heah it is."

He pulled a paper from the drawer and turned to catch the dim light from the skylights. "Lemme see now . . . lemme see. Nope. Can't help ya."

"Why not?"

"Says heah we got the order over the phone and they dropped off the check after hours. That's why we rushed it through the bank like we did." He looked up at me, his pale and narrow face betraying his interest. "Course, we was kinda nervous 'bout the distance an' all, too. I mean, it's a long haul from Northeast Texas to heah. Usually we don't go much further than Jackson or Baton Rouge."

I said, "Where's the car now?"

"Durned if I know. We brought it heah an' put a new battery in it an' drove it over to the old D.H. Holmes parkin' garage an' left it theah, just like the note said."

"Note? You got a note?"

"Sure. Right heah." He handed it to me.

It was written on white notebook paper with a black felt-tip pen. It was brief and to the point, with directions to the abandoned road where I'd found the Volvo, and instructions about replacing the battery and leaving the car at the parking garage. It described the location of a magnetic key holder under the rear bumper. It was in Mary Jo's handwriting. I stared at the paper for several minutes. Handwriting can be forged. But only two people on earth knew about that hiding place for the spare key: me and Mary Jo. The coals of smoldering anger flamed within me, fanned by this new evidence of betrayal. I fought the impulse to wad up the paper, and passed it back to the mechanic. It quivered slightly in my grip as I held it out to him.

I asked the man for the specific location in the parking garage where Mary Jo's car had been parked.

He said, "Your car ain't there, mister."

"How do you know?"

"They closed that place down the day after we drove it over. They gonna turn it into a shopping mall or sometin' like dat."

I thanked him and returned through the cavernous garage to the street. Strolling up Burgundy toward the Quarter, I turned the thing over and over in my mind. It made no sense. Why would Mary Jo park her car in the woods, leave the driver's-side door wide open, let the battery drain down, then hire a tow truck to bring it to New Orleans?

I remembered the brown stain on the carpet in the Volvo trunk, and the unmistakable smooth flowing style of her handwriting on the note to the garage. Then from out of nowhere a new possibility yawned before me, a wide and ragged chasm penetrating to the depths of hell. I stopped dead on the sidewalk beside a two-hundred-year-old Acadian cottage and prayed it wasn't true. But still my stomach felt like someone held it in a clenched fist.

Could Mary Jo actually be involved in the murder?

Chapter 25

ANCIENT LIVE OAK ROOTS, INTERWOVEN and shimmering with moss, bulged two feet high between the sidewalk and my rental car, like a bonsai on steroids. Monkey grass sprouted here and there from pockets of soil that had been carefully embedded up among the roots. On the other side of the oddly coiled tree, a black iron fence bordered a red brick sidewalk. Beyond the fence, straining to burst through the bars and spill onto the sidewalk, a lushly verdant tropical garden of broadleafed banana trees, amaryllis, and shade-dappled elephant's ears lingered in spite of the lateness of the season. From my position, hunkered down behind the steering wheel of the Pontiac, Doctor Melvin Milo's raised front porch was just visible through the gently swaying vegetation.

His antediluvian home in the Garden District was easy to find. I looked up the address in the white pages. Apparently, several other people had the same idea. About fifty feet in front of my car, a small group of men and women paced in sullen circles outside the Milos' gate. They held the usual signs. I had been watching their grim parade all day, not knowing what else to do.

Mary Jo's car was no longer parked in the garage, of course. I had walked the sixteen blocks across the Quarter, from the Crescent City Garage to the old D.H. Holmes building, knowing it would not be there. After returning to my hotel room, I had sat on the edge of the bed for an hour, head in my hands, elbows on my knees, staring at the carpet. Then I had remembered Mrs. Milo saying she was going to take her husband home.

I waited outside their house until about thirty minutes after sunset, then switched on the ignition to leave. The demonstrators had been gone for an hour. As I slowly rolled to the corner, I saw the light over the Milo's garage door blink on. The door began to rise. I pulled to the curb and turned off my headlights.

A dark green BMW 750i backed out of the garage. Plastered to the rear bumper were two bumper stickers: "Against Abortion? Don't Have One!" and "Capital Punishment Is Criminal." Shaking my head at the irony, I waited until the BMW was around the corner, then pulled away from the curb to follow. We made several turns for no apparent reason. Perhaps they were trying to avoid being followed, or perhaps they were unsure of their destination. Either way, it was a nice tour of the Garden District. Then we pulled onto Saint Charles heading west. I stayed several cars back all the way to Carrolton, where they turned left in front of a bar named Cooter Brown's, and then right onto Oak Street. The traffic had thinned, so I fell back almost a block. They made another right turn, then I lost them. I slowed to five miles per hour and inched along, searching left and right. A movement between two low buildings caught my eye. I stopped and reversed in time to see a man climb three steps and enter a side door off a driveway. The BMW was parked further up the drive.

I pulled to the curb and left the car, walking along the narrow sidewalk toward the building. It was an unseasonably warm evening, even for New Orleans. The crickets were singing. A low-slung car approached and slowed as it neared me. It swung close to the sidewalk and almost stopped about six feet away, infesting the evening air with a merciless rap bass beat. I began searching the area nearby for something to use as a weapon. Then the driver gunned his engine and it leapt on down the road, trailing high-pitched laughter from the open passenger side window.

I reached the sidewalk in front of the building. They had switched on the lights inside. I could see them moving from room to room. The building was set back from the street, separated by a strip of well-tended Saint Augustine grass and a row of azaleas along the wall below the windows. It looked familiar. After a moment's thought, I remembered seeing it on the television news the night they arrested Mary Jo. A dimly lit sign beside the door read "Milo Women's Clinic." I crossed the lawn and slipped between the shrubs to peek through a window.

Inside, Doctor Melvin Milo stood facing a woman. Her back was to the window. His eyes grew wide and he lifted his hand to his mouth, as if she were saying something he did not want to hear. He shook his head. She slapped his cheek and began to pummel his chest with her fists. He flinched and savagely pushed her away but she persisted. Lifting his arms to ward off her blows, he turned and walked to the far wall. He leaned against it, closed his eyes, and pressed his hand to his side, just above his waist. The pain from his wound was punishing him, but the woman obviously didn't care. She followed him, waving her hands violently. Through the glass I could hear her shouts but not the words themselves. His voice was low, too low to penetrate the window. Apparently he was placating her, because she stood quietly for a moment, suddenly calm. Then she turned and I saw her profile clearly.

I had seen her before.

I remembered her tears as she rushed down the hall alongside the doctor's gurney. They had troubled me. Why would a nurse, a medical professional, cry in that situation? Perhaps they were involved in an illicit relationship. But the body language between them was all wrong. These were not people who cared for each other. If anything, Doctor Milo and the nurse seemed more like enemies than lovers.

Turning from the window, I slipped across the lawn. I did not notice the man standing in the shadows of a tree beside the street until he spoke.

"What exactly have you got in mind?" he asked.

I stopped dead in my tracks. It was a darkly overcast night. I could not see details, but from his size and the way he stood with his feet spread and his weight forward, I knew he was ready for me. I took one step back and said, "I don't know what you mean."

"Oh, come on, son. I've been standing here watching you for five minutes."

"So?"

"So. I'm just wondering what you're planning to do next."

"I'm planning to get in my car and leave, if you'll get out of the way."

Suddenly, he glided to the side and swept his left arm in an arc above the sidewalk. He bent at the waist in a brief but courtly bow. "Be my guest."

I stepped onto the grass to walk wide around him. He chuckled as I passed. I looked back several times on the way to my car. He stayed where he was. As I was about to open the car door, he called to me. "Whatever you're planning, it's not the way."

Staring at his vague form across the top of the Pontiac, I said, "I don't know what you mean."

"Son, I've been watching this place for two years now, trying to keep you people from going too far. What you want, it's the right thing to want. But breaking the law isn't the right way to get it."

"What do you mean—'you people'?"

"Come on, son. Don't play games with me. We both know who you are."

"You know me?"

"I know where you come from, and that's enough."

"And where do you think I come from, exactly?"

He sighed. "Look, just go back and tell those nuts from C.H.A.R.G.E. they'll have to come through me if they want to get to Elizabeth Harmony or Melvin Milo or their clinic."

"Charge?"

"You gonna try to tell me you're not one of them?"

"I don't know what you're talking about."

"Fine. Have it your way, son. Just tell them about me, all right?"

"And who are you?"

"For tonight, why don't you just think of me as your guardian angel."

I squinted through the darkness, but could not make him out. He wore dark clothing and had blond or gray hair. He was built like a heavyweight boxer or a swimmer, with wide shoulders and a trim waist. That was all I could see. I said, "I could use a guardian angel right about now."

His short laugh was loud against the backdrop of distant traffic noise and pulsing crickets. He said, "Couldn't we all?"

As we spoke, a Honda Civic pulled to the curb down the street. A woman emerged from the small car and hurried across the clinic lawn and in through the side door. The man said, "Oh, no," under his breath.

I said, "What's wrong?"

He turned toward the clinic for a moment, as if he had forgotten me. Then he seemed to make a decision. He said, "I'm going to tell you something about that woman. Maybe it will help you understand how wrong you are. I can't tell you her name, because I learned about her troubles during the Sacrament of Reconciliation."

"You're a priest?"

"Yes. And that woman is a parishioner at my church. She's a good woman. A mother of three wonderful children. Her husband is an accountant at a restaurant company here in town. I married them seven years ago. I baptized their kids. She cooks in the rectory some-times when our housekeeper is ill. He helps out with the yard work twice a month. They are good, God-fearing people."

"If she's so good and God-fearing, what's she doing here?"

"Two months ago, a man abducted that woman from the parking lot in front of a shopping mall. He forced her to drive to an industrial park, where he sodomized and raped her and beat her and left her for dead."

"My God."

"I'm afraid God had nothing to do with it."

"Did they catch the man?"

"I don't know. I don't think so. But the thing is, that sweet, kind woman's suffering has just begun. She's pregnant, you see. And her husband sits up nights with a pistol. She doesn't know if he's doing that out of some instinct to defend his family, or if he's suicidal. She's afraid for him. That's the kind of woman she is. *She's afraid for* him."

"How terrible."

"She told me the baby will mean the end of her life, of their life. I tried to talk her out of it, to explain that God must have a plan, but I don't seem to have convinced her."

I looked at the brightly lit windows of the Milo Women's Clinic. "You mean . . ."

"Yes. It must be. There's no other reason for her to be here."

We stood silently in the darkness as I pondered the tragic story. What would I do in that woman's place? Would I allow the unborn child of a sadistic madman to destroy my family? Could I prolong the agony for nine months? Could I do that to my husband and children?

The priest said, "So you see, it is not always easy. It is not always black and white, as you people seem to believe. Sometimes it boils down to a choice between two evils. And no matter which evil is cho-sen, the devil will have his way."

Chapter 26

ARLY SUNDAY MORNING IN METAIRIE,
Louisiana, is slow as molasses and empty as a
January cotton field. I almost had the road to
myself as I drove the little blue Pontiac out
Airline Highway. Following vague directions obtained at the
Hotel Provincial's front desk, I left the highway and meandered
along residential streets lined with weathered clapboard houses.
On either side of the road, randomly parked pickup trucks
dripped motor oil on bare patches of yard. A Confederate flag
draped across a front porch railing reminded me that these were
the people who had elected a high official of the Ku Klux Klan to
the United States House of Representatives.

After a wrong turn that cost ten minutes, I found the Slydels'
church, wedged between a cemetery and a chiropractic clinic. It
was a low building, probably built originally to house a retail venture of some kind—perhaps a convenience store. A flat stucco
overhang rested on slender steel pipe columns and sheltered a
brown brick facade. There were no windows. Above the stucco
facia, they had added a simple white steeple, about five feet tall.
Beside the single glass and aluminum door, a sign was screwed
to the brick: "Grace Charismatic Congregation." The small parking lot was packed with cars and trucks, none of them less than
five years old.

I was uneasy. These people spoke in tongues, that much I
knew. Did they also roll in the aisles? Did they heal each other?

Such things made me nervous. They were foreign to my Southern Baptist upbringing. I did not understand them. At the last minute, my nerve failed and I decided to wait outside in the car.

It was a damp morning. Dew collected on the windshield. The chill invaded the Pontiac and began to seep into my bones. I left the car and strolled over to the cemetery. It was good to be moving after spending a day cooped up in the car outside the Milo house.

The cemetery was relatively new. I found one headstone marked 1956. It seemed to be the oldest. Unlike New Orleans, they buried their dead underground in that part of Metairie. The sound of a hymn drifted through the thin walls of the church and across the field of tombstones. It was a comfort to me. I found a gray granite stone inscribed with the words, "Mary Elizabeth. Beloved wife of Henry Stiller." The woman had died in 1968 at the age of thirty-three. I envisioned a man standing beside the freshly covered grave, facing a life to be lived without his love. Perhaps his children had stood beside him. The cold stone words could not convey the anguish he must have felt. But I understood all too well. I was in limbo myself, waiting to see if I would suffer a similar fate. Closing my eyes, I bowed my head and prayed. *Lord, if there's any way to work it into your plan, please give me back my wife. Keep her safe from our enemies. Heal her cancer.*

But again the mocking voice whispered that I had no right to pray for Mary Jo, not when my heart was filled with so many doubts. The reporters who'd seen her drive away in her Volvo, the check she'd written for the tow, the note in her handwriting . . . all of it cried out against her. And I was listening to the accusations.

Why should God listen to a man whose faith was so riddled with doubts?

At the sound of conversation, I lifted my eyes toward the church. They were leaving already. It seemed too early. I checked my wrist watch. It was ten-thirty. Where had the time gone?

I hurried back across the cemetery, carefully weaving between the tombstones to avoid walking across the graves. As I approached the church, I noticed several patches of stucco on the blank side wall that were painted a slightly darker color than the surrounding areas. The fresh paint was an attempt to cover crudely scrawled graffiti, a typical sight in the Crescent City area, where an ongoing battle raged between shop owners and kids with too much spray paint and idle time. As I crossed the cemetery, the ghostly pattern of the graffiti became more visible through the thin coat of paint. They were pentagrams: five pointed upside-down stars, with oddly disturbing symbols scrawled between the points. I had seen the patterns before, written in blood on the hospital wall.

Ignoring the sudden chill up my spine, I averted my eyes and hurried toward the church.

Brother James Slydel stood at the door, smiling and speaking to three men while a small group of women chatted nearby and watched their children. A man with hair the color of wheat carried a large box-shaped object from the church across the parking lot. He stopped beside a huge customized pickup truck set up high on tractor-sized tires. An olive-green cloth draped over the object in his arms, like a cover on a canary cage. As I strolled by, the man stood on tiptoe to lift the object over the dented fender and set it gingerly in the bed of the truck.

I smiled and said, "Whatcha got there?"

The man glanced at me suspiciously and remained silent. From within the box I heard a sudden muffled rattle. I hurried on.

Everyone stood outside the church in formal dress, the men in simple gray and black suits with dull burgundy or blue ties, the women in pale cotton dresses with quiet patterns and dark wool coats. The women all wore hats. An isolated memory rose to the surface: my mother in a yellow and white polka-dotted dress, with a pillbox hat and white gloves. She clutched her purse and a well-worn Bible in her left hand and held my hand as she led me up the steps of the Mount Sinai Baptist Church. Her white fabric gloves felt soft and fuzzy against my tiny palm.

Faye Slydel spotted me standing across the parking lot. She wore a floppy black felt hat with a pink carnation tucked into the band. Recognition flashed for an instant in her face, then her eyes assumed the haunted look I remembered from that terrible day at the hospital. She glanced over at her husband. As I approached, she seemed to collect herself. She smiled, extended her hand straight at me, and said hello. I had forgotten her crooked teeth and the wonderful honeysuckle sweetness of her accent. I shook her hand.

She said, "It's good to see you again, Mister Reed, but I must say I am surprised."

"Really? Why is that?"

"Metairie is such a long way from home for ya'll."

"Since you came up our way last Sunday, I thought I owed you a visit today."

She smiled again briefly. "And your wife . . . Is she here with you?"

"No. I think she's over in New Orleans somewhere."

"Somewhere?"

"You know how it is. She has her interests and I have mine."

Faye Slydel glanced over at her husband. I followed her gaze and saw him kneeling beside a young boy in earnest conversation. James stood and reached down to shake hands with the boy. The boy held his chin high as he proudly clasped the preacher's hand. With her eyes on her husband, Faye's voice softened slightly. "And what *are* your interests, Mister Reed?"

"Please, call me Garr."

"All right. Garr. What can we do for you?"

I watched James Slydel approach us, weaving through the dwindling group of people still socializing in front of the church. He paused to speak to the man beside the truck. Together, they peered into the truck bed. The man lifted the cloth from the box he had carried. I saw a wire cage lined with straw. James rubbed one hand with the other and said something to the man. They both laughed. James clapped the man on the back and turned toward us, his face lit up with happiness.

I said, "You can probably guess why I'm here. What with the way things worked out."

Faye Slydel said, "Worked out?"

"Yes. You heard they charged her with murder?"

"We heard that. James and I are very sorry for ya'll, aren't we, dear?"

Brother James Slydel joined us in time to hear her question. He held out his hand. As I shook it, I saw two small puncture wounds in the fleshy area between his thumb and first finger. The wound was red and slightly swollen. I was careful not to squeeze too hard.

He said, "Yes, we are, dear. It's terrible. Just awful."

I said, "We'll get through."

Faye Slydel said, "Isn't it unusual for them to let your wife leave Mount Sinai?"

I smiled at her silently. James searched my face for a moment, concern obvious in the guileless brown eyes behind his glasses. His scalp showed white along the perfectly straight part in his hair. I watched his Adam's apple bob above his frayed shirt collar as he said, "Is there anything we can do?" The sincerity of the offer was undeniable.

"I'm hoping to get some information to help clear my wife."

"And you think we may be able to help?"

I shrugged. "Who knows? You were there. Maybe you saw something."

Faye said, "We went over all that with your sheriff. I don't think there's anything else to say."

The preacher touched her arm. "Now Faye, if we can help . . ."

"We got to get over to the Maxwell's for dinner."

He looked at her. An unspoken communication occurred. Finally, she said, "Perhaps Mister Reed could come by this afternoon."

James Slydel beamed at her for a moment, then returned his attention to me and said, "I'm very sorry, but I won't be able to see you then. I've got to prepare for this evening's service. But Faye will be leading a protest outside Doctor Milo's house later today. About three. She'll be glad to speak with you there, won't you, dear?"

She sighed and looked away and said, "I suppose."

James Slydel smiled candidly. "Did you really come all the way to New Orleans just to find us, Mister Reed?"

I said, "Not to find you. No. Not really."

After a few pleasantries, they said they were late for lunch and walked away, offering apologies. I was halfway to New Orleans before I realized I had forgotten to ask about the strange symbols scrawled across the side of the Slydels' church.

Chapter 27

BACK AT THE HOTEL, I FOUND I HAD SEVERAL telephone messages waiting from Mrs. P. After staring out the window at the river for a while, I sat on the bed and returned her call.

"Garrison," she said, "Why don't you return my calls?"

"That's what I'm doing, Mrs. P."

"Don't get smart with me. I meant earlier. Why didn't you call me back earlier?"

"I was out. I didn't get the messages until just now."

"Well, that a shame. That a real shame."

"Why?"

"'Cause now you waited 'til two in the afternoon. And you *know* I take my Sunday nap at two in the afternoon. Your brain 'bout the size of a chickpea, fool!"

"What?"

"Oh, not you, Garrison."

I thought I heard someone's voice in the background. I said, "Okay . . . well, I forgot about your nap time. Sorry."

"That's all right. Just remember the next time."

"Did I wake you?"

"You must get them ideas donated, sugar, 'cause you too dumb to think of 'em for yourself, but not dumb enough to pay for 'em."

"What did you say?"

"Oh, not you, Garrison, I tol' you I ain't talkin' to you."

"Should I call back later so you can finish your other conversation?"

"What other conversation?"

"Whoever you're talking to. That conversation."

"Ain't talkin' to nobody."

"Didn't you say you weren't talking to me?"

"'Course I'm talkin' to you. Who else I be talkin' to?"

"But just now, when I thought you said I was too dumb ..."

"Oh, that. Never mind that. I'm just paintin' my toenails an' keeping Rush in line, is all. Ain't nobody here but me an' my Maybelline coral blush."

I visualized Mrs. P., ensconced upon her easy chair, head cocked against one shoulder to prop the telephone against her triple chin as she pulled her foot up on the cushion with one hand and applied polish to her chubby toes with the other. She would be wearing an outrageous wig, or the fluffy foam turban with the little multicolored flower petals that waved in the air each time she moved her head. Her corpulent body would be lost beneath a flowing, riotously colored floral muumuu. That murmuring I heard in the background would be Rush Limbaugh or one of the other conservative radio talk-show hosts. Mrs. P. disagreed with almost every word they spoke, and took great pleasure in flinging insults at the radio as if the host or their guest were with her in the room.

"I thought you said you were napping," I said.

"How can I nap when you won't return my calls?"

"Are you saying it's my fault you weren't asleep when I called?"

"That's right."

"So you're mad at me for not calling, which kept you up."

"A little bit, yes."

"But if you were asleep and I woke you up, you would be mad at me for that, right?"

"Prob'ly."

"I see."

"Well, listen here, Garrison. I got to get on with these toenails, so let's move this along. The reason I called is ..."

"But I called you, Mrs. P."

"What's that?"

"I said, *I* called *you*."

"'Course you did, Garrison. What's the matter with you?"

I sighed. "Nothing, Mrs. P. What can I do for you?"

"That's not the question, Garrison. It's what can I do for you."

"Do for me?"

"Sure 'nuff. We tol' you we wanna help with this problem of yours. An' you down there an' we up here an' we ain't doin' nothin' useful, far as I can see, except for plannin' honeymoons an' all."

"That's nice, Mrs. P. I appreciate your wanting to help. How's the honeymoon planning coming along?"

"Don't you try to change the subject, Garrison. But since you mention it, everything's just fine. We 'bout decided on the location."

"I thought you said you were going to Wichita."

"That was before I changed our plans."

"Now where are you going?"

"Don't know yet. But I'm thinking Nashville."

"Why Nashville?"

"'Cause of the music."

"But you don't like country music. You hate it."

"Don't everybody? But at least it ain't that nasty polka stuff Leon likes."

"I think they call it *Tejano*, Mrs. P."

"What difference that make?"

"Well, none, I guess."

"It still nasty music."

I sighed. "Nashville is very nice, Mrs. P."

"It better be, sugar. Leon said he never been there, an' you *know* I never been near no cracker town like that. So at least it gonna be somethin' new for us to do."

"Will you go to the Opry?"

"They musta popped your head in a blender, honey, 'cause you more mixed up than a margarita."

"Mrs. P.?"

"What's that?"

"Are you and Leon planning to go to the Opry?"

"Why we wanna do that? You know I don't speak Italian. There now. I got that last toe done. Lemme put my glasses on an' see what I can see . . . oh my goodness! This shade look terrible! I got to go, Garrison. Good-bye."

"Wait!"

"What is it now?"

"You haven't told me why you called."

"See there, I tol' you I was the one who called."

"I meant earlier! I meant the calls that I returned."

"No need to get upset, Garrison."

"I'm not upset. I just want to know why you called."

"Well, at least we finally got that straight."

I placed the handset on the bedside table and rubbed my temples with both hands. Then I picked the handset back up.

"Mrs. P?"

"Yes, sugar?"

"Please tell me why you called earlier today."

"Oh, that. I just wanted to tell you 'bout a conversation I had with that nice Sheriff Davenport yesterday. Don't you jus' love him? I mean, ain't he a sight better than that no-count cracker Clyde Barker was?"

"Yes, ma'am. I like Ernie a lot better than Clyde. But I'm dying to hear what he told you."

"'Course you are. Well see, I was up to the office yesterday, puttin' in a little overtime, in case you want to know ..." She paused in case I'd missed the point. I hadn't.

"I'll remember that at the end of the year, Mrs. P."

"Oh, sugar, I know you will. Anyhow, in come that nice Sheriff Davenport. He say he woulda gone over to your place, but he had the feeling he might not find you an' Mary Jo out there. I just look at him sweetly, you know, waiting for him to tell me what he got on his mind. After a while he say he want me to pass along a message." Her voice trailed off, then she said, "You head so full of hot air, it a marvel it don' rise from you shoulders!"

"Mrs. P.? Mrs. P.? Could you sort of focus on the conversation here? Maybe turn down the radio for a minute?"

"Oh, that not necessary, Garrison. I can keep several conversations goin' at the same time."

I sighed. "All right. Then what was it Sheriff Davenport wanted me to know?"

"He said them C.H.A.R.G.E. people? You know the ones with the silly little red hats an' the little soldier outfits?"

"Yes?"

"He said the police down in New Orleans think maybe they blew up a clinic down there. Say he might spend some time gettin' to know those folks better if he was you."

I thought about that for a moment. Then I said, "Did you tell Ernie I was down here?"

"No, sugar. He know that already."

"Did he say so?"

"No. But he know anyway."

"Why do you say that?"

"Just the way he talk about you an' them crazy people. Like he know you have no trouble talkin' to them down there."

"Was there anything else?"

"No, Garrison. I got to go see can I get this awful shade off my toes before Leon come by."

"Thank you, Mrs. P."

"I take it back, honey. You head not full of hot air at all. In fact, you best stop talkin' and suck some in oxygen before it collapse from the vacuum. Good-bye, Garrison."

I hung up the phone and returned to the window to stare out at the river, considering what I had learned. If Ernie Davenport knew where I was, did he also know Mary Jo was missing? If so, would he tell the New Orleans police? Somehow, I didn't think so. If that was his intention, why would he bother to give Mrs. P. the message about the Slydels' organization? And what did he think I would do with such information?

After watching the immutable Mississippi for fifteen minutes I still had no answers. I turned from the window and crossed the room to go out for a stroll around the Quarter. Sometimes a walk helped to organize my thoughts.

Most of the antique shops and galleries on Chartres were closed for the day, but the street was lively all the same. An angular young man in blue jeans and a smudged suit coat stood in a recessed doorway playing poorly on a cheap guitar. Beside him, a mongrel dog, mostly border collie, was tied to the door handle with a piece of string. It lay with its chin propped on crisscrossed front paws, its baleful brown eyes turned up to follow my movements as I dropped a quarter in the open guitar case. The dog's bushy tail wagged once, slapping the slate pavement like a steel brush drawn softly across a snare drum. It was the only thanks I received from either of them.

Tourists wove their way between the iron poles and hitching posts along the sidewalk, gesturing and pausing to peer through the plate glass storefronts of the antique stores. Like bird dogs on point, they lined up below the wrought-iron balconies, hands cupped beside their faces to block the reflection in the glass, noses aimed at the treasures inside. If Mary Jo had been there, we would have done the same. I shook my head and made a conscious effort to avoid such thoughts.

A white Crown Victoria with "New Orleans Police" painted in blue on its side cruised by slowly, its occupants laughing and carrying on a boisterous conversation. One of the laughing officers stared at me as they drew near. His laughter did not reach his eyes. They were deadly serious, missing nothing. And they seemed interested in me—too interested. A mule with a straw hat impaled on its ears pulled a white carriage full of tourists alongside the police cruiser, blocking the officer's view. The fat black man driving the carriage wore a brown fedora and a baby blue polyester suit. He gave the reins a shake and muttered, "Go on, mule." I turned and strode along the sidewalk in the opposite direction. Half a block away, I looked back. The cruiser had continued down Chartres. Should I worry about the policeman's stare? Perhaps it was my imagination. Or perhaps Ernie Davenport had told them Mary Jo was gone after all.

As I passed a rusty orange *Times-Picayune* newspaper box chained to a fluted iron lamppost, I glanced at the headline. Three hundred and eighty-three murders so far that year, and it wasn't yet Thanksgiving. Oh, well. At least that included Algiers. On the other side of the street, a man tossed a bucketful of soapy water from an open kitchen door. The water spread steaming across the chilled slate sidewalk. I sighed and looked away, toward a three-story red brick wall. Ferns clung to pockets of softness in the clay bricks midway up the wall, their roots searching for the cracks; filling them, enlarging them.

It wasn't easy to walk the Quarter. We had so many memories wrapped up in the place. Even the steaming water on the sidewalk reminded me of Mary Jo. I thought of another scene, almost exactly like this one, but twenty years gone, when we walked these same streets together in misery . . .

• • •

FIRST WE SAT ON THE BENCH FOR OVER AN HOUR, silently watching our fellow students as they rushed from class to class across the Tulane campus. Then, when she was well past crying, I walked with her to Saint Charles where we crossed the street and stood on the neutral ground beside a sign that read "Car Stop." We boarded the electric trolley and rode to Canal Street. At Canal, we disembarked and shuffled alongside the Vieux Carre toward the Shelter. She spoke as we passed a Woolworth's.

"Do you believe in immaculate conception?"

I said, "The virgin birth? Sure, I guess so."

"No, not the birth. Just the conception."

"What's the difference? I never heard anyone separate them before."

Her voice became hard, edged with impatience. "Conception. Insemination. The act of impregnation. It's very different from birth."

"Okay. I can see that."

"So do you? Do you believe in immaculate conception?"

"Mary Jo, what's this about?"

"I'm trying to explain to you. I'm trying to tell you why we can't be married."

"It's a little confusing . . ."

"But you *do* believe?"

"I suppose so."

"Then you believe that God could come down and make a woman pregnant? Without her consent? Maybe even without her knowledge?"

I was growing uneasy with the direction of the conversation. I said, "I guess God can do anything."

She nodded once.

We paused at a stoplight. Two men in gray suits stopped beside us to wait on the light. They spoke softly. She stood looking straight across the street at the "Don't Walk" sign. Lowering her voice, as if she was mumbling to herself she said, "If God can do it, why couldn't the devil?"

I said, "*What?*"

The two men stopped their conversation and looked at us. The light changed and we set off again. She went on as if she had not heard me. "Is it possible that Satan could impregnate a woman?"

"Like in that movie? Like 'Rosemary's Baby'?"

"I haven't seen it."

I said, "It's about a woman who gets pregnant by the devil and these witches trap her in her apartment building until she has the child."

"That sounds horrible."

"It was pretty scary, actually."

"I mean, it sounds horrible for the woman."

I let a few paces go by before I responded. "It was just a movie, Mary Jo."

"So you don't believe it could happen?"

"Of course not."

Grabbing my arm, she stopped and said, "But *why*? Why don't you believe? It happened to the Virgin Mary!"

"That's different."

Staring earnestly at my face, she said, "*Why?*"

"Because . . . I don't know . . . it just is."

Mary Jo released her grip on my arm and lifted the back of her hand to her mouth, wiping her lips. Suddenly, she took off down the street again, marching quickly. I had to trot to catch up. We hurried on in silence for about a block, then she said, "If you believe in God, you have to believe in Satan. The Bible says he's real." She held out one hand, empty and palm up. She said, "You have up. You have down." She held out the other hand in the same way, as if measuring two imaginary weights. "You have light and shadow. Hot and cold. Rich and poor. Protons and neutrons. Good and bad. Everything has an opposite. There has to be a *devil*."

She was speaking to herself now, striding along the skid-row sidewalk arguing with herself like some homeless schizophrenic. "If there's a God, there has to be something opposite. That's all. And if you believe in one, you have to believe in the other."

She stopped in her tracks without warning. I took a step beyond her before I realized what she had done. I stopped and turned. Her face was a mask of torment. "You told me you were a Christian."

"I *am*." It was a desperate lie. I would say anything to win this woman.

She said, "Then how can you doubt God?"

"I don't doubt God."

"Then how can you say there is no devil?"

"Who said that? Did I say that?"

"So you believe Satan exists?"

"Of course I do."

She reached for both of my arms, squeezing them above the elbow as she asked the next question. "Then why is it so hard to believe that the devil could make a woman pregnant?"

I searched her eyes, looking for a reason for it all. I saw nothing there but naked pleading, a need for reassurance of some kind. I said, "When you put it that way, I guess I do believe it's possible. But why is this so important?"

She held my gaze for a moment longer, then released my arms and continued up the sidewalk. We turned at the next intersection and descended toward the wharves and the hellish neighborhood she called home. I could not speak. I had seen something in her eyes.

Was it insanity?

Confusion and pain rose high in my chest. I felt I would scream if I opened my mouth. I still carried Mary Jo's books, clutched tightly in my right hand. She walked at my left, her face set in the neutral street mask worn by city dwellers the world over. Her frizzy reddish brown hair was pulled back in a rubber band, her hands tucked into the front pockets of her bell-bottom jeans, her shoulders hunched forward. We went four blocks without speaking. What could I say? How could words express the fear and bewilderment I felt? After longing for her every moment since she'd refused my proposal of marriage, I was finally alone with her again. But this was a new Mary Jo, someone I did not know. Her intensity was frightening. Her words disconcerting. Yet something must be said. Something.

We reached the Shelter. Across the street, a skinny white woman threw a bucketful of steaming water onto the pavement. Steam rose like the sulfurous fumes of hell. The muffled sound of Lucretia's singing voice filtered through the clapboard walls, accompanied by the distant tinkle of her piano. The evening service had begun, the bums were inside, and we were alone on the cracked and littered sidewalk. Above us, God painted a masterpiece in the sky; streaks of deep ochre, rust, and sepia cast against a brilliant turquoise background. But black power lines stretched across the sunset, like cracks in heaven.

She asked for her books. I gave them to her. She stepped inside and stood with one hand on the open door. Without looking at me, she said, "Well. At least now you'll understand. Good-bye, Garr."

"Wait! Understand what? I don't understand anything."

Eyes on the concrete below my feet, she said, "I thought I made it clear. I can't marry you. I can't marry anyone."

"But why?"

"I have been cursed by Satan."

"*What?*"

"I was defiled by him."

"Are you saying *Satan* made you pregnant?"

In a tiny voice, she said, "Yes."

Without thinking, I whispered, "Are you crazy?"

She flinched. She actually flinched. Then, without another word, she closed the door between us. I knocked for twenty minutes before I gave up and walked home through the gathering night.

Chapter 28

THE PRIEST STOOD HEAD AND SHOULDERS above the others. His eyes were on me as he walked in the picket line along the sidewalk, coming closer and closer until he reached the corner a few feet from where I stood. He turned, following the picket line back the way he came. He carried a crudely painted cardboard sign that read "Stop the Killing." There were many more demonstrators than the day before. They walked slowly in a long loop, passing each other on the sidewalk in front of Doctor Melvin Milo's Garden District home. The house loomed over them like a beached paddlewheeler; with filigree trim and ornate columns on a wraparound gingerbread porch. A massive cornice hung above it all like a brooding eyebrow. Faye Slydel had not yet arrived. The priest seemed to be filling in for her.

Across the street, a small group of New Orleans' finest stood with arms crossed, impassively watching the procession. The protesters sang softly as they walked. Mostly they sang old hymns. They never stopped marching. Someone had explained it to me: as long as they kept moving, the police could not arrest them for loitering. I leaned against the trunk of an ancient live oak, taking my chances on the loitering charge. Several people stood or sat on the curb nearby; probably curious neighbors.

A battered Chevy Impala pulled to the curb several houses down. The driver's-side door creaked open and Faye Slydel stepped from the car, still dressed in her church clothes. She paused for a moment to brush at the wrinkles in her dress. Her floppy black hat was gone, and a slight depression ringed her straight brown hair where the hat had pressed it down. Ignoring the policemen, she walked straight to the marchers and took a place in line. She did not see me. As she reached the end of the loop near my position, I called to her. She looked around for a moment before she picked me out of the small crowd of onlookers. I gave her a little wave. She pursed her lips, detached herself from the line, and walked over to me. I said hello. She did not.

"Like I told you, Mister Reed, everything I know I shared with the sheriff in Mount Sinai last week."

"How's the march going?"

"I don't know what ya'll want from me."

"Do you think Doctor Milo's in there, peeking out at us?"

She stared at me for a moment, then said, "What do you want?"

"The truth. I want to know the truth."

"What truth is that, Mister Reed? I keep meeting people who seem to have flexible ideas about that subject. They try out different truths until they find one that fits. Today this is true, tomorrow it ain't. To them, the truth is a choice they make from time to time, like deciding what dress to wear."

"You disagree with that?"

"Oh, yes. I disagree. I believe the truth never changes, Mister Reed." She stared at the Milos' home for a moment, her eyes narrowing, her lips pursed. Then she spoke again, distantly, as if to herself, "The truth never changes."

"Well, right now the only truth I care about is who killed Father McKay and shot Doctor Milo." I waved an arm at the demonstrators. "You know these people. Watch them with me. Point out the hotheads."

"Hotheads?"

"Does someone in your congregation have a problem with their temper?"

Turning to face me straight-on, she said, "You think one of *us* shot that priest?"

"Who knows? It could have been someone from home, or it could have been one of you. All I know for sure is that it wasn't my wife."

She stepped close and pointed a finger up at me, like a schoolteacher warning a giant child. "You seem like a good man. So I'm gonna be as honest with you as I know how. We did *not* kill anybody. We do not *do* that kind of thing. And I'll thank you not to say so. Everyone does that, and it ain't right. We're *against* murder!" She moved her finger, pointing now at the picket line. In spite of myself I felt admiration for her passion. "Ain't you paying attention here? Read those signs!"

I glanced at the picket line. The tall priest was watching us closely. I said, "Faye, I appreciate what you're trying to do. I appreciate anyone who stands up for their convictions this way. But you better face facts. Chances are good that one of your people shot the doctor and murdered the priest."

"No! Not one of us." She shook her head stubbornly. Then she lifted her head, and in her eyes I saw a curious mixture of softness and tenacity. "But if we *were* to go after him that way . . . why, that butcher would be dead right now."

"Why is that, Faye? Would you have bombed his home?"

Her nostrils flared and her eyes went wide, exposing the whites around her irises. She planted balled fists on each bony hip and spread her feet apart. "Bombed? Oh, *now* I see. You've been talking to the police, getting an earful of their so-called theories. Well, Mister Reed, while you're making wild guesses, you best remember this: I despise that so-called doctor, and I didn't care for that priest—none of us did—but that don't mean we killed him. We're defending little babies here. We're on the side of the Lord. And if you defame us, you join the devil's cause." With that, she turned toward the picket line.

I clutched her elbow without thinking. It felt delicate, like a bird's wing. "Wait a minute," I said. "You *knew* Father McKay?"

The tall priest broke away from the line and hurried toward us, apparently concerned about Faye Slydel's agitation. As he approached, he ran a finger under his clerical collar, pulling it away from his neck. He stood tall enough to look me straight in the eye. A chaotic thicket of prematurely gray hair contrasted with the tanned, unwrinkled skin of his forehead and the youthful vigor of his square cleft chin. Jet black chest hairs peeked over the top of the collar. A merry twinkle lit his pale blue eyes. Something about him seemed familiar. He said, "What's the problem here?"

I released my grip on Faye Slydel's elbow and she yanked it away, casting a furious glare at me. I said, "We're just having a private conversation, Father."

"Faye, are you all right?"

"I'm just fine."

I said, "She was just about to tell me how she came to know Father McKay, weren't you, Faye?"

The priest said, "Why do you want to know about him?"

"You knew him too?"

He smiled. "Sure. Mike worked with me here at Sacred Heart for years."

The more he spoke, the more I felt I knew him. He said, "My name's John Kratz," and stuck out a hand. We shared a silent look of mutual respect. It's not often that I shake hands with a man whose grip is a match for mine.

"Have we met before?"

"I don't think so. Maybe you remember me from my former life. I played for the Saints in '71. Had one good season before I busted my knee. Or maybe you've been to Sacred Heart. Are you Catholic?"

As I opened my mouth to answer, a large silver candlestick crashed through one of the windows overlooking the Milos' front porch. The protesters stopped singing and faced the house. In the new silence, the candlestick rolled across the wooden porch toward the railing with a dull, hollow sound. Then a woman's voice screamed from beyond the broken window, "Garr! Garr! Help me!"

There was another instant of silence, then the air was shattered by a single gunshot.

Chapter 29

SOMEONE SHOUTED, "GET DOWN!" AND THE crowd fell to the ground with cries of fear. But I was through the protesters and up on the Milos' front porch before the police had even crossed the street. I tried the front door. It was locked. As I inched along the wall toward the broken window, I replayed the cry for help in my mind. Was it Mary Jo's voice? It had been so thin and far away. The cries of the demonstrators were too loud; it was impossible to hear what was happening inside. I reached the window jamb. With the report of the gunshot fresh in my memory, I was afraid to peek through the shattered glass. I squatted low beside the window. Just as I was about to risk a glance into the house, a man shouted from the street.

"You on the porch! This is the New Orleans Police! Stay away from the window! Return to the street immediately!"

I looked toward them. The officers had scattered, squatting behind the white van and peering around the huge live oak trunks beside the curb. One of them waved me over. I shook my head impatiently. Someone inside had called my name. It was a muffled woman's voice—maybe Mary Jo's. If she was in the house, I was going to help her. I turned my back on them and peered through the window.

The scene inside was perfectly normal; a well-furnished and unoccupied room. I leaned back on my heels to consider my next step. The candlestick lay on the wooden porch beside me. I picked it up. Too late, it occurred to me that I might be obscuring someone's fingerprints. Using the candlestick, I bashed in the remaining shards of glass. I took three quick breaths and rose and jumped through the opening.

My momentum carried me to a position behind a nearby sofa. I dropped to the floor. Somewhere in the room, a clock ticked loudly. It was a living room or a parlor, furnished with period antiques that could easily have been original to the house. With my cheek against the wooden floor, I peered below the sofa. Dustballs scattered before my heavy breath. I could see the bottom half of everything in the room. A shallow coal-burning fireplace, filled with a dried floral arrangement. A pair of ornately upholstered chairs. Two built-in shelving units flanking the fireplace, stacked with gilded leather-bound books. And over in the corner, a white metal exercise bicycle looking completely out of place.

I lay perfectly still for several minutes, listening. Then I peeked around the side of the sofa. The opposite wall was covered with color photographs in ornate frames. Melvin and Juliette Milo standing beside a dead water buffalo. Melvin kneeling beside a male lion, holding its lifeless head to face the camera. Juliette proudly displaying a row of limp doves on a string. Juliette beside a prostrate antelope. The Milos on safari with their kills.

Strange statues lined the bookshelves. Primitive wood carvings of creatures from a child's nightmare: a woman with huge breasts and the tail of a snake, a man with an open chest, exposing his heart, and a strangely formal statue of a thin figure in a black suit, with a top hat jauntily set on his grinning white skull.

Voices drifted into the room from some distant part of the house. I stood, still clutching the candlestick, and slipped quietly across the parlor to stand just inside the opening to the hall. I heard soft footsteps approaching. Raising the candlestick above my head, I waited. The ticking clock seemed to boom in my ear. The footsteps stopped. I heard them turn and head away from my position. I peeked around the jamb.

At the far end of the hall, a woman was striding away from me. I just caught a glimpse of her before she turned the corner into a room at the rear of the house. She was Mary Jo's size. Her hair was exactly the same color and length. But I had made that mistake before. Was it Mary Jo, or was it Juliette Milo? I followed her down the hall, careful not to let the heels of my boots touch the wooden floor.

As I neared the door to the rear room, another shot was fired. It was very loud this time, the report magnified by the confines of the walls and ceiling. I paused for an instant, unsure of the best course of action. The candlestick seemed to shrink in my hand as I considered using it against a gun. Then I heard a crash and the sound of a door slamming. I decided to risk it.

I charged around the corner and almost ran over Juliette Milo.

She stood beside a breakfast table staring out through a window toward the backyard, a brown and red silk cloth draped around her body like a Roman toga. Her hair was covered with a red turban. The bone necklace with the monkey claw hung from her neck. She clutched another candlestick, exactly like the one I held. Following her gaze, I thought I saw a gate swing shut on the far side of the yard.

Juliette turned to look at me. Raw fury flashed across her face. Her eyes flicked to the floor. I glanced down and saw a handgun lying between us. She looked at me again, and I saw her eyes narrow. Dropping the candlestick, she dove for the weapon. I stepped on it with my right boot. She rose to her knees beside my leg and pounded her fists against my shin. The necklace of bones around her neck clattered with every blow like dirt and gravel being shoveled onto a casket. I did not move. She began to babble incoherently, a stream of extraordinary sounds, like the guttural grunts of a barnyard animal. Then, in the midst of the gibberish, I heard, "Please. It is not me you want. Melvin does the abortions, I just live with him. Please. Do not kill me."

I looked from her to the view through the kitchen window, longing to run for the backyard gate, to catch up with whoever it was. Could it really be Mary Jo? But Juliette Milo now clutched my leg pathetically, sobbing and pleading for her life. I sighed and said, "I'm here to help you."

She did not seem to hear. She continued her tirade, alternating between scattered English words and what I now assumed was another language, like none I had ever heard. I stared down at her, fascinated. Suddenly, she broke into coherent English again, begging in her strange, lilting accent, "You don't understand. I try to tell him he should close the clinic. I tell him it is not right. He will not listen to me. He does not care about me. Please. It is not me who is the one you want."

I was careful to keep my boot firmly on the gun as I kneeled beside her. "Mrs. Milo, I am not going to hurt you. I'm here to help.

Someone called my name, and I came in to help. Please don't be afraid."

She raised her red-rimmed eyes. Involuntarily, I flinched at what I saw there. I had expected to see fear. But the mask of tight skin at her cheeks failed to conceal the depth of her hatred. Her eyes held mine almost hypnotically. Something inhuman seemed to gaze out at me. I found it difficult to look away. The room seemed to grow suddenly colder. Tearing my gaze away from hers, I quickly removed the gun from the floor, certain she would use it against me if she could.

We walked together to the wooden breakfast table. I held a chair for her and indicated that she should sit. I said, "There are a lot of police outside. I'll go tell them it's safe to come in. But first, will you tell me who that woman was?"

"You saw her. It was your wife."

It was then that I became aware of the sound. Perhaps it had always been there. Or maybe it had begun as a soft whisper and grown into that faraway murmur, like the distant chants of ancient monks. I told myself it was the protesters outside. Yes, surely it was that.

But why should I suddenly feel such fear?

"I only saw her back," I said. "Are you sure it was Mary Jo?"

Juliette Milo smiled, baring sharp white teeth. There was no hint of a smile in her eyes. They continued to smolder malignantly, glancing occasionally toward the automatic in my hand. She said, "Your wife called out for you when I escaped from her. After she shot at me. Who else is it who would call for you?"

"I don't know."

The sound of voices had become a steady undercurrent.

"Do you hear that?" I asked.

"What?"

"Those voices. Don't you hear them?"

She looked away, but I saw her eyes reflected in a mirror on the far wall. In that unguarded moment, I caught a glimpse of something horrible. It glared at me malevolently for an instant, then retreated behind the normal expression of her face. Frigid fingers traced a path up my spine. I had seen the true enemy. Suddenly, the tension seemed to drain away from her, and her eyes filled with wicked satisfaction. "You have been chosen."

"What? What do you mean?"

"The *Baron* will come. You have been chosen."

I backed away without realizing it. The chanting continued relentlessly. "I don't know what you're talking about."

Again, she bared her sharp white teeth. "You will," she said. Then she turned away from me, as if I no longer mattered.

I took the opportunity to examine the gun. It was a chrome-plated .32 automatic. A Smith and Wesson. I knew it well. After Lester Fredricks tried to break into her studio three years ago, I gave it to Mary Jo for protection. She'd been afraid of it at first. But when I took her deep into the woods and we fired several hundred rounds into the side of a fallen tree, she learned to hold it properly, to align the rear and front sights, to keep both eyes open, and to squeeze the trigger without jerking. And the last time I saw the gun was outside our house on a crisp morning just a few weeks earlier, when I awoke in an empty bed and searched until I found Mary Jo firing it across a ravine with tears in her eyes.

I left the breakfast room and walked through the old house, past the antiques and hand-blocked wallpaper and primitive wood carvings of demons and nightmares. Perhaps it was my imagination, but the chanting seemed to fade as I moved further away from the kitchen and closer to the front of the house. I stooped to place the handgun on the floor, opened the front door, and waved to the police, beckoning them in. Then I remained perfectly still as they approached with drawn weapons. Sure enough, the protesters had resumed their chanting out on the sidewalk. Their voices seemed warm and comfortable as I stood in the open door with handguns trained upon my chest. Perhaps the voices I had heard were theirs after all.

But then, wouldn't they have grown louder as I approached the front door?

Seconds passed like hours as the police advanced. I thought about mixed blessings. I thought about how fortunate Juliette Milo was that my wife never learned to hit her target.

And I wondered if Mary Jo had gone insane.

Then I thought about the voices I thought I had heard, and about the thing I thought I had seen in Juliette Milo's eyes, and I realized it might not be Mary Jo who was going insane after all.

Chapter 30

WHAT DO YOU MEAN YOU DON'T KNOW? YOU tryin' to tell me you don't know your own wife?"

Gazing out through the Milos' kitchen window, I watched the backyard gate, hoping against hope that Mary Jo would open it. The detective repeated his question. I tore my attention away from the gate and faced him.

"I never saw her face," I said.

The detective sighed and wiped a delicate hand across his face, stretching the skin like rubber. He said, "How long you been married, Mister Reed?"

I had to think. "Twenty-three years."

"Twenty-three years. And you don't recognize your own wife's backside?"

"She was running. And she was a long way off."

He watched my face intently. His soft black eyes shone with interest. He said, "Tell me about the voice you heard."

I wondered if he meant the eerie chanting I thought I heard when Juliette Milo first looked at me. How could he know? But then I realized what he meant. I said, "Someone called to me from inside the house."

"Called your name?"

"That's right."

"Did you recognize the voice?"

"No."

"But you ran up there and hopped through the window."

"That's right."

"Why did you do that?"

"I don't know . . . I guess I thought someone was in trouble and needed my help."

He looked at me skeptically. "Someone?"

I remained silent, staring at him. The detective was small, maybe five feet six inches, with extremely short black curly hair, a wide nose with flared nostrils, high cheeks, and thick lips. He wore a well-cut brown hound's-tooth jacket, pleated gray wool slacks, and a pair of Italian loafers that looked like five hundred dollars' worth of shoe leather. As he listened to my answers he scribbled notes on a small pad of paper. Each time he asked a question, he shifted position in the Milos' kitchen chair and tapped a dainty finger on the table to a silent inner rhythm. A small gold ring pierced his right ear. It seemed out of character for someone dressed like a member of the country club set. But then, people with skin as dark as the detective's still had a little trouble joining country clubs in New Orleans.

We had been talking for thirty minutes. He said his name was Lincoln Washington. Lieutenant Lincoln Washington. He stared at me when he introduced himself, hard black eyes daring me to laugh. The other officers called him Link. Or Lieutenant.

He said, "You were willin' to come in here after someone who had a gun, but you didn't recognize their voice or know who they were?"

"It sounds kind of dumb when you put it that way."

"It sounds like a crock to me, sir."

"I can't help that. It's the truth."

A uniformed policeman walked up to us and stood silently. The lieutenant looked up at the policeman and said, "Well?"

Leaning down, the patrolman whispered something in Lincoln Washington's ear. The small detective nodded curtly. He said, "All right," and the policeman walked away.

With his ballpoint poised above his tablet, the lieutenant said, "Where is your wife, Mister Reed?"

"The last I saw of her, she was back home in Mount Sinai."

"Is she there now?"

"I'm not sure."

"We just spoke with the authorities in Mount Sinai. They have checked your house. They tell us there's nobody home."

"Maybe she went out."

"Maybe she's here in New Orleans."

I said nothing.

Lincoln Washington sighed and stood. Closing the notebook, he slipped it into the inside pocket of his suit coat. He adjusted his tie and said, "You're staying at the Provincial?"

I nodded. It occurred to me that I had not told him where I was staying.

"How long you plan to be in town, Mister Reed?"

"I'm not sure."

"Seems strange to me, you being here alone when your wife is in such deep trouble back home. That have anything to do with your mother-in-law?"

"I'm here trying to find some evidence to clear my wife. What does my mother-in-law have to do with anything?"

"Why are you looking for evidence down here when the murder was up in Texas?"

"It seems like everyone involved is from here. Why did you ask about my mother-in-law?"

He looked at me blankly for a moment then said, "You seriously gonna try to say you don't know she's one of these C.H.A.R.G.E. people? One of their biggest supporters?"

"Supporters? I know she's against abortion, but what do you mean by support?"

"I mean she gives them money, Mister Reed. A whole lot of money."

It was my turn to give him a blank look. "That can't be true. She's poor."

Lieutenant Washington sighed and nodded. "Yeah, whatever. Will you please let me know if you decide to leave New Orleans? You've got my card. Call me anytime."

I said, "I will," and followed him through the old house toward the front door. We paused in the hall. Through the shattered parlor window, I saw a man in overalls out on the porch, measuring the opening for a new piece of glass.

Lieutenant Washington said, "Rich folks get fast service."

"How's that?"

"The Slydels had a mess of voodoo graffiti on the side of their church for two days before anybody painted over it, and here these folks get their window fixed in an hour."

"You know about the Slydels' church?"

"Oh, yeah. We know all about them Slydels and their little army."

"So why don't you investigate them? Maybe they're the ones trying to hurt the Milos."

"Jeepers. You really think so?"

"No need to be sarcastic."

"You're gonna have to excuse me, Mister Reed. I get that way when civilians start jumping through windows chasing after people with guns and trying to tell me how to do my job."

As we passed by the parlor, I saw Juliette and Melvin Milo perched side by side on the sofa, facing Father John Kratz across a coffee table. Everything about the Milos' postures expressed estrangement: legs crossed in opposite directions, heads tilted slightly away from each other, arms crossed over their chests. Doctor Melvin Milo spoke in soft tones to Father Kratz. "Nobody asked for your forgiveness."

Father Kratz said, "Mel, that's not what I meant, and you know it."

Milo said, "What then? You parade out there with those maniacs, then you come in here with your platitudes about Christian charity— who do you think you are?"

The priest said, "Someone who cares about you and Juliette."

Juliette Milo said, "It is a strange way you have of showing it."

With the assistance of makeup, a vestige of her youthful beauty lingered in her surgically altered features. She sat ramrod straight on the edge of the sofa, her rigid body emitting waves of tension. I noticed that the odd bone necklace was gone but she still wore the rest of her strange costume: the turban and the toga. As I stared at her, she slowly turned and looked straight back at me, as if she was aware of my scrutiny. Our eyes met, and I saw it once more: that thing that lingered just beyond the mask of her humanity. Taking a half step back, I dropped my eyes to the ground, praying for protection. When I raised them again, she too had looked away. But now her hard features were set in a little smile.

Beside her, the trauma of Milo's recent injury showed in the slackness of his jowls and the ashen pallor of his dark complexion. His eyes held a haunted look, a hunted look, a desperation that was perfectly natural under the circumstances. Dozens of people outside his home carried signs that suggested he was evil. Only a week before, someone had tried to kill him in Mount Sinai. Now they had come for his wife. His life was a disaster.

He said, "Juliette, at least John made the effort to come in here and ask about you. None of the rest of those so-called Christians out there seem to care."

She said, "I know." Then, looking at the priest, "But why do you have to help them? Why cannot you leave us alone?"

Father Kratz said, "Juliette, I think you and Mel are basically decent people. But you have to understand, I can't stand by and silently watch what you're doing. I believe it is very wrong. And I don't understand why you can't see that too."

Doctor Milo began to speak, but the priest held up a massive hand and continued, "Melvin, I think I know you well enough to say you're not doing this just for the money. There are other areas of medicine that pay as well, and you're not the kind of person who would violate principle for material gain. So I am left with the conclusion that you truly believe what you are doing is correct."

Milo spoke as if reciting a litany. "I am making it possible for poor women who have made terrible mistakes to continue with their lives without the burden of caring for an unwanted child. I am saving unwanted children from a life without love or compassion. I am sparing them the insults of poverty. I am not a murderer. The fetus is not a viable human life. But the mother *is* alive. It is my responsibility to make it possible for her to go on living with dignity." It was the first time I had heard him speak more than a sentence. I was surprised to hear the same lilting accent I had noticed in Juliette's speech, although his grammar was better.

Father Kratz said, "Is it proper for us to kill one person for the sake of another person's dignity?"

"I do *not* kill people! An embryo is *not* a person!" Milo said. "You and those maniacs out there are the ones who kill *people*. You have followed us everywhere, calling us murderers and worse things in front of our friends and neighbors. You print those so-called 'wanted posters' with my face on them, as if I am a common criminal. And now see what you have done!" Impassioned by his anger, he rose and clutched at his shirt, pulling the shirttail out of his trousers. "Would you like to see the wound in my side? It was put there by a *Christian*." He sneered the final word.

The priest said, "Sit down, Mel. I know what they did to you."

Juliette pulled at Doctor Melvin Milo's leg. He seemed to become calm immediately at her touch. Milo sank back to the sofa with his eyes locked on the priest. Father Kratz said, "I am an enemy of the woman who did that, Mel. I would help them convict her if I could. Did you know I have made it my duty to stand outside your clinic every night for almost two years to see that they did not bomb it? Do you really think I want harm to come to either of you? Do you really think I could support the person who killed Michael?"

Melvin Milo fell back against the cushions and closed his eyes. His arms lay limp in his lap. I pitied him.

Juliette Milo said, "We know better than that. Mel is just tired. He knows you care for us. He knows you cared for Father Michael, too. Melvin is sorry. He will apologize." She looked sideways at her husband and said, "You *will* apologize, Melvin."

Doctor Melvin Milo rolled his head toward her. Juliette and Father Kratz did not see it. Lieutenant Washington had walked on and missed it. But I saw the haunted look in Melvin Milo's eyes before he mumbled an apology to the priest, a look that spoke of deep-down suffering and misery and a spirit on the edge of insanity. It drove my mind back to another pair of eyes, so terrible and so deeply buried that I had not thought of them for years . . .

• • •

LUCRETIA GRANIER STOOD AT THE DOOR OF MY NEW Orleans apartment, her pale green eyes blazing with anger.

"How come you call my girl crazy, you?"

"Crazy?" I said. "I never called her that."

"Now you call her a liar, too! Shame on you!"

"What? I never said she was a liar!"

Lucretia pointed a finger at my nose. "She told me you didn't believe her. She say she explain what happened and you say she was crazy, you."

I had been holed up in my small apartment for two days, eating little and sleeping less. Even Ernest B. had been unable to interest me in the outside world. When Mary Jo's mother appeared at my doorstep, my heart swelled with hope. She was so kind at the mission. Perhaps she was here to help me work things out with her daughter. But now I was faced by a different Lucretia Granier, one who would become all too familiar in the years ahead, an angry woman, quick to judge and slow to forgive. Well, two could play that game . . .

"What do you expect me to say to her?" I said. "Am I supposed to believe this stuff about the devil making her pregnant?"

"De good book says demons lay with women in de time of Noah! I suppose you don't believe dat, either."

"That's just a story. Something we're supposed to read to learn a lesson. But you and that husband of yours are using it to make Mary Jo crazy."

"There dat word again!"

"Well, I'm not blaming her. *You're* the one doing the brainwashing here!"

"Dat's enough! My girl been cryin' for days now 'cause of what you said! And I'm here to see to it dat you take it back! Now, you come with me, you!"

At that, she clutched my arm and pulled me outside, giving me no time to lock the door before she led me down the steps and onto the sidewalk. I tried to get her to tell me where we were going, but she only said, "You gonna see soon enough, you."

We hurried along a series of streets until we reached Saint Charles. I broke into a trot occasionally to keep up with her long strides. On the boulevard, we caught a burgundy and hunter green trolley and rode to the turnaround near the Vieux Carre. There, she bounded from the car and set out along another series of back streets. I began to hope she was taking me to the mission to see Mary Jo—we seemed to be heading toward that neighborhood—but then she turned away from her home.

I followed Lucretia Granier into a neighborhood even more bleak and forbidding than the area around the mission. If I had not seen it, I would never have believed such a place existed in New Orleans. The buildings loomed above us with windows cracked and covered by cardboard. The few power lines still hanging from their poles did not branch off toward the abandoned structures. Foul smoke from the garbage can fires of vagrants drifted across the narrow roadway, obscuring the block ahead behind a haze of forbidding gray. I saw no human life. No dogs or cats. Nothing to indicate that this was the center of a large city. Except for the barely intact facades of stores and empty apartment buildings, it could have been the scene of a nuclear war.

Lucretia said, "This way," and tugged on my elbow, pulling me toward an alley no more than eight feet wide between two ancient brick walls. The end of the alley lay in darkness, as if a solid black thing squatted there, waiting.

"Wait a minute," I said. "Where are you taking me?"

She stopped and looked up at me, a sour amusement in her eyes. "Oh, is de big boy afraid of de dark? Strong enough to make my little girl cry, call her crazy and a liar, 'cause she believes in de devil, but scared of a little ol' dark alley? Who believe in de devil now?"

I shook my elbow loose from her grasp. "All right. Let's go."

She resumed her hurried pace, moving ahead of me as we threaded our way between mounds of stinking trash. I was almost relieved to see the garbage. At least it was evidence that we had not left all of humanity behind. Then I noticed three chickens, lying side by side on top of a heap of empty cans. All three were missing their heads and feet. But their bodies were intact, complete with bloody feathers. Who in this poor neighborhood would discard whole chickens, keeping only the heads and feet? I shivered.

The air seemed to cling to my skin. It grew damp and steadily colder as we neared the shadows at the end of the alley. The darkness did not recede before us as shadows usually do. We drew closer, only a dozen feet away, but still I could make out no details within the wall of blackness. It seemed solid, yet vaporous somehow, like a cloud or a filmy veil. Lucretia Granier reached the edge and paused to look back. She lifted her eyes toward the thin sliver of smoky sky still visible between the twin looming walls and said, "Lord, protect me and this fool. Shelter us under de wings of angels until we leave this accursed place." Then with a mocking smile, she slipped into the darkness and disappeared from view.

I lingered in the last of the light, my heart racing. From within the shadows, Lucretia's voice reached out to me, hollow and distant, "Well, don't stand there gawkin'. Come on!"

I stepped into the darkness.

As my eyes adjusted, I saw two vague forms several feet away. Hands out like a blind man, I fumbled along the alley toward them. When I was closer, I saw that one of them was Lucretia. The other was a smaller figure, that of an old woman, less than five feet tall, with an odd, crooked posture.

Lucretia gestured toward me and said, "Garrison Reed, I want you to meet Miss Harriet. She lives here."

I mumbled hello.

The old woman did not look up at me or acknowledge my presence in any way. Instead, she turned toward Lucretia and said, "Why you come heah?" Her voice was oddly sweet, enticing in a vague way. I remember wanting to hear her speak again.

"Dis boy does not believe in your kind," said Lucretia. "He thinks Satan is nothing but a boogeyman for children."

The old woman laughed. It was an evil sound. She said, "Is dat so?" This time there was nothing sweet about her voice.

Lucretia said, "Tell her, boy."

I cleared my throat. "I don't know what you're talking about."

Lucretia screamed at me then. "Don't lie to me! You call my girl crazy. Your puny brain can't accept de presence of evil in de world— real evil dat you can touch and feel! Well, here it is! You don't believe my daughter could bear Satan's child? Look at her, you!"

Lucretia laid hands on the old woman, spinning her toward me and screaming, "Look at her! She is a witch! A disciple of Satan! If you are a Christian, she is de enemy! If you are not a Christian, she is your future! You don't believe me, you? Look at her eyes!" Lucretia Granier savagely lifted the old woman's chin, forcing her to face me for the first time. What I saw then kept me awake for weeks. Indeed, I tried hard for months to forget it.

The woman was not old at all. Beneath the rags she wore like a scarf, she had the soft complexion of a teenager. And above her flushed pink cheeks, deeply sunken in twin pools of blackness, her eyes glowed red like a wolf's in the beam of a floodlight. But it was no reflection. No light shone on her face. There was no light in that evil place, except for the twin dots of red that stared at me from a child's face.

I turned and ran.

Seven blocks away, I finally stopped. Leaning against a filthy iron light post, I stood facing back the way I came, chest heaving for breath. Soon, Lucretia appeared, walking toward me with the same hurried pace she had maintained before. When she reached me, she said, "Maybe now you have something useful to say to my girl?"

I said, "What . . . who was that?"

"I told you already."

"Are you saying she was possessed by the devil? Or a demon?"

"You saw her. What do you think?"

I teetered on the brink of belief, but in the end my mind could not release its hold on the commonplace convictions of the physical world.

I said, "Whatever it was, it couldn't be what you think."

"Hah! You an even bigger fool than I thought. You see with you own eyes, you, an' still won't believe."

"But . . . if that's what it was, why weren't you afraid?"

She sighed and said, "I am in de Spirit, young man. As you should be." And gripping my elbow again, she said, "Come along."

I struggled to make sense of what I had seen as she guided me away from that evil place, toward the Prodigal Son Mission. I said, "Wait a minute! Are you saying God can protect you from the devil?"

"Of course."

"But Mary Jo said they're equals. Like two sides of a coin. Like up and down, or dark and light."

"She got it wrong. How can dey be equal? God made de devil! De devil, he cain't make nothin'! He just destroy."

Mary Jo must have seen us coming. She stood alone on the cracked sidewalk outside the old mission building, watching us approach. As we drew near, Lucretia whispered to me, "Boy, I expect you to do de right thing with my girl. Don't make me come lookin' for you again, me. You won't like it much if I do."

When we reached Mary Jo, Lucretia said, "You two have a lot to talk about." Touching Mary Jo's cheek, she continued, "Child, I can't let Alphonse stand in de way of your happiness. I know you prayed about this boy. Do as de Lord commands."

With that, Lucretia Granier entered the mission and left me alone with Mary Jo.

Chapter 31

EDNA BENOIT LIVED IN THE BARATARIA swamp with her five children, two large mongrel dogs, countless cats of various breeds, and a battered Dodge pickup she called Jules for reasons I never understood. She pronounced her name "Aidna." Her home was a pale gray shack with teardrop cypress siding and a deep front porch shaded by rusting corrugated metal on gnarled and twisted raw poplar posts. The floorboards were dotted by tin can lids nailed over the knot holes. Above the door hung a rope of garlic—for good luck, or to ward off evil spirits, depending on how you looked at it. Lucretia Granier would not speak to a daughter with such pagan beliefs. I was there in part because of them.

I parked in the open yard out front and walked to the porch steps, my boots crunching on the bleached white shells that passed for gravel in that part of Louisiana. As I waited for someone to answer my knock, I stared across the clearing toward the dense barricade of green that marked the edge of the swamp. Edna's yard was strewn with castaway pieces of household machines, bicycles with missing wheels, a low pile of empty RC Cola cans, a bald automobile tire, three forlorn clay pots sprouting weed-choked petunias, and a pair of filthy white plastic chairs beside a folding card table. The neon blue Pontiac I had driven down from New Orleans looked incongruous amidst the squalor; sleek and businesslike and thoroughly modern. I waited for a long time on the porch, then knocked again, more forcefully this time. The warped screen door rattled loudly. I hoped to find Mary Jo beyond the door. It was a faint hope at best. Edna Benoit was her oldest sister, but they never got along.

A tiny girl opened the door about six inches and peeked up at me through the rusted wire screen. Her eyes were wide and green. Her aunt's eyes. Mary Jo's eyes.

I said, "Hey there. Is your mamma at home?"

The girl did not reply. Her remarkable unblinking eyes took me in as if she had never seen a man before. Something brown smeared her face. I said, "Honey, go tell your momma Uncle Garr is here."

Softly, she closed the door. I turned and resumed my inspection of the clearing in front of the dilapidated cabin. About a hundred feet separated Edna's front porch from the dip in the land that defined the edge of the swamp. Only twelve inches of elevation stood between the dry land and miles of mud and standing water sheltered by cypress, water tupelo, and willow trees. Elephant ears, palmettos, and hyacinths lent a tropical ambiance to the undergrowth below the dense canopy. Giant blue iris and yellowtops sprinkled dots of color against the relentless background of green. A least bittern flitted through the trees at the edge of the clearing, calling softly. I heard the voices of a dozen other species of birds. Some, like the discordant squawk of the great blue heron, reminded me of home. Others were strangers to my ear. And beyond it all, underlying everything, was the insistent pulsing rhythm of an oil pump hidden somewhere off in the swamp; a harsh, unnatural, distant rumbling that siphoned peacefulness from the scene like a crying baby at a wedding.

Five minutes passed. I decided to look around. The right side of the cabin was much like the front, a weathered wall of wood, a pair of windows, one covered by a portion of a tin sign where the glass had been broken. I read "Doan's Pills" upside down on the sign as I walked by. Behind the house, Edna stood with her back to me, hanging clothes on a line. I sucked in my breath at the sight of her long auburn hair, hanging in a loose ponytail tied by a piece of green cloth. It was exactly Mary Jo's shade, but longer. She wore a white T-shirt tucked into a pair of bleached blue jeans. As she reached high to clip a child's shirt on the line, I saw my wife in the shift of her shoulders and the tilt of her hip. I called to her from thirty feet away. She flinched and turned quickly, another wet shirt clutched in her hands. I waved and smiled. The question in her eyes faded as she recognized me.

"Well, I declare. Look what I got in my backyard."

"Hi, Edna."

She dropped the shirt into a cardboard box that lay at her bare feet. I walked closer.

She smiled, looked past my shoulder, and said, "I suppose that sister of mine is round heah somewhere."

I felt hope die. "Well, to tell you the truth, I was kind of looking for her myself."

"What in de world you talkin' about?"

"You haven't seen her?"

Edna Benoit placed her hands on her hips and stared at me. Her hips were wide. Her proud chest pushed at the cotton shirt. The front of the shirt bore the colorful inscription, *Laissez Les Bon Temps Rulez*. She said, "Garrison Reed, you best tell me what you got on you mind."

I glanced at her house. "Could I use your bathroom? I've been driving for an hour and . . . you know."

She held her pose for a moment, searching my face with a puzzled look, then she said, "Surely. Come on in."

I followed her up three narrow wooden steps and across a screened-in back porch piled high with the kinds of things most people store in their garage or attic. She opened a door to the kitchen. The linoleum was worn through to the wooden subfloor in a spot just inside the door. Edna pulled a folding chair away from a small table and sat heavily. She sighed and pushed a loose strand of hair away from her sun-bronzed forehead. Pointing at a low opening across the tiny room, she said, "It's through dat door theah."

I walked through the house, taking the opportunity to look in every room. There were only three, and Mary Jo was not in any of them. When I returned, Edna had been joined by the small girl I had seen before, and a boy about seven years old. The boy wore a pair of blue-jean cutoffs, frayed at the legs. He wore no shirt or shoes. Mud caked his feet. His blond bangs hung ragged across his forehead. It looked like Edna had used a bowl for a guide on his last haircut. The brown substance still streaked the girl's face. Perhaps it was chocolate. If Edna could afford chocolate.

The girl climbed into Edna's lap and watched me with intense interest as Edna spoke. "All right, Garr. You best start at de beginning."

I paused, unsure of how to begin. I said, "Mary Jo left home last Monday. I thought she might be here with you."

Edna said, "Ain't seen hide nor hair of either one of you for five or six years. What made you think she gonna come here?"

"I guess I'm running out of places to look."

She idly stroked the little girl's hair. "Why she leave?"

"I don't know."

"I thought ya'll had a dream marriage." She accented the word *dream*, drawing it out, making it sound sarcastic. Edna had bad luck with men. Five kids with four fathers. Mary Jo and I had offered to help with the kids, but she rebuffed our offers of cash and clothes. The last time we came to visit, Mary Jo was so worried about the children's living conditions that she insisted on buying them each a new wardrobe and offered to move them all to another house. Edna took offense to our "uppity" offer and said several unkind things. Mary Jo left in tears.

"I don't think Mary Jo is gone because of anything to do with our marriage, Edna."

She said nothing.

"Have you heard about our legal problems?"

"Legal problems? What happened? Run over some white trash in you Mercedes Benz, you?"

I smiled. "I drive a pickup truck."

She waved a callused hand through the air and said, "Whatever."

The boy stood silently beside the table, his hand draped idly around Edna's shoulders. The three of them stared at me with Lucretia Granier's emerald green eyes. I said, "They arrested her for killing a priest and shooting a doctor. An abortionist."

She lifted the girl from her lap and set her on the floor beside the boy. She said, "Madelaine, you and Martin run outside quick, quick and see can you find Julieanne and Marie. Dey gonna be out in de *mariase* somewheah. Tell dem supper gonna be ready in 'bout thirty minutes. Tell dem *Maman* said don't bring no more catfish back home. We got enough of dem tings. *Sac-o-lait* be good, though. You tell them bring *sac-o-lait* if dey caught any. We'll eat it proper." They hurried from the kitchen together, slamming the screen door behind them out on the porch.

I said, "*Mariase?*"

"Din't dat sister of mine teach you anything, you? Dat mean swamp down heah."

I said, "Must be French."

"It Cajun. Nothin' wrong wit callin' it Cajun."

We were silent for a moment. Then I said, "Your children are growing up fine."

She rose and crossed the tiny room to stand at the sink with her back to me. She said, "We all doin' just fine, we is."

I watched as she removed some potatoes from a shoe box on the counter. The water ran brown for a few seconds when she turned the faucet. She waited for it to clear, then began rubbing the potatoes under the water. After a few minutes, she said, "Did she do it?"

"Of course not!"

Edna chuckled. "Just thought I'd ask. Don't get you back up, you."

"How could you think Mary Jo might do something like that?"

Edna set the potatoes on the counter and sliced them into wedges. Then she opened the refrigerator. It was an old refrigerator, about five feet tall with a single curved door. She took a plastic sack full of fish from the top shelf and dropped it in the sink.

"She got no reason to kill no priest, but abortion doctors . . . dat different. My baby sister got a good reason for dat. She and I both got a ting for them fellas. Yes, sir."

"Why? Because of the . . . the thing that happened to Mary Jo and Linda?"

Edna stopped filleting the catfish and turned to stare at me. "What you know 'bout dat?"

"Enough. I know they were pregnant. I know they had illegal abortions afterward. I know the abortion killed Linda."

"And? What else?"

I looked at her, wondering what else there could be to know. After searching my face for a moment, Edna said, "You don't know nothin', you. Nothin' at all."

"What does that mean, Edna?"

"If she ain't told you, ain't my place to."

For thirty minutes, I tried to persuade Edna to elaborate, but she refused. I pleaded as she selected a large brown grocery sack from a drawer and snapped it open. I watched as she poured corn meal, salt, pepper, and spices from an unmarked jar into the sack. Then, one by one, she placed the catfish filets in the sack and shook it violently to cover the fish with the seasonings. After all the filets were breaded and seasoned, she struck a wooden match on the side of a wall cabinet and lit the gas ring on her range. The propane burned steady and blue. She melted a large patty of butter in a huge black iron skillet, then scooped the potatoes into the skillet, stirring them often with a wooden spoon. When they were golden brown, she removed the potatoes and laid the filets delicately across the hot iron. The spices sizzled and the kitchen quickly became foggy with an acrid smoke that rose from the skillet. While the fish cooked, Edna carefully rinsed the empty plastic sack she had removed from the refrigerator. When it was clean, she draped it over the faucet to dry.

"You gonna want some supper heah?" she asked.

"No, thank you. I've got to get back."

As I spoke, a tall boy entered through the kitchen door. Edna said, "Jacques, you remember you Uncle Garr?"

The boy looked at me blankly. I said, "Jacques, you sure have grown."

He nodded and said, "Hey. Is dat you car out front?"

"Not really. I rented it in New Orleans."

"It shore is a pretty car."

"Yes. It is, isn't it?"

"Can I drive it?"

"Jacques!" said Edna. "You watch you manners, boy."

I said, "No. It's all right. Jacques and I can take a quick drive while you wait on the other kids."

"Well, I suppose dat be all right. I learned him to drive in Jules last year. Just don't let him get you out on the highway, you."

Jacques moaned, "Oh, Ma, Ma."

I laughed and said, "We'll only be gone a few minutes."

"See you back soon, you. This catfish ain't no good at all when it cold."

The boy and I walked out through the front door. I handed him the keys as we approached the Pontiac. He was about six feet tall and skinny as a pole. His sunken cheeks were peppered with acne. He wore faded blue jeans, a black T-shirt with a heavy metal rock band's logo blazoned across the front, and a red and white polka-dotted engineer's cap. When we were in the car, he fumbled around for the lever and scooted the seat closer to the steering wheel.

I said, "Where you want to go? Any place special?"

"Naw. Just wanna drive."

I thought for a moment and said, "All right. Let's head over toward Lafitte. There's something I want to do over yonder."

Jacques drove slowly and carefully. We cruised along raised shell roads between continuous walls of deep green. Soon, the vegetation on the right gave way to a wide band of water—the Intracoastal Canal. Houses stood between the road and the Canal. Giant shrimp trawlers loomed behind the houses, rocking against worn pilings in the backyards of their owners. Their names, neatly painted on their bows, said a lot about their master's outlook on life. *Risky Business*, *Lady Luck*, and *Home Free*. We crossed over a small bayou on a dull gray wooden drawbridge and passed into town. A sign proclaimed "Beaudreaux Bayou Restaurant" on the left. Other signs, hand painted and nailed to telephone poles, announced less ambitious enterprises: "Sally's Snow Balls" and "Junk Cars Towed Free." We passed Chavez's Boat Repair and Marina. Two men in gimme caps stood watching as a marina employee operated a small crane, lifting their outboard fishing boat from their trailer and slowly lowering it into the canal. Thousands of flecks of glitter embedded in the blood-red fiberglass of the boat sparkled in the sun. A tiny plywood pirogue lay in the bow. Up in the bayous along the canal where the dense vegetation and shallow waters made travel by any other means impossible, the fishermen would tie off their sparkling boat and pole the pirogue deeper into the swamp.

I read the names on the mailboxes and the street signs as we cruised slowly by, learning something about the history of Lafitte and the heritage of the people of the Barataria Swamp. Falko, Bleu, Guidreaux, and Boudrey. Factory Street and Yacht Pen Road. As we passed out of the fishing town, I said, "Pull onto that road up there. Go left."

Turning away from the Canal, the boy drove deeper into the swamp. Small wooden shacks on stilts lined the road. Beneath them, battered four-wheel-drive pickup trucks parked between the faded poles. Beside one of the shacks a small shrine stood atop a pile of soil. From below the gabled roof of the shrine, a concrete statue of the Virgin held a slender hand aloft in perpetual blessing. Dark-skinned men clutching bottles of Jax and Dixie stared down on us suspiciously from precariously supported porches. Beyond the shacks, an intermittent shimmer reached the eye through the dense undergrowth, a watery reflection where the South Louisiana sun filtered through the heavy canopy. For as far as I could see, stagnant water and jet-black mud sprawled at the roots of towering cypress stands. Spanish moss hung on branches above the road, a widow's laced veil draped across the intertwined limbs. Palmetto trees squatted on the high spots, surrounded by the oily black waters, stunted and oddly out of place, as if the prehistoric goo had flung them up through time itself. The swamp spread for miles in all directions, from just south of New Orleans and Metairie all the way to the Gulf of Mexico; a slumbering stew of vegetation and wildlife so dense that the cultural descendants of Jean Lafitte still managed to maintain smuggling operations within its bowels, as they have for two hundred years. In spite of radar, satellite photography, and every other high-tech innovation the law can throw at them, the Barataria Swamp and Atchafalaya Basin was still a smuggler's haven. Next to fishing and oil, cocaine transportation was the area's biggest industry.

Jacques reached down and twisted the volume control on the Pontiac's radio. He tuned in a heavy pulsing rhythm. Voices chanted relentlessly, following the beat without bothering to break into song. I couldn't understand most of it, but here and there I caught enough of the heavily accented lyrics to guess that they were shouting about the joys of gang warfare.

I said, "Hey. You mind if we don't listen to that?"

"That rap, mon. It good stuff."

"I get enough of it from the cars next to me in town. I'd rather not listen to it on purpose."

"It you car, you."

I tuned the radio in to a Baton Rouge station playing Frank Sinatra. Jacques wrinkled his nose but remained silent.

I said, "You got a job?"

"Yeah, mon. I workin' for de power company, me."

"What do you do for them?"

"Clean de moss from de power lines, mostly. An' lately, we been buildin' boxes for de cranes, high up on de poles."

"Cranes?"

He glanced sideways at me, amused at my question. "You know, you. De big white birds. It for dey nests. Up top of de poles. It some kind of government ting."

"Oh . . . I see."

The car was new. The suspension shielded us from most of the bumps in the road and the carpeted and padded interior muffled most of the outside sounds. Sinatra's no-nonsense delivery of *Come Fly with Me* pumped from the speakers. I glanced out through the side window and saw an old man lift a three-foot alligator from the bottom of a pirogue he had just poled to shore. The alligator's mouth was tied shut with hemp twine. He looked up as we passed. I waved. Holding the unfortunate reptile draped from hand to hand in front of his chest like an offering, he smiled a black, toothless smile. Sinatra sang, "Weather wise, it's such a cool, cool day." A towering off-road truck rumbled up behind us, just inches away. We drove for about a mile with the truck glued to our rear bumper.

I said, "You know who that is back there?"

Jacques glanced in the rearview mirror. "No," he said, "But I seen dat truck round a lot, lately. Seen plenty strangers from different place all round heah."

On the radio, Sinatra mentioned Acapulco Bay. The huge truck pulled even closer, looming above the little Pontiac like an elephant intent upon crushing its trainer. Jacques said, "What they doin'?" His knuckles grew white around the steering wheel.

"Don't get nervous, Jacques. Just keep your eyes up front and drive normally."

The truck's grill filled the back window. Its windshield was too streaked with mud for me to see the occupants clearly. In place of the front license plate was a Confederate Stars and Bars. Jacques's eyes darted between the road and the rearview mirror. He stepped on the gas. The little Pontiac pulled away, but the truck soon closed the gap and resumed its position just behind the bumper.

I said, "You've seen these guys before?"

"Yep."

"Just cruising around here?"

"Uh huh."

I glanced in the side mirror. "Make a left up there."

Jacques sneaked a sideways look at me.

I said, "Just start slowing down now, and kind of move over into the middle of the road. They'll have to back off a little."

The boy lifted his foot from the accelerator and the Pontiac slowed. I said, "Turn on your left turn signal."

The muddy truck backed away to a position about four feet from our tail. I said, "Slow down some more, and ease over."

"What if a car come up the other way?"

"Don't worry, Jacques. We'll be fine."

Jacques slowed to about five miles per hour. He began his turn, descending the side of the raised roadbed onto a primitive dirt path. A wide puddle of water stood in the ruts ahead. Behind us, the truck roared by. I twisted to watch them pass. Through their open side window, I saw the driver, a clean-shaven blond man with metallic sunglasses. Something about him was familiar.

We came to a full stop and the boy said, "You wanna drive now, you?"

"No." I smiled. "You're doing just fine. Why don't we back up? Get back on the road heading on the way we were going."

Jacques shifted to reverse, twisted in his seat, and looked back through the rear window. Soon, we were on the raised roadbed again. We continued below the deep green canopy until we reached another group of pole houses, much the same as the first. On the radio, they were playing a Sinatra medley. "My Way" was flowing from the dashboard.

I said, "See that road up ahead on the right? Just pull over to the side when we get there."

Jacques glanced quickly at me, then back at the road. He said, "Pull over?"

"Just slow down and stop, Jacques."

"But what if someone come through heah?"

"Park the car off to the side. They'll have room."

"I cain't get too far over theah. They's graves off to the side up theah."

Staring straight ahead, I said, "I know. That's why I want to stop."

Carefully, the boy pulled the Pontiac over. A pale white crypt stood less than ten feet from the edge of the gravel road. Beyond the crypt, a parish sign hung on a galvanized pole. It read, "No Dumping—$99 Fine," and was peppered with tiny holes from the blast of a vandal's shotgun. Dry land fit for burials is scarce in Barataria, so the Cajuns adopted a tradition long ago of laying their dead to rest in the narrow right-of-way between their homes and the roads. Large cemeteries are impossible, so some roads are dotted by the small burial plots every mile or so. It is not uncommon for a short driveway to pass between the graves, or for a front porch view to include a half dozen raised crypts just beyond the front yard fence. The old crypts were built of red bricks and coated with plaster. In most cases, much of the plaster has long since peeled away. What remains is dull green with algae. Where the bricks lie exposed, the elements have eroded the mortar between them, leaving gaping holes which are often filled with weeds or ferns. But the one I was looking at was newer, and built of precast concrete. The mortuaries called them "burial vaults," probably because "vault" sounds less macabre than "crypt."

While Jacques waited in the car, I walked the few feet to the gravesite. It lay just above the surface, its top slightly rounded to allow the rains to run off. A small, simple cross was cast into the top at one end above an engraving that read, "Linda Madelaine Granier—Born May 9, 1958, died September 22, 1974—Called Too Soon."

The name and inscription had been defaced by a circle of brown paint . . . or could it be dried blood? The circle was surrounded by symbols very similar to those I had seen in the hospital corridor and on the side of the church in Metairie. Outside the circle, the white concrete of the crypt was scorched black in three places, as if something had been burned there. Flies had settled on the wide brown lines, hundreds of them in constant motion. I waved them off and stooped to smell the markings. The faint aroma was unmistakable: rotten meat. It *was* dried blood. But what could it mean?

Mary Jo had brought me there less than a year after we were married. It was a ritual of closure for her; the first time she had visited Linda's grave since the funeral, the first time she had shared this place with anyone outside the Granier family. I remembered standing beside her in that odd cemetery, two graves deep and six across, cars and trucks rumbling by just a few feet away as she placed a bouquet of brown-eyed Susans across the curved top of the crypt. I believed then that Mary Jo had finally turned a corner on her misery.

Now I stood alone beside the tomb of her sister, pondering the twist of fate that had taken Linda Granier, freed her perhaps, while my wife was left with the memories of abortion. Abortion and . . . what? What else happened? Perhaps nothing. Edna might be toying with me, tantalizing me with hints of nonexistent secrets. But what if there was something Mary Jo had hidden all these years? I always believed she had bared her deepest shame that afternoon as we stood in front of the mission, describing the pain and humiliation of her abortion, offering up the details like a confession. It hardly seemed possible that her pregnancy was a demonic curse. But whether it was that, or something more earthly, I had always believed she did not recall the act of conception. I had always assumed she lived with a kind of selective amnesia. But now, after all these years, the glowing red eyes of the ragged girl in the back alley were alive again in my memory. Now I wondered if Mary Jo's experience was far more sinister than the sins of adultery or murder. We had never discussed it again. I told her then that those things were in the past, that they did not matter when it came to her and me. I did not want to know the details. It hurt too much to think about them. For more than twenty years I had assumed she told me the truth as she knew it, sparing me only the painful minutiae. Could it be that she harbored secrets all that time, even from me?

Standing at her sister's grave, I felt ashamed of the growing sense of betrayal rising within me. I was angry with her—there was no use in denying it. The unexplained trips, the incident with the gun, and the terrible threat in her note all chipped away at my confidence. I had begun to doubt Mary Jo. Would I doubt my own faith as well? I longed for a more certain belief in the love of God and of my wife. Yet the uneasy feeling grew.

What could Mary Jo have hidden? What could be so terrible that it slumbered for two decades, only to rise now to destroy our lives?

Through the open car window, Jacques called softly, "Hey. Hey look, you."

I turned and he nodded down the road. The mud-splattered truck was there, pulled to the side, facing us. I could just make out the silhouettes of two men behind the grimy windshield. Jacques and I stared openly at them. After three or four minutes, the truck pulled forward slowly, huge tires crunching on the shell roadbed. The blond driver turned his metallic sunglasses toward me as the truck inched by. When they had passed, he gunned the engine and accelerated away, but not before I read the messages on his twin bumper stickers— "Abortion: America's Holocaust" and "Trust Jesus."

As the flies on the crypt buzzed insistently in the background, joined by Frank Sinatra through the open window of the Pontiac, I remembered where I had seen the truck driver before.

Chapter 32

I DROVE BACK TO EDNA AND JACQUES'S HOME. Edna stood in the deep November shade of the front porch, waiting for us

She said, "You welcome to some supper if you want."

"Thank you, but I've got to get going."

"All right."

"Listen, we were just over at Linda's grave. There was something strange about it . . ."

"Strange? What kinda strange?"

"There were symbols painted on it. I think they were painted in blood. And someone's been burning something on it."

"Oh. Dat."

I looked more closely at her. "You know something about it?"

"Of course. I been doin' dat for years."

"Doing what?"

She cocked her head, as if considering her options, then said, "I don't see no harm can come of it. You come on in heah, you."

I followed her into the little house. She led me down the short hall and into a small room. On the far side of the room was an old double bed, piled high with crazy quilts of every color. A scarred oak dresser stood beside the right wall. On top of the dresser were a circle of burning candles, a small chipped plate containing a mound of dried beans, three stacks of dimes, and an amulet made of hair and beads. I turned to look at Edna, eyebrows raised in an unspoken question.

She said, "It the old ways, Garr. *Maman* and Mary Jo don't care for dem none, but dat don't make dem go way. I still believe, me. An I always gonna believe, me."

"Voodoo? Come on, Edna."

She bridled at the criticism in my tone. "What? You more right with dat dead man on dat cross? You got de three gods dat be one god, you, and de risin' from de dead. You got de birthin' babies without no lovin', and you gonna tell me de old ways don't make no sense, you?"

"I'm sorry. You've got a right to believe what you want. It just took me by surprise."

"Mary Jo and *Maman* done a good job, movin' out and hidin' their Cajun talk. When *Maman* married dat man, she turned from de old ways and become a Christian like him. But dat man wasn't my daddy. I was old enough to know about de old ways already. Old enough to stay here wit Benoit. I still remembeah everyting, even if some folks got too big for dey britches and forgot everyting."

"Why do you do those things to Linda's grave?"

Her face assumed an eerie quality, lit by the candles on the altar with long, upcast shadows filling the hollows of her eyes. She said, "Linda died a bad death, Garr. Her *ti bon ange* is floatin' out there, exposed to de *loas*. I got to protect her, to keep her from becoming a *zombi astral*. I been fightin' dem for twenty-four years." She looked away from me, gazing at the flickering candles. "Twenty-four years."

"I have no idea what you're talking about."

She turned back to me. "My sister got herself killed by de devil, Garr. By de devil hisself. An now, he want her soul—what we call de *ti bon ange*. He send de *Baron Samadhi* down heah for her. I seen him my own self, me, with his clean black coat and his nice tall hat and dem holes for eyes in dat nasty skull he got."

I remembered the carving in the Milos' living room. Edna was describing it perfectly. I remembered Juliette Milo, sitting at her kitchen table, smiling in satisfaction as she said, "The *Baron* will come. You have been chosen."

Edna said, "I seen him myself—the Baron of all de *loas*. You call dem demons, I think."

"So these symbols you paint and these things you burn, they're to keep the demons away?"

She nodded. "Mainly de *Baron Samadhi*. He de one I worry most about, me."

"Why is that?"

"Because he de one can take you soul to hell. Dat why."

I stood staring at the macabre altar, unsure of what to say. Finally I asked a question. "Have you ever heard of a woman named Juliette Milo?"

She stared at me, her eyes deep in shadow. "How you know dat name?"

"It's a long story. But you've heard of her?"

"Oh, yes. Everybody heard of de *Mamba* up in N'awlins."

"Mamba?"

She nodded. "A priestess, like. A woman who give herself over to the *loas*."

At first, I had been inclined to ridicule her strange beliefs. Voodoo seemed such a outdated cliché in a world filled with legalized abortions and purple Pontiacs and Frank Sinatra on compact disk. But now I remembered the thing behind Juliette Milo's eyes, and suddenly, I found myself listening more closely to my superstitious sister-in-law.

"You're saying Juliette Milo is a . . . uh, a voodoo priestess?"

"Uh huh. She a woman you don't wanna mess with, Garr. She a bad one."

"Why do you say that?"

"Stories I heard. 'Bout how she come heah from de islands, bringin' de old, wicked ways. She not our kind, Garr. She practice de other ways, the dark ways." Edna held both hands up to the flickering candle, as if warming them. She said, "You stay long, long way from her, you."

After a moment or two of silence, she nodded and led the way back through the tiny cabin. Out on the porch, she said, "Anything I can do for you and Mary Jo?"

"I'll call if I need you."

"Can't call here. They turned de telephone off. Have to call Boudoit's Bait Store down de road. Dey'll come get me. All right?"

"All right."

"Tell Mary Jo I . . . well. You know, you."

"I know."

She was inside the house before I started the car. I followed the raised shell road for almost twenty miles before it intersected with pavement. Barataria Boulevard led me to the West Bank Expressway.

As I drove absentmindedly through the thickening traffic, I thought about what Edna had said about Mary Jo losing her Cajun accent and converting to Christianity. I remembered the day I finally won Mary Jo's heart . . .

• • •

MARY JO PLEADED WITH HER FATHER. "PLEASE, Daddy. I just want us to be together. It would mean so much to me if you would perform the ceremony."

Alphonse Granier said, "You know I can't do that."

We stood in the narrow living room on the second floor of the mission. The Graniers lived simply. The room contained a threadbare sofa, two straight-backed wooden chairs, a bookshelf stocked with *Reader's Digests* and religious paperbacks, and a black and white television on a metal folding table. The yellowed plaster walls were bare, as was the wooden floor. A single frosted bulb hung by a wire from the ceiling, casting stark white light on everything. I stood beside Mary Jo, silently offering support as she pleaded with her father. He sat on the sofa with his legs crossed. He wore rustic leather sandals with tire tread soles, white bell bottom slacks, and a pale orange Nehru jacket. It was difficult to resolve the way the man dressed with the stark simplicity of his lifestyle and the rigid fundamentalism of his beliefs. There were many things that were difficult to resolve about Alphonse Granier.

Mary Jo said, "Don't you want me to be happy?"

His tiny eyes softened. "Little girl, don't ask such questions."

"Then why can't you be happy with me? I love Garr. We want to be together. We want your blessing, and I want you to be the one that marries us."

He looked at me. "Garr, I'm sure if Mary Jo has such strong feelings for you, you must be an unusual fellow. But what you want to do is wrong. Mary Jo can never marry. She was chosen by the Lord for a life of celibacy. A life of service, without the distractions of a carnal relationship. I hope you can understand."

Mary Jo did not let me respond. She said, "We all know what happened. Garr understands. He believes, now, too. We all know why you feel this way. But this is my life, Daddy. I'm the one who must decide what the Lord has in store for me. Can't you see? It's between me and him."

Alphonse Granier rose and crossed to the bookshelf. He selected a Bible and opened it, then turned to face us. "It's all in here, little one. The Lord's Word is clear. The purpose of marriage is procreation. The indulgence of carnal desires for any other reason is a distraction from the Lord's work. A failure. A waste. Read Revelation fourteen four. He has chosen a path for each of us. Yours does not involve motherhood. How could it, when he allowed you to be tested in that way? Therefore, his path for you does not involve marriage. It is very clear."

I was in over my depth. I did not understand any of it. I was not a believer, did not share their concern with pleasing an invisible God I only knew from childhood picture books. But I loved her, and my love was pure. I said, "I don't care about children. We don't have to have children."

"You've missed my point, son. If you can't have children, there is no reason to marry."

She said, "Oh, Daddy. Was having me and Linda the only reason you married Mother?"

"I also hoped to be a father for Edna."

"You didn't marry for love? Didn't you love her?"

He sighed and closed the Bible. "Your mother is a fine woman."

"You didn't answer my question."

"I think I did."

She stared at him. "It's because of what happened, isn't it? You think I owe God something because of what happened."

"We all owe a debt to the Lord. He saved us all. But he saved you in a rare way."

"You think I have a special price to pay, don't you?"

He looked at her, a strange, unsettling look. His eyes conveyed a message I did not understand. He said, "Perhaps we both do, daughter."

"Daddy, I believe I am forgiven. Jesus paid the price for me, because he loves me. And he wants me to be happy."

Her father smiled and tilted his head back to look up at her. Something in the curl of his lips seemed both amused and condescending. She continued, "Jesus knows Garr and I have a true love for each other. It's not based on sex. Not *only* on sex. It's real love, Daddy. I believe Jesus wants men and women to feel this way. I believe he wants us married, with or without children."

The Reverend Alphonse Granier said, "I forbid it."

"No, Daddy. Please. Don't make me choose."

"What you want is sinful in the eyes of God, and I absolutely forbid it. Be careful, child. The terrible thing that happened to you was just a warning. Do not deny the Lord. You have been set apart. Made holy. You may not marry, now or ever."

"But Daddy—"

"No! I will not discuss it further. Satan placed his mark on you and it was only by committing you in special service to the Lord that we were able to remove it. If you choose to disobey me, you dishonor yourself and God, and I will have nothing more to do with you. The choice is yours."

I said, "What's the matter with you? Don't you care about your own children?"

Mary Jo sucked in her breath. Alphonse Granier looked directly at her, snubbing me. He said, "There, you see? His true character surfaces at last. In my own home, in front of my child, he speaks disrespectfully to me, a man of God. How can you consider uniting yourself with him?"

Finally, I could restrain myself no longer. I said, "You take this so-called religion of yours and use it to hurt people. You fill your children's heads with outrageous ideas until they doubt their own sanity. You only care about yourself and your little kingdom here, about using that Bible to treat your family like slaves."

Mary Jo clutched at my arm. "No, Garr."

"Let me finish," I said as I removed her hand and took one step closer to her father. "I don't know much about this . . . this religious thing you're talking about here. But I know how to treat people. And what you're doing . . . what you've *done*, is not right. Do you hear me? It isn't right!"

He stared at me for a moment, as if considering a response. Then he turned to Mary Jo. "The choice is yours, daughter. I love you. But I cannot allow myself to be part of your life if you disobey the Lord."

Without so much as a glance in my direction, he left the room. Mary Jo and I stood in stunned silence, listening to the wooden floorboards creak as he descended the stairs to the mission below. I wanted to follow him. I wanted to beat him to a pulp, to split his impudent lip against his teeth with a stiff right jab. I visualized him pleading for mercy, begging me to stop.

I struggled to control my anger. Perhaps Mary Jo saw my thoughts in my face. She watched me with an expression of sorrow.

In the days since Lucretia Granier led me to the woman in the alley, I had begun to believe what I saw there was an illusion—a trick of the light. To believe anything else meant Mary Jo was in terrible trouble. I did not want to accept the possibility that the solution to her problems lay anywhere but in my heart. What other options were there? A mental hospital? Religious fanaticism like her parents?

I said, "Let's go away together. Now. Tonight. Let's leave this place and never come back."

She remained silent, her eyes searching mine, looking perhaps for something that was not there. I did not yet know the Lord. Possibly it showed. After a moment, she said, "You really think that would be best?"

"Of course. Just you and me. What else matters?"

"Oh, Garr. I hope you know better."

"What does that mean?"

"God's plan matters. It matters much more than you and me. Daddy's right about that much."

"Of course it matters. But I thought we had agreed that our love was part of his plan for us. I mean, since he *is* love . . ."

She interrupted me. "Don't you believe Satan exists, Garr? How can you call yourself a Christian if you don't believe that?"

"I do!"

"Then why can't you believe me when I say he made me pregnant?"

I took her in my arms, and for the second time I struggled to remember every Sunday school lesson, every sermon I had ever heard. I was never attentive in church, because I resented being forced by my parents to attend. But now I regretted those hours of inattention. Who could have known I would need to recall each tired old cliché the preacher uttered in order to court the woman of my dreams? I searched my memory, struggling to dredge up something that would help. Suddenly, a concept came to mind.

"Honey, remember when they accused Jesus of being possessed by the devil? Didn't Jesus say no man can serve two masters?"

"Yes . . ."

"And tell me: are you a Christian or not?"

"Of course I am, Garr!"

"Then how can you believe that Satan could have his way with your body like that?"

It was a good argument. I felt proud of myself for beating her parents at their own game. And as she thought about my point, I felt Mary Jo draw herself closer in my embrace.

Then she whispered, "You're right. I know you're right," and I knew I had her. We kissed passionately. Then she drew back to look up at me, hope and fear combined in her eyes. She said, "How about you, Garr? Before we go on, I have to know. Do you really believe in Jesus?"

I knew that everything depended upon my answer. I could not lose her. I had come so close and knew the misery that awaited me if I lost her now. So I lied.

"Yes, Mary Jo," I said. "I do believe."

Her eyes faltered. In them, I could see a battle between doubt and hope. She searched my face for an answer I did not understand. Then, wonderfully, hope took hold. She nodded once with a look of determination and said, "All right. We'll marry. But give me time to convince Daddy that we're doing right."

Mary Jo and I were married in a civil ceremony by a justice of the peace at the Orleans Parish courthouse. Our wedding took place in a tiny office with dark oak paneling, a cluttered bookshelf, and a single window. The judge stood with his back to the glass, silhouetted against the midday glare. He wore a tie clasp in the shape of a Thompson submachine gun. Deer and wild boar heads peered at us from wooden plaques on the walls. We faced him over the desk. Ernest B. Martin was there, and Mary Jo's older sister, Edna. It was a tight fit for the five of us.

For some reason, as we descended the courthouse steps, hand-in-hand for the first time as man and wife, I remembered the final question she had asked that night in her skid row Mission home. After she had agreed to marry me, we descended the creaky Mission stairs. Suddenly she paused halfway down, standing above me with one hand on each rail of the narrow stairway, her lovely brow knit in confusion.

"What is it, honey?" I asked, looking back.

"Tell me how it happened, then."

"What?"

"How did I get pregnant, Garr? How did it happen?"

I found I had no words.

After a moment, she nodded and said, "Maybe someday God will give me the answer."

And for the next twenty-three years, neither of us mentioned the subject again.

Chapter 33

I STOPPED AT A CONVENIENCE STORE AT THE edge of the city to look up the Slydels' home address in the telephone book. They lived in a section of New Orleans near Magazine. It was not a good neighborhood.

Nobody seemed to post their address out front. I rolled slowly down the Slydels' street, leaning forward to peer up through the windshield at the tall houses on both sides. They stood high on piers with their entries one floor up, remnants of the days when it was best not to trust the levees to hold the Mississippi at bay. Over the years, the residents had added walls and windows between the downstairs piers. The impromptu first floors were finished in a wide variety of materials—everything from plywood to concrete block. None of it matched the original houses, which were uniformly built of whitewashed wood siding with shady front porches accessed by concrete or brick steps. People of all races sat on the steps, chatting to each other, watching their children play in the hard scrabble front yards, drinking from bottles in brown paper sacks and staring at me as I cruised slowly by.

As it happened, I did not need to see the address to find the Slydels' modest home. Faye was on her hands and knees in the yard, planting tulip bulbs. I pulled to the crumbling curb and stepped from the car before she looked up to see who it was. I smiled and waved. She did not return either gesture.

"Hey, Faye. I'll bet you're going to have the best-looking flowers on the block."

Still on her knees, she snorted and said, "They gonna be the *only* flowers on *this* block. You can bet on that."

I looked up and down the street. She was right. Every house in sight had a front yard of concrete or bare dirt. I said, "Nice that you're fixing up the place. Maybe your neighbors will follow your lead."

"Be the first time in seventeen years if they do. What you here for?"

"I was just down at Barataria. Saw a fellow there I think you know."

"What makes you think I know anybody down that way?"

"I saw him at your church yesterday. Big blond fellow. Drives a big pickup. He was putting some kind of cage in the truck bed after the service, while we were talking out front."

"Cage?"

I nodded.

She turned back to the flower bed. Leaning forward, she removed a bulb from a low cardboard box and dropped it into a hole. Her hands were protected by a pair of dirty white cotton gloves. She said, "I don't know anything about no cage."

I stood one step behind her, looking down on her as she worked. "That's all right. I'm more interested in the man. What can you tell me about him?"

"We get a lot of people at our Sunday service. Could've been anybody. Maybe a visitor." Using both hands, she pushed a small pile of loose soil over the shallow hole.

I shook my head. "Nope. I don't figure it that way. A visitor wouldn't be carrying boxes or cages or whatever out of the sanctuary. I figure he's an elder or deacon. An usher at the very least. I figure you know the guy pretty well."

Without turning to look at me, she said, "Okay. Say I do—just for the sake of conversation. What is it about him got you so interested?"

"He was following me."

Faye Slydel lifted a small trowel from the ground beside her knee and began to dig another hole in the flower bed. Glancing around, I noticed several oblong brownish spots on the front steps of her house. They were faded, as if someone had tried to scrub them away.

I said, "Don't you think that's strange? I mean, I saw the guy over at your church on Sunday morning, and on Monday morning I see him fifty miles away in the middle of a swamp. In fact, I see him a couple of times. And he seems real interested in me."

She did not speak.

I went on, "Why was he following me, Faye? Does it have anything to do with the abortion thing? With my wife?"

"I don't know what you're talking about."

"You people are so charged up about this abortion thing . . . I thought maybe you—"

She whirled around, brandishing the trowel like a dagger. "This abortion *thing*? Is that all it is to you? A *thing*?"

"What do you want me to call it?"

"How about murder? Or infanticide if murder is too clear-cut for you."

"Don't you think that's a bit strong?"

With a visible effort, she calmed herself. Turning her back to me she clawed at the earth with a sharp trowel, stabbing it in time with her words. As I watched, several large flies landed on one of the brown spots on her steps.

"Mister Reed, you need to get this through your head: it is murderers we're fightin' against. The facts is simple. You can't argue with 'em."

"Tell me about it."

She did not respond. I thought she had not heard me, but then she began speaking in a strange, distant voice. The silken sweetness of her Southern accent somehow underscored the horror of what she said.

"A two-week-old embryo is large enough to see with the naked eye. The heart, lungs, intestines, and brains is developin' by the end of the sixth week. Most women don't even know for a fact that they're pregnant after six weeks. Give 'em six more weeks and the embryo's got arms, legs, eyes, just about everything. I seen pictures. A baby that's only twelve weeks along is just that: a baby."

She selected another bulb and gently placed it in the hole. In her hands, the bulb seemed like a small treasure. I could tell she loved what she was doing, loved the soil, and loved to be playing her small part in the continuing cycle of life. Beside her on the ground was a paper bag. She lifted it and carefully shook a bit of yellow powder over the bulb. When she looked up at me, her eyes squinted as if against the sun's glare, yet her face was in shadow. She pressed the back of her right wrist against her eye, rubbing the cleanest part of her cotton glove against the eyelid. A fly landed on her glove. I glanced over at the steps. The brown stains were completely covered by a shimmering black mass—hundreds of flies, drawn to the stains. She said, "They call 'em embryos until they's 'viable.' That's doctor talk for able to live on their own, maybe. They have a heartbeat you can hear by twenty weeks. One in ten babies that is miscarried or aborted during the second trimester could live with proper care. We tried to get the right to incubate aborted babies, to give them that chance at least, but the government said no. It's an invasion of the mother's *privacy*." She curled her lip around the last word, as if it tasted bitter.

"The government lets them murderers suck them out, or cut them out, or flood them out. I seen what they do to them babies. Some of them four and five pounds or more, with hair and eyes and tiny little fingers and toes . . ."

She began jabbing at the earth as she spoke, digging another hole. Each word was accompanied by a vicious blow. "They cut them up while they's still inside, or use a vacuum to suck the body parts out. Nobody likes to hear it said that way, but that's exactly what they do." Her trowel unearthed a grub worm. It glistened pale and white against the black dirt. She laid the trowel aside and plucked the grub from the soil. Holding it between her thumb and first finger, a few inches above the ground, she said, "Little arms and legs, heads and ribcages, sliced into pieces and sucked up and dumped into plastic bags like so much rubbish." She squeezed, and the grub worm burst, its glistening sides erupting with a tiny stream of mucus.

Again, she looked up at me. This time her eyes were opened wide and her cheeks awash with tears. "How can a woman let them do that? These babies ain't *tissue*. They ain't *cells*. By the time most girls decide to do it, their babies have heartbeats! They can *move!* They can see and hear! I can show you sonograms at fourteen weeks of so-called *embryos* sucking their thumbs! One minute this baby is safe in the womb, sucking its thumb, and the next it's chopped to bits and tossed into a garbage bag. How can you wonder if it's murder? How can you say the word *murder* is a little bit strong? What kind of Christian are you?"

I looked away, deeply disturbed by her tears and fierce question. What kind of Christian was I, after all? She was right about one thing: no Christian could condone murder, of course. But was it murder?

Was she right about the state of a human embryo? Did they really suck their thumbs at fourteen weeks?

And if that was true, why didn't the whole world know?

I thought of the group of women at the hospital, standing in support of abortion, faces tight with anger. Their fanatical feminist reputation preceded them. Foolish notions like deleting male pronouns from the English language and inflicting unisex rest rooms on the public did nothing for their credibility on abortion. But were the anti-abortion crowd any more believable? When the press showed video of angry mobs shouting at physicians, obstructing the sidewalks outside their homes, plastering their neighborhoods with grotesque posters of bloody babies and burning doctors in effigy, I couldn't help the negative associations that came to mind, of wild-eyed hippies defacing the Stars and Stripes, burning draft cards, and staging sit-ins on the university steps. Could I really trust the words of people who used those tactics?

And now this woman was questioning my faith. If I did not burn with an urgency to oppose abortion that matched her own, was I less of a Christian? Bodies floated to the sea every day in Guatemala, tortured victims of a brutal regime supported by American tax dollars just as surely as our American law supported abortion. But I had never heard a sermon preached on that subject. Should I then question my pastor's faith?

If Faye was right, if we were aborting fetal human beings even as they sucked their thumbs, was it a Christian issue, or did it concern everyone? Must one be religious to oppose abortion? Must one be a radical feminist to support it? I didn't trust fanatics of any kind, no matter what their cause. So how could I trust Faye's information? How could I know what was true?

And then, for the first time, it struck me that babies might be dying because the religious agenda of fanatics like Faye Slydel blurred the truth for Jews and Buddhists and atheists and agnostics. Were they afraid of her fanatical demand that faith be connected with the choice for life? Was it our own religious fervor that kept them from joining us at the picket lines?

"Suffer the little children to come unto me . . ."

"What kind of Christian are you?"

Was *this* how we served Christ?

Across the street, a small woman watched us from an elevated porch. Mildew stained the peeling white paint on the square columns to her left and right. Banana trees rose from the bare dirt of her front yard, trembling in the breeze, blocking her face from view, then lifting to reveal her casual stare again. As I watched, she bent and lifted a child from the floor, setting it in her lap. Her head bowed over the baby for a moment. Then in a fluid practiced movement, she raised her white T-shirt, exposed her left breast, and lifted the baby to suckle. She seemed to whisper to the child, then she turned her head and her eyes met mine. I saw no interest in her gaze, no acknowledgment that she had just exposed herself to me. I swatted my neck and smashed two house flies.

Still holding the trowel, Faye Slydel said, "What should we do? What would you do if someone threatened a baby with a knife? Answer me! What would you do?"

I said, "It's different."

"*Why?* Because the child is not protected by the skin of a mother's belly? Don't that seem strange to you—that it's safer outside in this evil world than in the body of its own mother? How can a Christian man say that?"

Faye Slydel's eyes were too much for me. I looked away again. The woman on the porch across the street gently rocked back and forth as she suckled her child. The cool autumn breeze parted the banana leaves and I saw a liquor bottle on the floor beside the woman's feet. She bent and lifted it. Her throat moved as she swallowed the amber fluid. I thought of the liquor passing through her body into the mouth of the baby at her breast. There was too much evil in the world to fight it all. I could only deal with my share. Surely that was work enough to please Christ.

I said, "I still want to know why that man was following me."

Faye Slydel stared at me for half a minute, her eyes full of an emotion I could not identify. Perhaps it was disgust. Then she said, "We want to help you."

"Help me? Help me how?"

"We want to help you find your wife."

Involuntarily, I took a half step closer. "Do you know where she is?"

"No. Not yet."

"Not *yet?* That sounds like you think you can find her!"

"We can find her."

I dropped to my knees and clutched her upper arm. She winced at the force of my grip, but I did not notice. I spoke through clenched teeth. "You explain yourself to me. *Now!*"

With her eyes locked on mine, she said, "Let go of my arm. You're hurting me."

I released her. "I'm sorry. You have to understand how it's been . . . I don't know what I'm doing half the time. I don't know what to do."

"That's all right. I guess I don't blame you for being upset." She rubbed her upper arm with a gloved hand and searched my eyes. For the first time, I thought I saw compassion in her gaze. "We can help you, Mister Reed. But you got to let us do it our way. We got good reasons."

"What do you want me to do?"

"There's an old parking garage a few blocks west of the Hotel Provincial. The old D.H. Holmes garage. Do you know it?"

I remembered the garage where the towing service had left Mary Jo's Volvo. Was this coincidence? Surely not.

"I know it."

"Be there tonight at ten. Go to the top level. Wait beside the elevator doors up there. We'll get in touch with you."

"You keep saying 'we.' Who else are you talking about? Your husband?"

She turned her back to me again, knelt, and resumed digging in her tiny flower bed. Again, I was struck by the tender care she gave to her task. "Just be at the garage at ten. Don't be early and don't be late." Several flies landed on the back of her blouse. "We ain't gonna give you two chances, so make sure you're there tonight. Wait by the elevator up on top, like I said. We'll explain everything then. Now go on back to your hotel and wait. Maybe take a little nap. You look to me like you could use some sleep."

I walked to the car, dusting the soil from my trousers. The banana leaves obscured the woman and her child across the street. As I drove away, depression seeped into my mind, numbing it like whisky, straight from the bottle. Was Faye right about my faith? Was I only fooling myself? Why did I feel this hesitancy about joining her cause? I placed such urgency on helping Mary Jo, probably for selfish reasons, yet I had never given the slaughter of the unborn a second thought. I wasn't even sure it was true. What kind of Christian *was* I?

Was I a Christian at all?

My spiritual doubts were so disturbing, I was halfway to the French Quarter before I realized there was one other question I should have asked.

How did Faye Slydel know that Mary Jo was missing?

Chapter 34

I SAT ON THE BED IN THE HOTEL PROVINCIAL, watching through the open window as the colors changed over Algiers. The roofs of the warehouses and wharves on the far side of the river faded to a uniform gray, their jagged silhouettes clutching at the edges of the heavens. The clouds were awash with the colors of passion and anger. Beyond the clouds, the cool turquoise of the open sky remained aloof, graciously surrendering to the moon and stars. And below everything, the unrelenting Mississippi glowed like a lava flow, black ripples crisscrossing the hot red reflection, binding it like a net, carrying the cargo of dying lights slowly south to the Gulf of Mexico.

Man played his part in the evening's performance. A tugboat crawled upstream, dragging a vee-shaped wake of darkness through the burning river. I heard the streets of the Vieux Carre begin to awaken. The calls of demons and saints rose from the ancient pavement below, as they had every night for three hundred years. A male voice screamed unintelligibly in the distance. Car horns roared at the impracticality of driving through streets designed for horse-drawn carriages. A trio struck up an impromptu jazz concert below my open window; a ragged saxophone, acoustic guitar, and string bass playing *Basin Street Blues*. The sassy melody was a perfect counterpoint to the majestic sunset and the irreverent stirrings of the French Quarter. It captured my attention, drawing me into the ebb and flow of the antique notes, concealing the sound of the pass key in the lock until it was too late.

They flung the door open and charged in with handguns drawn. In less than a second, three of them were in the room; two covering me with their weapons while the third entered the bathroom. They were big men, dressed like steel workers at a wedding, in ill-fitting plaid sports coats, open-collared white shirts, and porkpie hats. Before I could speak, Lieutenant Washington entered from the hall. He was half their size and obviously in control.

The third man emerged from the bathroom. Lieutenant Washington caught his eye. The man shook his head.

The Lieutenant said, "All right, Mister Reed. Where's your wife?"

"I don't know."

He glanced at one of the men standing over me and said, "Do it."

The man gestured with his gun. "Stand up."

With my eyes on the gun, I rose from the side of the bed.

"Put both your hands on that wall."

I turned my back to him and did as he said. He pressed his palm between my shoulder blades, hooked my ankles with his size thirteen wingtips, and kicked my legs back one at a time, until most of my weight pressed against the wall. I felt practiced hands flutter over my body; slapping my armpits, sliding along my chest and down the small of my back, quickly passing over my groin, down each thigh, and across my shins and calves to my ankles.

Lincoln Washington said, "Turn around."

I faced him and said, "I must be under arrest."

He flashed a smile. "Lucky guess?"

"Can I call my lawyer?"

"At the station. Cuff him."

The one who frisked me said, "Put your hands behind your back." I stared at Lincoln Washington as the big man slapped the handcuffs around my wrists. He returned my stare, a casual interest in his expression. One of the other two men began reciting my Miranda rights, reading from a three-by-five note card.

When the detective finished reading, Lincoln Washington said, "You understand all that, Mister Reed?"

"Yes."

"Good. Here's the situation: we asked the sheriff back in that little town of yours to find your wife. 'Cause if she's up there, then of course she can't be the one who almost killed Mrs. Milo down here.

But it seems she ain't around, and we got a problem with that, her being a murder suspect and all."

"How did he know she wasn't there? Maybe she just didn't come to the door."

"I'll ask the questions if you don't mind." He walked to the window and stared out at the lingering sunset. The last of the light glistened on his golden earring. Two of the three policemen watched his every move. One kept his eyes on me.

Washington said, "You tell me where she is, I can let you go right now, Mister Reed. Otherwise, I got to take you down for aiding and abetting."

"I don't know where she is."

Still looking out across the river, he said, "My people built this town. We piled that ground up along the river to hold the Mississippi back from the white folks' homes. We laid the brick in their streets. We plowed their land and picked their cotton for two hundred years. They whipped us and raped us and kept us ignorant and hungry. They forced us to learn their language and worship their god. Sometimes they murdered us, although that didn't happen often. You don't kill your livestock for no good reason." He turned to stare at me, allowing a silence to build in the room. He was dressed in an immaculate gray suit, like a man going to church. Or a funeral. "But the worst thing, the absolute worst thing they did to my people was to break up our families. Husbands and wives traded to different plantations. Children sold to city folks while their parents stayed in the fields."

One of the white policemen said, "Hey Link, what is this?"

Without taking his eyes off of me, Lincoln Washington said, "Shut up, Benny. I'm making a point here."

I said, "What point is that, Lieutenant?"

"My great grandmother was born a slave, Mister Reed. Nobody knows the importance of family better than the descendant of a slave. I understand what your wife did—why she did it—better than most. I wanted you to know that."

"She didn't kill that priest. It's a mistake."

"I still got to find her. Now, let's get on down to the station where we can talk without distractions."

The one he called Benny closed a hand like a vise grip around my upper arm and said, "Let's go." He led me out to the hall with Lincoln

Washington close behind. The other two stayed in the room. An elderly couple emerged from the tiny elevator when it stopped on our floor. They glanced at us. The friendly interest in their eyes faded to a neutral mask when they realized I was a prisoner. They hurried down the hall toward their room as we stepped into the elevator. It was a tight fit. Benny's stale breath was hot against my neck, his hand solidly around my arm. On the ground floor, we marched along the narrow hall and out to the parking lot.

The old buildings of the Hotel Provincial cluster around a central court paved with asphalt. Waiting for the large policeman to unlock the Crown Victoria, I felt as if someone stood at every window in the two- and three-story buildings around us, staring out at the handcuffs binding my wrists. I felt ashamed.

Lieutenant Washington sat in the front passenger seat and Benny drove. I had the backseat to myself. I leaned forward to avoid pressing my weight against my hands. The interior of the squad car smelled like a sickroom, lemon-scented disinfectant against an undertone of last week's vomit.

The hip-roofed Acadian cottages of the eastern half of the Quarter crawled by as we inched through the traffic. Men and women strolled the sidewalks carrying beers and frozen daiquiris in plastic cups. They wore shorts and newly purchased souvenir T-shirts with messages printed across their chests. *I Got Sleazy in the Big Easy*. The crowd grew thicker as we headed west. Benny muttered under his breath when a mule-drawn carriage turned the corner and cut in front of us. The carriage driver said something and his passengers laughed. The car's headlights picked out the name of the carriage company, "The Gay 90's," painted in flowery cursive script on a lacquered wooden panel behind the laughing tourists.

I said, "Can I crack a window back here? It stinks."

Lieutenant Washington said, "Windows don't open in back. Do like we do. Breathe through your mouth."

As we drew near the west end of the Quarter, the revelry intensified. Dixieland jazz spilled through the open doorways of bars, so loud it penetrated the glass of the car. Neon signs advertised everything from Two Dollar Hurricanes to Live Nude Girls. The promise of debauchery was everywhere, dangling in the air like overripe fruit. Pale-skinned tourists from Iowa and Wisconsin wandered between the doorways, tempted at every turn to stray from the straight and narrow, to accept the serpent's offering just once, there in that exotic garden so unlike home, so far from friends and family. Do it. You know you always wanted to. Who would know? Eat from the tree of knowledge.

History repeats itself.

Lieutenant Lincoln Washington said, "You think Oswald acted alone?"

The words penetrated my thoughts, settling down to the present like a pebble sinking to the bottom of a pool.

"'Cause Benny here, he thinks the Cubans were in on it. Don't you, Benny?"

The big man nodded. "Yep. It was the spics all right. Them and the wops was in it together."

Lincoln Washington said, "What do you think, Mister Reed?"

"I . . . uh. I don't know. Are you talking about Kennedy?"

"Well, sure." The lieutenant laid his left arm along the top of the front seat and twisted to look at me. The gray wool of his suit coat sleeve slid back to expose a large gold cuff link, a cluster of tiny nuggets with a diamond in the center. The stone had to be two karats. I wondered if it was real. He did not seem like the kind of man who would wear costume jewelry.

I said, "I guess he was probably alone."

The lieutenant shook his head. "See, that's where you're wrong. I've seen the trajectory analysis. There's no way he fired the second shot. It had to be a conspiracy."

We rode in silence for a moment, then I said, "To tell you the truth, I couldn't care less."

Benny laughed, a single bark that filled the car and was gone in an instant. Washington looked back at me. He said, "Funny. I would have thought you'd be real interested in conspiracies, Mister Reed."

"Why would you think that?"

His eyes searched mine; soft, brown, and interested. Then, apparently satisfied with what he saw, he turned toward the front again. I stared at the back of his head. His barber had cut the hair across the nape of his neck in a ruler-straight line, an inch above his crisp shirt collar.

I said, "What did you mean about conspiracies?"

"Just passing the time of day, Mister Reed. You sit back now. Relax and enjoy the ride."

Benny laughed again, a sudden explosion, over in a second. I shifted my stare to him. Rolls of fat creased his freckle-dotted neck. His porkpie hat clung to the back of his head like a straw halo. The front brim brushed against the fabric ceiling of the car. He hunched forward as he drove, looming over the steering wheel, making it look tiny beneath his massive hands. Behind my back, the handcuffs bit into my skin. I adjusted my position. With my right leg cocked up on the seat, I found I could rest my shoulder against the seat back and reduce the pressure on my wrists. I stared through the side window as we left the Vieux Carre and turned right on Canal, wondering what Lincoln Washington had meant. It occurred to me that I was going to miss my appointment at the parking garage with Faye Slydel. It occurred to me—for the first time—that I might never see Mary Jo again.

Chapter

35

THE BIG BLACK HANDS ON THE WALL CLOCK moved too fast. I sat beside Lieutenant Washington's desk and watched them pass from six-thirty to seven, thinking of Faye Slydel, up to her elbows in soil, offering answers, promising to lead me to Mary Jo.

"We want to help you find your wife."

Washington lounged with his right shoulder toward me, using the first finger of each hand to punch at a computer keyboard. He had draped his suit coat neatly on a hanger behind the door when we entered. He wore leather braces and a starched Oxford shirt with French cuffs, diamond cuff links, and a finely woven paisley silk tie. Plus the earring. For the fifth or sixth time, he said, "Why did you come to New Orleans, Mister Reed?"

I sighed and absentmindedly twisted the steel eyebolt that was screwed into the side of the ancient wooden desk. He had fastened one end of the handcuffs to the bolt when we first arrived at the squad room. The other end still encircled my right wrist. "I gave my mother-in-law a ride home."

"Did you give your wife a ride, too?"

I gave the eye bolt another twist. "No. When can I call my lawyer?"

"In a minute. I'm just trying to get a few of the basics down on paper. What's your phone number at home and work?"

I told him. When he turned to the computer screen, I twisted the eyebolt again. With each twist of the bolt, I rotated the cuff around my wrist to avoid kinking the chain. The bolt was almost out of the wood. I was desperate to find a way to meet with Faye Slydel. Her promise resonated in my mind, the importance of it overshadowing my arrest: "*We can find her.*"

Lincoln Washington stared at the computer screen. "Home address?"

His fingers slowly poked the keys as I answered his question. "Does your wife have any friends down here? People who agree with her viewpoint on abortion?"

"Not that I know of."

"How 'bout back home?"

"We have a lot of friends in Mount Sinai."

"Any of them feel like she does?"

"About abortion? Sure. Most of the people in our church, I guess."

"Where do you go to church, Mister Reed?"

I answered. He typed.

He said, "Can you think of anyone there who might have an . . . uh . . . Old Testament point of view on abortion? Eye for an eye kind of thing?"

"Are you trying to come up with another suspect?"

He looked at me but remained silent. I said, "There may be some people back home who think violence is all right in that situation, Lieutenant. I am not one of them. Neither is my wife."

"Who is? Give me some names."

"How would I know? It's not the kind of thing you talk about at church. At least not our church."

"And outside the church? Barbecues? Softball games? Anybody bring it up? Get mad about it? Make threats?"

I thought, *He's trying to help us.* I searched my memory. I remembered Lucretia Granier, standing in my kitchen, shaking her fist at me and Pedro Comacho.

"*It's a wonder to me that my girl had the strength to do what she did, burdened down by cowards and foreigners.*"

But I could not give her name to the police. Not yet. Harsh and bitter as she was, she was still Mary Jo's mother.

I said, "We don't associate with people like that."

He stared at me, something flashing in his eyes. Impatience, perhaps. "Did you know someone down here tried to shoot that doctor? Before he moved to Texas?"

I leaned forward. "Who?"

"If we knew that, you might not be sitting here."

"Do the police in Mount Sinai know about it?"

"Of course."

"Then why don't they try to find that person instead of going after Mary Jo?"

"What makes you think the killer wasn't your wife?"

"Isn't that obvious? We don't live here."

"She was here at the time."

I thought of the trips to New Orleans, the strange moods she brought home. I said, "How could you possibly know that?"

Lieutenant Washington returned his attention to the computer screen. "We know, Mister Reed. She's been down here a lot lately."

"Her mother's been sick. She's been coming down to check up on her mother."

He said, "Mrs. Lucretia Granier. A significant financial supporter of Christ's Holy Army Resisting God's Enemies—C.H.A.R.G.E."

"So that's what it stands for."

He typed something without answering. I said, "She didn't do it, Lieutenant. She's a gentle person. She believes in forgiveness and the power of love. Sounds corny, I know, but she really thinks that way."

"Maybe you're right, Mister Reed. But your wife was here, and she had a better reason than most to kill the doctor."

"Reason? What reason could she possibly have? She didn't even know the man."

"Now, that's not true. Your wife has known Melvin Milo for years."

"Known him? What do you mean?"

He stared at me silently, searching my eyes, accessing me. Then he seemed to make a decision. "You sure you want me to tell you?"

"Of course."

"All right. Can't see any harm in it. Did you know Mrs. Reed had an abortion when she was thirteen or fourteen years old?

I said, "She was older than that."

"Forget how old she was! The point is, she had an abortion, and Melvin Milo was the abortionist."

I stared at the stainless steel bracelet around my wrist. It lay sleek and hard against my flesh. Doctor Milo. I should have known. *Milo* was her doctor when she lived down here. Milo did the abortion. It fit. I hated that it fit so well. I remembered the words of the Jackson

County District Attorney as he pointed at Mary Jo: *"There were more personal issues at stake here ... this was a premeditated crime with roots in the defendant's shrouded past."*

I said, "Do your records show that she was probably raped? I mean, if it wasn't for Dr. Milo, she might have had a baby by the monster who raped her when she was just a child herself. Milo did her a favor. A big one, too, since abortions weren't legal back then, were they?"

"No, sir, they were not. Except when the pregnancy threatened the life of the mother."

"So how did you find out about it? You didn't find it in any hospital records."

"I suppose I can tell you that. Doctor Milo remembered your wife. He admitted performing the abortion."

"Then he must have told you about the extenuating circumstances. About the rape. The amnesia."

The policeman looked at me with a question in his dark brown eyes. "Our records do show there was a rape. It was reported to us and investigated."

"There. You see? Why would Mary Jo resent the doctor when it was him that helped to get her out of that mess?"

"It wasn't your wife who was raped, Mister Reed."

"What? Of course she was raped. How else would she get pregnant?"

"If she was, she didn't report it to us."

"Then, who was it?"

Without rising from his chair, he leaned to the side and fished a set of keys from his pants pocket. He swiveled to face a row of filing cabinets and used a key to unlock the nearest drawer. When he had removed a file and swung around to face the desk again, his keys remained hanging from the cabinet. He flipped open the manila file, and lifting several papers one by one, he scanned the typewritten forms. His lips moved as he read. He followed the text with the index finger of his left hand. The diamonds on his ring twinkled in the cold blue fluorescent light. He said, "Here it is. The complaint filed concerned an L. G., minor female, Caucasian, age fifteen." He looked up at me and continued, "Back then, we kept the full name of minors private. I'd have to look in a sealed file over at the parish building to get her given name."

I said, "Linda. Her name was Linda Granier. She was Mary Jo's younger sister. She died."

He glanced at the report. "Oh, yeah. Says that here. Victim perished. No arrest made." He glanced at me. "What happened there?"

"She bled to death in her bed at home after the rape."

He shook his head. "Shame. Terrible shame, way these things come back to haunt you."

"So you're saying Mary Jo shot Doctor Milo because of this . . . this thing? This thing that happened twenty years ago?"

"Sometimes abortions leave women with a deep-seated guilt, Mister Reed. I've been reading up on it. There are studies. Medical reports. Some women never really get over an abortion. Psychologically, I mean. Some women blame themselves. Some blame the man that got them pregnant. Some blame the doctor."

"So you're thinking revenge? After *twenty years?* You're reaching, Lieutenant."

"Maybe. But we got to cover all the bases."

"Lieutenant, she is a gentle person. You've just got to believe that."

"I hope you're right, Mister Reed. I really hope so."

"Listen. Say I was right. Say she was *your* wife and they were trying to do this to her and you knew she couldn't have done what they said. What would you do?"

"Find out who tried to kill the doctor and killed the priest."

"Where would you start?"

"The usual places. Motive and opportunity. Who else could have done it? Who else might have wanted to?"

I sat silently, considering his point. After a moment, he said, "Well? You got any thoughts on that?"

"What?"

"Do you know anybody else with a reason to kill Doctor Milo?"

I looked down at the band around my wrist. Again I thought about Lucretia. She could have done it. Lucretia was in Mount Sinai when I brought Mary Jo home from jail. How could she have known so fast? When did Lucretia arrive in Mount Sinai? Was she there before the murder? Was she there when it happened? Lucretia Granier was filled with hate. Hate for abortionists, for women who had abortions, for anyone who disagreed with her viewpoint on abortion. She might have the hardness of heart it would take to commit murder. But could I set the police on her? Would Mary Jo forgive me for that?

And Faye Slydel. She was in both places, too. I remembered her words. *"We can help you, Mister Reed. But you got to let us do it our way. We got good reasons."* I would not mention Faye Slydel. Not until I knew if she could really help me find Mary Jo.

I said, "How about that nurse? The one who works with Doctor Milo?"

He nodded. "Elizabeth Harmony. Yep, she was my first choice, too. But it wasn't her."

"How do you know that?"

"Your sheriff did a paraffin test on her right after the shootings. She came up negative."

"Paraffin test?"

"It's a way to test for residual cordite, from the gunpowder in the cartridge when you fire a weapon."

"Couldn't she fake it? Couldn't the test be wrong?"

"Sure. But I don't think it was. Your sheriff seems to run a pretty tight ship up there. I imagine he knows how to get around the test, and allowed for that." He leaned back in the chair and put his fingertips together. His fingernails were coated with clear polish. He said, "I was thinking more along the lines of someone you knew, maybe a friend of your wife's or an associate that worked with her in an anti-abortion campaign . . . someone like that."

In desperation, I offered the only person I could, the only other woman who was in New Orleans and Mount Sinai with Melvin Milo. I said, "How about Juliette Milo? Don't you always start with the victim's family? She looks a lot like my wife, especially from the back."

He turned his eyes toward the ceiling for a moment, then dropped them back down to me. "If it was Juliette Milo, who was that woman you saw running from her house the other day? Who fired those shots at Mrs. Milo?"

I remembered the woman in the hall. Auburn hair, Mary Jo's length. Mary Jo's shade. The police had the chrome-plated .32 that she dropped on the kitchen floor. Was there any way they could prove the automatic belonged to Mary Jo? Maybe there were fingerprints on the gun. They had Mary Jo's fingerprints in Mount Sinai, from when they arrested her. They would think of that.

I said, "Did you find fingerprints on that pistol? The one on the kitchen floor at the Milo's house?"

"Mister Reed, I'm not going to answer a question like that. But if you'll share your thoughts on this thing, if there's anything you want me to know about the murder, or the assault the other day at the Milo's house, anything that might steer me in the right direction, you should tell me now."

I stared at him for a moment, making up my mind. Then I said, "When can I call my lawyer?"

He let out a short, disgusted sigh. Pushing away from the desk, he said, "Have it your way. I'm going to the john while you talk. Give you and your lawyer some privacy." He walked behind me. He stopped. I was afraid he would see the eye bolt, almost loose from the wood. He leaned over my shoulder. His earring glinted against his chocolate skin. My heart rate quickened. He spoke close to my ear.

"I have a little sister. She's twenty-two and married. No kids. Last year, she got pregnant. They wanted to fix up the spare bedroom, but didn't know if they should paint it pink or baby blue, so they had a sonogram to find out. It was a baby girl. But it had a tumor growing in its head. The thing was almost as big as its brain, and getting bigger. They said it would kill her—my sister, I mean. The baby was already dead for all practical purposes.

"So they prayed about it. My little sister is a very religious person. So's her husband. They prayed and cried and finally decided that the Lord wouldn't want her to die for the sake of a child that might not live itself."

His breath was hot on my neck. He continued, "I helped them make that decision. They asked for my advice and I gave it. So they picked a place—it wasn't the Milo Clinic. It was another one. And they went over there for her abortion, crying all the way. I drove them myself.

"It was one of those lousy coincidences, I guess. Or maybe God playing a practical joke. But anyway, that clinic was surrounded by demonstrators when we arrived. We didn't know who they were until we were in the middle of them. Then a woman called out my sister's name."

He stood up straight, his voice much softer now. "They were from her church. Imagine that. And they screamed at her as I led her in. They called her a murderess. They said she was murdering her baby. That she was possessed by a demon.

"They had no idea. The pain she already felt, the way her heart was breaking. And now, my sister and her husband won't go near that church—or any church."

He reached across and pulled the old black telephone closer to my side of the desk and said, "I thought you should hear another side of it. Dial nine for an outside line."

I watched him cross the room and exit through a battered steel door. There were three other desks in the squad room. A young detective slumped behind one of the desks, mumbling into a telephone. He was dark skinned, with shiny black hair piled high above his forehead. The walls were covered with faded photocopies of official notices, taped to the cheap wood-grain paneling. The ceiling sagged in several places, stained with water marks. None of the desks matched. Piles of paper buried the desktops, some neatly stacked, some haphazardly strewn across the blotters. I picked up the telephone handset and punched Winston Graves's number.

The phone rang ten times with a comforting antique rattle that reminded me of my childhood. I was about to hang up when his voice came across the line.

"Yes?"

"Winston, it's Garr. Guess where I am."

"At a substation of the New Orleans Police Department."

"How did you ...? Never mind. You're right, of course. They arrested me about an hour ago. They know Mary Jo is gone. They think I know where she is. That I've helped her to run. That I'm hiding her."

I heard a hissing sound, followed by an abrupt cough. Winston was having his after-dinner cigar. He said, "Their allegations are untrue, of course."

I sighed. "I wish I *did* know where she is, Winston."

"Indeed. I assume you require my assistance in posting bail?"

I watched the young lieutenant finish his phone conversation and leave the room. The clock on the wall read seven fifteen. I remembered Faye Slydel's words, "*We ain't gonna give you another chance, so be sure you're there.*"

"Can you get me out of here by nine-thirty tonight?"

"Garrison, that is impossible. But their case for aiding and abetting is quite weak. To sustain a conviction, they must demonstrate that you knowingly associated with a criminal venture, participated in the venture, and sought by action to make the venture succeed. I assume they have no proof of this. With luck, I shall obtain your freedom by tomorrow afternoon."

"In that case, don't bother."

"Don't bother? Do you mean you will not require my assistance?"

Faye Slydel's voice whispered in my mind, *"Don't be early and don't be late."* I said, "No. That won't be necessary."

"Won't be . . ."

"Listen, Winston, I've only got a second or two. I need you to do something for me."

"If I can."

"See if you can find someone who had a reason to kill Doctor Milo. Ask around town. Get Leon Martinez and Ethyl Polanski to help. Also, they tell me someone tried to kill Dr. Milo down here before the shooting in Texas. See if you can find out when that was, and look for people from Mount Sinai who were here at the time."

"Intriguing, Garrison. Of course, I shall be pleased to be of assistance, but it may require significant time . . ."

"Remember to get Leon Martinez to help. And Mrs. P."

"Very well. Is there anything else?"

I twisted the eye bolt again. It came loose from the desk.

I said, "No. I've got to go now."

Chapter 36

THERE IS A STORY IN THE BIBLE ABOUT THE easiest prison break ever made. I'm not sure where to find it. Maybe in the book of Acts.

The apostle Peter was being held in a Roman dungeon, waiting for his day in court. By all accounts, his time on earth was destined to be cut short by the Emperor Nero. Angels woke him in the wee hours and led him from the prison. Every guard they passed was sound asleep. Every gate they reached unlocked itself and swung open, pushed by the hand of God. Peter strolled across town and presented himself at the door of a local Christian family. The disciples within the house were so astonished to hear his voice, they forgot at first to open the door to him.

The ease of my escape was perhaps second only to Peter's, in that I was forced to open my own doors.

With the handcuffs and the eyebolt dangling from my right wrist, I slipped around Lieutenant Washington's desk and removed the key ring he had left hanging from the filing cabinet. As I hoped, the key to the handcuffs was on the ring. I left both keys and cuffs on his desk and hurried across the empty room. With a quick prayer for deliverance, I cracked the door an inch and peeked out to the hall. It was empty. I glanced back at the desk. My wallet, rental car keys, and pocket knife lay on the desk in a paper envelope beside the computer. I closed the door, hurried back across the room, and collected my things. Heavy footsteps approached along the hall outside. I dropped into the chair beside the desk, turning my back to the door. It began to open. I stared at the handcuffs lying on the desk. Should I try to put them back on? Too late. Whoever was coming would surely see me if I tried. Better to hope for a miracle . . .

Before the door was completely open, I heard a distant voice call from down the hall, "Harry, you forget about that B and E hearing tonight, or what?"

Behind me, the man cursed and said, "Why didn't you remind me?"

"What do ya think I'm doin', ya big ox?"

I heard the latch click as the door shut again. After waiting perhaps half a minute, I rose and went to the door. Peeking out, I saw that the hall was empty again. It was now or never.

I slipped outside and hurried down the hall. At the end was a set of stairs. A hour before, I had climbed them with Lieutenant Washington's hand on my elbow. They led down to a large room filled with police and civilians; a bull pen where officers conducted the day-to-day business of their profession. I paused at the top of the stairs to listen. Voices surged up the stairwell. I descended to the intermediate landing and stopped. Stopping was a mistake, since it gave me time to think. What was I doing? Was this the right thing to do? If they caught me, they would add attempted escape to the aiding and abetting charges. It might mean no bail, no release until my trial. I could rot in jail for months, with Mary Jo on the outside, beyond my help. It was not too late to return to the chair in the squad room. Winston Graves would have me out by noon tomorrow.

But Faye Slydel had said they would give no second chances. And something, perhaps an angel of my own, seemed to whisper that I must not miss the ten o'clock meeting at the parking garage. Not if I wanted to see Mary Jo again.

Breathing deeply to settle my pounding heart, I raised my chin and walked down the final flight of stairs.

The squad room pulsed with activity. As I reached the bottom step, a uniformed policeman escorted a row of handcuffed women up the stairs past me. The women wore very revealing outfits. I turned away from them without making eye contact. One of the women said, "Hey there, honey. Whatcha doin' afterwards?"

"Aw, shutup, Wanda," said the policeman.

"I's just bein' friendly, Officer Wilson."

The policeman's friendly Irish face was set in a broad grin. "Sorry, mister. Some of 'em can't seem to stop working, ya know?"

I glanced at him. "Got the same problem myself sometimes."

Chuckling, the policeman led his charges up the stairs. Focusing my eyes on the filthy tile floor a few feet ahead, I strode along the aisle, passing between scarred wooden desks occupied by uniformed and plainclothed policemen and women. Those who were not interviewing a victim or a suspect were intent upon their computer screens or speaking on the telephone. Ceiling fans revolved lazily beneath the antique tin ceiling, doing nothing to dispel the cigarette smoke hanging in thin layers above the room like wispy clouds in a bleak winter sky. Phones clamored everywhere. A man on the far side of the room burst out laughing. Someone called a woman's name over and over, "Cynthia Travis? Cynthia Travis? Cynthia Travis?"

Only the sergeant in the bullet-proof glass cubical beside the exit seemed to notice me. She smiled and nodded and pushed a large red button on the wall. A buzzer sounded. I pushed open the door and stepped through. Her eyes followed me as I crossed the narrow vestibule. The ten-foot walk seemed to take ten minutes. At any moment I expected someone to stop me. As I reached the pair of outside doors, the last barrier to freedom, I saw two uniformed policewomen climbing the steps outside. I opened the right-hand door and held it for them. The first one stared at me hard as she stepped through, a flicker of doubt or suspicion in her eyes. The second one smiled and said, "Thank you." I returned her smile but remained silent. My heart pounded too much to speak.

Outside, the night was cool, yet muggy; a contradiction I have only experienced in New Orleans. But New Orleans is awash with contradictions. I turned to the right and strode along the trash-strewn sidewalk, hands in the pockets of my blue jeans. Police cruisers drove by at thirty second intervals, heading toward the station or leaving it. I turned right again at the first corner and picked up my pace, desperate to put as much distance as possible between myself and Lieutenant Lincoln Washington. A black and white taxi approached from the opposite direction. I flagged it down.

"Where you goin', mister?"

"Know the old D.H. Holmes garage?"

"Sho'nuff."

"Take me there."

"It closed."

"Yeah. I know."

Chapter 37

THE TAXI STANK WORSE THAN LINCOLN Washington's squad car, but at least the windows opened. I rode with my nose pointed out and my face in the breeze. A sudden elation enveloped me. I was free. I thanked God, then felt a stab of doubt. Had God really freed me? I had been taught that Christians should obey the law. Perhaps I had sinned by escaping. Then I remembered Peter's escape again and smiled. Obviously, in certain circumstances, God made exceptions.

We were in an area I did not recognize. Sinister two- and three-story brick facades flashed by as the driver weaved effortlessly along backstreets. Most of the buildings looked abandoned, with broken windows and plywood nailed across the entries. Many of the streetlights had been smashed; the few that remained cast yellow pools of light on cracked and barren sidewalks. There was no other traffic. Now and then we skirted the stripped carcass of an automobile: wheels gone, doors gone, seats gone, everything gone but the naked chassis and the axles resting on the asphalt. I was grateful for the cab. I was lucky to have found it. Nobody in their right mind would cross this neighborhood on foot.

Soon enough, we emerged onto Elysian Fields and followed it to the Vieux Carre. The Quarter was in full swing, bars packed and sidewalks jammed with boisterous tourists. The cabby hummed to himself as we crawled along. Near the garage, I checked my watch in the fleeting glow of a passing streetlight. It was nine-thirty. Faye Slydel had warned me not to be early. I said, "Let me out here, driver."

An eight-foot chain-link fence with a padlocked gate blocked the auto ramp entry to the garage. I loitered on the sidewalk outside the ramp for twenty minutes, checking my watch frequently. At nine fifty-five I glanced up and down the street. For the moment, I seemed to have the block to myself. Reaching up, I grabbed the chain link with both hands, scrambled to the top, and dropped to the pavement on the other side. The harsh slap of my boots hitting the concrete echoed through the garage.

I took several steps into the shadows and stopped, waiting for my eyes to adjust to the darkness. Something rustled in the distant recesses of the building. The sound whispered down the concrete tunnel of the ramp. A rat, or a piece of trash blowing in a draft, or the careless footstep of whoever waited for me on the floors above.

I held my hands forward, waving them in front like a blind man as I ascended. The ramp curved tightly up to the right. As it rose, the dim light from the street below gradually faded. It became impossible to see. I touched the cold concrete wall and followed its curvature. I had heard someone at the Hotel Provencial say that they planned to build several restaurants and shops in the building. Their plans probably included demolishing the ramp. Perhaps they had already begun, and I was feeling my way toward a hole in the floor. I could drop thirty feet. I slid a boot forward before every step, feeling the slab in front. The going was slow. Each step echoed against the hard walls, announcing my progress to whoever or whatever waited above.

At last, I saw a dull glow ahead. Gradually, it became possible to see the vague outline of my surroundings. I increased my pace. The curving tunnel opened onto a flat parking area. Dim light filtered in through openings along the far wall, about two hundred feet away. I could just make out the steel door of an elevator on the left.

In my memory, Faye Slydel knelt on the ground saying, *"Go to the top level. Wait beside the elevator doors up there. We'll get in touch with you."*

I crossed to the elevators and stood with my back to the doors, scanning the cavernous garage, alert for sound or motion. Minutes dragged by. Five minutes. Ten. Fifteen. I shifted from foot to foot impatiently. I backed against the elevator doors and bent one leg to rest a boot at knee height against the steel. The glowing hands of my wrist watch read ten twenty-five. Where were they? I sighed.

Just as I was about to walk across the garage to look down at the street, a single dong sounded behind me and I heard the mechanical whir of machinery. Startled, I turned to face the elevator doors.

"Mister Reed, please turn around and face away from the elevator."

The voice seemed to come from everywhere, bounced from surface to surface by the hard concrete. I said, "Where are you?"

"Just put your back to the doors, Mister Reed."

I did as the voice commanded. The machinery whined in the elevator shaft. I heard the doors open behind me.

"Mister Reed, for your own safety, do not turn around or try to look in the elevator."

"All right."

"We're going to blindfold you. Keep your eyes forward."

Someone touched my back. Hands reached over my shoulders and a piece of cloth was wrapped around my eyes. The disembodied voice said, "All right now, Mister Reed. Just turn and step onto the elevator."

A hand on my elbow guided me in. The doors closed and the cab began its descent with a sudden jerk. I heard the breathing of at least two people. I said, "Why all the cloak and dagger stuff?"

Nobody answered. I said, "All right, have it your way."

The lights were on in the elevator. I could see their glow through the fabric of the blindfold. Looking down through a slit between the cloth and my cheeks, I saw my own boots and the worn vinyl floor. I considered tilting my head up to try to get a peek at my companions, but decided against it. Let them play their games if that's what it took to find Mary Jo.

The dong sounded again. The elevator cab stopped suddenly. When the doors opened, a hand grasped each of my elbows and turned me around. They led me through the doors in silence. We walked quickly. I heard a car door open. One of them placed a hand on my arm and lifted. I got the point, felt for the door jamb, and stepped into the vehicle. It was a step up, so I knew it was a truck or van. I heard one set of footsteps walk to the other side of the vehicle before they closed the door. The other one got in beside me. Without a word, they started the motor and we drove away.

Chapter 38

WE DROVE FOR AT LEAST AN HOUR, CRAWL-ing through the labyrinth of the Quarter, stopping and starting in jerky motions, then quickly along what could have been Canal, then up an incline and very fast onto a freeway, with a rapid clump-clump, clump-clump as the tires slapped the joints in the pavement. They were knobby off-road tires. I could tell from the rumbling road noise and constant vibration. It was cold in the cab. The man beside me shifted positions now and then. Neither he nor the driver spoke.

The road sound of the tires changed, became more hollow. The cab tilted up slightly. We might have been passing over the Mississippi, possibly on the Huey P. Long bridge. Or else we were traveling the other way, across Lake Pontchartrain. My nose itched. I started to scratch it. The man to my right grabbed my hand.

He said, "Leave the blindfold alone." His voice was familiar. He pulled down on my elbow. I resisted, flexing my arm. He grasped my elbow with both of his hands and pulled harder. I have worked a lot of steel and concrete over the years. My arm stayed where it was. After ten seconds of trying, he released his grip.

I said, "I was only going to scratch my nose."

"I'll do it for you."

I laughed. "No, thanks. It's not that bad."

"Well, leave it alone."

The road noise changed again, back to a more solid sound. We were off the bridge, much too soon to have crossed the lake. We were heading south, then. It occurred to me that I might be able to recreate our route if I kept track of the time. I peeked at my wrist watch through the slit below the blindfold. It was too dark to read. I sighed and settled back against the seat. We drove on. Time was marked by the monotonous pounding rhythm of the tires slapping against the road joints and the high-pitched rumble of knobby tires on pavement, vibrating up through the chassis. I leaned to my right for a moment. The passenger's shoulder dug into my arm a few inches above my elbow. It was sharp and bony. He was a thin man, maybe five feet ten inches tall. Six feet at the most. I waited a few minutes to avoid being obvious, then leaned to my left. The driver grunted and drew back, but not before I got the feel of him. His shoulder seemed more muscular, but he too was smaller than I was. Most people are. Unless they were armed, I could probably take them both if this was some kind of trap.

An hour or so after we crossed the bridge, the truck slowed. We swung sharply to the right, then back to the left.

"Watch your knee." This time it was the driver who spoke. His voice was unfamiliar. His hand bumped my knee as he shifted the floor-mounted stick shift into a lower gear. We turned twice more and drove along a much rougher road, then turned again. The sound of gravel beneath the tires was unmistakable.

"Slow down heah." It was the passenger to my right. Where had I heard his accent before? "Theah it is."

The driver said, "I know where it is."

We turned once more and stopped. The passenger opened his door, got out, and closed it again. I heard the metallic rattle of a chain against metal, then a long scraping sound. The driver drove us slowly forward and stopped again. The scraping sound and the rattle repeated in reverse order. A gate. The passenger-side door opened and the man got in.

The driver said, "Did you lock it?"

"Of course I locked it."

"Well, praise the Lord. You remembered for once."

We drove slowly on. After perhaps three more minutes, the truck turned sharply left and stopped.

"Okay, mister. I'm gonna get out and you just slide over heah after me."

My boots crunched on gravel when I stepped from the truck. The passenger held my elbow firmly. I heard the driver walk around the front of the truck. He took my other elbow and said, "Let's walk."

The night call of a screech owl sliced the darkness into little pieces of insanity. I heard a familiar whisper in the treetops and sniffed the musky scent of decay. Crickets sang all around us. A sudden splash in the distance silenced their song for a moment, then they resumed exactly where they left off.

I knew where we were. We were in the heart of the swamp. The sounds and the smells drew me deep within myself. Something flitted at the edges of my consciousness, a memory brought on by the deep musty smell of rotting vegetation. I struggled to dredge it up, knowing it was important, even before I knew what it was. And then it was there, another piece of history, rising to the surface after all those years . . .

• • •

"WATCH DAT BOBBER."

Benoit pointed a grimy finger down at the cork ball floating in the dark green backwater. Roused from my lazy reverie, I sat up straighter and gingerly lifted the cane pole from its perch in the forked stick beside the shore of the bayou. I had been thinking about the new job at my father's construction company up in Mount Sinai. Fresh out of college and already I was suffering from career burnout.

"She nibblin', that one," said Benoit. "She thinkin' 'bout it, yessir."

He spoke in hushed tones, although both of us knew the precaution did not matter. This was no clear mountain stream brimming with skittish trout. It was an insignificant tributary of the Bayou La Fourche, a solid slab of a stream laden down with mud and algae, inching across dead-level swamp land. The creature investigating my baited hook might be brim or catfish or snapping turtle or alligator gar. Whatever it was, it would not associate our voices with a threat.

I watched tiny concentric ripples expand around the bobber. It dipped slightly. It dipped again. Suddenly, it sank below the surface entirely. I yanked hard on the pole, lifting it toward the canopy of deep green above us, watching with fascination as the tip arched and quivered and bowed to point unerringly at the invisible beast below.

"She a big one!" whooped Benoit. "Big big! Pull up, you! Pull up!"

It had been the same all afternoon. Whenever I got a bite, Benoit immediately pronounced it sizable and started giving orders. He knew I had fished all my life from boat and shore in Martin Pool and the Big Muddy, but Benoit figured that anyone not from Barataria needed close supervision when the fish took the bait. I humored him, since he was my brother-in-law.

"Don't let her work round dat snag yonder! She gonna go for it, sure. You pull this away, you. Pull!"

I stood and followed his advice, tugging with both hands and backing away from the shore. Benoit remained crouched beside the water, his bony shoulders eager beneath the sweat-stained cotton shirt, his tiny black eyes narrowly focused on the spot where my taut and quivering line danced across the surface with a mind of its own, like a willow branch in the hands of a water witch. I began to believe Benoit's prediction. It *was* a big one! I backed toward the edge of the sand bar, lifting with all of my might. At last it breached the surface, body arched and rolling, yellow belly flashing and black mouth gaping, putty gray and blood red at the gills, sharp fins splayed violently like the rigid sails of a Chinese junk. I yanked as hard as I could on the pole. Then the channel cat plunged below again and my line went limp.

Benoit rocked back on his heels and gave a disgusted snort. "She gone. Why you did that wit' de pole, you?" was all he said, but in his posture I read impatience with my clumsy effort. This was no casual sport for him. Benoit and Edna fed their children from the proceeds of the Barataria Swamp. They hunted the high land for deer, both in and out of season. Their traps yielded alligator, valued for its meat and hide. Crawfish netted in quiet pools, *sac-o-lait*, catfish, French duck, and mourning dove all found their way into Edna's gumbo or jambalaya or her poor man's *andouille*.

As I lifted the line from the water, Benoit watched closely. I saw him relax when my hook cleared the surface. Hooks cost five cents a dozen in those days, a significant sum to surrender to the lip of a ten-pound fish.

I set the cane pole on the sand and bent to remove the lid of a foam ice chest. Inside, empty Jax cans floated in frigid water. I said, "We're out of beer and the ice is melted."

He nodded, intent again upon his own bobber, a red and white plastic ball adrift beside the snag.

I said, "I'll go back and get another six pack."

He nodded again without turning. "I be here, me."

"How long you wanna stay?"

"Till dinner come. You go on, you. I be along directly."

"I could drive into Lafitte, buy us all some burgers."

It was a calculated risk. Edna and Benoit were proud, often too proud to accept such offers. I suggested it by way of compensation for my failure with the catfish, hoping he would understand and take no offense. Benoit could be vicious in defense of his pride. Edna often bore the bruised results of his overreactions.

He said, "No need, Garr. You go home, you. I be along soon enough. Got plenty fish already. Take 'em back to the girls. Maybe I bring one more pretty soon, me. We fry 'em up, pass a good time tonight."

Dusk slipped between the treetops as I wound my way along the path to the Benoits' shack with five pounds of fish hanging from the cord in my left hand and a seven-foot cane pole in my right. Perhaps it was the habit of silence I had gained from a day on the sand bar with Benoit, perhaps it was a premonition, but whatever the reason, I was quiet as I stepped from the tree line and approached the rear of the Benoits' humble home. The women's voices reached me across the clearing, soft and sweet to my ear. I was still a bridegroom, often caught unaware by the sudden joy of Mary Jo. Her lilting Southern accent joined the katydids and the tree frogs and the settling-down night chirps of the titmice and chickadees. She was a part of it all, a natural element like the wind and flowing waters. I stopped a few yards from the screened porch, listening in rapt attention as her voice joined the natural calls of creatures above and below, interwoven, rising and falling. It was a moment of absolute peace, a moment of connection with things I only faintly understood. For me she was the crowning jewel of nature, the center of the universe, unblemished, perfect, and peaceful beyond anything I had yet experienced.

Then the meaning of her words spoiled the moment, jolting me back to reality.

"Don't talk so loud, honey," she said. "They'll be coming back soon. You don't want them to hear us, do you?"

Edna Benoit said, "I don't care. I don't care who hears."

Mary Jo said, "Hush that talk, sister. You know we can't let them hear."

"I don't care 'bout dat. I just wanna kill him. When I think about it, I just wanna kill dat man is all."

"Oh, sister. You got to forgive. We both got to forgive. And try to forget somehow."

"Forget! How can I forget what dat man did to us? How *can* you forget, you?"

"I just try, Edna. I try my best every day."

Behind me, a deep-chested cough announced Benoit's approach through the swamp.

"Shush now! They're comin'. Wipe your eyes and help me get the rice on 'fore they get here."

We ate fried catfish, red beans, and rice around a picnic table in the clearing, surrounded by twinkling fireflies and Edna's wiggling babies. After dinner, Benoit played an ancient guitar while the women put the dishes away inside the house. I sat on a wobbly wooden chair watching the women pass to and fro in the yellow light beyond the open kitchen window as he sang ancient melodies in archaic French.

Later, Mary Jo and I lay awake in the afterglow of our lovemaking. I said, "Has Benoit been beating Edna again?"

She turned to me, fear and curiosity in her lovely green eyes. "Why? Did he say something to you?"

"No. I was just wondering if they still . . . you know."

Mary Jo shook her head firmly. "She wouldn't stand for it anymore. She'd leave him."

"But when we were walking up tonight, I thought I heard you and Edna talking about Benoit and all their troubles."

The silence lasted a long time. Then she said, "We were talking about old family things is all. Nothing new. Nothing important."

"That's good," I said as I rolled onto my back and stared at the whitewashed ceiling. Soon, Mary Jo's breathing softened and grew regular. I lay beside her, looking up at the moonlit cobwebs, listening to the night creatures outside the open window. What could it all mean? What did Mary Jo have to forgive? What was she trying to forget? They had shared their anger on the porch that night as if it stemmed from a common outrage. What could it be? And why was Mary Jo keeping it from me?

I turned onto my side, away from her. Eventually, the surging rhythm of the tree frog's song lulled me to sleep.

• • •

A BRANCH SLAPPED MY FACE.

"Hey! Will you boys be careful here?"

The one with the familiar voice said, "Sorry."

"Why can't I take this blindfold off?"

"Just one more minute."

"Well, just watch out for those low branches."

"All right. Sorry."

We walked in single file. Now and then, the one behind me grabbed my shoulders to steer me left or right. It was cooler in the swamp. The concrete of the city soaked up the sun and released it overnight, but here in the swamp the temperature was lower by ten degrees. I crossed my arms and hugged my elbows for warmth. A woodpecker gave its crazy laughing call from someplace off to the right. Another branch scraped across my cheek. That's it, I thought. That's enough. I reached up and removed the blindfold.

The one behind me saw it first when I glanced back at him and he looked up at my face. His features were ghostly white in the crisp moonlight. I recognized him as the man I had seen carrying the cage outside the Slydels' church, the man driving the truck that followed Jacques and me to Linda Granier's grave. He wore his wavy blond hair long and combed it straight back from his forehead. Below his long straight nose, a bushy mustache concealed his upper lip. He would have been handsome—movie star handsome—if not for his jaw. It hung below his face like the visor on a medieval knight's helmet, heavy and wide. When he saw that I'd removed the blindfold, he cursed and told me to put it back on.

The other one said, "Watch your language, Charles."

The blond man said, "But look what he done!"

"It's no excuse to cuss thataway. This heah's sacred ground."

"Sorry."

"That's all right. I guess he spooked you."

Charles looked up at me. "I ain't scared of nobody."

"'Course not. That ain't what I meant. You're the last man alive I'd 'spect to get scared."

"Well . . . should we make him put that thing back on?"

"Naw. He's seen us now. And they's no way he could find this place again, anyway."

"Yeah, but—"

"Come on, Charles. Let him be. How'd you like to walk through heah without being able to see?"

I turned to look at the other one, to thank him for his kindness. But when I made out his features in the dim moonlight, I forgot to speak. He was as skinny as a poplar sapling, with oily black hair and a day's growth of whiskers like smeared grease on his sunken cheeks. He returned my stare with eyes set back in deep shadow beneath a bony brow, like twin holes drilled into his pale countenance. His was a face I had seen before. As soon as I remembered him my heart raced with excitement. He was Elmer, the mechanic from the Crescent City Garage.

Faye Slydel had promised to help me find Mary Jo, and now here I was with the man who had towed Mary Jo's car to New Orleans.

It was no coincidence. Mary Jo was near. I knew it.

Chapter 39

ELMER LED US ON THROUGH THE SWAMP. Behind me, Charles muttered now and then, still upset that I had removed the blindfold. Fog settled into the bottom land, hanging motionless above the black pools to our left and right. Moonlight streamed through the trees, bleached bars of fluorescent white, piercing the vapor at crazy angles. The path followed a narrow ridge of dry land that rose slightly above the standing water. Spanish moss dangled limply from the overhead limbs of ancient cypress trees and tupelos on every side. Dense brush clung to tiny islands in the distance. Palmetto palms huddled near the mud, prehistoric and alien. Our journey left no trace; nothing seen or heard, except by the invisible beasts that screamed in the distance and splashed through the quagmire beyond the mist, tracking our progress.

I looked straight ahead and saw dim yellow halos flickering in the distance. We plunged straight toward them. The fog muffled the sound of our footsteps. As we neared, I heard the soft murmur of voices. The path widened. An eight-foot chain-link fence topped by concertina wire glistened like a curtain of razor blades in the moonlight. We entered a clearing through a gate in the fence. The mist parted for an instant and I saw the low-slung profiles of seven or eight house trailers flanking an angular structure of bars and boards. The structure looked like scaffolding, or perhaps a set of bleachers. A single yellow lightbulb glowed above the door on each trailer, the source of the halos.

I heard the unmistakable sound of someone working the pump action of a shotgun. Adrenaline shot through my veins.

"Who goes there?"

The sound and voice came from the tree line to our right. I looked that way and saw what could only be a guard tower, silhouetted against the night sky.

Elmer stopped. "It's me an' Charles. We got the guy here." He held his hands well away from his body as a beam of light flashed down to pass slowly over each of us.

The voice said, "Okay. Go on in."

I followed Elmer across the clearing and up a set of wooden steps to the door of a trailer on the left. *Mary Jo is in there*, I thought. It was all I could do not to push Elmer aside and race in to her. He held the door for me. I stepped inside and immediately looked both ways. Faye and Brother James Slydel sat to my right behind a rectangular wooden table, looking up at me. A single unoccupied chair faced them. On the table were three stacks of colored paper, a lamp with a green glass shade, a Bible, and a .32 automatic handgun. The walls were covered with vinyl paneling. On the floor, the threadbare brown carpet was smeared with mud.

"Where is she?" I asked.

James Slydel rose and extended his hand across the table. The light from the lamp shone on his chest and lower body. He was in shadow from his shoulders up. I took his hand. It was like squeezing a lump of dough. I repeated my question.

"The lady is here in the compound, Mister Reed. Please, have a seat."

He released my hand, sat down, and indicated the chair. I remained standing and said, "I'd like to see my wife first."

He wrinkled his brow. "Your wife?" His Adam's apple bobbed once per word.

"Yes. I'd like to see her now."

He looked at Faye. "Did you tell him his wife was here?"

"Of course not."

I stared at the straight white line of the part in his hair, at the deep smudges below her eyes. James Slydel turned his naive features my way. I searched his eyes for some sign that he was toying with me. Their guilelessness was magnified by the lenses of his wire-framed glasses. "I apologize if we gave you the wrong impression, Mister Reed," he said. "We don't know where your wife is. Not yet."

"What does 'not yet' mean?"

"Please, be seated."

I stared at him a moment longer. He inclined his head to return my look. The glowing green lamp shade flashed in his glasses. I sat.

He said, "Mister Reed, we asked you here because we believe we have a mutual problem. You want to locate Mrs. Reed. So do we."

"How is it you know she's missing?"

He smiled. "I'll let Faye answer that."

Faye Slydel said, "That day, at the hospital, Mary Jo told me she wanted our help. She said she would come to us for protection."

"Protection? From what?"

"Don't you know?" she asked. "I would have thought it was clear as day."

Brother James Slydel said, "She wanted our help to escape the forces of Satan, Mister Reed."

Faye nodded. "I knew it soon as they come for her. I knew that was what she was talkin' about."

"Satan? Satan's forces came for her? What are you people talking about? Are you crazy?" The same words I had whispered to Mary Jo, so long ago.

James Slydel seemed unaffected by my question. "Satan's forces are often disguised."

"I see. What disguise did he choose this time?"

"Deputies. Officers of the law."

"You mean my wife asked you to hide her from the police?"

Faye Slydel nodded.

"Tell me again. When did Mary Jo bring this up, exactly? And what did she say?"

"It was while we was sittin' out front of the hospital. A few minutes before you come along."

"*Before* they came to arrest her?"

She nodded again.

I said, "That's impossible."

James Slydel cocked his head, considering my response. He said, "Impossible? Why is that?"

"Because that would mean she knew about the murder before anyone else. That she knew they would come for her. Arrest her."

"Yes?"

"But how could she know that?"

Faye said, "Another obvious question."

James said, "She knew about it because she did it."

Faye nodded.

I said, "No."

"I'm afraid so, Mister Reed. It is the only explanation."

"How did she ask for your help exactly? What did she say?"

James and Faye exchanged a look. James nodded slightly and Faye turned back to me. "Your wife told us that a sister suggested she ask for our help. She said she wanted to join our holy crusade. That she was willing to do anything to help us."

"Edna Benoit told Mary Jo to ask for your help?"

James looked puzzled. "Who is Edna Benoit?"

"Her sister. You said her sister told Mary Jo to ask for your help."

Faye Slydel said, "No. I said *a* sister. One of our sisters in the Lord told her to ask for our help, and she said she was ready to join us."

"That hardly sounds like a request for asylum."

"She said she needed to get away from Mount Sinai. That she had done somethin' she was afraid would ruin her life."

Looking beyond them, I focused on the plastic wood-grain pattern of the paneled wall, thinking again about the dawn target practice and the sudden trips to New Orleans. Was it possible they were telling the truth?

I said, "None of this explains how you know she is missing."

Faye said, "We sent a sister to your town to collect her, to wait until she was released on bail and then bring her to us. But she disappeared before our sister could bring her here."

"Who was this 'sister' you keep bringing up?"

"I'm surprised you don't know, Mister Reed," said James Slydel. He picked up one of the stacks of colored paper and, holding it with both hands, began tapping the edge on the tabletop, aligning the sheets into a neater pile. They were flyers announcing a protest at the Milo Clinic. He replaced the pile upon the desktop, adjusting it to ensure that it lined up with the edge of the desk. He said, "Your family is not very close, are they?"

"What does that have to do with anything?"

"We sent her mother, Mister Reed. We sent our sister, Lucretia Granier."

I nodded. It explained so much. My mind chased the implications like rats through a tenement. Some I caught. Some slipped into cracks before I could grasp them. Lucretia had arrived in Mount Sinai so soon after the killing ... perhaps the Slydels really were telling the truth.

I pointed at the automatic on the table. "What's this for?"

"Security."

"Security from what? Alligators? Snakes?"

James Slydel smiled. His smile was wonderfully naive, like the toothless mirth of an infant. Even Faye Slydel bared her crooked teeth briefly, then she closed her mouth and covered it with her hand. Her fingernails were short and dirty. Gardener's hands.

James said, "We have enemies, Mister Reed, but the snakes are not among them."

"I don't doubt that for a second."

His smile flickered and faded to a frown. He adjusted the position of three pencils, placing them so that their points were aligned perfectly. As he tinkered with the objects on his desk, he said, "We asked you here to help us deal with one of our enemies."

"I thought you brought me here to help me find my wife."

"Happily," he said, "in this case, problems may share a common solution."

"Maybe you better explain this place to me. What is it? Who are those people outside?"

He said, "We call ourselves C.H.A.R.G.E. It stands for 'Christ's Holy Army Resisting God's Enemies.' Rather appropriate, don't you think?"

I did not reply.

Faye said, "We've organized to fight the murderers of innocent children."

"Is that why everyone has a gun?"

James Slydel said, "As I said, we have enemies. I can't tell you more than that." He leaned back in his chair and crossed his arms across his chest, lifting his chin to stare at me. "So, the question is, will you help us find your wife?"

"Of course. But what can I do?"

"We're not sure. You'll have to ask her."

Suddenly angry and tired of their double-talk, I stood and leaned over the desk. Placing my hand next to the gun and my face less than six inches from Brother James Slydel's nose, I said, "Ask *who*? Quit fooling around and tell me what's going on here or you will have made yourself a brand-new enemy, Brother Slydel."

His Adam's apple bulged as if he had swallowed a hand grenade. I almost felt sorry to be intimidating such a helpless-looking man. "Calm yourself, brother. We're all on the same side here."

"I'm beginning to wonder."

Faye Slydel said, "We oughta show him."

I looked from one of them to the other. "Show me *what*?"

James Slydel stood abruptly. "A daughter of Satan, Mister Reed. An evil woman who claims she knows your wife's whereabouts and will speak only to you."

"Lead me to her."

He lifted the handgun from the table, self-consciously tucked it into the waistband of his camouflage trousers, and squared his narrow shoulders. "Come along, Mister Reed. And prepare to meet the enemy."

Chapter 40

I FOLLOWED THE SLYDELS OUT INTO THE MIST. In front of me, James moved with what he probably thought was a military stride across the hazy moonlit clearing. To me, he looked like a boy playing soldier. Faye seemed to drift through the fog, her upper body strangely without motion, arms rigid, head forward. It was like following a zombie. I was reminded of Edna Benoit's story of protecting her dead sister's *ti bon ange* and the symbols drawn in dried blood on Linda Granier's crypt. We hurried by the structure between the trailers, a crescent-shaped array of low wooden bleachers, arranged around the far side of a peculiar depression in the ground. The circular basin was about thirty feet across and choked with thick fog, like the white cotton lining of a cheap casket. For some reason, it reminded me of a miniature version of the Roman coliseum. I thought of Nero feeding Christians to the lions.

Perhaps it was a premonition.

We passed fifteen or twenty men and women sitting in small groups around the clearing. Their voices rose and fell in dull murmurs. In the upcast light of flickering kerosene lanterns, their faces resembled demons in a medieval painting, their eye sockets deep in shadow, empty and forbidding. Most wore berets, like the ones I saw on the morning it all began back in Mount Sinai. Some of them held rifles. There were deer rifles and shotguns and even a few M–16's.

James Slydel spoke as we neared another trailer, his large Adam's apple marking the pace of his words like a metronome.

"This woman has assisted in hundreds of murders in Orleans Parish. Maybe thousands. She is surely possessed of the devil."

I said nothing.

"She has resisted our efforts to purge her of the evil thing possessing her soul. She denies her guilt. She even claims to share our calling."

"What calling?"

He spoke in a monotone, as if reciting the words, "We exist to serve the Lord, to protect the unborn, to stop their murderers, and to destroy their slaughterhouses."

"Are you the ones who have been bombing abortion clinics?"

"The word *clinic* implies the practice of medicine. The practice of medicine exists to heal, not to destroy. We prefer to call them slaughterhouses."

"Does changing what you call them make it all right to burn them down and blow them up?"

"Did you know the Hippocratic oath specifically forbids abortion?" His voice slipped into the monotone again as he recited, "I will give no deadly drug to any, though it be asked of me, nor will I counsel such, and especially I will not aid a woman to procure abortion.' That, sir, is a direct translation from the ancient Greek."

"Does the oath call for a punishment for doctors who violate that provision?"

Faye Slydel said, "God almighty orders the punishment. We just carry it out, is all."

James pushed his glasses up on his nose. "Now, dear, that's not quite correct. We do not punish or judge. That is for God alone. We simply do what we must to defend the babies. To see that they are born in peace."

"Does that include trying to kill Melvin Milo?" I asked.

"We already told you, Mister Reed. Your wife shot him, not us. We do not judge her for it. In fact, we are prepared to defend her from those that do. With us, she will have sanctuary until the godless heathens are driven from control of our government or the Lord returns at last."

Faye Slydel lifted her palms toward heaven and said, "Come, Jesus."

Ignoring her, I tried again. "Did you try to kill Doctor Milo several months ago, here in Louisiana?"

James Slydel said, "We have done, and will continue to do, what we must to serve the Lord, Mister Reed."

We stopped outside the trailer. A tall man in camouflage gear and a red beret stood near the door. He held an M–16 at port arms. "The woman is within this building," said James Slydel. "Before we enter, you must know a couple of things. First, she should be considered dangerous. When we captured her, she had just attempted to murder Doctor Milo's wife in her own home. I believe you were there at the time. So watch yourself, Mister Reed. Do not turn your back to her. Second, she asked for this meeting. She said she knew your wife's whereabouts and would reveal that information only to you."

"Couldn't you beat it out of her?"

He smiled. In the dim moonlight I wondered how such an innocent smile could come from someone in charge of such a place. He said, "We have not touched her, except as necessary to ensure her captivity and to protect ourselves. If we must, we will allow the Lord to secure the truth in his way, but that will be a last resort. We hope you can convince her to reveal your wife's location of her own free will."

"All right."

"There is one thing more. We believe she was planning to arrange Mrs. Milo's death in a way that would have implicated us or you. We want to know why, and if there were others involved in her plan. Perhaps you can gain her confidence, learn what motivates her, determine if she had confederates."

Faye Slydel repeated the word, "Confederates," rolling it around on her tongue like a sip of wine.

I stared at her. She looked back at me, her face eager, like a child's on Christmas morning.

Turning away, I peered into the hazy distance beyond the moonlit tree line and wondered, *Where did they come from?* These impassioned fools, ready to bomb and kidnap and suffer imprisonment or death in the name of their cause? Was there a place for them in heaven, alongside the martyrs? Or was their profession of faith a masquerade, a clever sham that fooled everyone—even themselves? Such strength of purpose, such intense concern for the rights of other people's babies was easy to admire. But I was reminded of people who build their homes on the riverbanks, then work like Trojans to shore up the levees with sandbags when the water rises. It seemed so much wiser to build on higher ground.

One could lose one's perspective as the raging torrent neared the crest. One could panic, casting about for anything to pile up against the flood—even the corpses of enemies.

I took a deep breath, inhaling the fog and the musty odor of the swamp. Turning my eyes toward the aluminum door of the trailer I said, "I'll do what I can."

Chapter 41

SHE WAITED ON A COT IN A CORNER OF THE small windowless room, hugging her legs to her chin. Her dull blond hair hung limply across her face, obscuring her features. She wore a man's white cotton shirt, several sizes too large, with the sleeves rolled up. The shirttail almost covered a pair of blue shorts. Her legs were long and well toned, the muscles of her thighs firmly defined below her encircling arms. On the floor beside the cot lay a pair of deck shoes, caked with dried mud. Her bare feet were pale against the blue-and-white striped mattress. A thin gold chain encircled her right ankle. Her toenails were painted blood red. To my surprise, I realized I had seen her twice before.

I said, "Aren't you Elizabeth Harmony?"

She lifted her head and stared at me through a cascade of hair. The single naked bulb hanging from the ceiling shone starkly on her face. I sucked in a breath. Above her full lips and proud cheekbones, a pair of deep green eyes peered up at me. Eyes like Mary Jo's.

She said, "Lizzy. I go by Lizzy." Her voice was surprisingly deep.

I said, "You work for Melvin Milo."

Swinging her legs around to set her feet on the floor beside the cot, she said, "Have you got a cigarette? I'd prefer a Marlboro, but at this point, I'd even take a menthol."

"Sorry. I don't smoke. Don't you work for Doctor Milo?"

"Oh? You've been to the clinic? Maybe you were one of those fine Christian fellas who pounded on the hood of my car every morning for two years? Or one of those who wrote kind little messages on the windshield when I left it parked on the street? Such sweet little notes." She cast her eyes up toward the low ceiling. "Lemme see, I remember a couple of them . . . oh, yes. 'Murderer' and 'Baby Killer'?" She looked back down at me. "Was that you?"

"I've been there, but I never did any of those things." I remembered watching through the window as she fought with Melvin Milo. I remembered the merciless way she beat him with her fists, how he held his wounded side and fought off her blows.

She cocked her head, considering me. "I know who you are. You're Mary Jo's man."

I took a step closer. "They said you'd tell me where she is."

She giggled. I liked her laugh. It was husky and honest. "Slow down, slow down. We got all the time in the world. Don't you think we ought to get to know each other a little bit before we do business?"

I sat on the opposite end of the cot. There was no other furniture in the room. "All right. We'll do it your way."

She smiled. The smile lit every part of her face except her cold emerald eyes. It was difficult not to stare blatantly at such beauty. She said, "That's better. Now then, tell me what took you so long?"

"What does that mean?"

"I asked to see you ages ago. It wasn't nice to keep me waiting."

"How long have you been here?"

"That depends. What day is it?"

I checked my watch. It was two-thirty A.M. I said, "It's early Tuesday morning."

"Then I think I've been here two days."

"Have they mistreated you?"

She laughed again. Such a delightful sound. "They've kidnapped me. Does that count?"

"Tell me how it happened."

"You mean how I got here? I was walking along the street minding my own business when these maniacs grabbed me and threw me into a van and drove me to this awful place."

"Which street were you walking on?"

"Why does that matter?"

"It matters."

She shrugged and told me the street name. It was one block over from Melvin and Juliette Milo's house in the Garden District. I said, "What were you doing there?"

"You don't want to know, Garr." She smiled again. "May I call you Garr?"

"All right. But tell me why you were there."

"No. I mean, seriously, Garr. You don't want to know."

"Why not?"

"It'll burst your bubble about your precious Mary Jo."

"Tell me anyway."

She said, "We were there to kill Melvin Milo."

I leaned back against the wall. The cot creaked beneath me. "Who's 'we'?"

"Me and Mary Jo, of course."

"Mary Jo was there? To kill Doctor Milo?"

"Oh, dear. She didn't tell you? Don't you people talk?"

"Let's pretend we don't for a minute, Lizzy. Fill me in about why you and Mary Jo went to the Milo's house."

"Why, she wanted to finish what we started. She went inside with her gun while I watched the back door."

I remembered the voice that called my name from inside the Milo home. I remembered the flash of auburn hair through the garden gate. I remembered finding Mary Jo's chrome-plated nine millimeter on the kitchen floor. Suddenly, I found it difficult to breathe.

I managed to say, "Why should I believe you?"

She shrugged. "Believe what you want."

I watched her for a moment. She seemed to enjoy my scrutiny, pulling her hair back with both hands and twisting it into some sort of knot. She arched her back, stretching her arms toward the ceiling, thrusting her bosom tight against her shirt. My eyes dipped briefly, then returned to her face. She held my stare, aware that her beauty had diverted my attention, if only for an instant. There was mockery in her look.

Anger rose within me. I said, "You said she wanted to finish what 'we' started. Who is this 'we'?"

"Me and Mary Jo, of course."

"And what did you start?"

"Oh, come on. We don't have time for this."

"Do you mean the shooting at the hospital?"

"Well of *course*."

"You were in on that?"

"Sort of. I helped Mary Jo get inside the hospital." She smiled. "But don't quote me."

I remembered something. "Why were you crying?"

"What do you mean?"

"Later on, when you and Harry Attwater were pushing Doctor Milo down the hall on a gurney, why were you crying?"

"Oh, were you there?"

"You passed right by me."

"I was crying for Mary Jo," she said. "I'd just heard they caught her. Poor dear."

I snorted. She looked up and said, "Don't laugh! You have to understand, Mary Jo and I have become very close. We made a pact. We're like sisters."

"When did the two of you do all this sisterly bonding, exactly?"

"It all happened so fast. We met in New Orleans a few months before the thing at the hospital. She was outside the clinic. I was trying to get to my car and they were threatening me, standing in the way and yelling horrible things. She came out of nowhere and helped me. She must have seen something in me. She saw I wasn't one of those murderers. I was only there to try to stop them. Working from the inside." Lizzy Harmony squeezed her hands together. "Mary Jo saw the truth right away. I wonder why those people out there don't? Why don't they believe me?"

"Are you telling me you've been trying to stop Milo by working in his clinic?"

Her hands were in constant motion now, rubbing, squeezing, folding one into the other. She said, "It seemed like the best way. I could talk to the women before they did it, try to talk them out of it. I could work on Doctor Milo, keep up the pressure, try to convince him in a thousand little ways . . ."

"So why the switch to violence?"

She glared at me, her hands clasped so tightly I saw the knuckles turning white. "It wasn't working! He wouldn't listen."

Again I thought about the scene I had witnessed between Doctor Milo and this woman. Her anger. Her violent blows against his chest. This story she was telling might explain all that.

There were two doors in the room, the entry and another. I rose, took three steps, and opened the other. It led to a tiny bathroom. Aluminum foil blocked a small window high on the wall. I turned toward Lizzy Harmony and said, "You must have some idea why these people don't believe you."

"I'm not a good *Christian*." She spat the word across the room. "I won't believe in their little god, so they can't see why I would care about the babies." She gave a short laugh. "As if only Christians care! I hate them all."

"I am a Christian. Mary Jo is a Christian."

She looked at me curiously and said, "You think so? Then why is she so afraid of dying?"

I crossed the room to look down on her. "What do you mean?"

"Why is she so afraid of the cancer?"

"She told you about *that?*"

"Of course. We're almost sisters, like I said."

"And she said she is afraid?"

"Yes. Poor thing, she's in so much pain."

I leaned down and grabbed her shoulders. "*Pain?* What pain?"

"Let go of me!"

I shook her once, hard. Her head snapped forward and back like a broken doll. I shouted, "What pain? Tell me!"

She said, "The cancer. The breast cancer. It's starting to hurt her."

"But they just found it! It's in an early stage. How could it hurt?"

Lizzy Harmony's shoulders were firm beneath my hands. She looked up at me. There was no fear in her eyes. She said, "I can't answer that, Garr. I'm a nurse, not an oncologist. All I know is it hurts so bad she cries sometimes. So bad she begged me to get her some painkillers from the clinic."

With my hands still on her shoulders, I said, "And you did that?"

"Of course. I hate to see anyone in pain. It's against my nature."

"So you know where she is?"

"Oh yes."

That was when I lost control. Nothing mattered except finding Mary Jo. I shook Elizabeth Harmony again and again. Her head popped back and forth as I yelled, "Tell me! Tell me! Tell me now!"

I would have beat her with my fists, but for the smile on her face. Something watched from behind that smile, something like what I had seen in Juliette Milo's eyes. Whatever it was, it seemed to welcome the violence. I shoved her one last time and backed away until I was pressed against the opposite wall. Lizzy Harmony's smile grew wider. She rubbed her shoulders and said, "Oh my. Such a *strong* Christian man."

I rubbed my eyes with my palms and muttered, "I'm sorry."

"Here I thought you people were supposed to be the kind and gentle ones."

"I never said I was perfect."

"Then what's the point, Garr? My first husband beat me too, and believe me, he was no choirboy. I mean, if all that religion doesn't make a difference in how you *act*, why bother?"

"Please. Just tell me where my wife is. Please."

She straightened her shirt. "Oh, no. I'd much rather show you. You'll have to get me out of here, away from those fine Christian soldiers outside. Then I'll take you to her."

"How can I do that?"

"I haven't got a clue, but you better think of something, because Mary Jo is all alone, and she needs our help. I only left her with enough painkillers to last another day."

"Oh dear Lord," I moaned.

"Yes, well, you call upon the Lord, if that makes you feel better. Mary Jo did that too, and it didn't seem to do a thing for her. Just remember God helps those that help themselves." She yawned and stretched lazily. Then she said, "I feel much better myself, now that I know I have such a big strong man on my side. I'm going to get my beauty sleep. You'd better go get started working on a way to get me out of here."

"Please ..."

"No. You go find me a way out of this nuthouse. That's the only way I'm gonna help you. And for goodness sake, hurry up, Garr. I hate to think of Mary Jo in all that pain." She smiled up at me sweetly. "And I'm dying for a cigarette."

As I stumbled to the door and opened it, my heart churned with a toxic blend of grief at her description of my wife's pain and shame at my violent behavior. I fled the trailer, with the memory of Elizabeth Harmony's words pursuing me out into the night air of the Barataria swamp.

"... *all that pain* ... *all that pain* ..."

Chapter

42

THEY WOULD NOT LET ME SEE THE SLYDELS. James left instructions that I was to rest in one of the other trailers until morning. A small man in the now-familiar uniform of camouflage trousers, a black T-shirt, and a red beret stepped from the shadows outside Lizzy Harmony's trailer to escort me across the compound. We crossed the compound to an ancient aluminum Airstream trailer. Several men were already asleep inside, snoring on double decks of tubular steel bunk beds. Their uniforms were piled haphazardly around the trailer. Their rifles were locked in a wall-mounted cabinet.

Settling onto an empty bunk near the door, I lay on my side with my back to the aisle and folded my arms across my chest. I left my boots on, mud and all. Staring at the moonlit boomerang pattern on the vinyl wallcovering a few inches from my nose, I fought the gnawing worry about Mary Jo's cancer. It was important that I focus on the situation at hand. Maybe they would let me take Elizabeth Harmony away, but I doubted it. Outside were at least ten men with automatic weapons. There might be even more—it was hard to tell in the dark. Lizzy's trailer seemed to be guarded around the clock. If the idea was to let me take her home tomorrow, why treat her like a prisoner tonight? I rolled over. If necessary, could I help her escape? It would be impossible to slip her out through the tiny window in the bathroom. And even if I got her out of the trailer, how could we sneak past the guard tower at the perimeter fence?

I had to sleep. It would do no good for me to face tomorrow with a foggy and exhausted mind. But beyond the guilt and sorrow, something new troubled my thoughts. I rolled over again. Then I realized what it was. It was a new feeling of hopelessness, a new sense of desperation. The future had seemed bleak for days, but never without hope. What I felt had nothing to do with Lizzy Harmony's situation. It was not panic over Mary Jo's cancer—by now, that was a familiar sensation. The problem was me. I had betrayed my Ally, abandoning his ways and trying to deal with the situation in my own fashion. A vision of myself shaking Elizabeth Harmony flashed through my mind. Except for that vision, and the guilt that it brought, I felt hopeless and empty.

For the first time in many days, I felt truly alone with my fears, and the solitude itself terrified me on a level I could neither escape or ignore.

Oh, God, I prayed. *Please forgive me for losing my temper with that woman. Please forgive my violence. I don't know much about you. James and Faye Slydel know so much more. He's a preacher, and I'm just a beginner when it comes to knowing you ...*

I opened my eyes. It wasn't working. I could tell God wasn't listening. There was no sense of connection. I felt alone.

The men in the bunks around me snored loudly. I listened to them, sleeping like babies while I lay awake struggling with doubts. Perhaps I was the problem. Perhaps God was on their side, and I was wrong to have these doubts. With a grunt, I shifted positions. A metal spring poked my shoulder through the thin mattress. From where I lay, I could see the rifles in the cabinet across the room, illuminated in a single streak of moonlight from the tiny window. It would be a simple matter to slip out of bed and cross the room ...

Suddenly, like a whisper, I heard the voice of God say, "No."

I thought of Peter using a sword to defend Christ on the night before his crucifixion. Jesus stopped him and healed the man that Peter had harmed. It was Christ's last healing miracle before they nailed him to the cross. If he would not use violence or coercion to restrain the men who murdered him, would he allow us to protect our own children in those ways?

Again, I heard his voice say, "No."

My God was a loving God, even when it came to his enemies. *Especially* when it came to his enemies. And these people had no part in him. They were trying to solve an earthly problem with earthly tactics, when the real problem lay deeper down, in the soul of those who had become so lost that they would place personal convenience above the life of a child. What foolish conceit to think that demonstrations and lurid posters and publicity campaigns could affect the cause of such evil. What a sad mistake to struggle with our feeble human will against the symptom of this disease, when the love of our Lord was the only permanent cure. Suddenly, I remembered Pedro Comacho, staring across my kitchen at a furious Lucretia Granier, saying, "Lady, if I thought for one second that God wanted me to hate anyone—anyone at all—I'd know he was a false God and I'd never call myself a Christian again."

I prayed again, this time with the certain knowledge that every word was well received.

Lord, I understand. It is love you want. Love at all costs. And if you will help me, I will do what I can to see that you get it.

I felt peace settle over my mind and soon, in spite of everything, I slept.

Chapter 43

OUTSIDE, A MIGHTY CHOIR SANG THE CHORUS of "Onward Christian Soldiers" at the top of their lungs. Lying on my back staring at the bedsprings of the bunk above, I struggled to remember where I was. Then I thought of Lizzy Harmony on a pin-striped mattress, describing Mary Jo's pain. I saw my hands on her shoulders, and the strange triumph in her eyes as her head snapped back and forth. I passed a hand over my eyes, rubbing the sleep away and willing the image from my mind. Sometimes, when the Lord forgives you, the hardest part is yet to come. You must forgive yourself.

When I opened my eyes again, liquid golden sunlight flowed through the window across the aisle. The music faded and Brother James Slydel's voice boomed through the walls of the trailer.

"Rise and shine, rise and shine! This is the day that the Lord has made. Let us rejoice and be glad in it! Morning services will begin in forty-five minutes. And remember, there is a flyby in fifteen minutes."

A brief electronic crackle replaced his voice as the public address system was switched off, then merciful silence settled in. I swung my legs over the edge of the mattress. All around me, everyone else did the same; quietly rising from their bunks, pulling on camouflage trousers, lacing up combat boots, and strapping on olive green webbed belts. I remained seated as they filed past one by one to go outside. Some smiled or nodded. One or two said, "Good morning, brother." I nodded and did my best to look half asleep.

When the door swung shut behind the last man, I rose and strode down the short aisle in the opposite direction. Against the wall at the end of the trailer stood a primitive knotty-pine cabinet full of rifles. A steel bar ran through their trigger guards, fastened by a large padlock on one end and a steel hook on the other. I examined the hook. It was screwed to the side of the cabinet. With thirty minutes and my pocket knife I could probably unfasten the screws. But then I remembered my revelation of the night before. No guns. If there was any other way at all, I would do it without guns.

I was still looking at the rifles when the door opened at the other end of the trailer.

As I turned, Elmer from the Crescent City Garage stuck his head in and said, "Hey theah. Brother Slydel wants you to come by his trailer before the service. I'm supposed to walk you over." The red beret looked comical above his narrow features, like a caricature of a Frenchman. I thought of "Pe Pe Le Pew" and smiled. He watched carefully as I walked to the door. When I reached him, he said, "What was you doin' down theah?"

"I need to find a bathroom."

He glanced beyond my shoulder toward the gun rack, then up at my face, his eyes narrow and wary. "Well, they's only two or three trailers tied to the septic system so far, an' this heah ain't one of 'em. If you want, we'll stop by the latrines on the way over."

Blinking in the bright sunlight, I descended the wooden steps to the damp ground. The fog had lifted. With my first opportunity to take in the entire compound, I realized things were worse than I had thought. We were in a clearing the size of a football field, with the long dimension running east-west. At least two dozen house trailers of various sizes lined the edges of the clearing, all of them painted a dull olive green or sheltered by ragged camouflage netting draped across their roofs. Hemp rope held the netting in place and rough-cut poles hoisted the material twenty feet into the air like circus tents. Between the trailers, I saw the dull glint of wire against the deep green of the encircling tree line. The fence appeared to enclose the entire compound. There were three wooden towers like the one I had seen the night before, one at each end of the giant clearing and one in the middle beside the gate. They balanced precariously on spindly legs, a scant ten feet taller than the surrounding trees. Like the trailers, the towers were well disguised with netting and freshly cut branches. Two men with guns stood in each tower, watching the compound and the surrounding swamp.

Elmer led me away from the center of the clearing. We passed a group of men running in formation. Their boots pounded the soil in near-perfect rhythm. A cluster of wooden shacks with green and brown canvas roofs stood along our route. The wood was so freshly cut I could smell the sharp aroma of sap from ten feet away. At the east end of the compound, Elmer pointed to the latrine, a low wooden shed with a dozen doors along one side. Just beyond it rose a wall of deep green, the edge of the swamp, straining to burst through the dull silver cyclone fence and the glistening concertina wire.

I entered the latrine and relieved myself to the sound of sparrows chirping brightly just outside. The smell of new lumber did nothing to offset the outhouse stench.

With Elmer slightly ahead, we returned toward the center of the encampment. He wore a handgun in a black nylon holster clipped to his belt. His arm swung away from it as he walked. I knew I could easily take it away from him, but again, I remembered my revelation of the night before. Besides, what would I do then? Men, women, and children wandered through the trailers and shacks all around us, everyone heading in the same direction. Many of the men carried weapons. Taking the pistol would probably just get somebody shot. Most likely me.

Elmer led the way to the Slydels' trailer and without saying a word took up a position beside the steps. I entered to find James Slydel seated behind the same table as the night before. An ivory-colored curtain blocked the morning sunlight from the single window at his side. As I stood watching, he wrote on a legal pad in the glow from the green-shaded lamp. The straight white part in his hair looked like a bloodless wound. When he looked up, I saw red-rimmed eyes behind his thick glasses.

"Didn't you sleep?" I asked.

He smiled. "No. I spent the night in prayer."

"All night?"

"Yes."

"I could never do that."

He cocked his head slightly, like a curious dog. "No? Why not?"

"I don't know." I shrugged. "Just run out of things to say, I guess."

Checking his wrist watch, he said, "Ah, yes. I was once like that. Then I remembered to listen."

I was about to respond when he held up his palm toward me. "Wait a minute, will you, Mister Reed?"

He swiveled his chair around and opened a door on the cabinet behind the table to reveal a radio transceiver and a public-address system with a microphone on a spiral gooseneck. With his back to me, James Slydel pressed a button and spoke into the microphone. "Flyby in thirty seconds. Everyone in the open must take cover immediately." He waited silently, eyes on his watch. Then he pressed the button again. "Flyby in twenty seconds . . . ten . . . five, four, three, two, one!"

He flipped a switch and the strident sound of a choral group singing "Way Up Yonder" bounced off of the trailer walls at maximum volume. The bass notes pounded like a hammer, driving the spiked treble piano accompaniment through my skull. The window glass rattled in its frame. James Slydel swiveled around to face me with a manic grin on his face.

I covered my ears with my palms. "Turn it down!" I shouted.

He continued to grin and pointed at his ear, as if to say he could not hear me.

The voices rose to a strident finale on the last chorus. I considered shoving him out of the way to turn down the volume myself. Then, as suddenly as the music started, it was over. Slydel swiveled away from me again, grasped the microphone, and said, "All right, everybody. The flyby is over. You may go about your business. Remember, morning services in thirty minutes." He flipped off the switch and faced me, still smiling.

I said, "What in the world was that?"

"A flyby, Mister Reed."

"A what?"

He picked up the pen and legal pad he had been using and placed them in a drawer. "It was a flyby. A satellite flyby. We have them several times each week. The government is up there, Mister Reed. They're up there with their cameras taking pictures, and they'd like nothing better than to find us."

I watched him closely for signs he was joking. His bloodshot eyes returned my stare innocently. I said, "Do you really believe they are looking for you with satellites?"

"Satellites and spies. Oh, yes. I have the flyby timetable memorized. When they're up there, we must all take cover. If you are still with us on the next one, please see that you enter a trailer or stand beneath a net."

"Why the loud music?"

"It disturbs the heat waves, stirs them up, so they can't see us with their infrared technology."

I almost laughed. But then I saw that he was serious. *Dear Lord, I prayed, protect me from this madman.*

He rose and crossed to the small window to stand facing out with his hands clasped behind his back and his feet spread apart like a soldier at parade rest. "I believe Sister Granier told me you have no children."

"That's right."

"May I ask why not?"

I stared at his slender back. "That's pretty personal."

He nodded. "Yes. But I have good reasons for asking."

"Which are?"

"Children are a gift to God, Mister Reed. People have that wrong, you know. They say children are God's gift to us, but it is the other way around."

"I'm not sure I follow you."

"Oh, it's very simple, really. God needs us. He needs our help. So we must provide more people, more children, to serve him. And we have to pray so that he can do his part." He turned to look at me. "Did you ever ask yourself why God needs our prayers when he already knows everything?"

"Yes. As a matter of fact I have."

"He needs us, is why."

"I am not convinced."

"Oh really? Perhaps you have another theory?"

"I think he wants us to pray so we'll know who to thank when the prayer is answered."

His childlike eyes lingered on mine for a moment, bloodshot and curious. "That is an interesting thought, Mister Reed." He turned back toward the window and stood silently for a moment, staring out at a passing band of men in uniform. "An interesting thought . . ."

We stood for some time without speaking. I got the feeling he was deciding something about me. I broke the silence first.

"What was it you wanted?"

"Why do you have no children?" He asked it immediately, as if ready for my question.

"Why do you want to know?"

Turning abruptly, he crossed to the chair behind the desk and sat. Without looking up at me, he said, "I need to understand your role in the plan."

"What plan?"

"God's plan, of course."

"You find out, be sure to let me know."

"Do not make jokes about such things, Mister Reed."

"Who's joking? I've been trying to figure out what God wants from me ever since . . . well, for a long time."

"Can your wife have children?"

"That's none of your business."

"Perhaps not." Leaning back in the swivel chair, he considered me at an angle. "You did about as well as we expected with the Jezebel last night. Congratulations."

It was becoming difficult to follow the conversation. The man seemed to leap from thought to unconnected thought. But eventually, I caught up with him.

"Ah," I said. "You have her trailer wired."

"Of course."

"Then you know she wouldn't tell me where my wife is."

"Yes."

"And you know about the other thing. Getting her out of here."

A subtle smile danced at the edges of his lips. He remained silent.

I said, "So. How about it?"

"How about what?"

"Please don't play games, Brother Slydel. How about letting me take her out of here?"

"Perhaps. After this morning's service."

Patience, I thought. *Patience is the only way you're going to get him to agree.* I said, "I'd love to attend your worship service, but do you think it's wise to wait? She said she'd take me to Mary Jo. She said Mary Jo is in pain. I'd like to go as soon as possible if that's all right with you."

The chair squeaked as he shifted his position. "What if she lied, Mister Reed? She is a liar, you know. As all servants of the Evil One are liars."

"I'll find out."

He leaned forward, eyes burning, all sign of exhaustion gone. "How will you find the truth? With violence? Will you shake it out of her?"

"I apologized for that, to her and to the Lord."

"Good," he nodded. "It is good to confess our sins before the Lord. But the question remains: how will you learn the truth from her?"

I thought about it. "If she doesn't want to tell me the truth, I suppose there's nothing I can do."

"But the Lord knows her heart, Mister Reed. He knows her heart and he will share her inner thoughts with us."

"What are you trying to say?"

He rose and walked around the desk. I followed him to the door of the trailer, waiting for his reply. He opened the door and stood beside it, smiling up at me. It was a beautiful smile, full of peace. I saw why so many people were willing to follow him. Who could doubt that such unselfconscious serenity came from God? Yet the innocence in his eyes and in his smile was very difficult to resolve with his behavior.

"I've instructed Brother Elmer to show you our operation, Mister Reed. He'll take you anywhere you'd like to go. We have nothing to hide from a brother. In half an hour, the two of you will return to our little open-air chapel to attend our worship service. I believe the Lord may answer your questions then."

Elmer loitered near the bottom of the steps just a few feet away, with one leg propped against the wall of the trailer. His eyes were on something across the clearing, but I got the impression that his casual posture disguised an intense interest in our conversation.

I said, "Can I take Miss Harmony back to the city after the service?"

"Only the Lord knows."

I took a quick step toward him. Bending down to place my face less than six inches from his, I said, "Are you going to let us leave or not?"

From the corner of my eye, I saw Elmer's hand settle onto his holstered automatic. James Slydel glanced at him and shook his head slightly. I turned, looked down at Elmer and his gun, and stepped away from Slydel.

James Slydel smiled. "Good. We should not quarrel, Mister Reed. I have Lucretia Granier's word for it that you are a true believer. Faye and I know your wife is one of us. We want to help you and her."

"*If* my wife was one of you, whatever it is that you are, do you think she would want you to keep me hostage here?"

"Hostage?" His innocent eyes grew wide. "Oh, dear me. You misunderstand completely. You are free to go at any time."

"And Elizabeth Harmony?"

A fierce determination replaced the naiveté of his expression. "Her fate is in the hands of the Lord, as I have said."

"Would God want her held hostage?"

"The Lord will deal with that servant of Satan later this morning. He may force her to tell us the truth about your wife. He may not. He is merciful to us. His mercy may extend to her as well. But, Mister Reed, I want you to understand, if he chooses to withhold his mercy from her, it is not for us to question his will."

"Withhold his mercy? What are you talking about?"

"A trial, Mister Reed. A test if you will. The Harmony woman will pass through the Lord's fiery crucible, and woe unto her if he finds her wanting in faith or repentance, for she will surely die."

Chapter 44

ELMER TRAILED ME LIKE A PUPPY ALONG A well-worn earthen path between dilapidated house trailers and shacks. A few trees remained standing around the clearing, live oaks and cottonwoods mostly, some three feet across at the base and tall as a church steeple. A group of them sheltered two green canvas tents near the east guard tower. The aroma of frying bacon drifted from one of the tents, competing with the sour chemical smell of waterproofed canvas. Beyond the tents, we reached the perimeter fence, eight feet high and topped with razor-sharp wire. If Elmer understood that I was searching for a way to escape, he did not seem to mind. We strolled beside the fence for a hundred yards. At one spot a gully ran beneath the fence. Dull red rocks had been piled up to fill the gap where the ground fell away from the bottom of the wire. It was a possibility. I was careful not to turn my head as I passed, assessing the potential from the corner of my eye. Then, just beyond the fence, I saw the gully disappear beneath a solid hedge of thorny underbrush. Slipping through the barbed vines would be brutal, if it was possible at all. I would have to keep looking.

"Hey," Elmer called from several steps behind. "It's about time for the mornin' service. We better head over theah."

I turned and said, "Lead the way."

He squinted at me suspiciously. "You go on. I'll be right behind."

With a shrug, I continued along the path until it reached a fork. At Elmer's direction, we followed the left-hand trail back toward the center of the compound. We had the paths to ourselves for the first time all morning as we wove our way between the peculiar structures scattered around the clearing. When we reached the heart of the compound, I saw why. The Slydels' followers had packed the low wooden bleachers and stood three deep around the odd circular depression in the ground. As we approached them from the rear, they began to sing "Shall We Gather at the River."

Elmer and I took a position behind the crowd to the left of the bleachers. Looking left and right above the heads of the assembly, I searched for Elizabeth Harmony. Black automatic rifle muzzles sprouted like dead branches from the arms of a few men scattered at the fringes of the crowd. Overhead netting cast a grid of shadows on eager faces beneath blood red berets. The men and women in the bleachers rocked from side to side, marking the rhythm of their song. Faye Slydel stood in the center of the circular depression. From her position five feet lower than the ground I stood upon, she turned slowly with a thin-lipped smile and waved her arms to the beat of the music. A chubby man beside her massaged an ornate black and gold accordion in time to the music, fingers dancing along the pearl white keys like spiders leaping across a web. His eyes were tightly closed as his fat arms wiggled, pushing in and out on the instrument.

They sang one old hymn after another, rocking left and right to the bright Cajun tinged notes of the accordion. There were smiles all round. A festive mood rose from the strange amphitheater, fueled by the toe-tapping zydeco beat. Beside me, Elmer swung to and fro in time with the music, singing off-key. Their loud voices, full of hope and life, surged across the clearing and echoed back from the tall cypress at the edge of the Barataria swamp. In the background, I heard squirrels chattering, as if they too had decided to join in.

Brother James Slydel pushed through the crowd at the opposite edge of the pit and descended a set of wooden steps. Dressed in the usual paramilitary uniform, he stood in the center of the pit beside his wife, beaming up at the worshipers and clapping his hands in time to their final song. When it was over, Faye Slydel and the fat accordion player ascended the steps and James began to speak.

"Brothers and sisters, today is a great day! Every day is great when we live it with the Lord, but today he has something very special planned. Today, he will allow us to witness a miracle of salvation, or the swiftness of his judgment."

He turned slightly toward the side where I stood and nodded, his eyes on someone to my left. Over the heads of those around me I saw two large men lead Elizabeth Harmony through the crowd to the edge of the pit. Suddenly, the animals of the swamp were silent: no outraged squawk of the great blue heron, no tender coo of the mourning dove, no chattering squirrels. It was as if all of God's creatures feared the outrage that was to come. Each man grasped one of Lizzy's arms and, kneeling at the top of the wall, slowly lowered her over the side. I noticed that the walls of the depression were lined with smooth corrugated steel. James Slydel motioned for the woman to join him in the center of the depression. Looking up at the ring of people, she slowly crossed the dirt floor to his side. She still wore the oversized white shirt and short blue cutoffs. Her blond hair was limp and tangled. Her feet were bare and filthy. Her green eyes were wide with fear.

"Brethren, meet Miss Elizabeth Harmony. She may look familiar to some of you. Miss Harmony works at the Milo Women's Clinic."

There was an immediate reaction from the crowd, the sound of a hundred people sucking in their breath. Slydel held up his hands and said, "I understand. I understand how you feel, completely. But remember our calling of Christian love. And remember Paul's words in First Corinthians, 'If I speak in the tongues of men and of angels but have not love, I am only a resounding gong or a clanging cymbal . . . love keeps no record of wrongs.' We must deal with this woman with love in our hearts. We must offer forgiveness on behalf of the thousands of innocent babies she has so heartlessly murdered."

Beside him, Lizzy Harmony stiffened, turning her face down toward the hard-packed soil.

"For this woman claims she has been working with the butcher Milo in order to change things from the inside."

From the crowd came shouts of "No!" and "She's a liar!" Again, Slydel raised his hands for silence.

"Perhaps she is a liar as you say. But this morning, Miss Harmony told me she has decided to commit herself to the Lord. Although she has only now become one of us, she claims she was led to do what she did. She said she will prove this, in the way prescribed by Holy Scripture." James Slydel closed his eyes and recited, "And these signs will accompany those who believe: in my name, they will drive out demons, they will speak in new tongues, they will pick up snakes with their hands and when they drink deadly poison, it will not hurt them at all; they will place their hands on sick people and they will get well.'"

He opened his eyes and turned toward the woman, mumbling something under his breath. With a small nod, she knelt on the ground beside him. He turned back toward the crowd and said, "We have no sick people here, praise God, for all have been healed by his mercy." Shouts of "Amen!" rose from the bleachers. He continued, "Demons do not dare to dwell among us, for we are filled with the power of the Holy Ghost. We know that Paul warned us against trusting overmuch in the power of tongues. He warned us that Satan, the Great Pretender, can speak also through tongues. Let us pray." Like a priest christening a baby, Brother James Slydel placed one hand on Lizzy Harmony's head. He closed his eyes and said, "Lord, this woman has come among us claiming to be in harmony with our holy crusade. We earnestly pray that this is so. But we fear her, Lord. We fear that the Evil One may infiltrate our presence through this poor soul, sowing death and destruction as he has done for so long through the actions of those like her. We pray that you will test her according to your Word, which we have remembered here today. We pray that you will confirm your love for one of your own through the miraculous signs and wonders we have described. But Lord, if the Great Deceiver has brought her among us, we pray that you will rid the earth of her; that she may no longer cause suffering and death to innocent babies. Lord, as always, not our will but your will be done."

Without another word, James Slydel climbed the wooden steps to join the crowd. When he reached the top, two men knelt and lifted the steps out of the pit. Lizzy Harmony remained at the center of the depression, kneeling with her head bowed toward the earth. A man pushed his way through the crowd on the other side of the strange arena. As he drew near the edge, I saw that he was Charles, the blond man with the huge jaw who had driven me to their camp. In each hand, he clutched the handle of a covered box, like the one I first saw him place in the bed of his truck at the Slydels' church in Metairie. Behind the blond man, three other men followed. Each also carried two covered boxes. Suddenly, I guessed what was beneath the green felt covers and took an involuntary step toward the pit. Elmer's hand clutched my upper arm. His grip was surprisingly strong. Leaning near, he whispered, "You best stand still, Mister Reed. They don't need no help. They done this lots of times. Most of us been down there where that little lady is."

I turned to him. His eyes shone with excitement. He glanced from me to the woman in the pit. I followed his gaze and saw that she had risen from her knees. She turned in the center of the pit, staring up at the crowd, fear and defiance flashing from her grimy face, clenched fists held rigidly at her sides. She seemed to know what was coming.

The men removed the green felt covers, revealing the squirming mass of snakes each cage contained. They were water moccasins, natives of the swamp, dull brown and gray and undistinguished by any markings other than the vague crisscross diamond pattern along their backs, and the pregnant swelling of the poison at their jaws.

Elizabeth Harmony screamed and ran toward my side of the pit, frantically clawing at the smooth steel sides just below my feet. When she realized escape was hopeless, she backed away and turned her face up toward us, fury flashing in her deep green eyes.

She said, "You people are hypocrites! You stand there so high and mighty, talking about what an *evil* thing me and Melvin Milo do, and you bring me here to do the same thing. Worse! It's *worse* what you're doing, because you can see me. You can hear me. You know I'm here. I'm *alive!* Those things we take out aren't alive. You don't understand. They're nothing. They're like an appendix or a tumor; a lump of flesh that's got no life of its own. They're part of those girls' bodies, don't you see? It's up to those girls, what we do. They decide! We ask them! Nobody here asked *me!*"

Lizzy Harmony's eyes brimmed with tears. She searched the crowd in silence until she saw me. A communication occurred between us, unspoken but personal and strong. She stood still, with her back to the cages and her eyes locked on mine. Her appeal was clear. I was her only source of hope in that twisted nightmare, her one true judge.

My mind raced, searching for a way out, but the situation seemed hopeless. I considered overpowering Elmer and taking his weapon. But at least a dozen of the men in the crowd were armed with rifles or handguns. I wouldn't get three feet.

Across the pit, the three men set the boxes on the ground at the top of the metal wall. They slapped the sides of the cages, rattling the wire, enraging the snakes. Then, one by one, they swung open the tops of the cages and tilted them over the side, shaking them to dislodge the reluctant serpents onto the floor of the pit, five feet below.

If Lizzy Harmony heard the dull thuds of the water moccasins as they hit the ground behind her, she did not show it in her eyes. Her eyes remained locked on mine, silently begging, yet accusing me too, as if I played a part in the madness.

Behind me, Elmer sucked in his breath. I heard him whisper, "Why did they drop them all?"

I turned and hissed, "What do you mean?"

His eyes never left the pit. He said, "I seen them use one, or sometimes two when the Spirit is strong within a man. A real big man. But never this many. James must want her dead."

I swung back to the pit. On the far side I counted nine snakes, each between three and four feet long. They were molten rage, entangled, writhing, searching for an outlet for their fury. One by one they freed themselves from the living knot and slid across the hard-packed soil toward Elizabeth Harmony's bare legs. There was nothing I could do for her but pray.

I begged the Lord to save her. I reminded him that she was his, as much his as any other sinner there. I knew she was not a believer, and pleaded for her soul. *Please, dear God, don't take her before she knows you. Please let me show you to her.* Instantly, a sense of calm filled me, accompanied by a certain knowledge of what I must do. It was the Lord, speaking directly to me. I truly believe that now.

Elmer watched me closely, ready for anything, except for what I did.

Chapter 45

TAKING ONE STEP FORWARD, I DROPPED INTO the pit. The water moccasins paused at the vibration my boots sent through the hard black dirt. It gave me the extra second I needed to reach Elizabeth Harmony first. I lifted her like a child and turned to face the bleachers. James and Faye Slydel were there, front and center. I spoke directly to them.

"This woman does not believe, Brother Slydel. You know that. She has no faith to protect her. This is no test. It's a death sentence."

The first of the snakes struck me. I felt the whiplike impact against my shin. They could not reach Lizzy. I cradled her in my arms above their reach and said, "I haven't been a Christian for very long. I don't know what that Scripture meant—the snakes and tongues and poison and all of that. But I know my Lord. I know how he wants us to prove our love for him." Another moccasin struck, this time on my calf. Then another at my ankle. And another. And another. Staring up at the silent crowd I said, "You had me confused. You're a preacher, and I thought you must know better than me. I thought maybe God was speaking to you instead of me. I thought maybe I was wrong to feel sorry for Doctor Milo and his wife and the way you were treating them. But last night the Lord spoke to *me!* He told me that what he wanted us to do was to love these people. You prove the love of God by the loving way you treat your enemy," I lifted Lizzy an inch higher and said, "You can't change the world. Only the love of Jesus can do that."

Faye Slydel watched with something like fear in her face. James Slydel swallowed, his Adam's apple bobbing furiously. Then, for the first time, I saw hatred in his eyes. He screamed, "She is a Jezebel! A daughter of Satan! If you truly believe, set her down and let us establish her fate by the miraculous work of God!"

His voice echoed from the wall of cypress, repeating the name of God three times.

I returned his fierce stare silently, with Lizzy Harmony's arms wrapped around my neck as she sobbed against my chest. Five more times, the snakes struck my lower legs. The crowd was completely silent. I heard a dull thump each time the fangs sank through the fabric of my blue jeans. My arms ached with the weight of Elizabeth Harmony, her arms clutching tightly at my neck, her tears damp against my cheek. I wondered why I felt no pain. I thanked the Lord for that, and silently asked him to receive me. Knowing I was about to die, I lifted my face toward the sunny Louisiana sky and whispered, "'Father, forgive them, for they know not what they do.'"

A thin voice rose from the crowd. "Brother Slydel, theah's your miracle. Look at him! Ten strikes and still standin'! None of *us* ever took so much."

I turned toward the voice. Elmer stood at the rim of the pit, looking down with his red beret clutched against his chest. Without removing his eyes from the snakes at my feet, he dropped to his knees and said, "It *is* a miracle! Praise God!" Then, one by one, those around him removed their berets, kneeled, and bowed their heads as well.

James Slydel stormed away through the crowd, with Faye following slowly behind, casting furtive backward glances toward me. Elizabeth Harmony cried softly in my arms as they lowered the steps for us.

Chapter 46

I NEVER SAW A MIRACLE BEFORE."

I looked up at her.

She said, "I never believed in them."

I said, "They happen all the time."

"No. I don't think so."

"They do if you believe."

"Whatever."

We sat silently for a minute, alone again in the trailer where we met. Then she said, "Pull up those jeans. Take off your boots. I want to see where they bit you."

It was obvious when we looked. Twin parallel scratches scarred the dark brown leather from the ankle to just below the top of each boot. One pair of scratches began a mere quarter inch below the place where the thick leather stopped and the skin of my calf lay bare. I felt a familiar cold brush along my spine.

Elizabeth Harmony said, "See? It was just the boots. They couldn't bite through the boots. There's no miracle to it at all."

"Isn't there?"

"Well, of course not. Anyone could have done it."

I nodded, looking away from her. She said, "Hey. I don't mean it that way. It took a lot of guts to jump down there like you did. I wouldn't have done it. I'll never be able to thank you enough. It's just . . . well, for a minute I was thinking that maybe God really did work a miracle, sending you to save me. Protecting you from those snakes. Like magic, you know?"

"And seeing these boots changed your mind?"

"Well, sure! You're just lucky you were wearing them. There's no miracle to it at all."

Remembering the strong presence I felt the moment before I jumped into the snake pit, I said, "I guess it all depends on how you look at it."

Again, we sat silently, alone with our thoughts. I slipped the boots back on and leaned against the trailer wall. I was sitting on the floor. She sat cross-legged on the bed. James Slydel had recovered his composure soon after we ascended from the snake pit and ordered that we both be placed in the trailer and guarded around the clock.

Lizzy Harmony said, "I suppose a person could say that God made sure they didn't bite you above the boots. Or that he made sure you wore those boots today."

"You could say that."

"And a person could say that God made sure you were the one standing there when those maniacs did that to me. It could have been someone without the guts to do what you did."

"Lizzy, guts had nothing to do with it."

"Now you're being humble. Don't do that."

"I'm not being humble. I'm telling you the truth. Remember when I shook you yesterday? I almost lost it and beat you. That's the kind of guy I am when it's just me, doing things my way. God *did* work a miracle for us this morning. He gave me the strength to do what I did. I never would have done it on my own."

"If you say so."

Remembering my fury the day before, I said, "Oh, absolutely."

After another pause, she said, "I heard what you said down there. Just before they decided to let us up."

"What?"

"I heard what you whispered about forgiving them."

"Oh."

She swung her legs over the side of the bed and leaned close to me, placing her forearms on her knees. The bed creaked under her shifting weight. "How could you do that? How could you stand there with those crazy people trying to kill us and ask God to forgive them?"

"I couldn't."

"But you *did*."

"Not me, Lizzy. God. God did that through me."

"God asked himself to forgive them through you?"

I chuckled. "Yes."

"That's crazy!"

"Only if you don't understand it."

"What's to understand?"

"You want me to explain?"

Tossing her long blond hair back, she lifted her chin and said, "No, thank you. I'm not interested in a sermon today."

"I wasn't planning on preaching one."

"Sure you were. I can see it in your eyes. You people are all the same."

"'You people'? What people are you talking about?"

"You religious types."

"I'm not very religious."

"Oh, come on!"

"No, really. I hate religion."

"But you pray! And talk about God!"

"Is that your definition of a religious person? Because you're talking about God right now, aren't you? And are you saying you never pray? Not even when you get in a tough spot?"

Her eyes flashed, full of mistrust. After a moment, she confessed, "I pray sometimes."

"Sure you do. Most people do."

"It's not the same."

"What's not the same?" I asked.

"Just because I pray doesn't mean I buy into that religion stuff."

I smiled. "Exactly."

Eyes searching mine, lips pursed in concentration, she said, "So, why *did* you say that about forgiving them?"

"I told you already, it wasn't me."

"Don't give me that!" she spat. "I hate that!"

"Lizzy, I don't know what else to say. I'm trying to answer your question."

She beat the mattress with her fist. "You must be crazy!"

"Why?"

"To forgive that scum in the middle of what they did to us! You have to be nuts to say what you said!"

I shrugged. "If you say so."

"I do say so!" she screamed. *"I do!"*

I stared at her, surprised at her unexpected outburst. Since everything I said seemed to infuriate her, I decided to remain silent. And so time passed, maybe half an hour. Half an hour can feel like a day when you're alone in a small room with a furious stranger. Now and then, Elizabeth Harmony would let out a little sound, like a snort, as if she was conducting an internal dialogue and was upset at her own thoughts. After a while, I shifted position, the plywood floor hard beneath my buttocks. Stretching my legs straight out in front seemed to help. Outside the trailer, I heard loud voices, and the sound of booted footsteps nearby. At first, I reflected upon what we had just said, but eventually, worries about Mary Jo drove away all thoughts of my exchange with Lizzy. My mind drifted far away, to a sweet summer day back home at the lake—me and Mary Jo, alone on the pier, holding hands and watching the water ripple with the sudden strikes of brim feeding on the surface. For a few minutes, I forgot where I was and basked in the glowing memory. Then Elizabeth Harmony crushed my reverie with a short, sudden curse.

I looked up at her. "What?" I asked.

"All right. You win. Explain it to me."

So I did. I started with the years of pretending, of lying to Mary Jo about a faith I didn't feel. I told her about my old friend Ernest B.'s last day on earth, about the morning I heard him speak of Jesus Christ and forgive the man who tortured him. I told her about the empty feeling I had lived with all my life, the question I always feared to ask: What was it all about? Did anything matter? I told her how, when I was on the verge of despair, without any proof, with no reason I could touch or see, I decided to believe in Jesus, and my life was changed— the empty feeling was gone forever.

"Just believing is enough?"

"Well, you also have to ask him to forgive you for turning your back on him all your life, and you have to trust him to do that."

Her voice was harsh. "I never trust anyone."

"It really isn't hard. You just let go of yourself and believe."

"Believe what, exactly?"

"Well, you start with believing that Jesus is God. And he died in our place."

"Like you almost died for me this morning."

I shook my head. "More than that. He went to hell for us, in our place. Then he came back into the world, to prove who he is." Touching my chest, I said, "I don't really understand the details—why he had to do it, or how it works—but I know his spirit is alive today, here in my heart."

Screwing her face up tight, she lowered her voice to mimic me with an exaggerated Southern accent, "'His spirit is *a-live-ah!* Right heah in my heart!' What a laugh. You sound like some television preacher out for money."

Anger bubbled up within me, threatening to overflow. Fighting the temptation to return her sarcasm, I mumbled, "You asked me to explain it to you."

She lifted her palms toward the ceiling and spoke again in her mocking accent, "Lawd, I thanks you fo' sending this heah holy missionary to save little ol' sinful me!"

Blushing, I pulled my knees up to my chest and stared at the floor. I felt foolish and abused, as if she had somehow caught me doing something shameful. Where did those emotions come from? Was I embarrassed by my faith? *Dear God*, I prayed, *please forgive my weakness.*

Another thirty minutes passed. At first, Elizabeth Harmony chuckled to herself now and then. Finally she fell silent. This time I wasted no thoughts on pleasant memories, concentrating instead on trying to think of a way out of the camp. I was mentally reliving my early morning walk with Elmer through the compound when Lizzy interrupted my thoughts again.

"Look," she said, "I'm sorry. I just got frustrated. You weren't being straight with me."

I did not reply. After a minute, she said, "Okay, ignore me, then. But I said I was sorry, and I meant it. You shouldn't trot out all that mumbo jumbo when a person asks you a serious question."

Still, I remained silent.

"Look!" she said, "I already know why you jumped down there to help me. You didn't want me to die until I told you where your wife is. That's obvious. So don't try to pretend you did it just for me. But I still can't figure out why you said that stuff about forgiving them. And when I ask, all of a sudden you turn all holier than thou, like one of those maniacs out there."

"I'm not any holier than you, or anyone else."

"He speaks!" Again she rolled her eyes toward the ceiling. "Thank you, Jesus!"

"Cut that out!" I said. "Don't make fun of what I believe."

She stared at me for a moment, something new within her eyes. Suddenly, her mocking smile disappeared and she said, "Well, I'll be. You really *do* believe that stuff, don't you?"

"I believe."

"You really buy all that about Jesus being in your heart?"

"I don't 'buy it.' I know it."

"How? How could you possibly *know* something like that?"

"It's not something I can explain, Lizzy. There's just this . . . knowing that I have."

She stared at me for a long time. I looked away, embarrassed again, feeling like she thought I was an utter fool. When she spoke again, I was surprised at what she asked.

"What's it like to have God in your heart? Try to describe it to me."

"Why? So you can mock whatever I say?"

"No. I won't do that. I swear." She leaned forward, eyes intense. "Please. Just tell me what it feels like."

How do you explain the taste of crystal-clean water? The smell of pure air? The most eloquent words become grunts when we speak of the love of God. I swallowed and thought, *God, what should I say?* Then the words just came.

"I was numb before. Now I'm free to feel. I never knew why I was alive. Now I do. I was afraid to die. Now, when I really think about it, I'm not afraid of death anymore. I always felt alone. Now I feel his presence and I'm never lonely, at least not in the way I used to be. I know why I'm here, why the world is here. I know I have an important place in things. And—"

Without warning, the door crashed open, and Charles stormed in. Thrusting his ponderous jaw left and right, he assessed the situation, then he aimed a pistol at me and said, "Get up."

I rose from the trailer floor, my attention solidly on the barrel of his gun. He made a slight motion with the pistol and said, "Brother Slydel wants to see you. Come on."

As I was about to step outside, I glanced back at Elizabeth Harmony. Her eyes met mine, full of fear. I smiled. "Don't worry, I'll be back."

Charles prodded my back with the barrel of his gun and said, "I wouldn't count on it, hoss."

Chapter 47

YOU ARE A SPY, SENT AMONG US TO DO THE devil's work!"

James Slydel said it with a calm that did not match the intensity in his eyes. We stood facing each other in the center of their strange compound.

I said, "Was it the devil that protected me from those snakes?"

"Certainly! He has it in his power to imitate the Lord's signs on earth. We know this is true. Paul warned us of it."

"And if Elizabeth Harmony had been bitten and lived? Would you say she was protected by Satan or by God?"

James Slydel's Adam's apple danced in his neck like a hapless rodent in the belly of a python. I had him and he knew it. If he said God protected her, I would ask why God needed my help, an agent of Satan. If he answered Satan, then the "test" he had put her through was never intended to be fair. Live or die, it was the Slydels or Satan, not God, who had judged her guilty.

Faye Slydel looked at me strangely. Her lips were slightly parted, exposing the gap between her crooked teeth. Deep inside the sickly brown smudges above her sunken cheeks, her eyes glowed. She said, "James, we should send this man away."

"I'll send him to hell where he belongs!"

Charles stood behind them, clutching his pistol, ready to do whatever Brother James Slydel ordered.

Faye touched her husband's arm. "We oughta be careful. He might be what he claims."

"But he saved the Jezebel!"

"The Lord sometimes has a use for sinners like her. You know that, James. Now listen to me. When he was standing there, holding her up above the serpents, I had a vision. I saw a tree full of fruit. The fruit was being eaten by worms. A snake came and ate the worms and saved the fruit."

James Slydel looked at her strangely. She said, "Don't you see? The Lord was telling me that the serpent from the Garden must be used for good, to protect the tree of life! This man was that serpent. We must allow him to fulfill his role in the Lord's plan."

"And the Jezebel?"

Faye made a dismissive gesture with her bony hand. "She is unimportant."

Slydel stared at me for a full minute, his eyes wide and innocent behind the thick lenses of his glasses. Then he turned to Charles and said, "Take him out and drop him off somewhere so he won't be able to find us."

Charles moved behind me and pressed the muzzle of the gun into my back. He said, "Let's go."

I said, "What about Lizzy? Let her come with me."

James Slydel said, "She has not yet been tested."

I knew it was no use, but I pleaded all the same. "Brother Slydel, remember what she told me about my wife? Mary Jo may be dying. Only Lizzy knows where she is. Please don't hurt her."

Slydel ignored me. Looking at Charles, he said, "Do it." Then he and Faye Slydel turned and walked away.

The blond man said, "Head toward the guard tower."

We retraced our steps from the night before, out of the compound through the side gate and along the narrow ridge through the swamp. Thin bars of sunshine sliced through the gaps in the leafy canopy, illuminating the airborne pollen that hung in the air as thick as campfire smoke. Tiny dots of green algae floated on the oily black water beside the path, drifting slowly between the conical trunks of towering cypress trees. Strange animals screamed in the distance, their calls like tortured prisoners begging for release. Now and then, Charles poked my back with the pistol. I tripped on a cypress knee. Charles thrust out his massive jaw impatiently as I rose and dusted myself off. He held the pistol at an angle, not quite pointing it at me. Without thinking, I grabbed his wrist with both hands. He grunted and took one step back, throwing me off balance. As I struggled to regain my equilibrium, he kicked me hard in the shin. Pain spiked up my leg, bursting hot white in my brain. He yanked hard and pulled his gun hand free. With a backhand motion, he slammed the pistol against my head. I went down.

The blond man stepped away, breathing hard. "All right, tough guy. Get up!" he growled.

A fog of oblivion drifted at the edges of my consciousness. His voice seemed to reach out from some faraway place. I rose to my hands and knees. With no warning, he kicked me hard in the ribs. I grunted in pain.

"I said get up!"

I rose. He motioned along the trail with the pistol. As I walked I felt my side tenderly for broken ribs. A warm trickle of blood ran across my temple and dripped onto my filthy shirt. Charles stayed two steps behind me all the way to his truck, careful now not to let me get within reach of the pistol. At the truck, he held out the black blindfold from the night before.

"Put that on."

I complied.

"Now, turn toward the truck and put both hands behind your back." I turned, expecting him to tie my hands. Instead, I felt a short burst of blinding pain on the back of my head.

Then, darkness.

Chapter 48

I THINK I OPENED MY EYES.

My right cheek pressed into the putrid mud of the Barataria swamp. Before me, I saw the ground rippling like a bubbling cauldron of black oil. A loud buzz hummed in my ears. My legs sprawled below the surface of the motionless black water. My upper body lay in the mud, one arm cocked beneath my chest, circulation gone, feeling nothing. The world hung sideways, a primeval jungle of tangled vines, skewed cypress, and the nasty smell of rot. The sun was almost down. I could tell by the angle of the rays piercing the foliage. So I had been there most of the day, passed out cold, half in and half out of the stagnant water.

I tried to roll over, to free the arm beneath my torso. A scorching agony stripped away all thought, spreading around my chest like a ring of fire. Broken ribs. Maybe worse. I allowed myself to lie back against the pungent soil, a whimper escaping from my lips. After the pain subsided, I opened my eyes again. Why did the earth ripple and move so strangely? I willed myself to focus my eyes. Dear Lord, could that be? The soil around me was thickly covered by houseflies. Millions and millions of fat, shimmering, jet-black flies in constant, crawling motion.

"Hah!" said a voice behind my back. "I thought so, me."

My eyes closed against my will. Darkness settled upon my mind like the first shovel full of dirt in an open grave. I felt I had to fight it. I felt it was a matter of life and death. I did not know why.

The voice I heard was strangely hollow. It seemed to echo from the inside of my skull, bouncing around in the place where my brain should have been. It said, "You been a lot of trouble lately, you. But that all done now. Oh, yes. That done now."

I opened my eyes again. The scene had changed, become darker, yet I could see some things more clearly. Objects in the distance were obscured by a drifting smoke that seemed to rise from the water. How could smoke come from water? Preparing myself for the pain, I drew a breath and rolled to the side. It came again, in a tidal wave, almost drowning my consciousness. I struggled against the oblivion, knowing I must, knowing I would die if I let it tear me away. Rolling through the agony, I made it to a new position, flat on my back. The sky glowed sickly orange through the limbs above, clouds of glowing sepia drifting above the swamp like poison gas. The trees, the fallen logs, the palmettos, and the earth itself lay choking beneath the evil mantle of Satan—a shimmering coat of flies.

Something needed to be done. Something important. What was it? Oh, yes. That voice.

"Now then, boy. What make you think you any different, you? What make you think I not gonna come for you someday, me?"

Where was it coming from? After all the pain it took to get to my new position, I still saw no one. It didn't seem fair.

"I been watchin' you for long, long time, me. Watchin' close." A strange clacking sound occurred between the words, like dried sticks beating together. An image of Juliette Milo's strange necklace flashed in my mind. The string of bones. The monkey claw. I turned my head. Something was there, at the edge of my vision.

"An' we knew you'd come our way one of these days. Oh, yessss." It drew out the last sound, hissing like a snake. I turned my head further, looking up the bank, away from the water. He stood there, just five or six feet away, hands on his hips, glaring down at me. He was tall; almost seven feet tall, with the skinny build so common in those that reach that height. He wore black from head to toe, a plain suit coat and slacks that seemed impossibly immaculate in that filthy place. On his head, he wore a tall black top hat.

Beneath the hat, his face was a nightmare: a contorted skull, overlarge and draped with rotting flesh that curled away from the grinning teeth like the gaping edges of a gangrenous wound. Beneath the skull, where the suit coat fell open, I saw the rolling white parallel lines of his ribs, floating in a mass of bloody flesh. But more than the rest, it was the eyes that froze my heart with fear. They were twin pits of black, with tiny dots of red, glowing like the eyes of a wolf. I had seen those eyes before, twenty years before in the face of a teenage girl dressed in rags at the end of a New Orleans alley, and in the black silhouette of the woman who stalked me through the woods outside my home.

It spoke, teeth clacking together like a steam engine gone insane. "Oh, yessss. We here for you now. Gonna take you back where you belong. Gonna gut you proper. Take you *ti bon ange*. Make you nothin' but a shell for de rest of time. Do what *we* want now."

I lifted my head as far as I could and said, "Who are you?"

It threw back its horrible face and laughed, the same hopelessly evil, echoing laughter I had heard in that alley, so long before. It said, "I Beelzebub, me. I Lucifer. I de Prince of Darkness. But folk jus' call me *Baron Samadhi* round heah."

The flies climbed from the soil, a black plague, flowing up his fancy trousers. But then I saw what I should have seen all along. Everything in the swamp glistened like snakeskin beneath the thick black swarm—everything but me. The putrid flow of flies parted around me, avoiding contact with my form. Of everything I could see—trees, brush, logs, and mud—I alone was free of them.

Laying my head back against the mud I closed my eyes and smiled.

"What dat! What you do? You *smile*, you? You best watch you self! I heah fo' you soul, an' I mean to take it, me!"

One of my favorite Bible verses came to mind. Without reopening my eyes, I whispered, "'Get thee behind me, Satan.'"

Then I slept.

Chapter 49

DAT BETTER. DAT BETTER. YA'LL LIE STILL now."

I felt something cold and wet on my forehead. The voice seemed to grow from a source inside my mind. Grays and multicolored streaks of light swirled behind my eyelids. It was like living inside a kaleidoscope.

"You gonna be fine now. Dat a nasty knock on the noggin you got, but you head hard as a *bois d'arc*."

I opened my eyes. A woman's face floated before them. She seemed familiar . . . was it really her?

"Mary Jo!" I tried to sit up, reaching for her. Nausea rushed in. I clasped my head in my hands and groaned aloud. The woman frowned and pushed me down making shushing sounds with pursed lips.

"Ya'll lie still now. You know who I am?"

I fought a pain that throbbed in my head with every pulse of my heart. Squinting my eyes, I willed myself to focus. Her face grew clear. "Edna."

She nodded and leaned back. "Good. You be all right quick, quick. We worried theah for a while, though."

"How did I get here?"

"That a fine question. My little Madelaine, she strollin' over to the bayou an' she see a man lyin' face up in the shallows. She come cryin' so me an Jacques go see can we find him. Sure 'nuff we get theah, see that man you. Ya'll a big big man. It take Jacques an' me two hours to drag ya'll heah."

"What day is it?"

She had to think. "I believe it Wednesday evening."

A whole day gone. I closed my eyes again, struggling against the pounding in my head. Suddenly, I remembered the apparition in the swamp. The clicking bones, the hiss, the flies, and those twin dots of red in the depths of a grinning skull. Fear licked the edges of my consciousness. But I told myself it was a dream, a semi-comatose hallucination. Then I remembered what went before. Elizabeth Harmony in the trailer. "... *all that pain* ..." I pushed against the mattress to sit up and said, "Edna, you've got to help me. There's a camp somewhere around here, a bunch of people living together. They're some kind of crazy religious group."

"We heard of dem."

"Good. There's a woman there. She says she knows where Mary Jo is. We've got to find her."

"Oh. No need for dat. I already know where sister at."

Again, I tried to sit up without thinking. The pulsing in my head became so intense I almost lost consciousness. When the nausea had passed, I said, "What did you say?"

Edna removed the damp rag from my forehead. "I sent Jacques over to the store down the way to call *Maman*. To see do she wanna come pick you up. She say no. Don't like you much is what I think, me." Edna smiled.

"But what about Mary Jo?"

"*Maman* say some woman just called her. Say Mary Jo over to someplace called the Crescent City Garage, up in N'awlins. Say you most likely know where dat be."

Closing my eyes, I said, "I know where it is. Praise God, I know where it is."

"Yeah, well don't be praisin' him too soon."

"What does that mean?"

"De woman say something wrong with sister. Said Mary Jo feelin' poorly."

"I know that." I stared at the bare wooden ceiling. The jagged edge of an old water stain danced in the flickering light of an oil lamp on the bedside table.

"I've got to go now," I said, and I struggled to swing my legs over the edge of the bed. But it was too soon. Darkness dropped a curtain on my mind, and suddenly the image of a leering skull in a top hat loomed before me. I opened my eyes. It disappeared. Was it real? Was I dreaming? Had everything been a dream? But the creature in the swamp seemed so real, so frightfully real. What was true? What was a lie?

Edna was speaking as if she hadn't noticed anything.

"... 'Course you do, Garr. I told Jacques, make you up a bed in de back of ol' Jules. We gonna drive you into town good and proper." Turning her head, she called, "Jacques boy! We ready now!"

With Edna under my left arm and Jacques under my right, I stumbled through their tiny shack, past the pagan altar with the burning candles and the amulets, down the worn wooden steps, and across the white shell driveway to their antique pickup truck. The bed of the truck contained a thin mattress covered with threadbare blankets. The tailgate seemed to be a mile high, but with their help, I made it up onto the mattress.

Edna said, "Now, you lie quiet back theah, brother Garr. Jacques gonna get you to town quick. All I ask is dat you keep my boy from harm, you."

"Aren't you coming?"

"Who watch de little ones then?"

I nodded and lay back. Above me, stars peeped through the black felt ceiling of the Barataria sky. Jacques started the engine. Without looking at her, I said, "Edna?"

"Yes, Garr."

"When this is over . . ."

"I know, honey. I been too long without my sister. Too long without you, too."

She brushed the hair from my forehead. "Yes," I said. "Too long."

Chapter 50

TOWERING BRANCHES JOINED HANDS ABOVE the road like Olympian gods playing London Bridge. I lay on the mattress in the bed of the ancient truck watching the moon wink each time a limb sped by. It was a brisk evening. I was glad for the ragged blankets.

The crunch of gravel beneath the tires gave way to the whine of rubber on pavement. Other vehicles passed us. A streetlight flashed by, then we stopped. Grunting from the pain in my side, I clutched the cold metal wall of the truck bed and clawed my way upright to look around. We were idling at the only stoplight in Lafitte. It glowed green and Jacques accelerated out of town. I forced myself to remain sitting for half an hour more as he wove his way north toward Barataria Boulevard. As we drew nearer to the river and New Orleans, traffic thickened around us, like flies seeking a corpse. I tapped on the glass and waved Jacques over to the shoulder. He opened his door and stepped outside the cab.

"You all right, Uncle Garr?"

A semi tractor trailer roared by, the tailwind whipping at the blanket around my shoulders. Jacques held his polka-dot cap in place with one hand. I yelled to be heard. "I'm fine, son. You're gonna need me up front to give you directions to the garage."

"Can you make it?"

"Let the tailgate down and we'll see."

I inched my way across the truck bed and gingerly set my boots on the asphalt shoulder of the highway. Jacques came near but I waved him off. I had a feeling I was going to need to be mobile soon. It was best that I try to make it on my own.

In the cab, the heater made the blanket unnecessary. I shrugged it off as we topped the tall steel bridge above the Mississippi. The lights of New Orleans twinkled downriver, like sparkles in a harlot's jewels. Jacques followed my directions carefully, both hands on the wheel, diligently signaling his turns in advance, eyes never straying from the road. We reached Canal. A police cruiser pulled alongside us. I glanced down into the suspicious eyes of a uniformed cop, then quickly looked away. There was no way he could make me. I had walked out of Lieutenant Washington's squad room before they had a chance to take my photograph—or did they still call them mug shots? Either way, the cops on the beat probably had nothing but a general description to go by: six feet three inches, two hundred twenty pounds, brown eyes, no mustache, no beard, no distinguishing features except a slightly damaged right ear, hidden by brown hair worn a little long on the sides. Still, I kept my face turned away from the cruiser, thanking the Lord that Jacques was such a timid driver. The cruiser continued straight on Canal when we turned into the Quarter.

Jacques seemed distracted by the action in the streets. Two women yelled lewd invitations as we passed the corner of Chartres and Bienville.

"Pay no attention, Jacques. Keep your mind on the road."

"Yessir," he said, his face pale and young in the glow of a passing streetlight.

We rolled to the curb outside the Crescent City Garage. It was on the quiet east side of the Quarter in the *Fauberg Marginy*. Very few cars passed by at two in the morning. The sidewalks were empty. I said, "You stay out here, son. Keep these doors locked and don't open them for anyone. If you feel like you need to, start her up and drive away. Just be sure to circle around now and then until I come out."

I stepped from the truck. Standing with the door open, I said, "Jacques, did your momma give you some kind of a weapon to bring along?"

His eyes widened. "No sir."

"Do you have anything stashed in the truck that I might use?"

Turning sideways, he reached behind the seat and withdrew a five foot wooden handle with a large three-pronged steel fork mounted on the end. He passed it out to me. I turned it up to the light. The fork's prongs were viciously barbed. Glancing at Jacques, I said, "Frog gigger?"

"Yessir."

I balanced it in both hands. It would do. It would have to do.

Chapter 51

THE SINGLE OVERHEAD DOOR WAS DOWN and locked. Moving carefully to favor my ribs, I crossed the sidewalk to peek into the garage office through the grimy windows. Squinting between two pieces of paper taped to the other side of the glass, I could barely make out the interior in the light trickling down to the wooden plank floor. A car approached along Burgundy. I straightened and faced the street. The car did not pause. Jacques's face was white and scared inside the truck. I smiled and gave a little salute before trying the office door. The worn brass doorknob turned in my hand; I stepped inside. Standing with my back to the open door and the frog gigger at port arms, I surveyed the tiny office in the beam of light from the window and saw a paper-strewn desk, a calendar with cheesecake photographs of buxom girls holding mechanic's tools, half a dozen bad checks stapled to the Sheetrock next to a tax certificate, an ancient wooden swivel chair with a thin blue seat cushion, and two filing cabinets, one black and one putty gray, both scratched and scarred.

And a faint set of bloody footprints leading my way from the narrow hall.

Dear God, I prayed. *Watch over me and Mary Jo. Keep us safe if that is your will.*

Holding the gigger with the sharp end forward, I slipped down the hall past the time clock with its rows of time cards. I was careful not to step on the bloody footprints. At the rear door to the service area, I paused and took several deep breaths. Each one seared the muscles in my side, but I had to calm my heart. Finally, when I felt ready, I reached forward with my left hand and slowly turned the doorknob. The click of the latch slammed into the eerie silence like a wrecking ball. I paused, half expecting bullets to tear through the door. Two or three minutes passed. Nothing. I opened the door and stepped into the cavernous garage.

Moonlight streamed through the antique skylights high above. Cars of every description lined the walls of the huge building, some on the ground, others frozen in the air on pneumatic lifts. The row of wooden filing cabinets remained standing on the left. Across the garage, the parts racks loomed above the concrete floor, stacked with long boxes like caskets in a mausoleum. Centered in a beam of moonlight halfway across the wide empty slab, a woman lay face down on the concrete. I forgot caution and ran to her, the echo of my boots reverberating from the tall brick walls.

She lay in a spreading pool of her own blood, arms and bare legs skewed like a rock climber stretching for her next toehold. The footprints showed where someone had stood beside her after first stepping in the blood, then walked away. Her blond hair fanned around her head as if carefully arranged on a pillow. I knelt and said, "Lizzy? Can you hear me?"

A small nod. Perhaps I could do something for her. As gently as possible, I rolled her over and could not stifle a gasp at what I saw. She had been shot at least four times in the chest. I pressed both palms against the bubbling wounds, but it was useless. It was a miracle she was even breathing.

"I'm going to get you some help, honey. You hang on."

Using the handle of the gigger for support, I stood to go back to the telephone in the office. She mumbled something. I said, "What? I couldn't hear you."

She mumbled it again.

I knelt again, leaning over to place my ear beside her mouth. Her eyes were open, staring across the garage, an inch above the floor. She smacked her lips once, as if they were too dry to speak, then, very softly, she said, "I believe."

My heart leaped. Very slowly, very clearly, I said, "Lizzy, what do you mean?"

Again, she seemed to struggle to speak, working her mouth like someone dying of thirst. But it wasn't thirst she was dying of. Finally, she said, "Jesus . . . I believe."

I kissed her cheek and whispered, "Praise God."

Then, rising with a grunt of pain, I said, "Hang on, Lizzy. I'll go get you some help."

It was the strangest thing. I knew somehow that she was happy, even though she was dying on the cold concrete floor of a mechanic's garage. Joy and sorrow fought for control of my own heart, two halves of a whirlwind of emotion. For a few moments, I actually forgot why I was there.

Then I remembered. Throwing back my head, I yelled, "Mary Jo!"

My voice echoed from the antique brick walls and returned to me, empty. I crossed the garage toward a wall-mounted telephone. Dialing 911, I stood with my back to the wall and scanned the huge room. She might be anywhere. Lying behind a car, shot like Elizabeth Harmony, or floating in a bayou like I was when little Madelaine Benoit found me. A man's voice came on the line. I told him that a woman was bleeding to death on the floor in front of me, told him the name and location of the garage, and hung up, frantic to search the place for Mary Jo.

Five minutes later, after looking everywhere, I knew she was not in the garage.

I returned to kneel at Lizzy's side and said, "Lizzy. What happened here?"

She did not react.

"Can you tell me where Mary Jo is?"

Still she did not answer. I cradled her head in my lap and spoke to her softly. I told her about heaven, about the mansion waiting there for her. I told her she would see Jesus, that he would greet her with open arms and the most perfect love in his eyes, would prepare a place for her in paradise. I stroked her forehead and told her I envied her. She would be with the Lord that night, free of the troubles of the world, free of the pain and the insanity. Her eyes seemed to search the empty void above us as I spoke, flicking to and fro as if she saw something there. Perhaps she did. They stopped searching and fixed themselves in one position, focused and attentive. She smiled. Her arms moved just a little, as if she wanted to reach for whatever it was. Then she released her breath and lay still.

Sitting cross-legged on the concrete with Elizabeth Harmony's lifeless head in my lap, I cried. Emotions swirled out of control within me. I was miserable, I was joyful. I felt love and I felt sorrow. I praised God for Lizzy's salvation. But it was difficult to understand why she had to die or why I had to live without my wife. I closed my eyes and abandoned myself to the rapture and the misery, sobbing loudly. A hand touched my shoulder. I looked up into the dispassionate face of a man in a dark blue uniform. Behind him, a woman approached carrying a large black case. I was surprised to see them so soon.

"Give us some room, mister."

I gently laid her head on the concrete. Leaning heavily on the handle of the frog gigger, I stood as the medics went to work. A pair of policeman approached across the empty floor. The first one eyed the gigger warily. Standing ten feet away from me with his gun pointed at my chest, he said, "Drop the weapon."

The wooden handle clattered against the floor, like *Baron Samadhi's* clacking teeth.

I said, "How did you get here so fast?"

"Never mind that. Just tell us what happened."

Beginning with the bloody footprints in the office, I described my experiences in the garage. When I finished, the lead policemen said, "But what were you doing here at this time of night?"

I sighed. It was over. I said, "Maybe one of you should call Lieutenant Lincoln Washington. He'll want to hear this, too."

The policeman was about to respond when the female medic said, "Hey fellas. Look at this."

We all turned. She pointed her flashlight to the concrete, a few feet away from the spot where Elizabeth Harmony lay. Illuminated in the stark beam was something I had missed in the darkness. But it was something I had seen before, on the side of the Slydels' church, on the top of Linda Granier's crypt, and on the hospital wall beside the place where Doctor Melvin Milo almost died of a gunshot wound. A crude five-pointed star surrounded by eerie symbols had been crudely sketched with Elizabeth Harmony's blood.

Chapter 52

"OU CAN GO NOW," LINCOLN WASHINGTON told the two arresting officers. They left me slouched in the chair beside a desk at the police station squad room. My hands were cuffed. The air reeked, a combination of body odors, burnt coffee, and the aftermath of a hundred thousand cigarettes. The lieutenant sat in front of a computer screen. All around us, men and women came and went, talking on telephones, typing at computers, hollering across the room. It was as if the last twenty-four hours had never happened.

He watched the patrolmen until they had left the squad room, then turned to face me.

"You're a slippery one, Mister Reed."

"I'm sorry."

He grinned. "Are you really?"

I remained silent.

He rose and walked around the desk and said, "Hold up your hands."

I lifted them. He grasped the chain between the handcuffs and fit a key into the locks, freeing my wrists one at a time. Returning to his seat behind the desk, he said, "There, Mister Reed. That oughta make it easier for you this time."

I rubbed my wrists. "Easier?"

"Sure. Must have been a problem getting those off last night."

I smiled. "No. Not really. You left your keys in that filing cabinet."

Turning to look at the cabinet behind him, he frowned. "Imagine that."

Suddenly, I understood. "You let me get away, didn't you?"

Amusement lit his eyes. "Well, I kinda hoped you would."

"But why?"

Leaning back in his chair, he glanced down at his chest and straightened his tie. "We needed your help, Mister Reed. We thought you might lead us to your wife, or else to those C.H.A.R.G.E. people's hideout."

I closed my eyes for a second and said, "Christ's Holy Army Resisting God's Enemies."

"You betcha."

"Why did you go to all that trouble?"

"You're the one took the trouble to say it all out like that. I just say C.H.A.R.G.E."

I stared at him.

He said, "Okay, okay. Just havin' a little fun. Those people will drive you crazy if you take them seriously. What do you want to know?"

"Right now, I want to know where my wife is."

"We're looking for her, Mister Reed. We've got every radio car in the city on alert. It's just a matter of time."

"You think she's alive?"

"Didn't find any evidence to the contrary at that garage. No signs of a struggle. Nobody's blood except that Harmony woman's. Are you sure about that call to your mother-in-law?"

"All I know for sure is what her daughter told me. But I trust Edna. And I can't think of any reason why Lucretia would lie about a thing like that."

He nodded. "Then we'll find her. It may take a while, but if she's trying to get home, chances are we'll find her, one way or the other."

"What if the woman who called Lucretia was Lizzy Harmony? Now she's dead. Whoever shot her could have taken Mary Jo."

"That's one possibility, yeah."

I held my head in my hands, eyes closed, afraid to give voice to the dismal alternative. Finally, I said, "I suppose it's also possible that Mary Jo shot her."

"We have to consider that, Mister Reed."

Something in his tone of voice made me look up. "You sound like you don't believe it."

"I don't."

I sat a little straighter. "Why not?"

"I've got my reasons. Best not to discuss them just yet."

"Lieutenant, I'm going crazy here. Please. Give me something to hold on to."

"I wish I could. Maybe later. When we know more."

I stood. I looked around helplessly. I sat back down and said, "What else can we do?"

"Nothing, Mister Reed. Just sit and wait while our men do their job. But I wouldn't worry too much if I was you. Things are heating up. They'll find her."

"Well then, while we wait, do you mind explaining why you thought arresting me and then letting me escape would get me to hide out with the Slydels?"

"Worked once before."

"What does that mean?"

Lincoln Washington said, "It means we did pretty much the same thing once before."

"You did? With whom?"

He shook his head. "Maybe we'll get into that later too."

"All right then, tell me why you wanted me to go to them."

"So we could follow."

"What is this? Riddle time? You want to play twenty questions?"

Lieutenant Washington smiled. "More fun this way."

"Fun for whom?" I picked up a pencil and bounced the eraser end on the desk. "Why did you want to follow me to the Slydels' camp?"

"They got a camp?"

"If you followed me you should know that."

He leaned forward, adjusting his tie again. "Ol' Benny lost you, Mister Reed. He lost you when they took you down that elevator." He made a dismissive gesture with his hand. His nails glistened with clear polish. "Benny's gonna have to attend a refresher course on how to run a tail. Where was this camp?"

"Somewhere down in Barataria. They blindfolded me, so I don't know exactly."

"Figures."

"They are very security conscious."

"How's that?"

"They blindfold their visitors, live deep in the swamp, wrap their camp with concertina wire, and have guards in towers with automatic weapons."

"Oh, boy. Wonder if they'll let us big boys play?"

I smiled. "Did you find any clues at the garage? Anything to give you a hint about where she is?"

"Which garage, the one where Benny lost you or the one where we found you?"

"Either."

He frowned and shook his head. "All we found was you and that Harmony woman and that screwy writing on the ground in there. Crazy thing to do, drawing in somebody's blood like that. And the craziest folks I know on this case are those C.H.A.R.G.E. people. How many men were at that camp?"

I pushed back in the old wooden chair and crossed my legs. "Tell you what. Let's trade. I'll answer that question if you answer one for me."

"All right. Maybe."

"Am I still under arrest?"

"That depends. Are you gonna give us any trouble about all this? You know—false arrest kinda thing?"

"I've got enough trouble already."

With a sudden bright and cheerful smile he said, "In that case, we have no record of you being under arrest. Ever. Now then, how many men were at that camp?"

"I'd guess about thirty. The rest were women and children."

"Children? Oh, that's just dandy."

"Why?"

"They'll use them to keep us from rushing the camp. Like those nuts over in Waco."

"Why would you rush their camp?"

"To arrest them."

"You could always wait until they come out. The Slydels don't stay there all the time. Faye Slydel just planted flowers in her front yard over by Magazine. And James is still preaching at that church in Metairie on Sundays."

"Problem with that is we can't arrest them for planting flowers and preaching." He smiled again. "Much as some people would like to."

"How about me? I could swear out kidnapping charges against them."

"That would do it, all right. But what about those ol' boys back in the swamp? What do you think they'd do if we go arrest their leaders?"

I thought about thirty men with automatic weapons. Men who made a practice of handling snakes, and hid from satellites twice a day. I said, "Things could get messy, I guess."

"Yeah. That's how I see it. They might come up here loaded for bear. We'll arrest the Slydels just as soon as they get back to town if you insist. But it might be better to wait and handle them all together down in Barataria where nobody else will get hurt."

"That's all right with me."

He nodded. "Good. You said they have guards with automatic weapons. How many weapons did you see and what kind were they?"

I closed my eyes, walking through the compound in my mind, visualizing men carrying rifles. "I'd say they have about twenty M–16's. The rest seemed to be armed with pistols and hunting rifles. But I wouldn't be surprised if they had more weapons stockpiled in there. Maybe grenades or homemade bombs. You know, it could have been them that killed Lizzy. And that's plenty of reason to go up against them. But I hate to think of anybody going up against them just because of what they did to me."

He said, "It's not just that. We think they're behind our problems here in New Orleans with bombs and threats and attempts on doctor's lives at abortion clinics. I told you someone tried to shoot that Milo fella a while back. And then there's those three clinic bombings. We like those so-called C.H.A.R.G.E. people for most of that."

Hope welled within me. "Do you think they killed Father McKay and shot Doctor Milo?"

He stared at me, making a decision. Then I saw something change in his eyes. Maybe that was when he decided to trust me. He said, "Yes. I do."

"So you think my wife is innocent?"

He nodded. "Pretty sure she had nothing to do with it."

I leaned forward, eager for the next answer. "Will you help me prove it?"

"Why do you think we let you go and followed you?"

"You thought I knew where she was? That I would go to her?"

"Crossed my mind."

An unconnected thought bobbed to the surface, then sank before I could fully understand its meaning. I said, "What did you mean when you said you've let someone escape to hide with the Slydels before?"

"We had a volunteer go undercover, pretend to be a suspect for a murder we thought the Slydels committed. The idea was to get them to hide our informant, then our informant would find out if they're the ones doing these bombings and murders."

"Then why did you need to follow me? Why not just ask your undercover guy where they were?"

"We would have, but we lost touch with her."

"Her? You sent a woman?"

"Yep. Maybe you saw her at that camp . . . about five six, late thirties, early forties, good figure, green eyes, auburn hair?"

I stared at him. He stared back. The thought forming in my mind was fantastic. But it explained so much.

"You're describing *Mary Jo?*"

Lieutenant Lincoln Washington said, "You betcha."

Chapter 53

I COULD NOT SPEAK. FALLING BACK AGAINST the chair, I stared at him while the implications raced through my mind. Mary Jo and the police? Together all along? But that meant she couldn't be the one who shot Doctor Milo . . . and they knew! They knew she was innocent! Relief rose within me, replacing the ever-present dread I had never fully faced. Dread of the possibility that Mary Jo had gone insane, was killing people.

Then, as rapidly as it came, the relief washed away before a rising flood of anger. How could she do this? How could she get involved in something like this without telling me? I stared at Lieutenant Washington as my sense of betrayal spun out of control.

Neither of us had spoken for several minutes when the phone rang. The lieutenant picked up the handset. With his eyes on me, he said, "Washington . . . All right . . . Where? . . . Bring the car around, will you? Three minutes."

He hung up.

"Speak of the devil. Looks like they found her."

"Where?"

Rising, he said, "She's at that mission her momma runs. Shots have been fired over yonder. We got a radio car in place and three more on the way. You can wait here if you want. I'll send word to you soon as I can."

I stood. "No! I'm going with you."

He looked up at me. I thought he would refuse, but then he nodded. "All right. But you'll stay in the car when we get there. Understand?"

"Yes."

"I mean that, Mister Reed. You give me any trouble out there, I'll have you arrested for obstruction."

"I won't get in your way, Lieutenant."

"All right then. So long as that's straight. Let's go."

I followed him down the stairs, through the smoke-filled squad room, and past the glass-enclosed guard post at the front doors. Outside, the dull yellow glow of the city stained the underside of the clouds in the night sky. Benny had the unmarked car idling at the curb. The tires squealed as we pulled away, with Link Washington in the passenger seat up front, and me in the back. The unmarked car still reeked of vomit and disinfectant. I stared at the back of Benny's head, at the freckles on his fat-creased neck, and the porkpie hat he wore tilted back so far it seemed ready to fall into the rear seat.

Washington said, "There's some things you should know, Mister Reed."

I shifted my eyes to him. "A lot of things."

"Yes. That's true." He stared forward, out through the windshield. The golden earring dangled limply against the side of his chocolate brown neck. Benny was really pushing it. The engine whined as we hit sixty on the narrow two-lane road. Washington said, "We were desperate. Those maniacs were blowing up a clinic every three months. A woman over in Algiers went to work early and missed walking in on a bomb by thirty seconds. It exploded while she was pulling into the parking lot. A brass doorknob blew through her windshield and buried itself in her passenger-side headrest."

Benny took a hard left turn. My right shoulder slammed against the door. I adjusted my position, spreading my feet and gripping the door handle. Washington leaned forward and flipped a toggle switch on the dashboard. A siren's harsh wail filled the car. Without turning, he continued to speak, raising his voice above the siren. "We knew who was doing it. James and Faye Slydel's bunch was picketing every clinic that got bombed, parading around in their silly uniforms. But they're pretty good. You can buy the ingredients they used in their devices at any gun shop or hardware store in the parish. Never left a footprint or a fingerprint. No hairs. No fibers. Nothing. After three related bombings without a single decent clue, we realized the only way to catch them was from the inside. We tried to get somebody in their so-called

Holy Army to come forward. We made contact with a few members of their organization, but nobody would tell us anything. We're talking fanatics. Cult mentality."

"One person we tried was your mother-in-law. She claimed a twenty-seven-hundred-dollar deduction on her taxes last year for a contribution to the Slydels. We figured she might not understand what kind of people she was sending her money to. Maybe she'd help us."

I spoke loudly. "You picked the wrong person. Lucretia probably lit some of the fuses personally."

"Yeah. I figured that out after she called me a scion of Satan." He turned and his ivory grin lit the car's interior for an instant. "Been called a lot of things over the years. First time anybody ever called me a scion of Satan."

"She's from the old school, Lieutenant," I said. "Sort of inflexible about her beliefs."

"Shoot. I am too, when it comes right down to it. I don't like what they do in those clinics. Right's right, wrong's wrong. Fashion and politics shouldn't have anything to do with it. But sooner or later, the Slydels' bunch was going to make a mistake, blow somebody up along with the building. And like my mamma used to say, 'Two wrongs don't make a right.'"

"So Lucretia ran you off."

"Yeah. With a broom, actually. Kinda made me mad. Principle of the thing, you know. I decided to look a little deeper. Found out she was sending the Slydels more money than we thought. Lot of it was donated for the shelter here by churches and individuals. We figured we had her. You can't solicit funds for one purpose and use 'em for another. That's fraud."

I said, "Let me guess. You offered to overlook it if Lucretia would agree to spy on the Slydels?"

"You betcha. Brought her downtown to the squad room, sat her in that same chair where you sat, offered her a sweetheart deal. She darn near spit in my face. Some of the things she called me made scion of Satan sound like an invitation to dance."

"I wouldn't think threats would have much effect on Lucretia."

"You'd be right. We held her overnight. Spent twenty-four hours double-teaming her. Good cop, bad cop kinda thing." He shook his head. "Nothing worked. After a while, she wouldn't even answer us, except to quote Bible verses now and again. She knows some pretty nasty Bible verses. We gave up, booked her on fraud charges. Then the answer walked in the front door."

"Mary Jo?"

"That's right. She showed up to post bail for her momma at the same time Doctor Milo was in the station swearing out another complaint against the Slydels. I happened to be standing there. It was pretty clear from the look on her face that she knew him, and that she didn't care for him much. That intrigued me. So Benny and I asked her to join us upstairs. We spent a little over eight hours asking her about Milo. At first, she denied even knowing the man. But I saw what I saw. You get to where you trust your instincts about stuff like that. After a few hours, we got her to admit she was a former patient. One thing led to another, and here we are."

I took a deep breath and guessed. "You offered to drop the charges against Lucretia if Mary Jo would help you get evidence against the Slydels."

He nodded. "Seemed like a good idea at the time. Your wife had undergone an abortion at the hands of Melvin Milo. She had reason to hate him if you wanted to look at it a certain way. Her mother was one of the Slydels' biggest fans, so we had a solid introduction there. We found out Mary Jo was on a couple of pro-life mailing lists, which gave her even more credibility from the Slydels' point of view."

I stared through the windshield, thinking about her long trips to New Orleans. The early morning target practice. The morbid paintings. Benny cursed and slammed on the brakes as a car pulled out in front of us. I braced myself against the seat back. We swerved hard left around the car and pulled back to our lane, just missing its front bumper. I said, "I can't believe you'd put her in danger like that."

The Lieutenant turned toward me, cocking his left leg onto the seat so he could face me directly. I saw intense sincerity in his eyes. He said, "It didn't happen that way. At first, when we asked her to do it, we never dreamed there'd be murder involved. We thought she'd go to a few Sunday services out at the Slydels' church in Metairie, get invited to some protests, work her way into their inner circle, and wear a wire so we could get something incriminating on tape. Then came that thing at the hospital in Mount Sinai. An orderly misidentified your wife as the shooter. So did Doctor Milo. And we realized we had a natural cover all of a sudden, if we could talk Mary Jo and that sheriff of yours into cooperating."

"So she was never really a suspect?"

"No."

"And she knew that? *She knew?*"

"That's why I wanted to be the one to tell you these things, Mister Reed. Your wife is a brave lady. She's been through a great deal to help us capture some very bad people. I'd hate to see her suffer at home because of what she's done."

I said nothing.

"You have to understand, there was nobody else we could use. The Slydels saw right through every undercover officer we tried. It had to be an insider, someone they felt came from their little family. But all of them are fanatics; no way they'd help us. Your wife was our only option. She was the only one who could save the men and women who work at those clinics. And believe me, Mister Reed, sooner or later, the Slydels' organization was going to kill somebody."

I remembered Mary Jo's silence at the dinner table the night I brought her home from jail. She barely spoke to Lucretia or me. I assumed it was exhaustion and fear. Perhaps I was wrong. Perhaps she remained silent to avoid lying. I clenched my fists, my fingernails digging into the flesh of my palms. Perhaps even her silence had been a lie.

Lincoln Washington watched me closely. We did not speak for several minutes as I stared through the side window, watching the streets of New Orleans flash by. Most of the cars had pulled over to let us pass. A few ignored the siren, forcing Benny to pull over to the oncoming lane to get around them. He swore each time this happened.

The Lieutenant said, "Does that make a difference to you? That somebody was going to die if your wife didn't do what she did?"

I started to speak, but something caught in my throat. I waited, staring out through the window into the night, then said, "Who would have died? Abortionists? Men and women who make their living by sucking living children from their mothers' wombs?"

He said, "Does that matter? What they do for a living . . . does that make it all right to let them die if it's in your power to save them?"

The window beside Washington was open about an inch. The damp New Orleans air roared in and blew back against my face. Each time we passed a building near the street, the siren's scream bounced off the facade and back in through the window, increasing the volume in the car just a bit. More to myself than to Lincoln Washington, I said, "No. I guess she couldn't let that happen." I turned to look at the detective. "I just wish she had told me."

He said, "If she said anything and we found out about it, the deal would've been off. Lucretia Granier would've gone to prison."

"Why? Why couldn't she tell me? I'm her *husband*."

"You have to understand, if word got out it would set our operation back two years. The Slydels would have had a field day with the press. Government persecution, freedom of religion, that kinda thing. Then there was your wife's safety to consider. Who knows what they would have done to her?" Lieutenant Washington shook his head. "No. We made it very clear that she was to tell no one. And we mentioned you specifically. I have to admit I'm surprised she kept it from you, though. Especially after the murder."

Again, I thought about the terrible night that Mary Jo disappeared. The last thing she said was that we would speak later, after Lucretia went to bed. Was she planning to tell me? I remembered her exact words. *"There's something we've got to talk about."* Her face had been clouded with an emotion I could not identify. I'd thought then that it was worry. Maybe I was wrong.

Benny said, "Link. We're there."

I looked through the front windshield. Up ahead, two police cars were parked at odd angles across the street, blocking it off about a block away from the mission. The street façade of the mission was starkly illuminated by searchlights mounted near the driver's-side door on the four police cars. A small group of people lingered on the sidewalks on either end of the block. Near the cars, a cluster of uniformed policemen stood facing away from us, toward the center of the block. I saw two young women with them. Both of the women were clearly pregnant. Benny parked next to the cars. A uniformed policeman ran up to Washington's side of the car. The lieutenant opened his door and stepped out into the night. Benny did too. Then Washington leaned back in.

"Stay right there, Mister Reed. Remember what I told you about getting in the way."

I nodded. He closed his door and turned to face the patrolman. I listened to their conversation through the gap in my window.

Washington said, "Tell me, Sergeant."

The policeman's white cheeks blushed with twin spots of red. His eyes flicked back toward the mission as he spoke. "Shots fired inside, Lieu. It's that old gray building down there on the right."

"I know which one it is."

"Okay. Well, we got a couple of women here, say they've been living there for a few weeks. Say a man and a woman arrived about thirty minutes ago. The man was bleeding. Then someone started firing from the street. Put three through the door. Everyone hid in a sort of chapel room they got in there. Then someone, prob'ly the shooter, came in through the door and walked right into the chapel. The two we got here were hiding in a dining room across the hall. They ran outside after the shooter entered the chapel."

"Did they see the shooter?"

"Naw. Just heard him open the door and walk down the hall."

"Any more shots fired since the shooter went inside?"

"Yeah. Four, they think. One of these girls is pretty sharp. Said it sounded like two different calibers. One of them sounds smaller than the other."

Washington turned toward the mission. "We got witnesses can tell the caliber of a weapon by ear?"

The policeman shrugged. "Tough neighborhood, Lieu."

"Yeah. So what's our disposition?"

"These two cars here, with two more at the far end of the block. That's Thompson and some rookie over yonder, plus me and Calvin up on this end. I know Lewis and Spinoza are down on the far end. Not sure who came in the other car down there. Plus I got O'Connor up on the roof of that brick building across the street from the mission with a rifle, and James back in the alley watching the rear door."

The lieutenant nodded. "Good. Lemme see if I can get them on the phone."

The sergeant and lieutenant walked toward the two police cruisers, with Benny trailing just behind. I opened the car door and stepped out. From a standing position, I looked over the top of the cruisers. Centered in the glare of the spotlights, I saw another car half a block away in front of the mission. It was an old white Impala, parked at a strange angle, halfway up on the sidewalk. Both the driver's and passenger's doors were standing open. Behind it, the clapboard walls of the Prodigal Son Mission seemed to bulge outward, as if the pressure of the misery and evil they contained strained against them, building up pressure. The rest of the block was empty. No cars, no people. Just a huge pile of trash bags across the street from the mission, and twin rows of empty two- and three-story buildings flanking the street. A foul aroma rose from the mound of garbage sacks. High above, a spider's web of power lines crisscrossed the night sky. Most of the windows in the brick and faded wooden buildings had been replaced by plywood panels. Patches of asphalt had crumbled away to reveal an underlayer of orange clay bricks here and there along the street. Multicolored graffiti covered everything. Very little had changed since the day so long ago when I stood on the sidewalk here as Mary Jo told me she was pregnant by the devil.

I leaned against the hood of the unmarked car and crossed my arms. The lieutenant stood behind a cruiser a few yards away, speaking on a cell phone. Occasionally, he waved his free hand in time with his words. He also spent a lot of time listening and nodding. Three more cruisers arrived, and the sergeant dispersed the new men to locations around the mission. A television van pulled up to the police line on the far end of the block. Three men emerged from the van, two in T-shirts and jeans, one in a dark suit. The satellite dish on top of the van unfolded with a mechanical whirring sound. One of the men in blue jeans shouldered a video camera, flicked on a battery of lights, and aimed it at the man in the suit. A policeman strung bright yellow tape across the street, just beyond the parked radio cars. Black words on the tape read, "Police Line Do Not Cross."

Everyone settled in to wait. The lieutenant remained on the telephone. I asked a passing patrolman if Washington was speaking to someone inside the mission, but the patrolman ignored my question and kept walking. I slid up onto the hood of the unmarked car and hooked the heels of my boots behind the front bumper. Enough time had passed for the engine heat to cool. My stomach growled. I realized I hadn't eaten anything in almost twenty-four hours. I crossed my arms in front of my belly and pushed in. That felt a little better.

Patrolmen in dark blue uniforms stood behind the cruisers at each end of the street with their handguns drawn, facing the mission. The old building almost seemed to ignore them. Time crawled. My lower back started to ache. I slid from the hood of the car and walked over to the lieutenant's side. He ignored me.

"Of course. Anybody would feel that way," he said, speaking into the cellular telephone. "Somebody shoots your husband, you're gonna feel angry about that."

"Who is it?" I whispered.

He frowned at me and shook his head, waving me away with his free hand. A patrolman gripped my elbow and said, "Sir, you're gonna have to step back."

I returned to lean against the side of the unmarked car, watching the lieutenant closely. His hand motions seemed to be more animated than ever. That was strange. He'd been on the telephone for over an hour. You'd think the conversation would become calmer as time went by. Suddenly, he raised his voice. I heard him say, "Wait a minute! Wait a minute!" Then whoever it was must have hung up, because he removed the phone from his ear with a single curse, and slipped it into the inside pocket of his jacket.

Washington crossed his arms and placed one hand against his cheek, Jack Benny style, staring at the Prodigal Son Mission. He stood like that for a long time, with his back toward me. Suddenly, he swung around and looked straight into my eyes. I saw determination in his face, as if he'd been considering his options and had made a decision.

And that decision included me.

Chapter 54

"HE SAYS SHE'S GONNA START SHOOTING people one at a time unless we send you in."

I turned from Lieutenant Lincoln Washington to stare at the peeling facade of the mission, as I considered what he'd just told me. Juliette Milo was in there. She held Mary Jo and Elmer and Lucretia and a dozen young pregnant women at gunpoint. She had seen us arrive. She knew it was me sitting on the hood of the brown car at the end of the block. And she wanted me to join her little party.

I said, "Then I'll go."

"No, you won't," said Lieutenant Washington. "That would be suicide."

"Not necessarily. Maybe she just wants to talk."

"She wants to shoot you in front of your wife, Mister Reed. Just like her husband got shot by Mary Jo."

"You don't know that for sure."

"I'm telling you what she said."

I stared at him. "You believe her?"

"Got no choice."

We stood beside the police cruiser that the lieutenant had taken over as his base of operations. Seven or eight patrolmen leaned against the hoods and trunks of radio cars around us, their handguns still out and aimed at Mary Jo's childhood home. Other than our conversation, the only sound was an occasional crackle from the radio in the cruiser.

Then the uniformed cop closest to us called softly, "Hey, Lieu. Check that out."

Washington's eyes followed the policeman's nod toward the mission. The front door had opened. As we watched silently, a man emerged blinking into the floodlights. He took four steps out to the curb and stopped beside the Impala that was parked there. He raised one hand to shade his eyes. His other arm hung limply at his side. It was Elmer, the skinny Crescent City Garage mechanic who took me out to the Slydels' camp in the swamp. Lieutenant Washington cupped his hands around his mouth and yelled, "Come this way!"

Elmer seemed confused. He looked toward us. He turned and looked back at the mission. Then he looked our way again.

"Come on, sir! Come toward the cars!"

Again, Elmer turned back toward the mission. He seemed to take a deep breath. Then he took a step toward us.

A single shot shattered the silence. Elmer spun and dropped to the asphalt. He lay still. The front door of the mission slammed shut.

Lieutenant Washington cursed and slammed his fist against the top of the car. I could not remove my eyes from Elmer's fallen form. Washington and I stood silently, watching him for a sign of life. Benny shuffled over to us, moving carefully, crouched and hurrying between the patrol cars. He carried a small set of binoculars in one hand and held his porkpie hat on with the other.

"That ol' boy's had it, Lieu. You can see with these things if you wanna. Top of his head's pretty much gone."

He held the binoculars toward the lieutenant, who waved them away.

"Keep 'em. I believe you."

The three of us stood silently staring at Elmer's body. A counterfeit peace settled over the street, brought on by the shock of what we had all seen. Suddenly, a shrill ringing pierced the silence.

Washington reached inside his jacket and removed his cell phone. He extended the antenna, sighed once, then punched a button on the phone. Lifting it to his ear, he said, "Wish you hadn't done that."

He listened.

Then he said, "You won't have to. We'll give you what you want. But look, don't you think—"

Removing the phone from his ear with another curse he turned toward Benny and said, "She hung up."

Before he could speak again, I said, "I'll do it. I'll go in."

"No."

"Lieutenant, you can't let her keep shooting people."

"Of course not. We're gonna rush her," he said. Then he turned back toward Benny. "Get the S.W.A.T. team leader over here, will you?"

I said, "But what about those people? What if they get hurt?"

"She'll kill them if we don't take control of this situation, Mister Reed. She just told me the pregnant girls are next. Now you best move back over to the car and let us get to work."

"She won't shoot them if we give her what she wants."

"Probably even then, Mister Reed. That woman sounds like she's crazy to me. Now, please move. I'm not gonna ask you again."

I walked the few yards to the unmarked car deep in thought, my mind seized by a vision of Mary Jo, cowering before Juliette Milo, terrorized at having just witnessed the murder of a man. It was simply unacceptable for me to remain out here, watching. Unacceptable for me to allow Washington's men to storm the mission, when for all I knew, a murderer held the muzzle of a gun to my wife's temple. Everything I knew about Juliette Milo told me that she would kill Mary Jo at the first sign of a police attack. I remembered the photographs in the Milos' home, of Juliette and her quarry in Africa, Juliette Milo cradling a bolt-action rifle and kneeling beside a cheetah, an antelope, a lion. I remembered the specter in the woods outside my home, firing round after round into the tree an inch above my head. Juliette Milo would not hesitate, and she would not miss. If they stormed the mission, Mary Jo was a dead woman.

It was unacceptable.

I turned and walked back toward the cruisers. None of the policemen paid any attention to me until I stepped between two of their vehicles and ducked under the yellow tape.

"Hey! Get back here!" yelled a patrolman close to me.

I ignored him and strode directly toward the front door of the mission, past the inert body on the pavement.

Chapter 55

THE PRODIGAL SON MISSION DOOR SQUEALED open on unoiled hinges, destroying any hope that my entry would be unnoticed. I stepped into the dimly lit corridor and closed the door, silencing the voices of the police outside who still called for me to return to the safety of their barricades.

Standing with my back to the door, I listened. A muted whimper drifted down the hall. Someone was crying somewhere, and trying to do it quietly. I slipped down the corridor toward the dining hall, trying to move silently. But with each step, my boots echoed hollowly against the worn wooden planks. Since there was no longer any hope of sneaking up on her, I decided to take the opposite approach.

"Juliette? Juliette Milo?" I called. "It's Garr Reed. I'm here, just like you asked."

The distant whimper continued, but nobody answered my call. I reached the cased opening that led into the dining hall and peered around the corner. The room was unoccupied. It contained rows of folding tables with dull brown plastic tops and gray metal folding chairs. Against one wall stood a line of tables stacked with stainless steel warming pans and soup pots. It all reminded me of that day so long ago when I first met Lucretia Granier. Many years had passed since I set foot in the mission, but very little had changed.

I called again. "Juliette Milo! Answer me!"

There was only the distant weeping for an answer.

I continued down the hall toward the chapel. The sobbing grew louder as I approached. Reaching the wide opening that led into the room, I bent to peek around the corner. Like the dining room, the chapel was much as I remembered from my last visit. There was the low plywood platform against one wall with the ancient upright piano and the rough-hewn pulpit. Rows of cheap metal chairs filled the rest of the room. Crudely painted Bible verses and evangelistic slogans covered the walls like blood-red graffiti. Everything seemed just as it was, except for the old wooden cross on the wall behind the platform.

The cross hung upside down.

A dozen young women of several races huddled together in the front three rows of chairs. Several of them held each other as they sobbed. Others sat isolated from the group, stiffly facing the front with hands clasped in their laps or resting on their swollen bellies. Shock registered in their vacant expressions. Many wore long, oversized T-shirts draped around their bare knees like dresses. A few, not so far along in their pregnancies, wore blue jeans. Some had small gold rings piercing their nostrils. One had a streak of green dye in her hair. Another's head was shaved. Many were tattooed. All were terrified.

In the front row, Lucretia Granier and Handy sat side by side, holding hands. Both of them bowed their heads. I saw the old black man's lips move, and realized they were praying.

"Lucretia," I whispered.

She turned to look at me. What I saw in her hard bronzed face froze my heart with fear. The old familiar defiance was gone. Something had purged the stiff self-righteousness from her eyes and replaced it with total defeat. What could overpower her spirit so completely? Lucretia Granier had seen drunken debauchery, senseless violence, and wasted lives on a massive scale for most of her life. But those bitter flames had merely forged her austere severity and made her heart and her religion hard. Now something had made her abandon all hope. What could it be?

"Handy," I said. "Get these women out of here."

He looked at me as if I was mad. "How we gonna do that?"

"Just do it. Take them to the front door. And hurry, before she comes back."

"But they're out there."

"What?"

"They're out there in the hall."

"There's nobody here, Handy."

He cocked his head oddly. "I still hear them."

I stood silently for a moment, but heard nothing. "Ladies," I said, "y'all get up and come this way. Right now."

All of them stared at me, some still sniffling, others with questions in their eyes. But nobody moved.

I said, "What's the matter with you people?"

One of the girls, the one with the shaved head said, "They're right behind you."

I spun to look back. Nobody was there. I turned toward the girl again, angry at her cruel joke. But the raw fear in her eyes stopped me before I spoke. Her gaze was solidly fixed on the thin air just beyond my shoulder. I looked back again, but saw nothing. What did she see?

When I entered the chapel and walked up to the front row, each step sent a hollow echo bouncing against the stark white plaster walls. Kneeling in front of Lucretia and Handy, I spoke softly. "There's nobody out there right now. Trust me. We've got to get these girls away before Juliette comes back."

Lucretia's head remained bowed, but Handy looked me in the eye. He touched my shoulder, as if assuring himself that I was real. Then he said, "You sure they're gone?"

"Yes."

"Was a bunch of them. Evil, evil."

"Well, they're not out there now, Handy. But if we don't hurry . . ."

The old man stared at me for a moment, then he nodded and rose. "Ladies," he said, "let's all get up and move to the hall."

Three of the women wailed loudly. Handy inclined his head toward them and said, "Abby, you help these sisters. Jean, why don't you help too? The rest of you, follow me. Come on now. God is with us. We got to trust him."

The bald woman rose and whispered to the crying girls. Handy bent to place a gentle hand on Lucretia Granier's elbow. She rose stiffly, with her head still bowed toward the floor. This broken shell was all that remained of the loving Lucretia Granier, the fearless woman who once led me through an abandoned alley to confront a girl whose eyes were aglow with evil. I wanted to shake Lucretia and scream, "See? See what your bitterness has done to you?" But what would be the point? She had already made her choice, banishing the holy source of her courage with her hardness of heart.

Together, Lucretia and Handy shuffled toward the corridor. As they neared the opening, Handy leaned forward into the hall, looking left and right. Satisfied, he turned back and nodded to the small cluster of women. "It's clear, ya'll. Let's hurry."

I brought up the rear, following the three tearful women to the front door. Handy opened it, and the glare of the floodlights spilled into the hall. He held the door open as they filed out past him. Finally, when it was just me and him, Handy whispered, "Hurry up, Garr. We don't wanna be here when they get back."

"You go ahead. I'll be along."

He shook his head. "Garr. You gotta come with us. There's nothing you can do against them."

"Did you see Mary Jo?"

"Yes. She came in with that fella who got shot. Just before the *mamba* came."

"Where is she now?"

Handy shook his head again. "Don't know, Garr. The *mamba* took her out of the chapel a few minutes ago. Left those others to guard us."

"Where did the others go?"

"I got no idea, Garr."

"Well, how many were they? Were they armed?"

"I didn't see them, exactly. There was just a . . . sound. It's hard to describe. Like a wind, or a swarm of locusts." He stared back down the hall fearfully.

"I know. I've heard it too, Handy."

Clutching my arm, he said, "Then you know we've got to get moving. Let's *go*."

"I can't leave Mary Jo."

He looked toward the police line at the end of the block. I saw how badly he wanted to leave. But he said, "You want me to stay and help?"

I touched his hand on my arm, removing it. "You go on. Take care of Lucretia. She looks bad."

He nodded. "The *mamba* . . . she made Lucretia say some bad things."

"Go now," I whispered. "Go take care of her."

He stared at me, then nodded and stepped out into the police lights. When I closed the door behind him, it took a moment for my eyes to adjust to the darkness.

Chapter 56

I FLIPPED A SWITCH BESIDE THE DOOR AND A row of bare bulbs hanging from thin black wires doused the hallway in stark white light. As I stared down the long corridor with its worn wooden floor and yellowed plaster walls, Handy's warning reverberated in my memory.

Evil. Evil.

I thought of the eerie sounds of something passing through the moonlit woods outside my home. And of the whispered chants in the Milos' Garden District house. An inexplicable dread almost overwhelmed me. I felt an urgent desire to flee from that place. But Mary Jo was there. Handy had seen her, not fifteen minutes before. So I pressed the fear into the furthest corner of my mind, focused on my wife, and took a step away from the door. The next step was easier. And one step at a time, I searched the ground-floor rooms of the mission for Mary Jo.

I turned on every light as I went. If Juliette Milo was going to fight me with something more than just a gun, I would not allow her to do it in the dark.

Reaching the rear of the building, I peeked into the small room where Alphonse Granier once sat behind a desk and told me about Mary Jo's infertility. The desk was gone, and Alphonse's office had been converted to a storeroom for donated clothing. I was glad to see that something had changed, after all.

But as I pondered the painful past, something was rising beyond my consciousness like the slow, unnoticed advance of cancer. I moved to the bottom of the stairs, standing with my right hand on the banister, staring up at the darkness on the second floor. And then, when I finally became aware of its presence, I knew it had been there for some time, growing inconspicuously, until the eerie humming of it permeated the very atmosphere around me. The strange sound seemed to flow like a current, receding and advancing. The buzzing faded, but just when I thought it had merely been a natural ringing in my ears, it returned again, this time sounding more like the hiss of a hundred snakes. Then it changed again, assuming the frantic crackle of a swarm of locusts. I climbed the first step. The noise spiked suddenly, as if warning me away. Gripping the handrail, I continued to climb. The crackling faded, then returned like a black wave against a barren shore. And now it contained the unmistakable sound of voices: the distant chanting I had heard before, in Juliette Milo's home.

I flipped on the lights at the top of the stairs and entered the small living room on the left. It was in this room that Mary Jo's father forbade our marriage. A housefly buzzed past my ear. I searched the entire second floor, the kitchen and bedrooms, the single bathroom. Everywhere I went, I turned on the lights. There were flies in every room, dozens of them, but no sign of Mary Jo or Juliette Milo.

With each step I took, the fearful noises became stronger; unexplainable, yet undeniable, mocking me without words, whispering incoherent warnings, eroding my courage. I told myself to ignore it. I told myself it was merely the buzzing of the flies. And yet the terror rose. I don't remember making the decision to do it, but suddenly I realized I was praying out loud as I searched the rooms.

"Lord, protect me. Lord, protect Mary Jo. Lord, remove this evil from this place . . ."

It was a prayer I repeated again and again. My words had no effect upon the eerie sounds, but my confidence returned. I felt the hand of God upon my shoulder, encouraging me to continue. I was still afraid. I was deathly afraid. But I had been reminded that whatever happened, I would not face it alone.

At last, when I had searched every other room in the mission, I stood at the bottom of a steep set of stairs, almost a ladder, which led to a wooden door high above. Up there, beyond that door, the attic huddled beneath the tall gabled roof. It was my last hope and my greatest fear. The mere thought of climbing those steps seemed to drive the unholy whispers to a fevered pitch. But I grimly seized the handrails and began the ascent. Shrieks and wails resonated against my skull. Were they coming from the room around me, or were they only inside my brain? I screamed my prayers now, trying to shout above the vile voices.

"Lord, protect me. Lord, protect Mary Jo. Lord, remove this evil from this place ..."

My arms and legs felt heavy, encased in lead, pressing against my every movement. A thick cluster of shiny black flies clung to the attic door, vibrating ecstatically, as if feasting on a carcass. I reached for the old brass doorknob. It was like sticking my hand into a barrel of snakes. The wails and screams rose to a crescendo, louder than anything I had ever heard.

But then, as soon as I touched the knob ... silence.

The door swung open.

Drifting particles of dust shimmered in a diagonal column of moonlight just inside the attic. The crisscrossed bars of the dormer window muntins carved a grid pattern in the light, dividing it into nine intense squares of white that struck the rough-hewn timbers of the floor at my feet. A woman lay on her back, framed in that geometric rectangle of light, eyes closed, face deathly pale, hands clasped just below her breast like a corpse in a coffin.

The woman was Mary Jo.

I sucked in my breath and took a quick step forward.

"Get back!" hissed Juliette Milo.

I lifted my eyes from the prostrate body of my wife and saw Juliette for the first time. She stood in the shadows beside the single window. In her right hand, she held a dull black revolver. In her left, the strange, carved stick I had seen before at the Jackson County Hospital. She seemed to lean on the stick, as if for support. Her head was covered by a yellow turban. A multicolored batik toga wrapped her slender form. And around her neck, I saw the familiar bone necklace with the shrunken paw of a monkey.

"I said get back!" Her face was twisted, like a fearful mask. Her lips curled back from her teeth. Her nostrils flared impossibly. And a smoldering hatred glowed behind her eyes. Compared to the raw evil I saw dancing there, the gun she pointed at my chest seemed inconsequential.

"Why are you doing this to us?" I asked.

"Step back. You are too close."

I did not move.

"Step back I said! Or I will kill you where you stand."

Her finger tightened slightly on the trigger. Carefully, I backed up one step. Any further and I would fall over the edge of the ladder, twelve feet down to the second floor.

I said, "What do you want?"

"You!" She aimed the weapon at Mary Jo's body. "And her."

"Why? Why us?"

"You fool! You think you can come against me with your puny god and I will not respond? You think you can oppose my will and survive?"

"I don't know what you're talking about."

"Do not play the games, Mister Reed. It is just we three and the *loas* here. We have no need of the deceptions."

"I'm telling you I honestly do not know what you're talking about. You say Mary Jo and I have come against you. But we have done nothing to you."

"Nothing! This female almost killed my husband. It is she who shot him, no? And you! You cannot let him be in peace, even in his hospital room. There you try to finish what she started!"

It was pointless to argue. I looked down at my wife. Very softly, I said, "What have you done to her? Why won't she open her eyes?"

"She has been prepared. Those who resist *Samadhi* must be taken by *Samadhi*."

"What does that mean?"

The smile that flickered upon her tortured countenance was horrible to behold. "Soon you will see. You will be first. She shall watch. Just as she tried to make my Melvin first."

The woman's eyes fell on Mary Jo and she uttered a string of words in a language I did not recognize. At the instant she stopped speaking, Mary Jo's eyes opened. They stared straight up at the dark wooden beams and the gray and blue underside of the slate roof tiles. Nothing but her eyelids had moved. I called her name, but Mary Jo did not even glance my way. Looking again at Juliette Milo, I said, "Tell me what you've done to her."

"Silence! The time for you to speak is finished."

Again, she lowered her malevolent gaze to Mary Jo and spoke in the strange tongue. I watched the muzzle of her handgun, waiting for the right moment, but it never wavered. Remembering the fearsome accuracy of the shots she had fired in the woods, I decided to remain still. Her voice rose. The words began to sound repetitive, as if she was chanting or reciting a litany. Suddenly, she kneeled beside my wife's body, still aiming the gun at me. She extended her other arm rigidly, holding the strangely carved stick out above Mary Jo, then moving it back and forth over her body in time to the words that she spoke. When next I looked at Mary Jo's face, her eyes were focused on me. Nothing else had moved, just her eyes, resting on me with mute despair, and a single tear, which trickled from her eye to quiver on her cheek like holy water from a baptismal font.

Juliette Milo stopped speaking. Somehow, I knew my last chance had come. If I was going to do something to save myself and Mary Jo, it would have to be now. And so I decided to risk everything. It seemed the only way. I considered the best approach, and decided to go at her with my right shoulder tilted forward, hoping that the bullet would be deflected by the bones in my arm and ribcage, hoping that my heart would be spared. I marshaled my will for one desperate plunge toward the cold black muzzle of her gun.

But when the moment came I found I could not move. My body felt completely normal, but it did not respond to the commands of my mind. Perhaps I was paralyzed with fear. And so I watched in silent terror while Juliette Milo advanced toward me. As she drew near, I saw she had left the gun behind her on the floor. She clasped the carved wooden stick instead, holding it horizontally in both hands like the handles of a bicycle. When she was a mere three feet away, she smiled and slowly spread her hands apart. The stick seemed to break in two as she unsheathed a hidden blade, twelve inches long, double edged and tapered to a point as sharp as a serpent's fang.

I found I could still speak. Once again I prayed, "Lord, protect me. Lord, protect Mary Jo. Lord, remove this evil from this place."

Juliette's face erupted in hatred. "Nothing can your little god do for you here!"

She raised the blade above me in both hands, screaming words in the tongue of demons.

I seemed to watch from a great distance as my hands rose to grip her wrists. Their movements felt out of my control, like the hands of a puppet. Her shrieks continued as we struggled. Juliette Milo's countenance had altered unbelievably. Her eyes seemed to recede into black pits in her skull. Her lips curled back to expose her naked gums and her jaw shuddered violently as the incomprehensible words spewed from her mouth, clicking her stark white teeth together like the rapid-fire rattle of castanets in the hands of a diabolic dancer. Although she was barely half my size, she drove the blade steadily closer to my chest. Praying aloud for protection, I found I could move again, and pushed against her wrists. But I was unable to overpower the force within her. Slowly, the knife advanced until it pierced my shirt and entered my flesh.

I was not afraid of death. I was honestly not afraid to pass from this life. That is one of the glorious side effects of faith in Jesus Christ. But I feared for Mary Jo. I feared the things this woman might do to my beloved before she was granted the blessed relief of death. And so, even with the tip of the knife piercing my skin, I fought with all my might.

But it was no use. The woman's clattering incisors grimaced like the bared teeth of a rabid dog as she drove the blade ever deeper, ever closer to my heart. For some reason, a calm settled over me. I knew it was my time to die. And so, even as I struggled, instead of screaming in pain or rage, I found I had the presence of mind to speak three simple words aloud:

"Take me, Lord!"

Something in those words startled Juliette Milo. For just one second, she relented. And in that instant, I thought I saw a flicker of weakness in her eyes. So I pushed one last time with every bit of strength I could muster. This time, my arms seemed to explode outward, driving the madwoman back as if she was shot from a cannon. Waving her arms wildly to regain her equilibrium, she stumbled over Mary Jo's prostrate body, and I watched in horror as, completely off balance now, Juliette Milo backed through the plate-glass attic window.

She fell three floors to her death, screaming curses all the way down.

Chapter 57

WE LAY INTERTWINED, BASKING IN THE afterglow of our passion, her head on my bare chest. Wordlessly, we listened to the sounds of the French Quarter drifting through the open window, together again in her favorite hotel. My eyes searched the dimly lit ceiling. The plaster was crisp and white, not mildewed or cracked like you might expect in a two-hundred-year-old room. Outside, someone was driving around the block, honking a custom car horn. They had it rigged to play the first twelve notes of *Dixie*. A crowd of people cheered each time it played. I heard the sound of breaking glass, followed by a woman's high-pitched laughter.

Mary Jo said, "Garr? Are you all right?" She rolled to her belly and propped her chin on her fist, staring deeply into my eyes.

I touched her cheek. "Sure, baby. I'm just so happy and so . . . angry. Both at the same time, you know?"

Her eyes grew serious. "Angry? With whom?"

I thought about it for a long time before answering. I didn't want to answer. But she was right beside me, her eyes searching my face. And I had spent too many years lying about my faith to continue lying to her now. "Mary Jo, I don't understand why you didn't tell me the truth."

"They had Momma in jail, Garr. What was I supposed to do?"

"Tell me! Let me be a part of it!"

She rolled away, drawing the sheet up to cover herself. "I thought Lieutenant Washington explained all that."

"About him warning you not to tell me? Yes, he filled me in. But since when do we let other people force us to keep secrets from each other? I don't care what he told you to do. It still doesn't excuse the way you hid things from me. The lies you told—"

"Lies! You're one to talk!"

I stared at her, indignation rising within me like the inevitable flood of the Mississippi when the storms upriver have raged for too long. But, truth be told, I felt angry at myself, too. Because she was right . . . I had lied to her all those years, faking my faith to win her, and faking the life of a believer to keep her. Besides, this was not how it was supposed to go tonight. I had promised myself I wasn't going to do this. All those days of searching for her, hoping for the best, dreaming of this moment when we could be together again at last . . . and here we were, about to start a fight. I reached out to touch her bare back, rubbing between her shoulder blades as I spoke.

"Listen, Nibbles. I'm sorry. I don't want things to be this way tonight."

She did not respond, not even to my use of her most private name. I tried again.

"Can't we just be together? Leave it at that?"

Without turning, she said, "You're the one who's mad."

"Yes, I am a little. But give me some time. You did a hard thing. I wish you hadn't, but I think I understand why you did. If my mother was alive, and they threatened her . . . maybe I'd make the same decisions."

Turning toward me, she said, "So why the anger?"

"I'm not sure yet. Maybe I'm mad at fate."

"No such thing as fate."

"I know."

"Everything's in the hands of God."

"I know."

She knit her brow with concern and said, "You mustn't be angry with God."

Pushing her lovely auburn hair away from her forehead, I looked into her eyes and said, "I know that, baby. Don't fret."

The telephone rang. Who would call our room at three in the morning? I said, "Don't answer it."

Rolling across the bed, she reached for the handset. "It might be important."

Lifting the infernal machine, she said, "Hello?" Her body stiffened. She slid her legs over the edge of the bed and sat upright, listening. She said, "Uh huh" a few times. After a pause, she said, "Yes, I thought it was them, too." Another pause, then, "I see. All right. Thank you for calling." She hung up.

I said, "Who was that?"

Without turning, she said, "Lieutenant Washington."

I stared at her naked back, worried and still angry, but trying to put that away, at least for now. Her silence bothered me. What had Washington said? What next? Finally, she turned to look at me. I saw she had begun to cry, the tears flowing silently from her emerald eyes.

"It's all over now, Garr."

"What do you mean?"

"He told me they dropped the charges. For the murder up in Mount Sinai."

"Thank God!"

"That's why he called. To say they dropped the charges. He figured we might still be up, and he wanted to let us know before it comes out in the papers tomorrow. They decided it was Juliette Milo who tried to kill her husband."

"But that can't be!"

"Why not?"

"Because she thought *you* were the one who tried to kill him."

"Well, the lieutenant told me just now that they found a note at her house. It said she was going to kill Elizabeth Harmony and then kill herself. Because Elizabeth was sleeping with her husband. At least that's what she thought."

"Juliette Milo didn't seem like the suicide kind."

"I know. She seemed too . . . full of herself for that, didn't she?"

I nodded. "And this note Washington said they found, it said Lizzy and Milo were lovers?"

"That's what the lieutenant said. And Juliette found out, so that's why she killed Lizzy."

"And why she tried to kill Milo?"

"I guess so."

"What was that part on the phone about, 'thinking it was them too'?"

"The lieutenant said he always thought the murderer was the Slydels or one of their people. He said that's why he let them get away with accusing me over in Texas. To draw them out, maybe get them to incriminate themselves somehow when they tried to help me. But of course he was wrong. It was that Milo woman, all along. He apologized."

I thought about it for a moment. Juliette Milo tried to murder her husband and succeeded in murdering his mistress, intending to kill herself afterward. It did make sense. But it still felt wrong. Juliette was so filled with hatred in the attic of the Mission. Personal hatred, for me and for Mary Jo. Surely anyone who felt that strongly about anything wouldn't consider suicide. And there was something else that didn't add up. I said, "If she never really believed that you shot her husband, why did she try to kill you?"

"I guess because Elmer and I were witnesses to Lizzy's murder in the garage."

"So Elmer was there at the garage when Lizzy got shot?"

"Yes. He and Lizzy came to her apartment and let me go."

"You were at Lizzy's apartment all this time?"

"As far as I know. She kept me pretty well doped up most of the time."

"But why? Why would Elizabeth Harmony want to kidnap you? I mean, she never asked us for a ransom."

"I don't know."

"Was it personal? Did you know her? Meet her on one of your trips down here?"

"I don't know why she did it, Garr. I really don't. I never met the woman in my life."

"And she never offered any explanations?"

"No. She burst into my studio that night and pointed that shiny little pistol at me and made me write that note and drive her away in the Volvo. She ducked down so those reporters out at the gate wouldn't see her, and then sat up and gave me directions to this deserted road down by the bayou."

"I found the car there."

"Really? Is it all right?"

"No. Elmer's outfit towed it down here and left it at the old Holmes garage. I went to look for it, but it was gone."

Mary Jo said, "Oh, I loved my little Volvo. Every time I drove it I thought about you giving it to me on our fifteenth anniversary."

"Who cares about a *car*, baby? Finish telling me what happened."

She idly stroked the hair on my arm as she spoke. "There's not much else to tell, really. She made me get in the back of a van, and gave me an injection. I was terrified she was poisoning me, but it just made me all hazy, and then I guess I passed out. The next thing I knew, I woke up in a dark little room—I think it was a walk-in closet because the clothes rods were still there—and I was lying on a mattress and handcuffed to this steel ring in the floor. I screamed and screamed, but she had lined the walls with more mattresses, so I guess nobody could hear. After a while, I just lay awake in the dark, praying."

I clenched my teeth. My voice was hoarse with emotion when I asked, "And she never even hinted at why she did it?"

"I asked her over and over what she wanted. Every time she opened the door and gave me food or water or carried out the bedpan I asked her. At first she ignored me." Mary Jo drew a ragged breath, the memories threatening to overwhelm her. We sat for a few minutes in silence, as she fought to regain her composure. Then she continued. "I kept begging. 'Tell me what you want.' Finally, she got angry and threatened to shoot me if I kept asking. But I kept at it. Then she must have drugged my water, because I started sleeping again."

Aching with fury at what Elizabeth Harmony had done to Mary Jo, I said, "But she fed you okay? And gave you water?"

"I guess so. I'm still alive, and I haven't lost much weight." She smiled. "Darn it."

"Don't you remember *anything* after that? How about Elmer? Did he come around Lizzy's apartment while you were there?"

"I never saw him before tonight, when he and Lizzy let me go. I don't even remember him very well from tonight. When they came to get me, I was still feeling groggy from whatever she put in my water."

"Is that why you wouldn't move when Juliette had you up in the attic?"

"I don't know, Garr. I don't remember much about that, either."

"But you must remember *something*."

Raising herself onto her elbow, she pressed her chest against a small bandage above my heart. It covered the fourteen stitches that closed the cut where Juliette Milo's knife had stopped just short of my lung. She said, "Listen, buster. If I did remember anything, do you think I want to talk about it now? Let's just be together tonight like you said, and count our blessings."

I smiled and stroked her hair. She pressed her cheek against mine and we lay like that while everything she had said coursed through my mind. Elmer and Lizzy came together to free her. Why? Why kidnap her? Why release her? Was Elmer in on it from the beginning? After all, he did tow Mary Jo's Volvo . . . but then I remembered how I first met Elmer. In fact, I drove down to New Orleans because of the check he cashed for towing Mary Jo's car. Elmer hadn't seemed simple-minded enough to take a check for stealing someone's car.

I said, "Did Lizzy make you sign a check for the Crescent City Garage?"

Without moving, she responded, "No. I mean I don't think so. Why would she do that?"

"I don't know, but it was written in your handwriting. It's how I knew Elmer's garage towed the Volvo."

After a pause, Mary Jo said, "She could have told me to write anything, Garr. I wouldn't remember it. You have to understand, it's like the last two weeks didn't happen. I just have bits and pieces."

"I know, baby. I know." Again, I stroked her hair. "Maybe it's for the best. Would have been a lot harder if you were awake all that time."

I thought about Lizzy's last words of faith. I remembered Elmer on his knees beside the Slydels' pit, red beret clutched in his long bony fingers, gazing down upon me as I lifted Elizabeth Harmony above the reach of the snakes. Could Elmer have come to his senses because of that? Freed Lizzy and helped her to escape? Could Lizzy have freed Mary Jo in turn?

Suddenly it came to me that Elizabeth Harmony might have kidnapped Mary Jo in self-defense. Maybe she was afraid Mary Jo would try to kill her, as she assumed Mary Jo had tried to kill her employer, Doctor Milo. To Lizzy, Mary Jo must have come across as a deranged pro-life fanatic, capable of anything . . . a mortal threat to anyone who worked at an abortion clinic. After all, that was the kind of woman Lieutenant Washington had forced my wife to impersonate. And Mary Jo had done it all too well. Even Lucretia Granier thought Mary Jo shot Doctor Milo.

Then again, if the motive was self-defense, why not just kill Mary Jo? Why kidnap her? Surely Lizzy didn't intend to keep Mary Jo captive forever. Maybe the original idea was to kill my wife, but Lizzy found she couldn't do it. Or maybe she was waiting for some reason, planning to kill her later.

But then Lizzy and I survived the snake pit together. And I shared the faith with her. Maybe she believed, and could no longer justify keeping Mary Jo captive, even in self-defense. So when Elmer offered to help her escape, she asked him to drive her straight home, where she freed Mary Jo. But why did they go to Elmer's garage?

"Baby?"

"Umm?"

"Why did they take you to that garage?"

She sighed. "I remember there was a problem with a truck. Something about the tires. Maybe it was his truck, I don't know. Anyway, her apartment was near the garage, so they helped me walk over there. Probably to get a car."

"You don't remember what was wrong with the tires?"

"No. Wait. I remember Elmer kneeling by the truck. Lizzy was holding me up, sort of. And . . . yes, I can see it. They were flat. The tires were flat."

"Could they have been slashed, maybe?"

"I guess so."

"So maybe Juliette Milo was waiting outside the apartment, and she slashed the tires?"

"Who knows, Garr? Can't we talk about this tomorrow?"

"Sure, baby. I'm sorry."

"Mmm," she said, nuzzling into the crook of my arm.

My mind continued to race through the possibilities. Juliette Milo thought her husband was having an affair with Elizabeth Harmony. Maybe she staked out the apartment building, and saw Elmer and Lizzy go in. Maybe she slashed Elmer's tires, thinking . . . what? Maybe she wasn't thinking. Maybe she just did it because she could. Or maybe she thought they'd call her husband for help and she'd kill Lizzy and Milo together, right there. But then Elmer and Lizzy set out for the garage instead, probably with Mary Jo between them, leaning on them. And at the garage, Elizabeth Harmony died. Then Elmer and Mary Jo took that white Impala and made a dash to the Mission. After what Lieutenant Washington had put Mary Jo through, and with Elmer unsure whether he was wanted for my kidnapping, neither of them could trust the police. Juliette Milo followed, with her revolver and her hidden dagger, intent upon killing the witnesses to her murder of Elizabeth Harmony.

And there, in that attic room, I was forced to become her killer instead.

Suddenly, the thought that Juliette Milo had died at my hands rose from a graveyard of regrets, seizing my mind in its ice-cold grip. A bone-numbing sorrow settled upon me, wrung from the memory of the fear in her eyes as she'd backed through the attic window. It was the first time I had allowed myself to think about what I'd done. In that terrible, silent moment after Juliette's fall to death, there had been the joy of my first embrace with Mary Jo. Then came the slow walk down two flights of stairs to step through the front door into a cacophony of shouting police and the blinking brightness of the floodlights. I had not even glanced at the body on the sidewalk as Lieutenant Washington led us toward his car. I had focused only on Mary Jo, and the fact that she was safe once again in my arms.

But now, hours later, it was no longer possible to avoid the horrible truth of what I had done . . . what I had become. In the instant that my arms propelled Juliette Milo through that third-story window, a dull ache had settled on my mind. I tried to hide from it, avoiding it, focusing on Mary Jo and the fact that Juliette had given me no choice. But the pain was still there. Whether or not she deserved what happened, the reality was that I had killed someone.

And the worst of it was, none of it had had to happen.

If Mary Jo had just told me the truth in the beginning, we could have stopped it all, gotten a good lawyer for Lucretia—maybe Winston Graves would travel to Louisiana for us. But no! Mary Jo had to lie to me. To hide the truth from me for all those months as she went again and again to New Orleans, masquerading as some fanatical cult member. To render meaningless and petty the self-righteous indignation she had shown, months ago, when she discovered I'd been lying for years about my faith. In spite of my earlier resolution, I felt the resentment rising again, bearing my good intentions away on a river of recriminations.

Stop it! Think about your wife. Think about how close you came to losing her.

The voice seemed to come from beyond my pain and resentment, a tiny voice of reason amidst the rancor. Was it God?

I forced myself to think of something else . . . anything else. Focus on the mystery again. Something didn't fit. What was it? My mind searched through the betrayals and the assumptions until it came to the missing piece of the puzzle. Mary Jo said the police had found a suicide note. If Juliette was planning to kill herself, why would she bother to kill the witnesses to her murders?

My thoughts were distracted by a wetness against my chest.

"Hey," I said. "Are you crying?"

She reached up and wiped one eye, then the other. Sniffling, she said, "I was just thinking . . . how it may not even matter. With the cancer, even though they won't put me back in jail, it may not matter much . . ."

Suddenly, she began to cry in earnest, her shoulders rising and falling with each deep breath, her words coming out in choppy phrases, spaced between the sobs.

"It's . . . been . . . so . . . terrible! I can remember seeing that woman get killed in that garage. And that other woman, the Milo one, she shot at me and that man . . . Elmer? I can remember how it happened. We were almost in the car but Lizzy dropped something, I think it was Elmer's hat, and bent to pick it up. Then the shot came. She fell and just laid there. I saw that woman walking toward us, holding a pistol with both hands. She was firing slowly. I mean, she took a lot of time between shots. I don't know how close she came, but I heard the bullets, Garr. They went right past my ear." Mary Jo's eyes locked on mine, overflowing with tears as she repeated, "I heard the bullets."

"Hey. Hey." I tightened my hold on her. "You're fine, baby. You survived."

She sat up, swinging her legs over the edge of the bed, turning her back to me. "But they're all dead! Elizabeth and that man and that Milo lady. All dead!" The fear in her voice was heartbreaking. "Oh, Garr. I can't stop thinking about the cancer. Am I next? Am I going to die too?"

I rose and wrapped her in my arms. She pressed her cheek against my chest. We sat that way for several minutes. I rubbed her back as she sobbed, remembering the bullets slamming into the tree a few inches away from my head, that night in the woods back home. The slow, measured way Juliette Milo squeezed off her shots. She had been so sure of herself, so comfortable with the weapon. I remembered her voice, strangely accented, calling from so close by when I hadn't heard her coming. *"You see? I can kill you easily."*

My mind was a boiling cauldron of raw sensations. I didn't know *what* I felt. Just as I began to settle upon one emotion, another rose to replace it. I felt furious and tenderhearted. Resentful and protective. Devastated and vengeful. Guilty and indignant. Mary Jo had never deliberately lied to me before. It hurt like nothing I'd ever felt. But mixed together with the pain of her duplicity was the inescapable sorrow I felt for killing Juliette Milo, and an overwhelming rage at all of the people who had driven Mary Jo to do what she'd done. Lieutenant Washington, the Slydels, Juliette Milo, Elizabeth Harmony, Lucretia Granier . . . at that moment, I hated them all. In spite of my anger at her lies, I felt a primal urge to protect Mary Jo. But that protective impulse was thwarted by the fact that all of the people who had hurt her were dead or well beyond my reach.

And then, the cancer. The terrible frustration of knowing it was just beneath the skin, threatening her life, and there was absolutely nothing I could do about it. So impotence joined the swirling pot of pain within me. I clenched my fist as it lay upon Mary Jo's back.

"Listen," I said, whispering in her ear. "They said they caught it early. They said your chances were real good."

"But it hurts. It hurts, Garr."

Her words impaled my heart. "Your breast? It hurts?"

"Yes," she sobbed.

I pulled her closer. Rocking her back and forth, I resolved to forget the betrayal. To forget her lies. To stand with her. To lift her up if I could. To be whatever she needed until this thing was over, one way or the other.

She murmured against my chest. "Why shouldn't I die too? Why shouldn't I?"

"Don't say things like that." I touched her lips. "Shhhh."

She pulled away. "I know you're angry. I can feel it. But they're all dead. So there's nobody left to be angry at, unless you change your mind about me."

I pulled her close and buried my face in her softly scented hair, basking in the warmth of her flesh against mine and remembering the girl who ran over my feet with her bicycle, the girl who shared her paintings with me in the Tulane studio, the girl who refused my advances on a pier beside the Cajun shack after our bayou boat ride, and rejected my proposal in the crowded restaurant on Canal. I remembered the girl who trusted me with her darkest secret on a lonely sidewalk on St. Charles, surrounded by the desolation and debris of her skid-row mission home.

My lips touched her ear.

I whispered a secret to the girl I loved.

I said, "I'll never change my mind about you."

• • •

LATER THAT NIGHT, JUST BEFORE DAWN, I LAY AWAKE, listening to Mary Jo's soft snoring. Outside the open window, the street party had died down. I turned my head. Through a narrow gap between the black silhouettes of two ancient buildings across the street, I could just make out the running lights of a container ship cruising slowly up the Mississippi. I closed my eyes and willed myself to relax. In a few hours, there would be beignets and cafe au lait on the hotel patio, a gurgling cast-iron fountain, smoothly competent waiters in crisp white aprons, and Boston ivy on the brick courtyard walls. Life at its sweetest in the Vieux Carre.

But I could not relax. Something was unresolved. Something I could not name. There was the cancer, of course, but this was something else, probably worse. I knew it as surely as I knew that my wife lay sleeping beside me at last. I replayed the events of the last few days in my mind, searching for the inconsistency, the missing piece. Finally, when it came, I felt foolish for having overlooked the obvious.

If Juliette Milo tried to murder her husband, why did she stalk me with a handgun in the woods? Again, I remembered her words, *"I won't let you hurt him anymore."*

I almost woke Mary Jo in my excitement. But her childlike face was lit by a perfect moonbeam, her hair a soft halo spread like powdered rubies across her pillow. I forgot about my questions and gathered her into my arms. She murmured something softly, then settled back into her dreams. I simply watched her sleep.

It was a perfect moment, marred only by a tiny voice in the background. I knew I shouldn't listen. I tried to ignore the words. But I could not suppress the recurring refrain. None of this would have happened if Mary Jo hadn't agreed to help the police. The weeks of suffering, of frantic searching, of worry, of doubting God and my own faith. None of it had to happen. But it did happen, because Mary Jo did not tell me the truth. And now I had to live with the fact that I had killed a woman. Because Mary Jo lied to me.

Lied to *me*.

The words refused to be ignored, rebounding through my soul like the ricochet of an assassin's bullet. And in spite of that part of me that longed to simply love her, I felt the anger rise again. But I had obligations to a wife with a life-threatening disease. So this time, I decided to guard my anger carefully, holding it very close.

Even closer than I held my wife.

Chapter 58

"HEY, NOW. DON'T WORRY, BABY. THE LORD'S gonna handle this."

Mary Jo squeezed my hand, reassuring me as I stood beside her bed in the Jackson County Memorial Hospital. Behind me, sleet tapped at the window. It had been a hard winter in East Texas, with one storm after another. Now, two months after the tempest in New Orleans, we faced the worst storm of all. Mary Jo had suffered through minor surgery and two months of chemotherapy, but the cancer was worse. They were going to take her right breast.

I said, "I know it's a sin to worry, but—"

"No buts. They do this operation all the time. I'll be fine."

I felt a sudden shame. Although she lay waiting for the disfiguring knife of the surgeon, with her head wrapped in a brightly colored silk scarf to conceal the patchy baldness inflicted by the drugs, it was *she* who comforted *me*. I bent to kiss her cheek, my emotions swirling like back eddies along the Big Muddy Bayou. Love was chief among my feelings, followed closely by respect. And anger. Try as I might to ignore it, deep down, there was still the anger.

Forcing myself to smile, I searched her eyes from inches away. They were huge and held the emerald-colored universe for me. Why couldn't I forget?

I whispered, "It doesn't seem fair. I almost lost you, and now—"

"Shush now, honey. No matter what happens, there's a reason."

"I know."

"Remember the way he took care of me that time?"

I nodded, thinking of the miracle in New Orleans. Only God's will could explain Elmer's sudden change of heart, his willingness to betray the Slydels and release Lizzy. And it wasn't chance that led Lizzy Harmony to free my wife. It was the miracle of her newfound faith.

The door opened and an orderly entered, pushing a gurney. Behind him was a nurse. She wore a surgical smock and head gear. Her shoes were covered by lime-green paper with elastic at her ankles.

"How ya'll feeling, Mary Jo?" she asked.

"A little groggy, I guess."

The nurse nodded. "Good. That's the sedative kicking in."

From the bedside table, she lifted a black felt cowboy hat I had bought for Mary Jo as a joke. The hat's crown was almost a foot tall. Since she'd lost her hair, my wife had tried to remain bright and upbeat, but the image in her mirror took its emotional toll. I had purchased the huge hat along with several scarves, hoping the silliness would help her to forget, if only for a while.

The nurse said, "What in the world is this thing?"

"It's my good luck hat," said Mary Jo.

The nurse smiled and replaced it on the table. She leaned over the bed and looked closely at Mary Jo's eyes. "I'd say you're about ready. Shall we get going?"

"All right."

I couldn't seem to let go of her hand. As they shifted her onto the gurney, I squeezed it three times: I love you. She squeezed my hand twice: me too. Then she smiled at me—a firm, courageous smile. They helped her onto the gurney and rolled her out of the room. I started to follow. The nurse turned and said, "Now, don't ya'll worry, Mister Reed. We're going to take real good care of her. Why don't ya'll wait down the hall? She'll be at the I.C.U. before you know it. The doctor said he'll come by as soon as he can."

With a dreamy smile, Mary Jo said, "Take care of my hat." Her words were slow and slurred.

"I will," I said. The same words I spoke at our wedding.

As the orderly pushed Mary Jo past the nurse's station, Leon Martinez and Mrs. P. rounded the hallway corner and almost collided with the gurney. Leon dropped a bottle of cola. It spilled onto the vinyl floor. The wheels of the gurney passed through the liquid and rolled on, trailing twin lines of soda on the shiny vinyl. The nurse stepped in the cola, too, tracking a dull brown footprint for several steps. Suddenly, I remembered the bloody footprints in the Crescent City Garage. I shook my head to clear away the grisly image and watched as they pushed my wife through a pair of elevator doors, past Leon as he bent to wipe at the soda pop on his clothes. When the elevator doors closed, I turned toward the waiting room and steeled myself for one of the longest waits of my life.

Mrs. P. waddled up to me, an uncharacteristic smile on her face. "Sugar, we here to keep you company."

I was surprised at the relief I felt. With my elbow firmly clutched in her pudgy fingers, she led me down the hall to the waiting room. The television on the wall was tuned to a soap opera. A woman in a pink evening gown whined about her sister's boyfriend, while a broad-shouldered man in a tuxedo mixed a drink behind an art-deco bar. As I reached up to turn it off, Leon trailed us through the door, still wiping cola from his trousers.

"Hey, *compadre*. Want some company?" He smiled, but his rugged face was tight with concern.

I said, "Sure. Let's walk around a little. This room gives me the creeps."

"All right," he said, turning back toward the hall. "Ya'll wanna follow this little blue line on the floor? See where that gets us?"

"Lead on."

With Mrs. P. on my left and Leon on my right, we set out through the maze of hallways. After a minute or two, Mrs. P. said, "Honey, Leon an' me been wonderin' 'bout that business in New Orleans." She looked up at me. "You mind talkin' about it?"

"No. Might get my mind off things."

"You sure?"

"Yes."

"'Cause if you ain't up to it, don't make me no never mind."

"No, it's okay."

"I don't wanna pry."

"Go ahead and ask, Mrs. P. It's all right."

"Well, if you're *sure* that you are *sure*."

"Mrs. P., I'd tell you anything."

"Well, honey, if you really wanna talk about it ..."

"That's funny, I thought *you* were the one who wanted to talk about it."

Leon made a strange sound, covering his mouth, eyes dancing above his hand.

She stopped in the middle of the hallway, clenching her pudgy fingers into fists, which she planted solidly on her hips, sending ripples up and down her corpulent body. "All I'm tryin' to do here is be sensitive to your needs, Garrison Reed. Ain't no call for sassy talk like that there."

"I'm sorry, Mrs. P."

She stared at me silently, her head tilted back to allow an angle of view up at my face. The seconds ticked by. I began to squirm. Finally, she said, "All right then. If you're *sure* you don't mind me asking ..."

Leon burst out laughing.

Mrs. P. turned to him, hands still on her hips, and said, "Leon, I tol' you and I tol' you. This here weddin' is off if you keep on laughin' at me thataway."

"I'm sorry, sugar cakes," said Leon, struggling to contain himself. "I'm not laughin' at you, I'm laughin' with you."

"Humf! Sugar cakes, huh? Laughin' *with* me, huh? Leon Martinez, if you laughin' with *me*, you laughin' your way out of a night of *sweet* romance at the Nashville, Tennessee Holiday Inn. 'Cause ain't nobody else laughin' round here but some sorry old numbskull don't know he's 'bout to go honeymoonin' without his good thing if he keep it up."

Leon turned away for a moment, hand back over his mouth. I said, "Mrs. P., what was it you wanted to know?"

Eyes still locked like gunsights on her amused fiancé, she said, "Where was your wife at all that time?"

"You mean when she was missing?"

She turned to me, deliberately facing away from Leon Martinez as if he no longer deserved her attention. "Of *course* that's what I mean. What you think we been talkin' 'bout?"

"I wasn't sure exactly." Her eyes flared and I hurried to say, "Mary Jo was locked in a closet at Elizabeth Harmony's apartment."

Ethyl Polanski clucked her tongue and shook her head. Her cheeks kept vibrating long after her head was still. "Mercy. She musta been bored to tears, cooped up like that for almost two weeks."

"She was drugged most of the time."

Leon said, "Poor thing."

"And who shot the woman that kidnapped her?"

"Juliette Milo."

"The doctor's wife?"

"That's right."

"You sure 'bout that?"

"Well, that's what the police said."

"Huh."

"What do you mean, 'huh'?"

"Nothin'."

"The police were kind of surprised it was Juliette Milo too, Mrs. P. They always thought James and Faye Slydel were behind everything."

"Nope. Wasn't them neither."

I stopped walking. "You sound like you know something about it."

"Maybe I do. You did ask me to investigate 'round here, after all."

"I don't remember asking you to do that."

"That what Lawyer Graves tol' me. Said you asked for our help."

Remembering my telephone conversation with Winston when I was in the New Orleans Police Department squad room, I said, "Oh, yeah. I forgot."

"Forgot! I been sneaking 'round town like Mattie Harry all this time an' you *forgot*?"

Leon said, "That's true, Garr. Ethyl's been doin' a lot of sneakin' lately. Wearin' sunglasses indoors and everything."

I laughed.

Mrs. P. said, "Leon Martinez, I tol' you that was 'cause of my complexion."

"Yeah, I know. But I never understood that. Explain it again, will ya?"

She stared at him suspiciously, then said, "The light on my eyelids causes wrinkles."

"But you were indoors."

"Light is light, honey."

"And you were pretending to read the paper. Hiding behind it, like."

"I tol' you, Leon. I was reading the obituaries."

"Hidin' behind a corner down in the hospital lobby, wearin' sunglasses, holdin' a newspaper right up under your nose and peekin' around is what you were doin', Ethyl."

"*Peekin'?* I never peeked in my life!"

"Now Ethyl, you know you used to peek at me all the time before I asked you out."

"*What?* I never hardly noticed you! Why, I just went out wit' you as a favor!"

"Droppin' hints. Starin' at me when I wasn't lookin'," Leon grinned at me. "She wanted me bad, Garr. Real bad!"

Mrs. P. inhaled deeply, her bosom exploding dangerously as it always did when she was about to embark upon a substantial round of insults. I decided to intervene in the interest of Leon's continued good health. "What did you discover, Mrs. P.?"

She ignored my question. She fixed her hard black eyes solidly on her intended, who fidgeted like a bug in a jar. It appeared that all was lost. Then she turned toward me, deliberately giving Leon her back. Crossing pudgy arms across her chest, she looked up at my face as if her fiancé were the furthest thing from her mind. But I think we all knew she would deal with him later.

"Actually, I did detect a few clues, Garrison."

I waited. Finally I realized she wanted me to ask, "What did you detect, Mrs. P.?"

"Well, there was a new nurse 'round here at the time of the crime."

"Elizabeth Harmony?"

"That's right. And they's some who say she wasn't too nice to that doctor who got shot."

"Who told you that?"

"I can't reveal my sources, Garrison."

We began to walk again, Mrs. P. and I walking abreast with Leon trailing behind. I said, "What did they say, exactly?"

"Say she an' the doctor had a fight. Like cats an' dogs. Say it was a nasty thing."

"What were they fighting about?"

"Didn't know. But it was pretty clear she didn't have no use for the man."

"When was this fight?"

"Don't know exactly. But it was sometime that day."

"The day of the murder?"

"That's right."

I remembered the night in New Orleans when I followed Doctor Milo to his clinic and stood outside the window there as Elizabeth Harmony beat him with her fists. And once again, I thought about Juliette Milo's words as she threatened me with her gun. Warning me to stay away from her husband. As if she was protecting him from me. Why would she do that if she was the one who tried to kill him? It had been bothering me for two months. I had even considered the notion that Elizabeth Harmony was involved. Yet she hadn't killed Mary Jo in spite of the fact that my wife was at her mercy all that time. Lizzy Harmony just didn't seem like the murdering kind. But there was no doubt that Juliette Milo was a cold-blooded killer. I remembered her teeth, bared like a mad dog's as she tried to drive her blade into my heart. And she had certainly killed Elmer and Lizzy ... but why? What motive could she have had for killing them, and trying to kill her husband and Mary Jo? And me?

For that matter, did Elizabeth Harmony have a motive?

We turned another corner and found ourselves entering the maternity wing. On our left, a young man and a middle-aged woman stood arm in arm, staring through a wide glass window. As we approached, I could see they were watching a nurse swaddle a newborn baby. The man turned to face us, his eyes alive with excitement.

"Here," he said. "Have a cigar!"

Leon and I each took one and mumbled our congratulations. Mrs. P. said, "Hey. What about me?"

The young man laughed and said, "Sure. Why not? How about you too, Momma? You want one too? Let's *all* light up." He handed Mrs. P. a cigar, but his mother, giggling and patting his arm, declined.

Leon eyed the blue wrapper. "Had a boy, huh?"

"And how! Eight pounds, ten ounces. He's a keeper."

"What's his name?"

"We named him McKay. McKay Emery Johnston."

I said, "I don't think I ever heard of anyone named McKay. Except as a last name of course. Is it a family name?"

The man said, "It was our priest's name."

"Michael McKay?"

"That's right. Did you know him?"

"No. Just heard about the ... thing that happened."

We fell silent, the five of us, watching through the glass as the nurse laid tiny McKay Johnston in his clear plastic crib, wrapped now in a powder blue blanket from toe to chin. The child was beet red from his first bath, his thin black hair plastered to his scalp. After a moment, the man spoke under his breath, with his eyes locked upon his son. "Thank God we listened to him."

I said, "Excuse me?"

He turned to me. "What?"

"I thought you said something."

"Oh. I guess I did. I was just thinking. Emma, my wife, and I, we weren't doing too good. We thought about . . . you know . . . some alternatives." He wrapped his arm around his mother's shoulders and continued, "When we mentioned it to Mom, she sent Father McKay over to talk to us. He seemed so . . . I don't know. Kind. And wise, I guess. We heard him out and changed our minds." The man turned back to the glass, a slow smile spreading across his face. "And now we have McKay."

"He's a good-looking boy."

"Yes, he is, isn't he?"

Mrs. P. said, "How's your wife doing?"

"She's upstairs sleeping. I think she's gonna be just fine. I think we're both gonna be all right."

McKay Emery Johnston screwed up his features and let fly a high-pitched wail. It sounded thin and forlorn through the plate glass. The man laughed and hugged his mother.

We wished them luck and moved on.

Chapter 59

S HE CAME HOME FIVE DAYS LATER, NOT BE-
cause they released her, but because she had
stubbornly refused to remain in the hospital
for the next round of chemotherapy. I rented
a wheelchair and an electrically powered adjustable bed and
hired a home nurse to sit with us after each administration of the
chemicals. When Lucretia Granier learned about the nurse, she
arrived without warning and announced that no stranger was
going to take care of her girl. And Lucretia stayed. Mary Jo felt
terrible for the first couple of days after each chemotherapy ses-
sion, then her health returned like an Indian summer, sometimes
for as long as a week. Then, always, the pain returned.

Mary Jo had cut her own hair in the late fall, soon after our
experiences in New Orleans. She trimmed it first with the pair of
scissors we kept in a kitchen drawer, then used an electric clip-
per she'd purchased at the Wal-Mart store. She did it herself
because she did not want the local hairdresser to spread rumors
about her health. I knew what she was doing, and waited on the
back deck to view the results. The shock must have registered in
my face when she emerged from the house, in spite of our
solemn and unspoken agreement not to acknowledge the little
changes we were making to accommodate the cancer. She lifted
one hand to touch the back of her head and did a little pirouette
beneath the golden canopy of post oak leaves. Keeping her voice
light and playful, she said, "It's not that bad, is it?"

"No. It's not bad. I mean, I like it very much," I lied. "You should have changed it years ago."

Then, for sixty mornings, we tried to ignore the short hairs that covered her pillow when she rose. The first round of chemotherapy was unsuccessful. The weeks we lost in New Orleans appeared to have given the cancer enough time to spread into her lymph system. By the time they performed the radical mastectomy, she was almost completely bald beneath her brightly colored silken scarves. Even silly gifts like the foot-tall ten-gallon hat I bought for her weren't enough to bring a smile. They said her hair might grow back a different color. It might be straighter, or more curly. Mary Jo tried to keep her chin up. She even said it might be fun to have a different "do."

I prayed that she would be given the chance to grow it back at all.

Leon and Mrs. P. watched over the construction business while I spent more and more time at home. Work was impossible for me, but, incredibly, Mary Jo found the energy to paint on her better days. Her work changed, of course. She seldom had more than two sessions in a row without the nausea and terrible weakness, so she adapted her style to her limitations. The usual level of detail gave way to broad simple bands of color, deft brush strokes that hinted at the core of her subject matter, boiling it down to the essentials and ignoring everything else. The result was an impressionistic shadow of her former style. I liked it very much. The new technique contained a lightness and sanguine flavor that was irresistible.

I made the mistake of assuming that this new optimism was a reflection of Mary Jo's true inner feelings. Then, late one afternoon, when Mary Jo and I were at home alone, the telephone rang as I stood by the stove waiting for a pot of water to boil. I was making fetuccini with a creamy mushroom sauce. The phone rang as I unwrapped the noodles. It was Julie Berger, Mary Jo's agent and gallery representative in New York.

After the usual pleasantries, she said, "Garr, I've been struggling with my conscience for days now, and I'm still not sure that this is the right thing to do ... it's a bit of a violation of my relationship with Mary Jo. But you *are* her husband after all, and there are some things that rise above the normal way one must deal with life. I mean, there are times when one shouldn't concern one's self with the short-term view. That is, some things tend to supersede the day-to-day. We certainly can't allow business to interfere with . . . with a thing like this. But that's why it's taken so long for me to call. I mean, I *thought* about keeping this to myself. I must confess I—"

I interrupted her. "Julie, you're rambling. Just tell me what you called to say."

"Rambling? Oh, I suppose I am. Sorry. It's just . . . the thing is . . . you see, it's Mary Jo. I am worried about Mary Jo."

The line hummed in my ear. After a moment, I said, "Is that why you called?"

"Well, no, actually. There is something more. This is quite difficult. I feel as if I'm violating a trust here, Garrison. You must understand, it is only concern for her welfare that leads me to this decision."

"Julie. You are a fine friend. I have no doubt that whatever it is, you are making the right choice."

"Yes. One hopes so. At any rate, one hopes one's motivations will be taken into account."

I decided to remain silent. She would tell me eventually. As I watched, the pasta boiled nicely near the top of the pot. With the telephone handset cocked against my shoulder, I opened the refrigerator and removed a stick of butter and a half pint of heavy cream. I quickly unwrapped the butter and sliced about a teaspoon of it into a sauce pan. When it had melted, I stirred in a quarter pound of chopped mushrooms, some finely diced yellow onion and two cloves of fresh garlic. Through all of that, Julie Berger remained silent.

Finally, she said, "Two weeks ago, I received a rather large consignment of oils from Mary Jo. You may know she has moved in a new direction with her work?"

"Yes."

"Of course you do. It's really quite . . . refreshing isn't it? Such energy and enthusiasm. I was delighted. And apparently, Mary Jo has been withholding these most recent works for some time, long enough to establish a rather respectable series."

It was time to add the cream and flour. Stirring them slowly into the pan, I said, "She's been working quickly. Producing them in a tenth the normal time. Sometimes less." I opened a drawer, selected a stain less steel serving spoon, and stirred the fetuccini, just as the frothy mixture bubbled dangerously close to the rim of the pot. It receded. Julie Berger said, "I see. Well, it shows in the spontaneity, doesn't it? The excitement. The *joie de vie*."

The fetuccini was swirling nicely, roiling in a constant stream of bubbles. I realized I would have to speed the conversation along. "Julie, I'm sort of in the middle here. If you don't mind, could we please get to the point? You don't have to sell me on Mary Jo's work."

"My apologies. Force of habit I suppose. At any rate, I received a note along with the paintings." She paused. When she continued, her voice was softer, more personal. "Garrison, did you help her pack the paintings?"

"Yes."

"And the note? Did she show you the note?"

"No."

"Oh, dear. I'm afraid this may be difficult news, Garrison. I do wish we could speak face-to-face, but . . . here it is. In her note, Mary Jo included the usual instructions for framing and presentation. She gave me some small insights regarding her motivation for each work. You know: why she chose the subject, what she hoped to say with the painting and so forth. Collectors love to know such things. All of this was quite normal—the kind of thing she has sent along with every shipment over the years. But the end of the note was different. It was the first time I can recall that she failed to request a specific sale price for each canvas."

"Maybe she forgot. We've had a lot on our minds lately."

"No. She did address the subject of pricing, but in a way which, frankly, has caused me to be quite anxious."

"Julie, I don't mean to be rude, but I'm cooking dinner here . . ."

"Oh, I *am* sorry. But this is so delicate. You see, her instructions with regard to pricing were quite specific. She wants me to hold the paintings because, as she quite correctly mentioned in her note, the works will command a premium at auction after her death."

My hand tightened on the telephone. "Her death?"

"Yes."

I stood silently beside the stove. After some time had passed, Julie said, "Garrison? I am quoting directly from the note, you see. It seems rather, ah, macabre, I suppose, so I thought I should call."

I turned to stare through the kitchen window. Mary Jo sat sideways on the porch swing outside, enjoying the unusually warm winter afternoon. She wore a thick wool sweater with a bold geometric pattern of jagged horizontal stripes, like an Indian blanket. Her legs were up on the swing, covered by a pale green afghan. She held her face toward the sun, drinking it in with her eyes closed. The red and yellow scarf around her head seemed to sparkle in the crisp clear light.

I said, "Julie, I think you should do as she said."

"Of course. That was never the issue. It was—"

"I understand. You wanted to let me know about her . . . state of mind."

I heard her exhale. "Yes. Exactly."

"Thank you. You are a good friend."

"I want to be." Her voice rose and fell too quickly and ended with a sob. "I do so want to be."

"Let's keep this conversation between us. All right?"

"Certainly, Garrison."

"And Julie? Don't worry. I think she's going to make it."

"Yes. Of *course* she will."

Outside, Mary Jo seemed to feel my stare upon her back. She turned and forced a smile, her eyes dull and vague above the dark smudges that had sunken into her cheeks. I said good-bye to Julie Berger and hung up the telephone. Just then, Lucretia wandered through the kitchen and stopped to look at me. I waved to Mary Jo and returned her smile.

Lucretia said, "What on earth is de matter with you, boy?" She was pointing at the fetuccini, boiling over onto the stove top.

Chapter 60

"LET'S NOT MAKE A BIG DEAL OUT OF THIS," she said.

Nodding, I stared into the woods. Somewhere out of sight beyond the bare tree trunks, a woodpecker drummed staccato on a hollow branch. The rat-a-tat pierced the bright winter air in short bursts, interspersed with longer periods of silence. Suddenly, the limbs in the treetops shivered and the silence surrendered to the north wind's resonance. God's rosined bow caressed the high branches, an omnipotent cello moaning high above the earth, lonely and sorrowful. It was a perfect counterpart to the overwhelming misery enveloping my heart.

I said, "It's hard for me, not to talk about it."

"It doesn't do any good."

"Mary Jo, I need to understand why you wrote the note."

She sighed. Then, wrapping her arms across her wounded chest, she shivered. I waited for her answer, but heard only the duet of the woodpecker and the northerly breeze in the high branches. I said, "Is it too cold? Do you want to go inside?"

"No. I'm fine."

The sun shone clear and warm on the porch where we sat. I said, "You've got to explain it to me."

"Oh Garr . . . it's simple, really. If I don't make it, you'll get more money for the paintings after I'm gone. Julie should wait. She'll sell them for you after I'm gone."

I said nothing.

After a while, she said, "I'm just thinking of you. Planning for the future."

"Planning for the future? Mary Jo, you're planning for dying."

"We have to be honest about the possibility."

"All right. I know that. But we don't have to live like it's preordained." I leaned toward her with my hands clasped together. "You have to fight for our future, honey. All I can do is help. It's mainly up to you. Maybe the Lord has other plans for us."

The woodpecker loosed another volley of blows. The sound reverberated through the trees. I stared at Mary Jo's profile. Her cheeks showed no effects from the chill in the air. On wintry days in years gone past the cold had given them a healthy blush. Today they were simply pale. The brightly colored scarf around her head was no protection from the cold, no protection from anything.

I said, "Why don't we go inside?"

Without looking at me, she said, "Whatever."

I rose. Mary Jo faltered halfway up, clutching my upper arm for support. I bent and lifted her to her feet, passing one arm around her back. Slowly, we crossed the leaf-strewn deck. As I pulled the door closed behind us, I heard the woodpecker's lonely cadence rattle through the woods once more.

I searched the woods to catch a glimpse of him. But instead, I saw the cold blue of the water down at the foot of the hill. And for some reason, it reminded me of another time when Mary Jo was in pain, and there was nothing I could do for her.

• • •

IT WAS THE SUMMER OF OUR SEVENTH YEAR TOGETHER. We drifted in the center of Martin Pool, a thousand feet away from the shoreline of our property, watching the sky catch fire. Back then, we owned a sixteen-foot Galaxy with a split windshield and padded benches in the bow. She sat on one bench, I sat on the other. Both of us reclined against the windshield, not talking, relaxed, enjoying the Sunday evening and each other.

A great blue heron on a stump fifty feet away heaved itself into the air and slowly crossed the sky, gliding toward its treetop roost. Martins skimmed an inch above the lake, dipping now and then to pluck a water bug from the mirrored surface. The sound of distant voices reached us from the public campground on the far shore: city people, packing their gear to head home to all that traffic and concrete after a weekend in the country. I felt sorry for them.

"Momma called," said Mary Jo. "She said Daddy's getting worse."

Water lapped against the hull. The boat rocked slightly. There was nothing to say.

"They want to move him back home."

I sipped my wine, letting a moment pass, then I said, "I don't see how Lucretia can take care of him."

"They're going to have nurses over every day. She'll rent a hospital bed. The kind that adjusts."

"I see."

"You know why they're sending him home?"

I looked at her. Her eyes were on the horizon. It was a beautiful sunset.

I said, "He's almost gone."

She nodded.

We sat silently for a long time after the sun dropped below the distant treetops. The aquamarine sky faded to pale turquoise as, one by one, the clouds flared orange and sepia. Their reflections flickered in the smooth water, an armada of burning galleons adrift in a lake of liquid fire. I heard the campers slam their doors and drive away. The sounds carried clearly across Martin Pool, although the opposite shore was a quarter mile away. The turquoise sky darkened, and the moon appeared, a ghostly sliver of a smile above the East Texas piney woods.

Or was it a frown?

I rose and walked around the windshield and fired up the motor. We cruised home at idle speed with Mary Jo in the bow trailing her fingertips in the water. When we docked, she set out up the hill to start dinner while I slipped the elastic edges of the canvas cover all around the boat, pulling tight. After checking the position of the straps beneath the hull, I flipped the switch to start the electric boat lift. When the boat was well above the surface, I stopped the winch. With one hand on the aluminum ski ladder, I leaned over the water behind the boat to remove the drain plug. The boat swayed against my weight in its wide cloth stays. When I pulled the plug, filthy bilge water streamed through the hole in the stern, spewing an oily sheen across the still surface of the lake. I watched as the tiny slick fanned out from the boat house.

Life jackets, water skis, inflatable floats, and other paraphernalia of a summer weekend on Martin Pool lay scattered around the pier. I gathered everything together in the boat house closet and closed the door. A hollow cracking sound caused me to glance toward the shore. In the last dim light of dusk, I saw Mary Jo standing at the tree line, watching me. She had stepped on a dry branch. I called to her, "I thought you went on up."

She did not respond.

The pier wobbled underfoot as I walked toward the shore. I said, "Hey, Nibbles."

She smiled at my use of her most private name. When I reached her, she held her arms wide and said, "Hug."

We embraced at the edge of the forest, swaying slightly as we listened to the calls of the night creatures. She pressed her cheek against my chest. I bent to kiss her softly scented hair. A dove cooed forlornly from somewhere up the hill. After a while, I released my hold, but she squeezed me tighter.

I wrapped my arms around her again. "Tell me."

"It's hard."

"I know."

"No. I don't think you do."

"Of course I do, honey. I've already lost my mom and dad. I know what it's like."

She said nothing. Finally, I released her and she let me go. Holding hands, we climbed the path up the hillside to our house, our footsteps muffled by a blanket of pine needles as we wound our way past familiar trees and rocks, wordlessly following the trail my father cut through the woods, fifty years ago.

We cooked dinner together, a simple meal of panfried steaks and mashed potatoes, with fresh tomatoes Mary Jo had purchased at a farmer's fruit stand up the road. She played Vivaldi's "Four Seasons" on the stereo. Sitting together at the kitchen table, we ate and listened without speaking. There was no need to speak. It was the comfortable silence of two people in love.

She rose and collected the dirty dishes and carried them to the kitchen sink. Standing with her back to me, she said, "I can't cry for him."

"You will. Sometimes it takes a little while to sink in."

"No, Garr. You don't understand. I can't cry for him. I don't feel anything for him."

"It's shock."

"No, it's not caring. I've tried, but I just don't seem to care."

I stared at her slender back, unsure of what to say. After a moment, she turned to me. "How about dessert?"

I said, "Do you want to tell me about it?"

She walked to the refrigerator. "There's nothing to tell, really. It's just that I keep waiting to feel something. But it never comes."

"I think it will."

"Maybe." Facing the open freezer door, she said, "How about some ice cream? Or a piece of that buttermilk pie from the other day?"

"No. I'm too full of steak."

She took out a carton of Bluebell vanilla, set it in the sink, and began to dig out big globs, shaking them into a bowl on the counter. I said, "You never talk about him. Why is that?"

She shrugged. "I don't know. Maybe because I don't think about him much."

"Why not?"

"What would be the point? He's not a very nice man."

"He's done a lot of good."

She looked at me over her shoulder, still scooping out ice cream. "You think so?"

"Sure. The Mission and all . . ."

"Yes. The Mission."

After a moment, I said, "You say that like it's nothing special. Lucretia and Alphonse have a lot to be proud of. All the men they've fed. Kept off the streets. Helped to sober up."

"Garr, believe me, nobody knows what they've done better than I do." She returned the ice cream carton to the freezer.

"So why would you say your father's not a nice man?"

Sitting across the table from me, she leaned close to her food, spooning ice cream into her mouth as fast as she could. One arm coiled around her bowl as if to protect it. I had long since learned to ignore her unusual table manners. They were understandable. After all, she ate most of her childhood meals in a mess hall surrounded by people on the verge of starvation.

I repeated my question, "What's wrong with Alphonse, exactly? He's always very civil to me."

Without looking up, she said, "Momma said he's been cursed."

"Cursed?"

"That's right. She thinks they've called *Baron Samadhi* down on him."

"That sounds more like sister Edna talking."

She glanced up. "You don't think Daddy believes in voodoo?"

"He's a preacher, Mary Jo. He hates everything about it."

"What does hating have to do with believing? Jesus saved the man possessed by Legion. Sent the demons into a herd of pigs. Angels and demons fight for our souls—it's in the Bible. God cast Lucifer down from heaven." Her lovely green eyes narrowed and she said, "And now Lucifer is among us."

"But voodoo . . ."

"It's just another word for Satanism. Christians fight it every day."

I shifted my gaze out the window. It was summer and the trees shrugged beneath their weight of green. I said, "What I meant was how could Satan curse a Christian man?"

She did not answer.

"He's a preacher, Mary Jo."

"Let's not discuss him anymore."

"You're the one who brought all this up."

"I know. But let's just drop it."

We sat silently for a moment, not looking at each other. I said, "Are you all right? I want you to be all right."

"I'm fine."

"You can be sad, you know."

"I'm not sad."

"But if you were, it would be okay to let it show."

"Oh, thank you."

I looked at the top of her head, bowed over the ice cream.

I said, "That sounded a little bit sarcastic."

"I asked you to drop it and you won't. What do you expect?"

"I'm just trying to help, Mary Jo."

She dropped her spoon into the empty bowl. It clattered loudly against the fragile china.

She looked at me with haunted eyes. "Did I say anything about needing help?"

I rose and walked away, anger bursting in my brain like fireworks. As I crossed the living room, she called after me, "Satan is down here with us now, Garr. Never forget that."

Chapter 61

EON LOOKED UP FROM THE *DALLAS* MORNING News. *"Says here they arrested that Slydel fella an' his wife at their church over in Metairie."* I said, "I saw that."

Glancing down at the paper again, he said, "They raided some place outside New Orleans and found a bunch of bomb parts. Same kind of bombs they been findin' at abortion clinics around the country."

"That figures."

He read out loud, "'Police Raid Barataria Camp. Informant Reveals Location.' Was that you?"

"Yes. I'm surprised they waited so long."

He laid the paper down on the worn tabletop. "You gonna testify against them?"

"If I have to. Somebody should tell what they did to Elizabeth Harmony."

"The snake pit thing?"

"That's right."

He said, "Lots of folks at church think they oughta get a medal for what they did. Not the snake part, but the demonstrations and blowin' up the clinics and all."

I looked over at him. "What do you think?"

He drained his coffee cup before answering. "I don't know exactly. Abortion's a terrible thing—I know that. It's like what the Nazis did to the Jews if you ask me, what's going on in those abortion clinics. But somehow it don't feel right using violence and intimidation to stop the doctors. It almost seems like those C.H.A.R.G.E. people are as bad as the ones they're tryin' to stop."

I nodded. "That's the way I feel about it. We've got to fight our enemies without becoming so wrapped up in it that we forget they're just sinners, like us. Otherwise what's the point?"

"Yeah. That's it exactly."

Rising, I said, "Want some more coffee?"

"No thanks. Two cups is my limit."

"Since when?"

He grinned. "Since Ethyl told me so."

I crossed the squeaky wooden floor of Pedro Comacho's cafe. Stepping behind the dining counter, I helped myself to a cup of coffee.

Pedro was perched on a stool beside the ancient cash register, reading a Spanish language newspaper. The headlines were two inches high and printed in blood red. Without asking permission, I lifted the plastic lid from a pastry display and took a donut. Pedro shook the paper and turned a page. I tried to decipher the headline. It didn't have anything to do with James and Faye Slydel.

Leon called from across the dining room. "Hey, Garr, bring me one of those, will ya?"

I took a second donut and replaced the lid. As I walked behind him, Pedro said, "They're two days old."

"So give me a discount."

He snorted and continued with his reading.

I returned to the table. Leon and I used these early breakfasts to get caught up on a few business details. With Mary Jo going through a new round of chemotherapy every two weeks, I was working mostly from my study at home. Even with Lucretia around to help out, I still felt I had to be there with Mary Jo every day. Since Leon worked out on job sites most of the time, I missed him whenever I dropped by the office, so it was best that we meet face-to-face a couple of times a week. Besides, spending all day at home with Lucretia was driving me crazy. It was good to get away, even if only for an hour or two.

I handed Leon his donut. Indicating the newspaper, he said, "I see those Slydels hired some fancy New York lawyers. A whole team of 'em. Where'd they get the money for that?"

Thinking of Lucretia Granier and the donations from her mission, I said, "They must have money coming in from all over."

"From churches?"

"Mostly."

He bit into the donut. Chewing, he said, "Bombs and hidden camps in the woods . . . funny way to spend church money."

"Well, the times are strange."

"Man, that's for sure." He glanced down at the paper. "Tell me again why the snake lady kidnapped Mary Jo?"

"We'll never know for sure."

"Didn't she say anything to Mary Jo about her reasons?"

"No. Remember, I told you she kept Mary Jo sedated and locked in a closet most of the time? Mary Jo doesn't remember much."

With a severe, Mayan frown, Leon said, "One thing I still haven't figured out: if she was worried about defending herself, why kidnap Mary Jo? Why not just go ahead and kill her? It would have been a lot simpler."

I looked out through the storefront window. Across the street, the huge oaks around the plaza stood naked and cold against the spreading dawn in the January sky. A tall pine Christmas tree still twinkled in front of the courthouse, decorated with lights and strings of ornaments made by local school children. I had been regretting that Mary Jo and I could not have children. It was an old and hopeless lament, something I had pushed from my mind years ago. But now it was back again. My parents were dead. I was an only child. If I lost Mary Jo there would be no close family left for me on the face of the earth.

Leon watched my face. "Hey, I'm sorry."

Still looking out the window, I said, "No. It's a good question. I've been asking it myself. Killing her would have made more sense." I returned my attention to Leon. "Maybe Elizabeth Harmony just wasn't the murdering kind."

Leon said, "She sure murdered a lot of little babies."

I passed my hand across my face. If only we could have had children. It would have been so much easier to bear. How could they kill them in the womb when we wanted a child so badly?

Leon stared hard into my eyes, his forehead wrinkled with concern. He said, "What? What did I say?"

I forced myself to smile. "Nothing, nothing. I was just thinking . . . it's probably different, when you can see the person who's about to die. Less abstract. Harder to rationalize."

"Sort of like the difference between droppin' a bomb from a mile in the air and pushin' a knife between somebody's ribs, up close an' personal."

"Yes. Something like that."

We sat silently for a moment, chewing the donuts. They tasted all right for two days old. I remembered the dullness of Mary Jo's voice as we talked on the deck. The pale white of her cheeks in the brisk morning air. The gray-brown smudges below her eyes. She was planning for death, making arrangements to sell her art for the higher price it would bring after she was gone. Art is a morbid business. How many times had we heard it in the galleries of Dallas, New York, and Santa Fe? "That painting is a fine investment. The artist died recently, you know. The value is climbing."

I had to do something to cheer her up, to make her fight again. I thought of a wig. Maybe if she could look in the mirror and see herself as she was . . .

Leon said, "Listen, I'm sorry to keep bringin' this up, but it still doesn't make sense to me."

"That's all right. What is it?"

"Well, everyone's sayin' the Milo lady killed the nurse, then that C.H.A.R.G.E. fella, then tried to kill you?"

"Uh huh."

"And she left a note?"

"Yes. It said Elizabeth Harmony and Melvin Milo were having an affair, which is why Juliette tried to kill Doctor Milo at the hospital, and why she killed Lizzy at the Crescent City Garage."

"Okay. So none of this had anything to do with abortion, like all the television people was sayin'?"

"Nope." I shook my head. "It looks like it was a simple case of jealousy and revenge."

"All right then, here's what's got me so confused: If the doctor got shot by his wife, why would he claim it was Mary Jo who shot him and the priest?"

"That gets a little weird. The Milos were into a strange religion. Part voodoo, part *Santaria*. Juliette Milo was a priestess in the religion, what they call a *mamba*. When Harry Attwater, the hospital orderly, arrived on the scene, he saw a woman running away. He saw her from behind, which is why he identified her as Mary Jo. Juliette Milo looked a lot like Mary Jo from behind. I made that mistake myself one time. Plus Juliette was dressed kind of like Mary Jo. Anyway, after the woman turned a corner, Attwater ducked into a room to call for help. When he returned to the hall, Juliette was back, crouched beside her husband, drawing symbols with his blood. The official theory is that she ran away to hide the gun, then returned to play the part of hysterical wife, and maybe to make sure Milo was dead. Harry Attwater probably saved Milo's life by being there. The police figure when she realized her husband might live, Juliette used his blood to draw a symbol that terrified Melvin Milo. When he heard Attwater identify Mary Jo to the police, he went along out of fear of his wife's spiritual powers."

Leon smiled. "He was afraid of being cursed? Like, turned into a zombie or something?"

"It isn't funny. More people believe in that stuff than you think."

Leon crossed himself. "Who's laughing? I got cousins in Monterey who do that *Santaria* stuff. They think the saints are gods. They think demons can be called upon for good or evil. It's a bad thing, is what I think."

I remembered Lucretia Granier's words so long ago. *"Your puny brain can't accept de presence of evil in de world, real evil dat you can touch and feel!"* I remembered the strange stains on the Slydels' porch that would not be washed away, and the circle of blood on Linda Granier's crypt. I remembered the glowing red eyes of the girl dressed in rags at the end of a dark New Orleans alley, and the awful visions I had seen in the Barataria swamp. Visions of the trees and ground swarming with flies, and a hissing voice emanating from a grinning skull. The horrible shrieks and whispers in the woods, in the Milos' home, in the Mission. Maybe these things were dreams or hysterical delusions. Certainly there was nothing I could prove. But before I'd allowed the Lord to enter my soul, I'd laughed at Satan and thought him nothing but a boogeyman used by the superstitious to scare their children. I'll never laugh at him again.

"You're right," I said. "It is a very bad thing."

We finished our donuts and helped ourselves to more coffee. By the time we were done reviewing the upcoming business day, the sun shone brightly on the courthouse plaza across the street. More cars and pickup trucks arrived, mostly the owners and employees of the small businesses around the square. Steam rose from tailpipes and nostrils alike. Leon and I stood to go. I fished around in the pocket of my blue jeans for some money.

He said, "Hey. Didn't you tell me that someone tried to shoot the Milo lady in her house? You went in and chased them out?"

Remembering the scene just before I crashed through the Milos' front porch window, I said, "Yes. That's right."

"So who was that?"

I looked at him. "Who was who?"

He shrugged into his jacket and said, "Who'd you chase out of the house? Who tried to shoot Mrs. Milo?"

It was a fine question. I felt foolish for not asking it myself. I said, "It was a woman. Someone who looked like Mary Jo from behind."

"Are you sure?"

"Of course. I saw her running away."

"Like in the hospital? When the orderly saw Mrs. Milo running away and thought it was Mary Jo?"

"Yes . . ."

Leon said, "So it was Mrs. Milo you saw at the house? The woman that looked like Mary Jo?"

"No. Mrs. Milo was in the kitchen when the woman ran outside."

"Then there must have been *another* woman who looked like Mary Jo from the back, right?"

I sat back down. I had been having trouble concentrating lately, my mind clouded with fear and self-pity. But still, I should have seen it earlier.

There were *two* of them in that house at the same time. So there were three, really. Three look-alikes: Mary Jo, Juliette Milo, and *someone else*.

Suddenly, none of the theories made sense anymore.

Chapter 62

OW STRANGE, TO FIND THE ANSWER TO everything within a modest plywood shack teetering on concrete blocks in the East Texas woods.

The lavender walls of Kathy's Kuntry Kuts clashed violently with the pink trim, green asphalt shingle roof, and traditional reds and greens of the Christmas decorations hanging from the front porch eaves. A wall of pines towered above the small clearing, their tops swaying slightly in the winter wind. Wondering if I was doing the right thing, I stepped from my pickup and zipped up my jacket.

Early on, when her hair first began to fall onto her pillow and shoulders, Mary Jo's doctor suggested she should be fitted for a good quality wig. It would help to keep her spirits up.

But Mary Jo said no, thank you.

Later, as we walked away from the doctor's office, I tried to change her mind. The doctor's suggestions made sense to me. Why not go ahead and buy a wig now, so she could start getting used to it? Her angry reaction took me by surprise.

"I will *not* be controlled by this thing, Garr. At least no more than I have to be. Maybe I can't do anything about the pain and the nausea. But wigs and makeup make me feel like somebody else. Like I'm wearing a disguise."

I started to speak but she cut me off.

"Garr, I've never worn those things, and I won't start now. No matter what happens, I am going to be myself."

That was when I bought her the funny cowboy hat with the foot-tall crown. At first, I admired her high-chinned determination. My Mary Jo, fighting the traitor within her body without a flinch. But time and constant pain had replaced the resolve with something worse than any disguise that she could wear. And funny hats could not distract us from the most terrible truth of all.

She had given up hope.

I had never seen the side of Mary Jo that could arrange for paintings to be sold after her death. My Mary Jo lived in the here and now. The woman who tossed fitfully in our bed at home under the tender care of Lucretia Granier was someone else. And whoever she was, whatever she had become, I was willing to risk her anger to get my Mary Jo back.

I climbed the wooden steps and opened the door. Inside, a propane heater beside the door belched hot dry air into the room with a constant hiss. Pink wooden cabinets lined the wall to my right. Above them, mirrors rose to the ceiling, which was so low I had the feeling I should duck. To my left, two plastic chairs flanked a shiny aluminum Christmas tree. The walls that weren't covered with mirrors were plastered with faded unframed posters of young women modeling outdated hair styles. The centerpiece of the room was a chrome and red leather barber's chair. A woman lay semireclined upon the chair, while another woman sat on a rolling stool at her side. A man's whining voice oozed country and western from a huge black radio on the pink cabinet, something about drinking away his troubles and blinking away his tears.

I assumed it was Kathy on the rolling stool and a customer on the barber chair. Both women turned toward me as I closed the door. The reclining woman's face was caked with a thick substance the color of mildew. Her hair was fire engine red. Her eyes peeked out through twin holes in the dull green mask, dipping to my boots and rising slowly to linger for a moment just below my belt. When the inspection reached my face, I returned her stare until she rolled her head toward the ceiling again. Kathy followed all this with a smirk, her eyes large behind thick-lensed glasses. She chewed gum nonstop while the clicking scissors in her hands performed an intricate ballet above the woman's head.

"What can I do for you, big boy?" she asked.

Muddy face giggled.

"I'd like to look at a wig."

"Well, I'll darn sure sell you one, but it seems a shame. You got a fine head of hair, honey. Shouldn't let that touch of gray bother you none. It gives you a certain experienced look—know what I mean?"

Another twitter from muddy face.

"Besides, you can always color it. Ain't no problem at all. Some folks change color just about daily, don't they, Sally Jean?"

The woman giggled again. "What color *am* I today, anyway? I forget."

I said, "It's not for me. It's for my wife. And it needs to match her hair color pretty closely."

The beautician looked closely at me through her large glasses. "You Mary Jo Reed's husband?"

"Yes."

"Thought so. I seen you two together over at Pedro's Cafe a couple of times."

Kathy returned her attention to the woman's hair. I pointed at her customer and said, "Then you know it needs to be an auburn color, sort of like hers, but not as red."

"Hear that Sally Jean? This fella likes your color." Her jaw worked furiously on the wad of chewing gum. Smack. Smack. Smack.

The reclining woman said, "I don't mind. Maybe we'll leave it this way for a day or two. Whatever color it is."

Kathy laughed, a big, horsy sound.

I said, "Should I come back when you're not so busy?"

"No, no. We're done here for a while anyway. Sally Jean's got to let that mud soak in, don't you, honey?"

Muddy face said, "Every little bit helps."

Kathy gave the woman's shoulder a pat and rose. She was taller than I expected, almost up to my chin, and very thin in a pair of burgundy colored blue jeans and a western-cut shirt with a red leather fringe around the yoke. The dusty beige makeup coating her face had smeared onto the top half of her glasses. Heavy false eyelashes dangled from her upper lids.

"Come on to the back room, honey. That's where I keep my stock."

I followed her through a doorway into a larger room. Shelves lined two of the walls from floor to ceiling. White plastic heads lined the shelves, each wearing a wig. There must have been fifty different styles in a dozen colors. It was cold in the back room. I put my hands in the pockets of my blue jeans.

Kathy said, "Now then, you got your three kinds of wigs. Your custom-made, customized, and ready-to-wear. Your custom-made is the most expensive. They're gonna run anywhere from fifteen hundred up to about thirty-five hundred dollars. But they look real good 'cause we'll fit it right and get it made just for your wife. An' they're a hundred percent human hair. Nobody's gonna be able to tell she's wearin' it, I can guarantee you that. Plus they're more comfortable. They got a nice lace foundation that breathes real good. A customized wig is almost as nice lookin', but the foundation is made of nylon and they get a little hot and scratchy in the summer time. 'Course you'll save about a thousand dollars. I don't recommend a ready-to-wear, although I stock 'em. They just never fit right, and that synthetic hair's so fake lookin'."

She turned to peer up at me. "I hate to pry, but could you tell me why you're buyin' this wig?"

"My wife has cancer, and the chemotherapy . . ."

"Oh, thought that might be it. Someone was tellin' me about Mary Jo." She fell silent for a moment, then said, "You won't want the custom-made, honey. It's too much to spend on a temporary . . ." Her hand flew up to her mouth. "I'm sorry. I didn't mean to say she wouldn't be . . . that is, she'll only need it 'til her hair grows back, right? It'll be a temporary thing. Just 'til she gets better?"

I said, "That's right. Until she gets better."

Kathy turned toward the wall of plastic heads. Smacking her gum and waving her arm, she said, "But you do want her to feel good about it, right? So I recommend one of our mid-priced customized products. That's them on those shelves over yonder. Go ahead and look 'em over. Let's talk style while you look. See anything here that she might like?"

I stepped closer to the wigs and found one similar to Mary Jo's original style before she cut it short. "This one's about right. But the color's wrong."

"Okay. Which one's colored right?"

It was more difficult to pick the color. I searched the shelves, finally selecting a pageboy that had the right combination of brown and red. "This is about it," I said.

"Okay, honey. I'll go ahead and order it this afternoon. Let's go back up front and make an appointment."

"Appointment? What for?"

"Why, for the fitting, of course."

"You mean she has to come in for a fitting?"

"Why sure, honey. How else am I gonna get it to look right?"

"That's going to be a problem. I wanted to surprise her." I knew there was no way I would get Mary Jo to set foot in that place. My plan was to present the wig to her as a done deal and hope she would give it a try.

Kathy said, "I see. Well, maybe we can figure something out . . . I know, bring me in one of her hats. I'll adjust it from that and you can bring her in for the final fitting after the big surprise. Will that work?"

"I think so."

As she led me back to the front, Kathy said, "Funny how things come in bunches. You're the third person in three months to come in here looking for a wig like that."

My pulse quickened. I said, "Oh, really?"

"Yep. First it was Ethyl Polanski. She picked the exact same style and color." Kathy chuckled. "Ethyl's a lady of color, you know. She's all the time buyin' wigs in here, and don't none of them look right on her. I mean, she must have three dozen of 'em, and only two or three designed for black people. Looks funny, runnin' 'round with long straight hair."

"I know her. She's a friend of mine."

Kathy turned, eyes large behind the thick lenses of her glasses, and said, "Oh, I did it again, didn't I? That sounded wrong. But I'm just sayin' she's a little bit eccentric in her fashion sense."

"I know what you mean. She really looks strange in her double-braided Indian-style wig."

Kathy giggled. "I remember that one. She said she was gonna get her a man with that one."

"It worked."

"You don't mean it. Some fella *liked* that look on her?"

"Yes. Another friend of mine. Leon Martinez. They're going to get married. But you know, I haven't seen her wearing the kind of wig I just picked out."

"That's because she never came in to get it. I held it for her for almost four weeks, then this fella came in and bought it for cash. I hated to sell it out from under Ethyl, but you know what they say, 'Take the cash and keep the credit.'"

We went back up front. The woman in the mud mask sprawled across the barber chair, snoring. I whispered, "You sold Mrs. P.'s wig to a man?"

"Yeah. That's kinda funny, ain't it? I mean, selling the exact same style three times in a row is one thing, but selling two of them to men . . . that's downright weird. I hardly *ever* get any men in here."

She opened a drawer and removed an order form and pencil.

I took a deep breath. "Do you remember the other guy's name?"

"No. I don't think he told me. It was a cash deal, so I didn't ask." She began to fill in the blanks on the form. Her jaw rose and fell, chewing the wad of gum relentlessly as she wrote.

"Could you describe the man to me?"

"You're sure a curious fella, ain't ya?"

"I've got good reasons."

Still writing, she said, "Oh sure. Don't doubt that, what with everything I been hearin'."

I waited. She kept writing. Finally I said, "So? What did this guy look like?"

"Well, he was a different-lookin' fella, sort of skinny, dark complexion, like black kinda, only different. Bald on top. Told me the same thing you did. Said it was a surprise for his girlfriend, which was why she wasn't there."

All of a sudden, the pieces fit together. Sometimes you spend days thinking about it, rolling it around in your mind, looking at the angles from every which way, and still you never see it. Other times, it comes to you in a flash of inspiration. That's how it was for me. As Kathy described the man, everything fell into place.

The beautician continued to write the order for Mary Jo's wig at a leisurely pace. I fought for patience. It was all I could do to stand beside the snoring woman, watching Kathy's laborious efforts. I wanted to dash out to the truck, burn rubber back into town, and tell Sheriff Ernie Davenport that I finally knew who shot Melvin Milo.

Chapter 63

ON MY WAY INTO MOUNT SINAI I CALLED Father Kratz in New Orleans. I drove much too fast, with both hands on the wheel, my head cocked to the right to support the cellular telephone handset. I passed a muddy logging truck, piled high with stripped pine trunks. I wanted Ernie Davenport to hear what I had to say. I wanted to set the record straight. But first I had to talk to the priest.

"Father? It's Garrison Reed. Do you remember me?"

After a brief pause, he said, "Of course, Mister Reed. You're the gentleman I met at the Milo house that day."

"Actually, I think we met before that, didn't we?"

"I'm afraid I don't recall."

"It was late at night outside the Milo Woman's Clinic. We spoke on the sidewalk. It was very dark. You were guarding the clinic. I'm afraid you took me for a mad bomber."

There was a pause, then he said, "That was you?"

"Yes, Father."

"I hope you weren't offended. I felt I had to be somewhat aggressive."

"No problem. I just wanted to ask you a question. It might help to clear an innocent woman's name if you can give me an answer."

"Fire away."

"Did Father McKay know Melvin or Juliette Milo?"

After another pause, he said, "Yes, he did. They're from Haiti, you know, and Mike was assigned there several years ago."

"Did Father McKay ever stand guard with you at the Milo Clinic?"

"Yes. Well, not exactly *with* me. We took turns on alternate evenings."

"And did he ever see anything unusual?"

"What do you mean?"

"You know ... something out of the ordinary. Perhaps a fight between Doctor Milo and Nurse Harmony, like the one you and I saw that night."

"If Mike ever saw such a thing, he never mentioned it to me."

"But he could have seen something?"

"Yes."

"Father, did you ever see anything unusual yourself?"

Another pause, longer this time, then, "Mister Reed, maybe you'd better tell me what this is about."

"So you *did* see something? Will you tell me about it?"

"Why are you so interested, Mister Reed? I understood that your wife was cleared of the murder charges."

"That's true, Father. But something has come up here. Something that makes me think this may have been more than a simple jealousy murder. It may be something Father McKay saw that got him killed. Perhaps you saw it, too."

The priest said, "I don't think either of us saw anything that important."

"Maybe you just didn't understand the importance at the time. If you'll think back to the last few weeks before Father McKay was given the position here at Mount Sinai ... was there anything unusual? Anything at all?"

After a long pause, he said, "Well, now that you mention it, there was the one time ... About two weeks before he left New Orleans, Father Mike came back to the rectory in the early morning as usual. We had breakfast together. He seemed excited. Happy. I asked him why, and he told me he'd found a way to stop the abortions. Of course, I asked him what he meant, but he wouldn't say."

"He never told you?"

"No. He said it was better if I didn't know. Do you think he was in some kind of trouble?"

"Father, I think he was in the worst kind of trouble there is."

Chapter 64

I WAS AN IDIOT NOT TO SEE IT COMING. THREE days had passed since I told Ernie Davenport how the murder was done, and who did it. Ernie took me seriously—seriously enough to call Lieutenant Washington down in New Orleans to ask for help. Washington said it was a pretty good theory and promised he would look into things.

I should have known they would stir him up with their questions and surveillance. I should have known Melvin Milo would come for us.

Still, it was a surprise that stormy Sunday night when an insistent pounding on our front door woke me up. The clock on my bedside table read two A.M. I left Mary Jo alone in bed upstairs as I descended in my night robe, rubbing the sleep from my eyes. I opened the door before I realized he held a pistol.

A sudden flash of lightning lit his malevolent features. He pointed the weapon at my stomach and said, "Where is your wife, Mister Reed?"

I stared at the dull black revolver and said nothing. He waved me back into the entry hall and stepped inside, closing the door with his free hand. A drop of water clung to the tip of his nose.

Wiping his free palm across the top of his naked scalp, he said, "Oh, come now, Mister Reed. You may as well cooperate. I'll find her eventually anyway, and we don't want this to take all night, do we?"

"What do you plan to do?"

"Actually, I'm afraid I am here to kill you."

I stared at him, thinking hard. "What do you want with Mary Jo?"

"Your lovely wife must go, too. I *do* apologize. But the authorities are leaving me no choice."

"What does that mean, leaving you no choice?"

Melvin Milo advanced two steps and pressed the muzzle of the gun against my temple. He was almost as tall as I was, able to place metallic death alongside my ear with ease. He said, "Mister Reed, I'm on a bit of a tight schedule. Mustn't let the New Orleans police know I'm not at home. My alibi depends on it, don't you know? So if you insist, I will search for your wife without your help. But I'm afraid that means you will have to die right here in the foyer." He pronounced it the French way: "foy-yay."

I heard him cock the pistol. He pressed the muzzle tighter against my skull. I closed my eyes. If he fired, the sound would bring Mary Jo and Lucretia. He would kill them as they ran down the stairs. I had to buy them some time.

I said, "I'll take you to her."

"Excellent! I thought you might reconsider." He lowered the revolver. "Now then, which way shall we go?"

Without looking at him, I said, "She's night fishing down at the lake."

"In this storm? At this time of night? Come now, Mister Reed. I am not as foolish as that."

"She's taking chemotherapy. It keeps her up. So she does things— paints or cooks or fishes to pass the time."

He searched my eyes carefully, then said, "I had heard of her cancer. Such a painful way to die. No doubt she will view me as a blessing. Where is she, exactly?"

"She's fishing inside our boat house. We feed the crappie there."

"Ah, a sporting girl, eh? Admirable trait in a woman. I wonder if she is having any luck. Shall we go find out?"

He shoved against my temple with the revolver. I led him through the house toward the back door, praying that Lucretia and Mary Jo would remain quietly sleeping upstairs. As we walked, I said, "I figured it was you. Once I found out about the wig, everything was obvious."

"Is that so? My congratulations on your powers of deduction, Mister Reed. How did you learn that Juliette was falsely accused? What was your first clue?"

"I wouldn't call it a clue, exactly. More of a contradiction. Whoever murdered Father McKay was a lousy shot. At such close range, to accidentally shoot the priest when you were the main target, then to give you a superficial wound . . ."

Milo interrupted. "That 'superficial wound,' as you call it, could have been quite serious. It missed my kidney and stomach by less than one inch."

"Yes, but it did miss. It missed everything vital. That was surprising, since I knew that your wife was an excellent shot."

"How did you know that?"

"Two ways." I would go on talking forever to keep that cold muzzle away from my temple. "She demonstrated her skill with a handgun in the woods right outside this house. She stalked me, came within ten feet of me without a sound, and fired a tight pattern of rounds into a tree about three inches above my head."

Melvin Milo laughed softly. "Did she really? She never told me. But that is my Juliette, all right. She was never one to make a subtle point. What was your second reason?"

"The trophies and photographs inside your house. She is an accomplished hunter. Nobody with such success against moving targets in the wild could miss so terribly in a confined space like that hospital corridor."

"Very good, Mister Reed! You amaze me. But perhaps my Juliette's shots hit exactly as she planned. Did you think of that?"

"Of course. If she was the killer, with her weapons skills, she would have placed her shots exactly where she wanted. She might have wounded you in a non-vital area to make her point, and killed the priest deliberately since he was a witness."

He said, "But that would leave me in a position to testify against her."

"Yes. That didn't make sense, until I remembered the symbol she drew in your blood. A voodoo curse would never make Father McKay hold his tongue, but it might be enough to keep you quiet about what she had done. That is, if you believe in voodoo."

"Oh, I believe, Mister Reed. After the things I have seen, I have no other choice."

"I thought so. You had a house full of *gris-gris*, and there was that altar in your hospital room."

"*Gris-gris?* You know what that is?"

I nodded. "It's what you call your dolls and your potions and so forth."

"So you know something about voodoo."

Remembering Alphonse Granier's private war on voodoo and Mary Jo's unshakable belief that she was pregnant by Satan himself, I said, "I had cause to study it some time ago."

"Interesting," he said. "But you informed the authorities that they were wrong to suspect Juliette. They have reopened the case. They follow me everywhere. They have searched my home and office. What made you tell them Juliette was not the murderer?"

"It was partly because of what she said in the woods that night. She said, 'Stay away from Mel. I won't let you hurt him anymore.' I asked myself why a woman would try to kill her husband one day, and defend him so violently a couple of nights later."

"Perhaps she was simply insane. Completely illogical."

"That's what I thought at first. But then I began to wonder, why would she pick a hospital corridor so far from home? She could have killed you much more easily at home." I glanced at his gun and back up to his empty eyes. "On the other hand, it occurred to me that perhaps you were never her primary target. Perhaps she intended to kill the priest from the beginning, and you simply got in the way."

Milo indicated the door with his pistol. "Open the door and step outside very slowly, Mister Reed."

When we were both out on the porch, he said, "Why would Juliette want to kill the priest?"

Out on the porch, the rain beat a violent rhythm against the shingles above and thunder rumbled in the distance, like a locomotive, relentlessly rolling our way. The storm was going to get worse before it got better.

I said, "I have no idea."

"So your theory was a dead end."

I had to yell be heard. "Yes. Until I learned about the wig. You bought a wig that matched my wife's hair. And since Juliette and Mary Jo had the same hairstyle and color, the wig matched Juliette's hair as well."

"This was significant to you?"

"Of course. I knew that Elizabeth Harmony was involved somehow. She kidnapped my wife, after all. I followed you to the Milo Clinic one night and watched through the window while the two of you argued. Everything made sense if it was Lizzy who wore the wig. Especially if the rumors were true about your affair. She would be mistaken for your wife. You would allow her to shoot you to establish an alibi, then claim Juliette did it. If anyone saw Lizzy running away, they would assume she was your wife and back up your story. The only catch was the hospital orderly. He saw Lizzy running away from the scene of the crime as you planned, but he didn't identify her as Juliette. He identified her as Mary Jo."

Melvin Milo laughed, his dark features lit by a distant flash of lightning. "So near and yet so far, Mister Reed. You're quite correct about the wig, of course. Lizzy did wear it that day, and we did hope she would be mistaken for Juliette. But you still have no idea what happened."

"Why don't you tell me?"

"Why should you care, Mister Reed? Whatever occurred, you will soon have no further need of facts or curiosity."

"Come on, Melvin. Indulge me."

With a twitch of the pistol, he pointed at the back porch steps. "Let's continue, shall we? You go first. And don't make the mistake of running. I am a far better shot than my dear Juliette."

I descended the steps into a wall of rain, feeling the spot on my back where his pistol was aimed. It felt like a hot poker prodding my skin. As he followed, he said, "You really are quite astute, Mister Reed. My compliments. But you haven't put the pieces together properly." He pushed the pistol against my spine. "Shall we move on to that lake you mentioned? Carefully now."

I led the way to the path. The rain fell like liquid ice, soaking my hair and robe. Occasional rumblings of thunder followed distant flashes of lightning. It was a perfect night for murder.

Behind me, Melvin Milo spoke loudly to be heard above the storm, "It was never about abortion, of course. It was a simple case of survival. I was being blackmailed. I had to defend myself."

"Blackmailed? Who blackmailed you?"

"I should have thought that was obvious to someone with your powers of deduction, Mister Reed. It was Father McKay. Father Michael McKay. He's the one who started everything."

Chapter 65

AS WE DESCENDED THE HILL TOWARD THE boat house, Melvin Milo's voice rose to a near shout in competition with the storm. "You see, my wife was an unkind woman, Mister Reed. When I married her in Haiti many years ago, she made it clear that her family fortune would remain under her control. There were lawyers. Papers were signed. I was a fool to agree to her conditions, but the thought of living in her father's *maison*, of dressing well, and dining on the finest imported *cuisine* every night . . . well, suffice it to say that I was not well off when I met Juliette. Actually, I was living a desperately poor existence, trying to work my way through medical school as a janitor at a local cinema. Let's see . . . before I met Juliette, I believe I was living on nine dollars per week, plus a cot in the projection booth. Her wealth was an irresistible temptation. She even offered to send me to Paris for my residency. Such things held a great appeal."

A crack of thunder shook the ground beneath my feet, followed by a searing white flash of lighting. The violent center of the storm approached like a marauding army.

Milo continued, "As time wore on, I realized the price was very high. She made it clear she would not play the role of doting bride, nor allow me even a semblance of the role a man should have in marriage. She made every decision, often without consulting me. In fact, it was her choice to move from Port-au-Prince to New Orleans. I first learned of it when I returned home from the hospital one day to find men packing our belongings. Three days later, we were here. She did not care that I had been offered a promising position at the hospital in Port-au-Prince. She did not care that I had made many friends in Haiti, men of influence and prominence who respected my work. I know now that she was jealous of them, of my impending success. It is why we came here, so I would be separated from those who would have elevated me to the position in society that I deserved.

"I am glad she is dead, Mister Reed. I hated her for the way she withheld her family fortune from me. I hated her for using her powers to enslave me."

I shouted, "What powers?"

"She was a *mamba*, Mister Reed. A priestess, in your language. She had a position of social authority in Haiti. Men and women feared her. I feared her. She had great power.

"I had hoped that our move to New Orleans would cut her off from her followers. A *mamba* obtains strength from those who believe, from the *ti guinin*. But she found a new . . . how do you say it? Congregation? She found a new congregation in New Orleans. I had lost everything, my friends and associates and my work. I was powerless without my work. But she grew stronger. And to make matters worse, Juliette had turned from the *rada* to the *petro* ways. Do you understand? For you, I suppose it would be as if she had turned from your Jesus to your Satan."

The forest shivered as streams of rain battered the leaves and branches all around us.

"I lived in fear of her, Mister Reed. Do not laugh! You cannot conceive of the power a *voodoo mamba* wields. Once, I defied her. Only once. She had money in her purse. A great deal of money. I stole it and packed some things and took a room at the Hotel De La Poste, planning to fly to Paris the following day. But that night, the walls of my room moved inward and the ceiling began to sink. I felt my *ti bon ange*—my soul—straining to escape. It was as if *Baron Samadhi* himself had come for me. As if I lay within a coffin, waiting to arise. And when I escaped from that room, the *veve* lay just outside, drawn in gunpowder! It was in the shape of a coffin, so I knew it had been the *Baron* after all.

"I returned to our home in the Garden District. Along the way, I saw the *Baron* several times, in the face of a streetwalker and the face of a child. Do you know how fearsome she looked?"

Remembering my vision at the Barataria swamp, remembering the terrifying nightmare of a figure dressed in black with a face pale as death and glowing empty holes for eyes, remembering the child in a pitch-black New Orleans alley dressed in rags with burning eyes, I said, "Yes. I've seen such things."

He inclined his head as if to say he had not heard. I shouted it the second time, raising my voice above the furious storm, and he nodded his understanding.

"Then you understand my fear. I was trapped, *mon Dieu*, how I was trapped! It was my lot in life to be her pet, or her slave. Without money, I could never escape. Only distance can weaken her powers. I needed money to travel and live. And I had to separate her from the *asson*. With the proper *asson*, she could reach me anywhere."

I said, "*Asson?*"

"A rattle, made from a gourd. Or a carved wooden stick. They are what she uses to call down the *loas*, the creatures you might call demons. With her *asson*, she is very powerful. Without it, her powers are limited."

The rain fell freezing cold on my neck. I clutched the wet robe closer. "Why didn't you just take it away from her?"

Melvin Milo laughed. "You are naive, Mister Reed. Steal her *asson?* To do such a thing is to tempt the demons of hell. I had no choice but to stay with her. I had no money to escape, and even if I went as far as Paris or Quebec, she could reach me so long as she possessed the *asson*.

"I was miserable. Then I began to think that perhaps Juliette cared for me in her own way, because she did a strange thing. She built a clinic for me, complete with all the equipment I could ever need. She gave it to me with only one proviso: I was to operate it without profit. She did not want me to accumulate resources, you see. She would support the clinic with her fortune. No patient was to be charged. I suspected she had some dark motive, since she had never before shown such kindness. But whatever her reasons, I was glad to be at work again.

"Then one day, about three months after I opened the clinic, Juliette brought a patient to me, a young girl in her third trimester of pregnancy. This was before Roe versus Wade, you see. The young lady had very few choices. It was my first abortion. Juliette assisted me. And when we were done, she took the fetus away, leaving the girl child in my care.

"There were many other abortions that year. At first, Juliette brought the patients to the clinic herself. Then one night, a man appeared, leading a pregnant girl. I knew the man. A tall man with no hair or eyebrows and a ring of gold through his ear. He was a *hounsih ventailleur*—the one who collects sacrifices for the *ge rouge*, the red-eyed demons. Like Juliette, the *ventailleur* stood by as I performed the procedure. Like Juliette, he took the fetus when he left."

Again, thunder exploded above our heads, accompanied by an instantaneous burst of lightning, like the white-hot finger of Satan. A tree one hundred yards to our left erupted in flames, suddenly engulfed in an inferno from top to bottom. The fire seemed impossible in such a downpour. Melvin Milo continued as if nothing had happened.

"I knew then why Juliette had built the clinic. I understood the horrible truth. But understanding made no difference. I was still trapped. I was an unwilling accomplice in their unholy rituals.

"Then something happened that I thought would lead to my salvation. A woman arrived at the clinic with her daughter. She had heard I performed certain services. Her daughter was pregnant. She asked me to help. Would I do this thing? After the abortion, the woman astonished me. She pressed fifty dollars into my palm and begged me to remain silent. Fifty dollars that Juliette did not know I had! Imagine my excitement.

"And soon, other girls and women came. I raised my price. One hundred dollars, two hundred, three hundred dollars. They would pay anything. The money began to grow. I began to hope again, to believe escape would be possible. Then, I heard the worst possible news. Your Supreme Court declared abortion to be legal. What a disaster! Soon, the women no longer hid their condition. They asked openly for my services. I could no longer take their money in secret. All hope of saving enough to escape was gone.

"I labored under those conditions for many years. On a lucky day, I might steal enough money from the petty cash drawer to eat an occasional meal away from Juliette. I was forced to pretend I enjoyed her company, traveling to Africa and South America when she wanted to hunt, and always, always, there were the midnight abortions with the fetus carried away for some evil purpose I dared not imagine.

"Then, I got a second chance. My darling Lizzy applied at the clinic for a nursing position. We fell in love. I told her of my plight, and she laughed! She called the voodoo "mumbo jumbo" and called me a fool to let such superstition ruin my life. She drove me wild with pleasures I thought I would never experience again. She pressed for a divorce. But, as much as I loved Lizzy, still I could not divorce Juliette. It would mean a terrible fate for me, although I hoped Lizzy's unbelief would protect her.

"We lived a life in the shadows for years, Lizzy and I, hiding our passion from Juliette. It was not the best of lives, yet all was well until the protesters began to appear.

"They were like a devil's curse. Following me from home to work, standing outside my house day and night, driving me crazy with their wild accusations of murder. If this is the way of Christians—to persecute and harass, to destroy reputations, to turn neighbors and friends against people like me . . . I will worship the *loas* in the old ways of my people and be glad not to be a part of your pagan religion!"

He stared at me as if expecting a response. I returned his stare, ice-cold rain streaming down my face, saying nothing.

"You have nothing to say in defense of your brethren, Mister Reed?"

I shouted to be certain he could hear. "They were wrong to treat you that way. We are supposed to be loving in everything we do, loving toward everyone. They think their love for the unborn justifies their abuse of the living. I disagree. So do many other Christians."

His black eyes examined my face for a moment, vacant windows to an empty soul. "Then you do not condemn me for what I do?"

"Only God can condemn. You are just a sinner, like everyone else."

"Ah, Mister Reed, not many of your brothers seem to agree. What a pity. If the priest McKay had your outlook, perhaps none of this would have happened."

"Tell me the rest of it."

He nodded and indicated with his revolver that we should continue our descent through the raging tempest. He yelled his words from just behind my ear. "One night a few months ago, that meddling priest called me on the telephone at home. He said he had seen Lizzy and me through the window at the clinic. The nerve of him! A priest, behaving like a common *voyeur!* My time with Lizzy had been limited before, but when you so-called *Christians* began your persecution, Lizzy and I found it was only possible to see each other late at night at the clinic. Yet even there, we were allowed no privacy. This priest had seen us, and now he threatened to tell Juliette unless I stopped the abortions. She had known him in Haiti, he said. She would believe him. So, to the crime of harassment he added extortion! I tried to explain that Juliette would never allow me to stop, that she was the reason the abortions were performed from the beginning. The priest would not listen. I was trapped."

Flinging my words back over my shoulder through the driving rain, I shouted, "I can't believe a man of God would stoop to such a thing."

"Such a thing? Say the word, Mister Reed! Blackmail! That is what he did! And why not? When *Christians* printed posters of fetuses posed in trash cans and slipped them under my neighbors' doors for their children to see, was that more acceptable? When *Christians* put my photograph on a wanted poster and stapled it to telephone poles, knowing that the last man to have his face on such a poster was murdered, was that more acceptable? Where would you draw the line, Mister Reed? Was it acceptable for *Christians* to follow my wife to her beauty salon where they stood outside the window chanting until Juliette ran out the back door in tears?"

Melvin Milo threw back his head and screamed into the downpour, "Murderess! Murderess! Murderess!"

Eyes wide with hate, he lifted the pistol, aiming it squarely at my face. "Would your Jesus have done such a thing? Would he have slipped a lurid photograph of me in a blood-stained apron under the windshield wipers of every car in the parking lot at our country club, as if I perform procedures with a butcher knife? Where would your Jesus draw the line, Mister Reed? The line between what they did and what I do? I seem to recall that all sin is the same in the eyes of your god. Does that apply to harassment, persecution, extortion, and blackmail?"

He had drawn closer as he shouted through the rain, his eyes wild in the night, revolver almost touching my forehead. Now he lowered the gun a few inches, and, more quietly, lips inches from my ear, he hissed, "In the practice of voodoo, we sacrifice animals, it is true. We call upon the *loas* to change the course of fate. It is a simple faith. Many say it is based on nothing more than feathers and hollow gourds. But we do not say one thing and do another, Mister Reed. We take no delight in forcing our ways upon others. We would never tell the world we believe in *love* and *goodness*, then persecute those who disagree with our beliefs. Where is the love in what you *Christians* do, Mister Reed? Where is the goodness? You call voodoo a pagan religion. Such hypocrisy! Look at what you *Christians* say, then look at what you *do* and tell me, Mister Reed: *who are the true pagans?"*

His eyes were wide with anger, his mouth a thin tight line. I could think of no response to his question; in fact, I was ashamed at the seed of truth it contained.

I said nothing.

He stared at me for a long time, the rain dripping from his bald forehead into his eyes, unnoticed. Minutes passed. Finally, he continued, "I told Lizzy we would have to stop seeing each other. She scoffed at my fears. She said she had a better plan.

"They called us killers. Very well! We would kill McKay and frame Juliette for the murder. In this way, the priest would be silenced forever. If we managed things properly, Juliette would never suspect us. She would be out of the way behind bars. The law would separate her from her *asson*. And Lizzy and I could live as man and wife, with free access to Juliette's fortune. We could escape your persecution. Escape your *Christianity*." He spat the word like a condemnation. Then he said, "Best of all, they would not allow Juliette to keep her *asson* in prison, or practice the rites of the *petro*. So, even if Juliette discovered the truth, she could not trouble us. We would be free of all of you.

"The priest McKay had already moved to Texas. To kill him, I had to pretend to be interested in a residency here at your hospital. Juliette agreed to consider the move to escape the harassment. You see how your *Christian* campaign of terror played into my hands? It would give me an excuse to be near him. We made several trips to Mount Sinai. I bought a wig for Lizzy to wear so she would be mistaken for Juliette. I made certain that several people at the hospital were introduced to Juliette so they would identify her later. The disguise Lizzy wore, the auburn wig, blue jeans, and T-shirt was to match what Juliette would wear that day. Unfortunately, your wife wore similar clothing. And that meddlesome orderly identified your wife before I could claim it was Juliette who did the shooting."

We were almost down to the lake. I could see the boat house light twinkling through the naked branches. The scent of pine whirled in the roaring wind. I tried to slow down, to buy time, to think of a plan for escape, but Milo's pistol nudged me again.

"Let us pick up the pace, Mister Reed."

Watching the muddy ground to avoid falling, I said, "Why did Elizabeth Harmony shoot you? Was it just for an alibi?"

He laughed. It was like the hollow sound of ice cracking beneath my feet.

"Do you think I would actually allow her to shoot me? Come now, Mister Reed. Give me more credit than that."

"If the killer was not Juliette, or Elizabeth Harmony, then who shot Father McKay and you? Was it Faye Slydel?"

Again, his empty laugh defiled the cold air. "That silly woman doesn't have the courage."

"Who then?" I asked. "Who shot you?"

"I did, Mister Reed. I shot that accursed priest twice through the heart. And then I shot myself."

Chapter 66

DOCTOR MELVIN MILO SCREAMED THROUGH the storm: "Only a surgeon could find the exact entry location, the proper trajectory to pass the bullet through the fleshy muscle without damaging vital organs. And before I was reduced by that evil witch to playing the common role of abortionist, I *was* a surgeon, Mister Reed! I was a respected man!"

He seemed to lose himself for a moment, his eyes staring far away, as if seeing a life he could have lived. Then, in a softer voice I barely heard above the rain, he said, "So when I had killed the blackmailer McKay, I turned the gun inward and fired it through my side." He looked at me and smiled. "It was the perfect alibi, don't you agree?"

It was a perfect alibi, indeed. Who would think of testing the victim's hands for cordite? Who would bother checking the victim's fingerprints to see whether they matched those on the gun?

I led him on through the dripping woods, shivering and praying for a miracle. Then I saw the end of the boat house pier ahead through the trees. Time was running out. When we reached the boat house, he would see that Mary Jo was not there. Would he kill me then?

I said, "Was Elizabeth Harmony the one who hid the gun?"

"But of course. The orderly saw her running away, just as we planned. Then the disaster occurred. Juliette came around the corner from the other direction. The witch! I'd given her enough sedatives to make a normal woman sleep for twenty-four hours. She was to have remained in our motel room, without an alibi that entire day." Melvin Milo shrugged, an almost Gaelic expression of fatalism. "But . . . Juliette was no normal woman. The thing was done. It was not possible for Lizzy to masquerade as Juliette.

"Still, when the orderly identified her as your wife, I was prepared to contradict his statement. I was prepared to say, 'No, you are wrong. It was my wife who has done this terrible thing.' But just as I was about to speak, I looked down to see that Juliette had drawn the *veve* of life on the floor in my blood. Or almost drawn it. She was rubbing her finger along the floor, about to make the final sacred sign that would determine if the *loas*, the spirits, would bring life or death to the one who offered the blood used to draw the symbol. I'm afraid my nerve failed. I told the police I was unsure. When they showed me a photograph of your wife, I confirmed the orderly's identification.

"Lizzy was furious, but we immediately began to make other plans. When your wife was released on bail, we would kidnap her to make certain there would be no last-minute alibis this time. Then we would kill Juliette and frame your wife for the crime. In a way, it was better than the first plan. We had McKay off our backs. We still got rid of Juliette. And would do it in a way that exposed the Slydels and your wife and those other C.H.A.R.G.E. maniacs for the self-righteous hypocrites they are.

"We even made the attempt once at my home. While the protesters conducted their outrageous charade in front of the house, Lizzy slipped in the back. She was to shoot Juliette with the gun she took from your wife. When she saw you standing out front with the Slydel woman, she even thought to call your name, as if your wife wanted your help. But Juliette was difficult to kill. Lizzy barely escaped without being discovered."

I said, "But why would Mary Jo want to hurt your wife? Just because you gave her an abortion twenty years ago? Nobody would buy that!"

There was a brief pause, then Milo said, "So you do not know? My dear Mister Reed. Did she not tell you?" I stopped and looked back. Milo stood above me on the trail, smiling widely, his malevolent smirk illuminated by another flash of lightening.

"Mister Reed, I assure you she had the best of reasons to want me dead. Personal reasons. Mary Jo Granier and I knew each other very well at one time. Intimately, in fact." He leaned forward, almost touching my face with his. His breath was tinged with garlic. In his eyes, I saw a strange, hot light. He said, "You see, your wife once carried my child."

Time froze. I will never forget the evil joy in his eyes. They were hypnotic, staring into my soul with perfect malice. I stood as if paralyzed by the new fear rising from deep within. *No*, I prayed. *God, don't let it be true.*

"I suppose it was over twenty years ago. My, how time flies. I remember it as if it was yesterday. She came to me first for a routine physical. Her lovely young sister came as well. I found the early stages of displacia in both cases. I scheduled a procedure to remove the affected cells. When she returned, I sedated her. We were alone in the operatory. She was completely nude beneath the white gown. She was unconscious, she was beautiful . . ." He shrugged and smiled at me. "I am afraid I allowed my baser instincts to get the better of me, Mister Reed. And then I did it again with her sister."

Chapter 67

IT ROSE WITHIN ME FASTER THAN I COULD control, erupting from somewhere deep inside. I screamed and charged up the hill at him, my fury driving away all fear of his revolver. He fired one shot. It whistled past my ear. I froze in a half-crouched position, ready to spring again, staring at the empty black eye of the muzzle of his gun. For an instant, I actually considered taking a bullet to get to his throat.

He screamed, "I missed you deliberately, Mister Reed. Do not expect me to do it again. Are you in such a hurry to die? I thought you would want to hear the end of the story."

Slowly rising from my crouch, I spoke through gritted teeth, "Tell it to me. Tell me everything."

"There's not much left to say, I'm afraid. Do you believe in coincidence, Mister Reed? But of course, you Christians call it providence, do you not? Well, no matter. Call it what you will, I was amazed to see your wife's face on the photograph that the police brought to me as I lay in the hospital bed. When they left the room, I laughed out loud at the humor of it all. I would have known her anywhere. I remembered her—all of her—so clearly. How could I forget such a beautiful woman, especially when I had known her so . . . intimately? The irony! You see, here was a woman who had the perfect motive and I hadn't even known she lived in Mount Sinai. How delightful! They said she was active in the so-called pro-life movement. They believed the shooting was done to stop my professional activities."

His wide smile carved an ivory gash across his face. I fought the fury within, willing myself to wait. The moment would come. I knew it would come. I felt no vestige of Christian forgiveness. I would have died to kill him.

Standing silently in the falling rain, I stared up at Doctor Melvin Milo as he said, "I told the authorities, of course. The district attorney was quite interested in my story. I explained that this was no murder based on cold philosophy. Oh, no! This murderess had a very personal reason to want me dead. She had waited twenty years to kill me. Your friend, the sheriff, was quite amazed to hear of Mary Jo Granier's colored past."

"Reed."

He cocked his head as if to hear me better and said, "I beg your pardon?"

I growled, "Reed. Her name is Mary Jo Reed."

"Ah, yes. The ties that bind. I suppose they will get it right on her tombstone, Mister Reed. Never fear."

I sucked in air through my open mouth, staring at him with eyes that surely showed the emotions of my heart. He seemed to revel in it, to enjoy the pain and anguish I exposed to him. The impotent rage. I thought of Mary Jo's tears in Mandina's restaurant, that terrible night when she refused my proposal of marriage. I remembered her shame as we sat side by side on the Tulane campus bench while she revealed the secret of her sterility. Her hysterical reaction when I touched her at the crawfish shack on the Bayou Beau Bois so many years ago. Her eyes wide with fear when she spoke of demons, of immaculate conception, of Mary, the mother of Jesus, of Satan.

And now, here before me was Mary Jo's incubus.

It was all true, everything she feared so long ago. The rape she could not recall. Impregnation by evil itself.

True. All true.

Chapter 68

THE STORM WAS GROWING. MILO HAD TO scream at the top of his lungs to be heard. "I see we are near the water. Is the boat house close by? I am so looking forward to having a word with Mary Jo before I kill her."

I yelled, "You raped her!"

"Rape?" He cocked his head and considered me. "You know, I never thought of it that way. Rape implies violence, don't you think? And I was gentle, Mister Reed. Quite gentle, I assure you. After all, it would be unwise to leave physical evidence."

"You did leave physical evidence. You got her pregnant. And when you found out she was pregnant, you gave her the abortion that sterilized her for life. I always thought it was God's will that we live without children. But it was you, all this time."

Something slipped behind his expression, veiling it, hiding his thoughts. He said, "Interesting."

I screamed above the gale, "What? What now, Milo?"

"*Doctor* Milo, if you please."

"All right, if your ego demands it. What now, *Doctor* Milo?"

He leaned closer to be heard. "She really hasn't told you, has she?"

"Told me *what?*"

But he was not to reveal that final secret. He seemed about to speak, opening his mouth, and then, with a small shake of his head, closing it. He wiped the sleeve of his raincoat across his face. We stared at each other for a moment. Then he said, "Enough talk, Mister Reed. Enough mystery. I must return to New Orleans before dawn." With a small twitch of the revolver, he indicated that we would continue down the windswept path.

I turned and descended, following the narrow trail between swaying undergrowth on both sides. Over the last fifty years, first my father and then I had done our best to prevent erosion on the trail, building stone steps at the steepest places, and shallow ditches carved into the soil to divert the run-off. But the footing was tricky all the same, with slick muddy patches and pools of cold water settling in behind the stones at each step. The rain was unrelenting, flowing down the hill between my feet and washing over my hands when I grasped the smaller tree trunks for support. I was completely drenched, my thick flannel robe clinging to my back, heavy with frigid water. My bare feet ached with every step, the cold seeping deep into my bones.

High above, the center of the storm had arrived. Lightning seared the heavens, starkly illuminating the woods, followed more closely now by cracks of thunder. In the instant of every thunderbolt's brilliance, I searched for a stone or a fallen branch, anything to use as a weapon. But fate, or providence as Milo said, would not accommodate me. Perhaps that was best, if he was as good with a gun as he claimed.

We reached the tree line. Just below us the ancient pier careened across the angry waves of Martin Pool. Out on the lake, the rain was a living thing, changing shape even as we watched. At first, it was a solid wall of water, angling down, leaning toward us. Then, like a rippling curtain, it parted to reveal the boat house, just for an instant, visible at the end of the pier.

I paused, stalling for time. With his mouth just behind my ear, Milo yelled, "Mister Reed, I believe you lied to me. Your wife would be insane to fish in this deluge."

I turned to shout over my shoulder, "She's inside the boat house out of the weather, fishing in the boat slip. Like I told you, we drop bales of alfalfa there for the crappie." It was a lie only someone from the city might believe.

He jabbed the muzzle of the revolver between my shoulder blades, pushing hard. I got the message and stepped onto the pier. The waves crested just beneath our feet, rocking the framework of the rickety wooden wharf with every surge. Milo gripped the back of my robe in his fist, following a half step behind with the pistol now touching my head. As we drew closer, the boat house seemed to materialize again at the end of the pier, no longer shrouded by pale sheets of rain. The old shack leaned a few degrees to the north, as if resisting the howling wind. Rain crashed against the rusted metal roof, atomizing on impact into a fine mist that hovered above the little building like fog on a hilltop. I knew there were many weapons inside. A frog gig. A wooden paddle. A fishing knife. Even a shotgun, last used by Mary Jo to kill a cottonmouth.

But could I reach the shotgun in time to stop Milo from ending my life with a bullet? And if I did, would he force me to pull the trigger? I hoped not. I sincerely wanted to avoid pulling that trigger, not because of Christian charity, but because I wouldn't know until that moment if the shotgun was loaded.

With Milo unseen behind me, his presence reduced to the hard pressure of a gun barrel against my head, I felt the bloated corpse of fear swell inside my chest. Each step closer to the boat house was a step closer to death. It would be me or Milo. There was no other way. And if the Lord was going to take me now, who would care for Mary Jo? Would she survive the cancer? Would she survive Milo?

I would never know, and somehow that was the cruelest fear of all.

Chapter 69

THE DOOR FACED ME NOW, INCHES AWAY, water streaming down the rough cedar planks. I visualized the interior of the boat house. Cobwebs in a yellow light. Shelves to the left, overflowing with odds and ends: fishing gear, boating paraphernalia, and tools. The sour smell of stink bait. The boat hanging above open water to the right, swaying slightly in the straps as the whole boat house shook in the terrible wind.

Please, God. Please. Don't let him do this.

To live, I would have to position myself close enough to the shelves to grab a weapon—maybe the shotgun—before Milo realized I had the opportunity. But would he be foolish enough to give me such a chance? Doctor Melvin Milo had shown himself to be anything but a fool. It was almost too much to hope for. It would take a miracle.

So that is what I prayed for, even as I grasped the handle of the door. *Please God . . .*

"Stop!" yelled Milo.

My hand froze in place.

Still facing the door, I screamed into the wind, "What? What is it now?"

He pulled against my shirt and yelled, "Turn around and go in backwards, facing me!"

My heart sank. Milo was giving me no chance—no chance at all.

The water streamed into my face as I turned toward the wind to place my back against the door and face him. We were inches apart. His gun pressed against my stomach. The deck shook beneath our feet, assaulted by the writhing waters of Martin Pool, as I stared into the empty windows of Melvin Milo's soul. Then, something moved on the pier just beyond him. I glanced over his shoulder. At first, I thought the rain in my eyes explained the thing I saw. I blinked and looked again, but still, it was there.

It came slowly across the planks, one arm outstretched as if beckoning me, the other leaning on a rod or staff of some kind. It wore a tall black hat, strangely unaffected by the wind. Its face—if face it was—was ghostly white, almost translucent, like the bleached pale countenance of a skull. A black robe or suit coat covered its body completely. The wind whipped at the folds of the coat. I saw a white shirt underneath. Where its heart should have been, something blood red glistened, raw and gaping like an open wound. It seemed to advance without legs, gliding above the wharf rather than walking. It was a horror I once thought only came in nightmares, a demon in human form.

It was the voodoo *loa, Baron Samadhi* himself, come to take someone to hell. And this time, there was no mistake. I was not delirious or dreaming. It was here.

"Dear God, protect me," I whispered.

Melvin Milo could not hear the fear in my words above the roar of the wind, but what he saw in my face was unmistakable. He wavered for an instant—was this some trick? But the emotion in my eyes could not be a lie.

He turned, and in that instant, a thunderbolt cracked across the sky, searing the puny mortals below with blinding light. The apparition loomed clear and undeniable, defined by the lightning in a world of searing white, staring at us with empty black holes and grinning a long-toothed grimace of agony or unholy rapture. A gust of wind had pushed back the tall black hat, exposing the naked skull beneath.

And Milo knew.

He knew what it was and who it had come for.

Milo spun and fired his gun. I dropped to the deck, almost blinded by the flash of lightning. Something exploded. I sensed a shaft of pale yellow light surging toward me through the darkness. Bracing myself, I felt nothing. Milo screamed in a language I did not understand. He fired again and screamed, *"No, Samadhi!"* I heard pounding feet and the splash of something large hitting the water.

Kneeling on all fours, I blinked rapidly, frantically willing my vision to return. I was sure death would come in an instant, with a bullet or something worse. But nothing happened. Finally, the light in my eyes cleared away, and I lifted my head to gaze across the pier. Melvin Milo was gone. The *Baron Samadhi* was gone.

And I was alone with Mary Jo.

Chapter 70

THE TEN-GALLON HAT FELL FROM HER BALD head into the raging water when I lifted her in my arms. Leaving the shotgun she had leaned upon behind, I carried Mary Jo up the hill to the house. It had been her, of course. My brave, brave woman, come to save her man.

Mascara streamed from her eyes, filling the already deeply sunken sockets with blackness. Her chest wound bled from the strain of fighting her way down the slippery path in the storm. The hat and her long black raincoat had been precious little protection from the cold, leaving her pale as a corpse, with lips curled away from chattering teeth.

I was afraid she would die before I reached the top of the hill.

As I climbed the treacherous path, I prayed aloud, "Please, dear God, in Jesus' name, please don't take Mary Jo!"

The last four words became a chant, repeated over and over with every straining step through the storm. *Please don't take her. Please.*

Thighs burning from the strain of the climb, I struggled to the back door. Lucretia flung it open, her eyes wide with fear.

I screamed, "Call the hospital!"

Lucretia ran to the kitchen phone as I carried Mary Jo into the living room and laid her gently on the sofa. Her eyes opened as I placed her there, seeking mine and growing warm when I looked into them deeply. It was then I knew the Lord had heard my prayer, as he always does. It was then I knew he had taken pity upon me. He would allow my lovely one to live.

I rose to get a blanket, but she stopped me with her hand on my arm. "Garr," she said, "I'm a murderer."

Thinking she had Melvin Milo in mind, I said, "I hope so."

Agony flashed across her face. Behind me, the rain streamed in through the open door unnoticed. She tried to rise but I pushed her back. The dark red stain on her nightshirt had spread. I went to be sure Lucretia had asked for an ambulance. She covered the mouth-piece and nodded to me, whispering, "Get back in theah with her, Garr. She need you."

I returned to the sofa and sank to my knees beside Mary Jo.

She whispered, "Pray for me, Garr. I'm a murderer."

"It couldn't be helped, honey. You saved my life."

She reached for me then, fingers closing around my arm with surprising strength, eyes wide with pain or fear. "No! That's not what I mean!"

"Easy, Nibbles. Take it easy."

She released her hold and closed her eyes. Gently, I rolled her to her side and removed the wet raincoat. I wrapped a wool afghan around her and softly dried her face and naked scalp. In a tired, lonely little voice, she said, "Did he tell you?"

After pausing to consider the question, I said, "Yes."

Her eyes were still closed. She said, "They told me it was evil. We were in a war, a spiritual war. Anything could happen, but we were to stand strong for the Lord. He would protect us. Nothing the Evil One could do would touch us." She sighed, a long, shivering sigh that seemed to rise from someplace deep inside. "They were wrong. Or maybe I was too weak. The time came and went. At first I didn't notice, but then one evening, it occurred to me that I was late. I waited for three weeks, hoping all that time that it was something else. But a person knows. When a child is growing inside, a person knows, somehow." She opened her eyes and turned to me. "Isn't that strange?"

Lucretia stepped into the room, standing against the far wall with an age-spotted hand covering her mouth, as if she was afraid to come any closer. I said nothing, kneeling on the living room floor beside my wife.

Mary Jo whispered, "It was impossible! I never had sex with anyone until I met you, Garr. I swear!"

"I know, baby. I know."

"Momma and Daddy always taught us that evil was a real thing, a force in the world, like hurricanes and fire. I knew it *had* to be that. I knew it had to be Satan who made me pregnant. I was not worthy for the other . . . the other possibility."

"No. You were just a scared young girl with nobody to turn to."

Behind me, Lucretia Granier sucked in her breath.

Mary Jo didn't seem to know her mother was in the room. She closed her haunted eyes again and said, "I *was* scared. Really scared. I couldn't have the baby. What would it be? A demon? And even if I was pregnant some other way and it was a normal child, Daddy would have thrown me out. Such a sin inside his house?" She laughed once, bitterly. "He would never have spoken to me again. And Momma. What could I tell her? That I never lay with a boy? That I did not surrender to temptation, not once? She would have known, then. She would have known I was pregnant by a demon. Or maybe Satan himself."

Lucretia let out a single cry. Looking wildly around, Mary Jo tried to rise from the couch, but I pressed her back down. "Shhh. Nibbles, you lie back quiet now."

She began to shake, either from the cold and wet, or from something horrible inside that was clawing its way out to the light at long last. When she spoke again, it was a whisper forced through chattering teeth. "You have to understand! I was a *child*. My daddy spoke every day to the people from the street, telling them we were surrounded by evil, by demons. Daddy made his war on voodoo, speaking out against their gods as if they were real, like enemy soldiers in a real battle. I believed him. I believed every word!"

"And the hate in his eyes when he preached! The anger in his voice! He would never understand that I was not to blame. I could never tell him. It would have been better if some boy *had* lain with me!"

I said, "So you didn't tell Alphonse?"

"Oh no! How could I? He would have driven me away forever."

"And Lucretia? Did you tell her you were pregnant?"

"She would have told Daddy. She would have felt it was her duty."

A flush of pity tinted my thoughts, spreading warm and rosy like a sunrise. I pushed away the folds of the afghan and fumbled with the buttons of her blouse, my movements an excuse to avoid speaking. If I spoke just then, I knew I would cry, and my wife needed her man to be strong. Finally, when I had collected myself, I spoke in a casual tone, belying the depth of my emotions.

"Are you saying you went to get your abortion all alone? You went to Milo by yourself?"

She turned her head away, closing her eyes. I stared at her for a moment, then opened her blouse to reveal the damage her desperate struggle down the hill had caused. The stitches had torn. Blood streamed from the incisions, washing her rib cage in sparkling red. When I looked back up at her face, I saw tears flowing from her eyes as she stared blankly toward the ceiling.

"Oh, please don't cry, Nibbles. Please . . ."

"I thought you said you knew," she said. "I thought he told you."

"He did, baby. He told me everything."

"But the abortion . . ."

I touched her lips. "Shhh. Let's put that behind us, once and for all."

She lifted her hand and slapped mine away. "No!" she said, "I won't hide it anymore! I want it said!"

"What more is there to say, Mary Jo?"

"I did it! I killed my baby!"

"What?"

"I got rid of the baby myself, Garr."

A new fear formed within my soul. A fear for Mary Jo that went beyond death and physical suffering. I thought I understood her, and if I did, I feared for her very sanity. I whispered, "And Linda? What about your sister Linda?"

Mary Jo sobbed and nodded, lifting her palms to her face. "It was the same for her. The very same as with me. Both of us were pregnant, but neither of us knew how. So I took a wire coat hanger, and I . . . I did it to her. And when I was done, I did it to myself."

Behind me, a low moan rose from Lucretia Granier. It was a mournful sound, a dirge for the dead, a bitterly cold wind, blowing in from the wasteland of her frozen heart.

Mary Jo's hands dropped from her eyes, revealing twin windows into a tormented soul. "When they came to ask their questions, I told them lies about a boy who raped us. I told them he raped us and when we told him we were pregnant, he tried to cut it out of us. But she was never raped. And she never did it with a boy. She wouldn't do that."

Leaning forward, I said, "And Milo? What about Doctor Milo?"

Lucretia Granier answered my question, her voice a monotone in the background. "We took de girls to him, bleedin' like they was. He worked on dem. Tried to fix they bleedin', him. But it weren't no good for my poor baby Linda, no. It were too late for her."

I turned to stare at her. "Are you saying Milo tried to *help* them?"

She nodded, eyes focused on something far away, far beyond the confines of the room.

Looking back down at Mary Jo but still speaking to Lucretia, I said, "And you knew Mary Jo did this. All this time, you knew?"

"No," said Lucretia Granier as she stared at Mary Jo. "She kept dat to herself. All this time."

Mary Jo's pain-wrenched face swam in a waterfall of tears flowing from my eyes. All this time. To carry such a burden alone, all this time. I leaned across her and, taking care not to press against her wound, wrapped my wife in my arms as best I could, longing to draw some of the pain upon myself, to draw it from her heart into mine. She curled inward within my embrace, hugging tightly clenched fists to her chest and moaning aloud, "Oh, baby sister. Oh, baby sister."

There was a roaring sound in my ears. Perhaps it was the sound of God's Holy Spirit, because it was then, from behind me, that I heard Lucretia Granier's soft whisper.

"Dear God, forgive me."

I turned, and Lucretia came toward us, clutching her robe to her throat as if to ward off the horror of what she had heard. It was the last thing I wanted. Lucretia's self-righteous judgment could drive Mary Jo over the edge of a precipice from which she would never return. I stood to stop her, to protect my love from her mother's self-righteous indignation. But Lucretia's eyes contained something I had not seen for twenty years. Perhaps it was that same Something that held me back and whispered, "Wait." Perhaps it was that same Something that bade me watch silently as Lucretia settled to her knees beside the sofa and slowly wrapped her wounded daughter in her arms.

And then, that Something showed me a miracle I will never forget.

Lucretia Granier held Mary Jo with a tenderness, a kindness I thought the world had stripped from her forever. Lucretia Granier—judgmental, holier-than-thou, self-righteous zealot and hater of sinners—embraced the woman who caused her beloved daughter's death and gently washed the guilt away. She bathed my poor, poor wife with forgiveness, and banished her own bitterness with the simple gift of love.

Chapter 71

S PRING WAS SLOW IN COMING THAT YEAR. We seemed to live in a pocket of winter, while other parts of the country basked in sunshine. Mary Jo's confession never left our thoughts.

She responded to the chemotherapy at last. In late May, the doctor said her cancer was in remission. It was as if a heavy weight had been lifted from my chest. But Mary Jo did not even smile.

Lucretia Granier stayed with us for three months after that terrible, wonderful night. In all that time, I never heard her utter another hateful word. She became the loving woman who had led me back to Mary Jo through a haunted alleyway, all those years ago. At our parting, she cried and hugged me close.

She had remembered her reason to live—every Christian's only reason to live. She had remembered to love us all, no matter what we are, and to act upon that love.

Melvin Milo's body was never found. Sheriff Ernie Davenport's men dragged the lake for a hundred yards in every direction. They pulled up a muddy tackle box I had accidentally dropped overboard three years before, but nothing else of interest. It was everyone's opinion that the violent waters of the storm that night carried Milo beyond the dam and far downstream, perhaps as far as the Red River. Who knows? He may have drifted to the Mississippi and all the way home to New Orleans. My friend Ernie Davenport told me not to worry. Milo's body would turn up someday.

It was not a comfort.

I dreamed I was a college kid again, walking the levee beside the Vieux Carre. Milo's corpse rose from the Mississippi to clutch at my soul with bony fingers dripping blood from a thousand babies. I pulled away and stumbled over Mary Jo, lying cold and half buried in the ancient soil, surrounded by the bones of a thousand African slaves.

When she was able, we began taking boat rides up to the mouth of Martin Pool, slow, quiet cruises along the shoreline, watching as deer nibbled timidly at the tender new-grown shoots of grass and ferns along the banks. Up where the Big Muddy Bayou feeds in, the lily pads had begun their annual spread downstream—thousands of emerald islands dotting the surface, lifting brilliant yellow blossoms like hands of praise to the sky.

But even the beauty of another spring, a spring we thought we'd never see together, could not remove the shroud of misery from my darling Mary Jo. And anger at her lies still coiled around my heart. It was a cold steel suit of armor I longed to remove. But I was afraid to speak it, just as I feared to speak of the real cause of Mary Jo's pregnancy. It seemed cruel to bring those emotions to the surface until I knew she was strong enough to bear the truth.

Spring dissolved into summer, the intense Southern heat rolling up from Mexico to hover in the air like a living thing, intent upon sucking the breath from our lungs. We retreated to the air-conditioned refuge of our home, living more closely together than we had in the spring. It had been almost half a year, but still, Mary Jo's spirit wallowed in despair. I simply could not let her go on with the questions. And so, when the time finally seemed right and her strength had fully returned, I told her she had been raped by Melvin Milo.

Her face changed when she realized she had not been singled out by Satan—at least no more so than any other victim of rape. She went blank, devoid of all emotion, like a mannequin. She walked away and closed the bedroom door between us. I stood just outside in the hall, listening as she cried softly, praying she would come to me when she was ready, praying that when the door opened, she would be well again. And hoping that then, at last, my own healing could begin.

I stood silently beside the door, waiting patiently. It was almost an hour before she opened the door and greeted me with her first real smile in half a year.

I would have waited a lifetime for that smile.